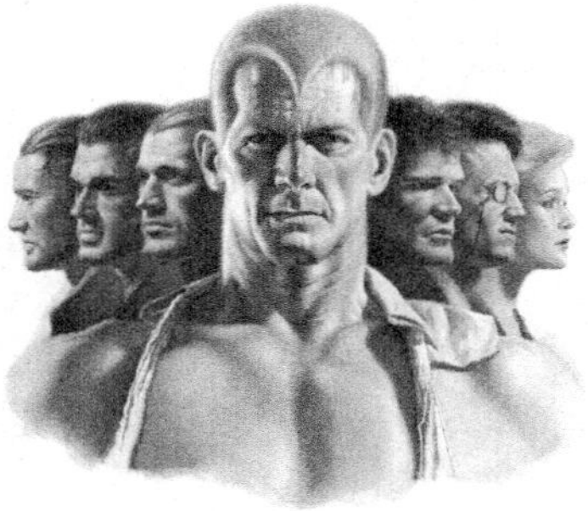

DOC SAVAGE

The Wild Adventures of Doc Savage

Please visit www.adventuresinbronze.com for
more information on titles you may have missed.

PYTHON ISLE
WHITE EYES
THE FORGOTTEN REALM
THE DESERT DEMONS
HORROR IN GOLD
THE INFERNAL BUDDHA
DEATH'S DARK DOMAIN
SKULL ISLAND
THE MIRACLE MENACE
PHANTOM LAGOON
THE ICE GENIUS

(Don't miss another original Doc Savage adventure coming soon.)

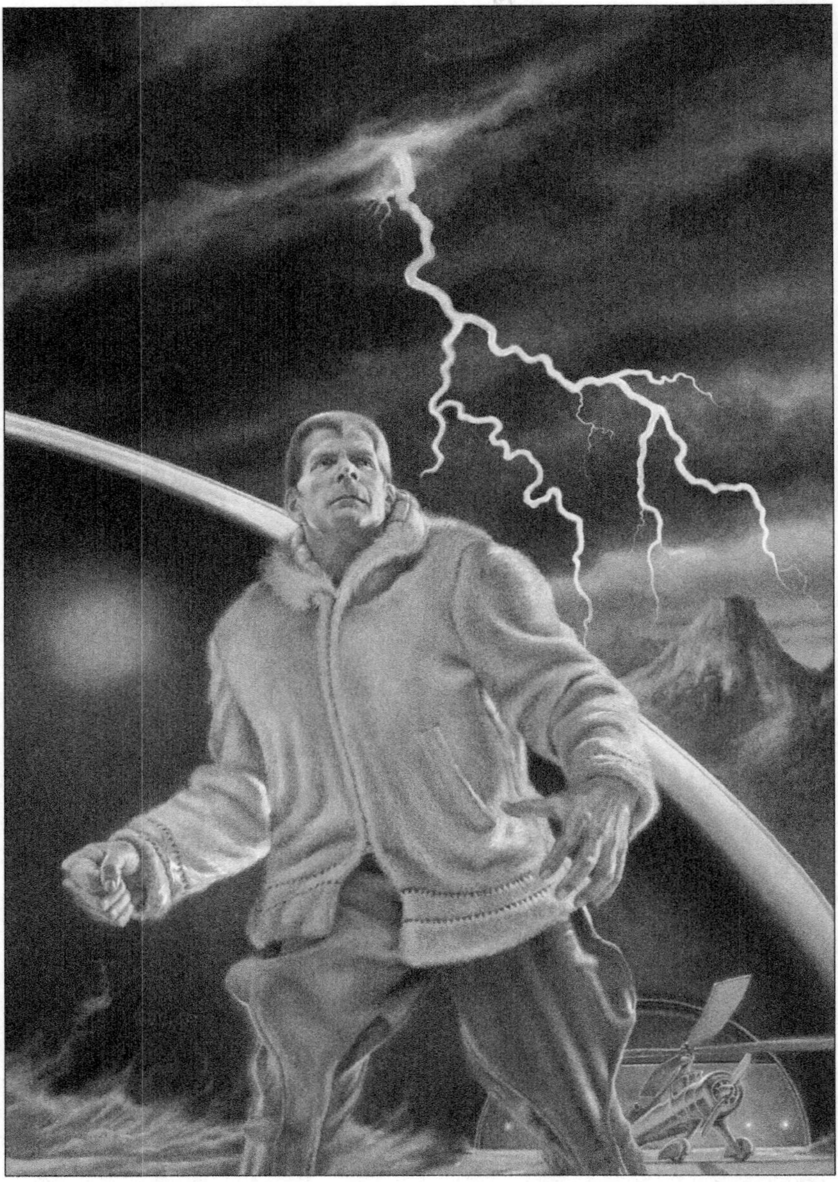

DOC SAVAGE
THE WAR MAKERS

A DOC SAVAGE ADVENTURE

BY WILL MURRAY & RYERSON JOHNSON
WRITING AS KENNETH ROBESON

COVER BY JOE DeVITO

ALTUS PRESS • 2014

THE WAR MAKERS copyright © 2014 by
Will Murray and the Heirs of Ryerson Johnson.

Doc Savage copyright © 2014 Advance Magazine Publishers Inc./
Condé Nast. "Doc Savage" is a registered trademark of Advance
Magazine Publishers Inc., d/b/a/ Condé Nast. Used with permission.

Front and back cover images copyright © 2014
Joe DeVito. All rights reserved.

*No part of this book may be reproduced or utilized in any
form or by any means, electronic or mechanical, without
permission in writing from the publisher.*

First Edition — April 2014

DESIGNED BY
Matthew Moring/Altus Press

SPECIAL THANKS TO
*James Bama, Jerry Birenz, Condé Nast, Jeff Deischer, Lester Dent,
Norma Dent, Dafydd Neal Dyar, Lois Johnson, Dave McDonnell,
Matthew Moring, Bill Pronzini, Ray Riethmeier, Jennifer Spencer,
Anthony Tollin, Mort Weisinger, Howard Wright, The State Historical
Society of Missouri, and last but not least, Ryerson Johnson.*

COVER ILLUSTRATION COMMISSIONED BY
Rick Scheckman

Like us on Facebook: "The Wild Adventures of Doc Savage"

Printed in the United States of America

Set in Caslon.

For Ryerson Johnson, who plotted
this story way back in 1935....

Friend, mentor, and now
collaborator. Thanks, Johnny!

The War Makers

Table of Contents

I	The Highway Horror	1
II	The Baron in Black	13
III	The Bronze Intruder	24
IV	Death Drop	40
V	Slaughter in Straight Lines	54
VI	Terror Trail	75
VII	Monk Gets His Teeth in Something	90
VIII	The Cellophane Chain	105
IX	The Lady in Beige	118
X	Park Ambush	128
XI	Milk Truck Trail	136
XII	White House Conference	145
XIII	Fire On the Water	157
XIV	Doom in Five Days	169
XV	The Great Lone Land	180
XVI	Arctic Attack	197
XVII	Fortress of Silence	209
XVIII	The Lethal Laboratory	217
XIX	Gliding Death	231
XX	Six Must Die	238
XXI	The Mad Maze	257
XXII	Sinister Genius	276
	About the Author—Ryerson Johnson	293
	About the Author—Will Murray	296
	About the Artist—Joe DeVito	298
	About the Patron—Rick Scheckman	301

Chapter I
THE HIGHWAY HORROR

IT WAS A red rubber ball that started the chain of events that shook America from coast to coast.

An ordinary ball of vulcanized rubber purchased in a five-and-dime store and given to a boy of eight for his birthday. It had been manufactured in Akron, Ohio, which was the rubber capital of the United States, and now it was being bounced by its owner on a quiet residential street in Peoria, Illinois.

The lad was nimble, but the ball got away from him. It went bouncing in the direction of vehicular traffic.

Thus far, nothing extraordinary.

All of that changed in a twinkling.

Seeing his birthday ball bounce off, the boy naturally took on a look of dismay. His reflexes were good, even if his judgment was not.

The tyke darted after his scarlet prize, heedless of automobile traffic.

It happened that the boy had been conducting his youthful calisthenics in front of his home, and that particular house sat on a busy street corner.

A traffic cop was directing the vehicular flow. He had been watching the child in between waving his arms and pirouetting in place as he skillfully stopped and restarted impatient motorists on their way to work. For it was morning of a warmish autumn day.

One watchful eye on the boy was prudent. But it was not

enough to curtail a tragedy. Before the officer's horrified eyes, the lad chased the red rubber ball into running traffic.

Abruptly, the ball stopped rolling—stopped dead, as if all the natural bounce had been leached out of it.

The cop blinked in disbelief. Autos whizzed smartly by. He was no longer paying attention to his traffic duties.

The ball simply sat there, dead and unbouncing.

In the act of lunging for the ball, the boy suddenly fell. It was unnerving, the manner of his falling. He flopped to the blacktop, like a trout being landed by a fisherman.

Except that the youth did not move after he fell. He lay stunned.

Up the street charged a shiny green roadster, traveling fast.

Snatching up his whistle, the traffic cop blew a long blast. He was running, too. Running hard. But the space between the helpless boy and himself was too great to make a difference.

For the interval between the approaching green auto and the unresponsive tyke was shrinking by the second.

The cop, seeing the inevitable, dropped his whistle. The chromium-steel bumper was bearing down on the boy like the blunt teeth of some voracious mechanical monster. That was how the roadster appeared at that frenzied moment—a glassy-eyed demon about to devour a helpless child.

Sickened, the cop halted, squeezed his anguished eyes to unseeing slits, and turned his head. For there was nothing that he could do.

A fragment of a prayer escaped his trembling lips.

The sound of the roadster lurching to a halt was strange. The cop would always remember it. There was no screeching of brakes, no squeal of rubber. No sound usually associated with a braking vehicle.

There was, however, a horrid thump. The thump haunted him forever.

When he forced himself to look, the trembling bluecoat saw

what passing motorists had witnessed, but could not believe.

The roadster had slammed to a stop so violently that the driver was thrown half way through the windshield. The man was obviously stunned, but he must have possessed a hard head because he levered himself back into the driver's seat.

The windows, still in their steel frame, lay atop the hood, ruined.

Before the chrome-plated bumper—in fact half under it, but not near the tires—lay the boy, still unmoving.

The cop rushed up, knelt down, and felt the small body all over.

"Glory be!" he muttered. "Not a scratch on him!"

The white-faced driver had stumbled out from behind the wheel, was coming around to the front of the machine now. He was afraid to look. One could see that on his slack expression. His eyes were sick. A tendril of scarlet began creeping down from his scalp. It soon became a fat red worm.

"Is he—" croaked the driver. He swallowed hard, tried words again. "How is he?"

"He'll get a good paddling from his mother, once I fill her in, but otherwise he's intact," growled the policeman.

For the boy was batting brown eyes open. He seemed confused.

The cop turned on the youthful driver and seemed to want to chew him out. But the near miss with death had, for the moment, frightened all the starch out of him.

"I ought to run you in, buddy. But you did such a sweet job of stopping, I'll skip it this time. What kind of brakes you got on that car anyway?"

The copper had realized that this spotless green machine was a model he had never before laid eyes on.

"It's a Huron Speedster," muttered the driver, holding his aching head. "New model. Not on the road yet. I'm a test driver for the Huron people."

The officer blinked. The Huron Motor Company of Detroit was the largest in the nation. It sold more autos than any other manufacturer. In addition to their main plant, the Huron concern operated nickel mines in Montana, Kentucky coal mines, and rubber plantations in Brazil—all to feed their ceaseless assembly lines. They were the biggest of big shots in the automotive industry.

"Well, you were speeding, and that ain't right," snapped the cop, prudently swallowing a bit of his righteous anger.

"I'll be more careful in the future," promised the driver.

"See that you are," returned the mollified officer, tenderly picking up the boy. "I'm going to get this little feller home to his mother. There's a garage up the road half a mile. You'd better get that busted window replaced."

"Yes, sir," said the driver in a dazed voice.

THE HURON DRIVER was still in a dazed frame of mind when he sat down to a lunchroom counter and ordered a cup of steaming black coffee for his nerves. He had been tempted to enter a nearby saloon and treat himself to a stiff belt of something stronger, but he was on duty and didn't think the drink would help any.

Webster Neff had been speeding all right. He admitted that much to himself. The road ahead had been clear and he was anxious to finish his run to Detroit by nightfall. So he had been a little lead-footed. They don't hire old ladies to test-drive new machines at Huron. It was a weakness he had. Speeding, that is. Web Neff was young, under the age of twenty-five, and had the impetuousness of a three-year-old colt.

What the shaken driver failed to comprehend still haunted him as he took his first sip of strong, bracing coffee.

Neff was reliving the moments before the accident. He had not noticed the red rubber ball bouncing into traffic. He had seen the pursuing boy, however. But too late to brake in time. He was certain of that part. His foot had slammed against the brake pedal, but it refused to budge.

An instant before it would have crushed the young child to death under his wheels, the Speedster had slammed to a halt. On its own!

"Maybe," Web muttered to himself, "maybe I managed to engage the brakes before I went flying."

But he didn't think so. He was certain the car smashed to a stop, hurling him through the windshield. Smashed as if it struck a stone wall. But there was no wall, of course.

It was inexplicable.

But there it was.

Web Neff did not know that the red rubber ball and the running boy had also slammed to a quick and unexplained stop. Everything had happened so fast.

Three cups of steaming black coffee went down his aching throat before a mechanic came over from the garage with the news that his windscreen had been replaced and Webster Neff was free to go on his way.

He wasted no time. The test driver was anxious to leave this sleepy town behind.

AT LOGANSPORT, INDIANA, the still-rattled young man stopped for lunch. It consisted of more black coffee and a piece of apple pie. Web had very little appetite.

A radio was blaring music in a corner of the eating establishment. It was old-time music and, since Webster Neff preferred more modern stuff, the melody went in one ear and out the other. Anyway, he had a headache from the accident. Maybe a mild concussion. His ears had rung a little, but that annoying noise had finally settled down.

The music abruptly stopped. An announcer cut in, speaking in an urgent tone.

"We interrupt this musical program. Flash! In the town of Divernon, Illinois, just an hour ago, a passenger bus turned over

when the brakes locked, according to the bus driver, for no apparent reason. Injuries are reported to be minor. Three persons were taken by ambulance to the city hospital. Authorities are investigating the incident."

The announcer went away and the music resumed, but Web Neff had no more ear for the melodic strains than he had before hearing the alarming report.

"Peculiar," he muttered to himself.

"What was?" asked the pretty waitress as she laid down his second cup of molten java.

"Today isn't Friday the Thirteenth, is it?"

"No, it's Friday the Eleventh. Don't you know that?"

"It's coming back to me," muttered Web.

The pretty waitress eyed him skeptically. "Why did you ask such an odd question, mister?"

"Must be a big day for accidents involving brakes."

"Do you need a newspaper?" she asked.

"What for?"

"You might," she said tartly, "wish to read your horoscope, talking as you are."

Web Neff lost himself in his coffee and pie, still not feeling right. He frowned, a growing unease taking hold of him.

WEBSTER NEFF ate a steak dinner in Toledo, Ohio, his appetite having returned. There he purchased a newspaper. There was no radio installed in his test car, so he was starved for news. His mind had been racing as much as his eight-cylinder engine.

The headlines screamed of a rash of automobile accidents. A sedan had smashed into a delivery truck in Dayton, Ohio. The driver had complained of his brakes. A touring car had sideswiped another in Palmyra, Missouri. Again, the motorist blamed his machine, not his driving skills.

Everywhere it was the same. Strange, unaccountable accidents. And in almost every reported case, an automobile that had rolled off the assembly line of the Huron plant in Green Creek was involved.

Peering out the restaurant window into the parking lot, Web regarded his own streamlined Speedster with a growing suspicion. It, too, had been assembled at Green Creek.

Getting into his immaculate emerald machine, Web tested the brakes with his right foot. They seemed to have just the right amount of resistance.

Still, he drove gingerly as he left the restaurant parking lot, and for the remainder of the evening Web drove well under the posted speed limits.

Web Neff was not a superstitious man, but the peculiar rash of auto accidents—beginning with his own—had rattled him.

IT WAS near dusk when the test driver approached the city limits of Detroit.

An advertising blimp was plodding along. It belonged to a famous rubber tire company. Its silver side, only beginning to catch some smoldering fire from the setting sun, captured Web's alert gaze. He watched it with pleasure.

There was something about the sight of an airship, looking like a man-made cloud marching along the sky, that was something to behold.

Overhead, a red-tailed hawk circled, seeking prey. The majestic bird held his attention for a bit.

While his eyes were still on its outspread wings, Web Neff watched in amazement that turned to baffled shock as the hawk seemed to lose all animation without reason.

Neff had done his share of hunting. Deer. Duck. Even bear. He knew how a bird on the wing behaves when it is struck by birdshot.

This hawk suffered no shot. It simply stopped cold, folded up its wings and plummeted to earth, to all outward appearances dead before it hit the ground. Dead from no apparent cause.

Along came the blimp. Had the operator seen the distressed hawk? That was never known.

As the blimp approached the zone of air where the hapless hawk had folded up in mid-flight, Web Neff felt a growing tension that made the muscles of his neck tighten up. He couldn't take his eyes off the silent blimp loafing along in the sky.

"I hope what I fear for is only my imagination," he undertoned.

But it was not.

As Web watched, the blimp seemed to strike an obstacle in the air—an invisible something. Then it rebounded slightly. Its propellers churning, the airship tried to advance along its placid course.

For no reason that Web could see, the blimp abruptly gave a weird lateral twist, and then it began falling....

Horror can do funny things. It can make a man turn his head from the sight of it, as it did the traffic cop during the morning incident with the little boy and his wayward rubber ball.

Conversely, it can hold another man fixed and rigid, oblivious to everything but a dread fascination with an unfolding and unavoidable tragedy.

This was the case with Web Neff. He could not take his eyes off the spiraling airship.

It nosed down behind some trees, and there was hardly any sound audible over the throaty moan of the Speedster engine, but the blimp made a hard landing.

A pall of grayish-black smoke told that much.

Not taking his attention off the event meant that Webster Neff had no eyes for the road ahead, nor mind for his driving.

When he snapped out of it, Web discovered to his shock that he had drifted over to the other side of the macadam roadway—the wrong side!

Around the curve ahead came an oncoming sport coupé, a powerful machine with a long, streamlined hood.

Web snapped one foot off the gas-feed to tromp the brake. It was snappy work. The converging automobiles were coming at one another—head on!

Both stopped dead. Stopped as if a great invisible hand had reached down to prevent a collision.

Web Neff never knew if he successfully crushed the brake pedal. His tow-headed skull went rebounding off the windscreen for a second time that day.

Fortunately, the new windshield held. It didn't even crack. The rest was a blur of wild action in which the Speedster swapped ends at least once.

Web was sitting hunched in his seat, clutching his aching head in both hands, when two peculiar men stepped from the other machine and raced over to him.

Only then did Webb Neff realize that his test machine had turned over. He was upside down in a ditch. The tires were still spinning.

One of the men reached for the car handle and gave it a twist, pulling open the door.

"Out of there, buster," ordered a squeaky voice that sounded like an actor in a movie comedy pretending to be a kid.

"He appears dazed," commented a well-rounded voice. This was the second man.

A hairy hand reached in and seized the Huron driver by his shirt collar. Strong fingers pulled him from the wreck that was the Speedster.

"If he ain't got a concussion after all that," muttered the squeaky-voiced one, "I'll be happy to give him one, so the accident won't be a total waste of his time."

After being hauled out of the wreck and made to sit by the soft shoulder of the highway, Web Neff looked up.

Two men stood over him. They were a pair. That is, they were the least likely duo Webster Neff had ever laid eyes upon in all of his twenty-four years of life.

One was well dressed and spoke as if he had had an excellent education. Harvard, judging from the affected accent. He was pointing at Web with a slim black walking stick. A cane.

The other was a short wide brute of a man, whose broad face looked more like a gorilla than some anthropoids Web had seen in the Chicago zoo. It was almost as though the second man was some sort of cross between man and gorilla, for his head was an apish bullet sitting on neckless shoulders. Under beetling brows, small black eyes twinkled in eye sockets that resembled pits of gristle. Hairy arms dangling at his sides were amazingly long, and as red as rusty shingle nails.

"I think I recognize you," Web sputtered.

"That so?" muttered the human ape.

"You have the advantage," clipped the cultured man. "Who are you?"

"Webster Neff. Test driver for the Huron works."

"My good man, it appears as if you were aiming this unresponsive vehicle in our direction," accused the well-bred individual.

"It was the blimp that distracted me. I saw it go down."

"We saw it, too," said the apish individual in a belligerent voice. "So what?"

"It was strange. It seemed to bounce backward, and then fall."

The well-dressed one remarked, "We saw it fall. I do not know about any bouncing."

"Before that, a hawk dropped dead in the sky."

"I think this man needs a doctor, Monk," said the well-dressed one in a clipped way.

Web suddenly understood. "You are Monk Mayfair, the chemist, and Ham Brooks, the lawyer."

"Correct," stated Ham—he of the Harvard accent.

"Associates of the famous Doc Savage."

"Also correct. What of it?"

Web mumbled, "I can stretch a point and understand that the brakes on a Huron test machine might jam, but I'll be hanged if I can understand the brakes in one of Doc Savage's ultra-modern cars gumming up."

"Nothing of the sort happened, my good man. I braked just in time."

"Nix, shyster!" said Monk.

"What do you mean, you ignorant gollywoppus?" demanded Ham.

The apish man displayed open hands. "You were so busy watchin' that blimp go down, you didn't see this guy's oncomin' car, any more than he saw ours. You didn't try to brake. Before you could, the car up and stopped dead."

"That's what happened to me, too!" exploded Web.

"Nonsense," insisted Ham. "My foot reached the brake pedal in time. I felt it."

"If that's so," flung back Monk, "how come neither set of brakes made any squealin'?"

Ham opened his mouth to argue, then shut it when he suddenly remembered that no sound of brake shoes attended the sudden stoppage of the two colliding cars.

"Perhaps my foot hit the pedal after we stopped," he grudgingly allowed.

Web Neff exclaimed, "He's right! And it's now happened to me twice in one day!"

Excitedly, the test driver recounted the story of his eventful day, beginning with the little boy with the bouncing red ball and the near fatality that had been narrowly avoided by some unseen agency.

"I think that Doc Savage should look into the strange stoppages transpiring in these parts," concluded Webster Neff, as they helped him to his feet.

"Mebbe so," said Monk. "But first we'd better take a look at that blimp."

They found the blimp smashed into a shapeless sack of rubberized fabric in the back lot of a manufacturing factory. Workers had already gone home. There was no one about, nor any other witnesses to the accident.

There was only one pilot aboard the blimp. He was quite dead, his neck broken, eyes open and goggling like automobile headlights. He had perished at his controls, apparently upon impact.

"Nothing for us to do here," mused Ham. "The police will be along in due course."

Web said sheepishly, "I could use a ride into town. I have to report to my bosses."

"Then your misfortune has abruptly been turned on its head," returned Ham Brooks gallantly. "For we are on our way to that very place."

Web started. "Honest?"

"Your superiors are ahead of you, it seems. They have asked for Doc Savage's help. We happened to be in Chicago, and came directly here."

"Yeah," added Monk. "We're pinch-hittin' for Doc until he can show up."

Web managed a shaky smile. "So I can hitch a ride?"

"You bet," said Monk, throwing open the door. "I wanna hear more of your story, cockeyed as it sounds."

Chapter II

THE BARON IN BLACK

LIGHTS WERE BURNING late in the executive offices of the Huron Motor Company, in Green Creek, a very few miles outside of Detroit, Michigan, where a tense discussion was in progress.

The unseasonably warm evening was well along. But from the strident words emanating from behind the closed doors of the sumptuous office of Huron President Phineas P. Slade, it might have been the height of the working day.

Days were long at the Huron Motor Company. Its great assembly plant operated day and night, toiling tirelessly to keep up with the enormous demand for the most famous and, by reputation, durable motor cars produced by an American automotive concern.

One would not know or suspect that success to hear the angry voice of Phineas P. Slade as he lit into his chief engineer.

Waving white sheets of paper in the other man's face, Slade bellowed strident words.

"Lawsuits filed against the company! For accidents sustained when the brakes jammed on Huron motorcars. What do you have to say about this, Frost?"

The man being addressed was diminutive in stature. Wiry, his black hair lay flat against his skull. This was in stark contrast to the stiff white bristles of his pointed mustache. Eyes as green as a tiger's smoldered with resentment, barely repressed.

The man attempted to defend himself. "Sir, I—"

"Shut up! I am not finished chewing you out!" roared Phineas Slade. He was just getting warmed up, it appeared.

"When we hired you to design the hydraulic braking system for our new line of cars," sneered Slade, "the idea was to improve our performance, not call it into question!"

"These brakes have been tested, and proven to perform according to the most exacting Huron standards," the other defended.

The executive's features grew redder. "Then what are all these screaming headlines about Huron accidents? Why have we received a flock of lawsuits in one single day?"

"I am sure that I do not know, for I do not understand what is transpiring. My new brake design is perfectly reliable."

"Reliable?" retorted Slade. "Reliable, you say! If these brakes were satisfactory I wouldn't need a platoon of lawyers to beat back the swelling demands for restitution."

Felix Frost swallowed with an effort. He did not sweat, nor was the placid expression on his face troubled by the yelling that was directed at him. He stood stiffly, a gaunt, springy-jointed individual with a trick mustache that had become very popular on the Continent, and had spread to America in recent years.

The mustache was thin, twisted at either end. Its artificial points brought to mind the stiff whiskers of an agitated feline. Frost looked barely forty.

The man had a reputation as an excellent engineer of automobiles. But Felix Frost was not well-liked at the Huron Motor Company. His slick hair, pretty mustache, and silent way of going about—as if he possessed the padded feet of a feline rather than human feet—had caused his co-workers to give him the nickname of "The Cat." No doubt his first name of Felix, which he shared with the popular movie cartoon character, had also prompted the unfortunate nickname.

It was a warm night; consequently the windows were open a crack. This had invited in a solitary blue bottle fly, and this pest began buzzing around the room, much to the annoyance of all concerned.

Noticing it, the vice-president in charge of sales found a flyswatter and began chasing the pesky insect about the office, with a noticeable lack of success. In fact, his rushing about the room, vainly attempting to smack the fly dead, only caused more commotion, adding to the unpleasant atmosphere of the meeting.

"Stop that!" snapped Phineas P. Slade angrily.

The vice-president in charge of sales meekly returned to his place on the rug facing the desk of the company president. He folded his hands behind his back, concealing the offending flyswatter.

A new man entered the room at this point—tall and craggy-featured, with a fine head of graying hair that seemed fuller than necessary. This man closed the door behind him as he stammered, "There has been another accident!"

All heads turned, eyes sharpening with concern.

"Involving one of our automobiles?" demanded Slade.

"Incredibly, yes. It involved—"

President Slade groaned, shaking his white head as if in disbelief. "Spare me the unpleasant details, Buffington."

"Yes, sir," replied Theodore Buffington, vice-president and chief assistant to the president.

The Huron President turned the penetrating glare of his attention back upon his chief engineer. This gaze, as he resumed speaking, became a dark glower.

"Consider yourself suspended, Frost," snapped Phineas Slade.

"I protest!" returned Felix Frost in a tense but even tone of voice. Mustache points quirked with suppressed indignation. "There has not even been the beginning of an investigation," he shot back, green eyes glowing.

"That investigation has already commenced," returned Slade coldly, pointing a finger quaking with rage. "You have been with us less than a year. All of your work encompassing that period of service must now be reviewed by our attorneys, as well as by outside engineers. The government will be down on our necks before you know it, demanding to know what has happened to Huron products. Has the quality of Huron automobiles slipped? That is the question that will be on editorial pages by the time the morning papers land on our desks."

"It is presumptuous to assume or assign blame before a proper investigation can be undertaken," asserted Felix "The Cat" Frost, voice as stiff as his bristly mustaches.

Theodore Buffington cleared his throat noisily. "This man has a point."

Turning to his assistant, President Slade directed his wrath in full. "I do not recall inviting you to this meeting, Buffington!"

Theodore Buffington flinched ever so slightly, and explained, "I did not invite myself. I was merely informing you of the most recent developments."

The man's reasonable response caused some of the spleen to leak out of Phineas P. Slade's truculent demeanor.

"Since you are here," said Slade in a more calm tone, "and the entire future of this company may be at stake, it is better that you know about developments as they unfold."

"Yes, sir."

For several long moments, no one knew what to say. The unpleasant enormity of the situation began to settle upon them, and now that hot words had been spoken, cooler heads were beginning to prevail. The most famous and popular motorcar company in the entire United States of America was teetering on the brink of a public relations disaster—if not financial ruin.

There were already lawsuits, and threats of lawsuits. If the rash of inexplicable accidents continued at the pace of this first day of the outbreak, it would not be long before the government would intervene. It was even possible that Huron would have to shut down until explanations were discovered and remedies put in place. It was a painful, sobering thought.

During the lull, the buzzing of the fly touring the office was again heard. The vice-president in charge of sales twitched his flyswatter behind his back, and looked as if he would like nothing more than to seek out and mash flat the offending insect, as if the innocent fly somehow lay at the heart of all their troubles.

In the near silence of the room, the winged pest wandered about, buzzing loudly. For it was quite large.

The insistent creature neared the spacious desk of the President of the Huron Motor Company. The vice-president of sales, watching closely, sensed that his opportunity to strike was coming.

But before the latter worthy could make a move, the wandering blue bottle abruptly dropped straight down on Phineas P. Slade's spacious desktop.

The fly's action seemed entirely unmotivated. One moment it was the center of attention, very energetically making a circuit of the desk, as if in search of something sweet to imbibe. The next moment it was lying inert on the desk, beside the onyx fountain pen and gold inkwell arrangement on the desk.

With annoyance tracing deeper worry lines upon his mature face, Phineas P. Slade flipped out a brisk hand to knock the helpless insect to the floor.

The gesture remained uncompleted. The Huron chief executive slammed his hard palm on the desk, completely missing the fat fly. The hand remained, pressing the desktop, not moving to complete the effort. It might had gotten stuck there.

All gazes tracked this odd display with a dawning curiosity that soon turned into myriad eyes widening in puzzlement.

PHINEAS SLADE'S hand might have been held in place by a magnet. That was the weird impression gained by his subordinates in the office.

That strange impression grew stronger as, with a grunting effort, the Huron president attempted to pull his palm away from the desktop, to no avail. His leonine face began to swell and grow pink, then red with frustrated exertion.

Peculiar sounds started emerging from his throat as the executive's efforts grew even more strenuous, but conversely more fruitless. The struggling effort etching itself into his face became difficult to watch. Sweat poured from his high brow.

Suddenly, the seemingly-stuck hand jerked clear. Slade lifted the member, raising it to his face. Eyes troubled, he searched the hand for signs of damage. Finding nothing overly disturbing, the executive began to feel the trembling digits with the fingers of his other hand.

"What is the matter?" demanded Theodore Buffington in a strained voice.

"I—I do not know," faltered Phineas P. Slade.

"You looked as if you could not lift your hand."

"That exactly describes it," returned Slade. "I completely fail to understand what has just happened to me."

"Perhaps," suggested Felix Frost, "the stress of the day's events are taking their toll."

"Frost may be right," inserted Buffington, grayish eyebrows knitting together.

Phineas P. Slade lowered his trembling hand, eyes growing round and a little bit stark. He began muttering. "Could—could I be suffering a paralytic stroke?"

"Nonsense," retorted Buffington. "You had a complete physical examination only last month."

"Yes, yes, I know I did. But how do you explain my inability to control my own hand?"

No one in the room had any explanation. Nor did they wish to offer theories that might only further depress their spirits, or take them away from the weighty matters at hand.

In that awkward silence, Felix Frost resumed his stout defense of himself and his engineering staff.

"Huron brakes are as mechanically perfect and sound as any on the market," he insisted. "It isn't only our brakes that are going wrong. It is happening proportionately to all makes and models of vehicles on the road. There happen to be more Huron cars on America's streets, that's all. Makes it look worse for us. But it is only a consequence of our enormous popularity as a maker of automobiles."

This all but mollified the others in the room. It was true that Huron was America's leading manufacturer in the automotive industry, but it also made the concern the largest target for lawsuits, and other criticisms—warranted or not.

"Well, I am not waiting for the roof to fall in on me any more than it already has," snapped Phineas Slade with a gruff belligerency. "I have sent for Doc Savage. If anyone can allocate blame, he can."

"Doc Savage!" thundered Theodore Buffington. "He rates very highly in Washington. Should we not keep this an internal matter? For the time being, at least."

"Mr. Buffington is absolutely correct," seconded Felix Frost. "My new brakes are sound. I am fully prepared and able to undertake the investigation of the manufacturing process. And if any flaws exist, I will root them out."

President Slade shook his head slowly. "No, Doc Savage is the man for the job. As for you, Frost, I will write a formal letter dismissing you from this company, pending a thorough and complete investigation of your work."

That said, Phineas P. Slade reached for his fountain pen. Gripping the onyx instrument by one hand, he attempted to remove it from its gold holder. Simple, easily accomplished. Yet no sooner did he touch the pen than the Huron executive began to grunt and strain once more. His expression grew frantic. More sweat poured forth.

The others watched with growing concern warping their features.

Theodore Buffington swallowed once, and started to speak. The words never came.

Straining to his utmost, President Slade jerked his arm angrily. The expensive writing instrument broke, the lower half remaining in its holder, India ink scattering in all directions, like black strings of octopus secretions.

Gasps raced around the room.

Theodore Buffington rushed up, leaning both hands against the desk. "Phineas! You *have* had a stroke! Look at you, you're a sick man."

Phineas P. Slade was a hard and capable executive. He had come up through the ranks of the Huron Motor Company. The old production wizard shook his head. Sternly, he said harshly, "No. Not a stroke! I'll tell you what the matter is. I didn't intend to say anything about it. It is all too frightful, too unbelievable. I did not believe it myself. But now I do! And I'll tell you—"

Theodore Buffington began to interrupt. Not in words, or if they were words, they became tangled in his involuntary cry of warning.

"Mr. Slade, there are some matters that are too confidential to reveal, even to insiders," he cautioned once he regained his iron self-control.

Slade hesitated, weighing his words, before resumption of his unexpected announcement.

Outside the closed office door, a long, feminine scream hammered at the panel. This was followed by the sound of a body falling with a mushy thud.

The assembled Huron executives rushed for the door, all except for Phineas P. Slade, who continued staring at the broken fountain pen in his hand, and the ink splatters that had ruined the top of his desk, blackening his well-manicured hand, and speckling the front of his otherwise immaculate coat and tie.

He wore the expression of a man who questioned his good health, if not his sanity.

Out into the hall tumbled Theodore Buffington, Felix Frost and the other Huron executives, eyes searching, raking the dimly-lit corridor.

The sight that greeted their questing eyes was a wholly unexpected one. None of the men, had they been questioned before exiting, could have clearly explained what they expected to discover. A woman had screamed, and there had been an unpleasant thud. What that amounted to would have been impossible to predict.

For on the hall carpet runner, they discovered the office scrub woman sitting on the rug, wildly waving her mop handle. The handle lacked a proper mop, it appeared.

The woman looked as if she might have simply fallen over on account of her weight, for she was on the plump side, as well as on the far side of fifty. She pointed a fattish finger at the dirty gray mop strands, which lay on the rug, leaking soapy water.

"Stuck to the floor like it's glued there!" she shrilled. "No reason for it, but it's stuck!"

"Talk sense!" insisted Buffington.

"I *am* talking sense. All of a sudden, it happened. I was mopping along, and the wet part of the mop became stuck to the floor. It refused to budge. I yanked the handle clear out, trying to move it. In all my born days, I never heard of such a thing!"

No one had. That went without saying. Although their thoughts were hurled back into the executive office where a few minutes before the president of the company had been unable to budge his own hand from the top of his own executive desk.

The vice-president in charge of sales was a forceful individual. While the others stared, he stepped forward.

"Stay back," Felix Frost warned frantically.

The vice-president of sales was unheeding. Apparently, he was also a stubborn man. He gave the equally stubborn mop head a savage kick.

The limp-looking mop head went flying once the man's polished shoe snapped out at it. There was nothing unnatural about its behavior in any way. It jumped into a corner, where it made a sloppy mess.

Theodore Buffington turned on the scrub woman, who was laboriously climbing to her feet, looking even more flustered than before.

"You better go home and sober up," he told the woman in a severe voice that promised future disciplinary action.

Muttering, the woman gathered up her mop and bucket and went huffily on her way. The expression on her doughy face as she took her departure indicated complete lack of comprehension on her part.

Turning to the others, Theodore Buffington said, "We must finish what we have started here."

As fate would have it, just as they turned to repair to the executive office, there came another unpleasant thump. It sounded almost exactly like the disturbance that had preceded the discovery of the confused scrub woman.

Buffington ran ahead of the others, flung open the door.

On the threshold of the executive office, he froze. The others craned their heads around him, the better to see the sight that greeted their popping eyes.

Gasps erupted from their throats.

Huron President Phineas P. Slade lay sprawled upon the expensive rug beside his executive desk. He was unmoving, one hand lifted like a clutching claw.

Theodore Buffington was the first to reach his side. He fell to one knee, reaching out a hand that was steady despite the situation and felt for a pulse. He found none.

Woodenly, he rose, turned to face the others.

One word only he pronounced:

"Dead."

Stunned silence held the group for over a minute. The events of the day had been terrible indeed, but this was the capper. The head of the Huron Motor Company was no more. He had been struck down. The only question was, by what?

The feline green eyes of Felix Frost searched the body. He pointed a slim forefinger and asked, "What is that sticking out of his pocket?"

Theodore Buffington intoned, "The very thing Slade was

about to reveal, the thing I fervently wished he would not reveal. But with Doc Savage on his way, there is no sense in further secrecy."

Buffington sank again to one knee, plucked out a piece of paper from Slade's breast pocket, where minutes before a crisply folded linen handkerchief had poked.

Returning to his feet, Theodore Buffington unfolded the sheet of paper. It was an ordinary piece of Huron Motor Company stationary. Nothing remarkable about it at all.

Except that there were blocky words written in black ink on the paper. They had long since dried. Therefore, they were not freshly made. The note had been in Phineas Slade's pocket all along. Possibly, he had attempted to pull it out in his death agony.

The typed words read:

"If you call in Doc Savage on this matter, you will *die*."

The note was signed, *The Baron in Black*.

Chapter III
THE BRONZE INTRUDER

THEODORE BUFFINGTON, AS befitting his position as capable vice-president to the late Phineas P. Slade, was an aggressive, hard-charging individual. These qualities, already in evidence, now came to the fore.

He spun on his heel and ordered the vice-president in charge of sales to summon the police.

That worthy sputtered, "Should I not call for an ambulance?"

"The man has expired," returned Buffington savagely. "An ambulance and all the doctors in the world would do him no good."

"What shall I tell the police?" stuttered the vice-president of sales.

"Tell them that Phineas P. Slade has suffered a fatal stroke, and in doing so struck his temple on the corner of the desk as he fell."

Disbelief greeted that pronouncement.

"A stroke? Are you certain?"

Stabbing a decisive finger in the direction of the desk corner closest to the dead man, Buffington indicated a clump of blood-clotted hair adhering to the oaken side, substantiating his claim almost beyond question.

Hanging back, diminutive Felix Frost maintained an ominous silence. His harsh green eyes ranged about the room, and he bounced on his feet nervously as if not sure what to do, or what his true place in the scheme of things was now that his superior was no more.

The letter of dismissal that Phineas P. Slade has been about to pen had never been executed. Technically, Felix Frost was still chief engineer of the Huron Motor Company—even if his immediate future was very much in doubt.

Seizing the telephone instrument in one firm hand, Theodore Buffington then began making urgent calls, alerting the Huron chief counsel, as well as heads of various departments, of this regrettable development. These calls were terse and to the point. Buffington was unsparing of the feelings of those with whom he communicated.

"I have many more calls to make," he snapped at one individual, whose voice, vibrating through the receiver diaphragm, bespoke of pain and disbelief.

Hanging up, Buffington inserted his blunt finger into the rotary dial and spun it several times, creating a new connection. Reaching his party, he began rushing through clipped explanations of the state of the Huron Motor Company this tragic night.

Sirens in the distance, caterwauling in the night, warned that the police were on their way.

The vice-president in charge of sales was shaking. "What if—what if Mr. Slade's death is not what it seems to be?"

In the act of hanging up on another call, Theodore Buffington focused cold, unsympathetic eyes on the agitated man. "How much evidence do you need to see the obvious?"

The man swallowed, his face sagging, his mouth so dry he struggled to reply.

The blue bottle fly that had earlier been buzzing about the room resumed its winged perambulations.

No one paid it any heed. It was as if their ears were capable of hearing no noise other than that of their own arguments.

In the face of Theodore Buffington's high-pressure insistence, the concerns of the vice-president of sales were momentarily stilled.

Between the wailing approach of police sirens, and the extremely active fly, other sounds were submerged.

The three stunned men were gathered about the body of their former president, Phineas P. Slade, their uneasy eyes going to his dead features, then seeking more pleasant sights, before being drawn back irresistibly to the dead man's frozen-faced countenance. It was all but unbelievable how quickly death had struck.

One minute the man had been vital and commanding, now he was but cold, common clay. The sobering sight robbed the others of some of their spark.

Faintly, a new sound came from behind them. It was so muted, it almost did not register on the eardrums.

Felix Frost, perhaps more sensitive than the others, was the first to react. He whirled on his springy feet, catlike eyes leaping toward the source of the sound.

A man was in the act of stepping into the room through the partly open window. Previously it had been open but a crack, but now it yawned widely.

The reason for its being so open was that the man who had entered the room in such an unorthodox fashion was a veritable giant. Bronze was the hue of his skin, and his hair, lying close to his skull, resembled a metallic skullcap only a shade darker than the distinctive fine-textured skin. He might have been a man constructed of flexible metal, forged in the furnace of the sun itself.

"It is impossible," hissed Felix Frost. "The outer wall is too sheer. No one could have scaled—"

"You see me," returned the intruder in calm, well-modulated tones.

The others by this time were reacting to the new entrant. The vice-president of sales dropped his jaw as if losing all control over his lower mandible.

Craggy-faced Theodore Buffington proved more in charge of himself. "Doc Savage!"

"But why—?" sputtered Felix Frost.

Doc Savage smiled enigmatically. "The unconventional entrance? Because your plant guards are sprawled in the yard below, stunned. The elevators are all inoperative. Doormen and elevator boys are lying unconscious on the floor. A surprise entrance seemed to be in order."

Shocked silence greeted this pronouncement. All had heard astonishing things about this wonder man, Doc Savage. But this, the ease and silence with which the bronze giant had breached the Huron executive office, where death had struck only moments before, all but took their breaths away.

It is doubtful if anyone in the room could muster up a syllable of commentary. The complete transference of interest was really indicative of the forceful personality of a unique personage.

That individual was perhaps one of the most astounding personalties in the world today. The Man of Bronze—as the newspapers styled him—was more renowned than the greatest scientists, statesmen or Hollywood celebrities who dominated the news.

Yet comparatively little was known about this renowned man of mystery.

DOC SAVAGE stepped forward. For just the barest second everyone in the room stood staring at the huge bronze figure. As one radio commentator had at one time expressed it: "There is something about Doc Savage that gets to you. I don't care how many times you see him, you always get a bang out of it."

Doc Savage was a prodigious giant of a man. As he filtered through the group, which shrank back to make way, his radiant vitality seemed to pervade the whole executive space. Actually, Doc was an even bigger man than he appeared. This was because his massive muscles were so evenly developed all over his body that they knit under his bronze skin as one perfect unit.

Tendons stood out on his hands like cables, his gigantic

muscles were as chrome steel. There was a silky flow to them. With equal facility they could have directed the threading of a nearly microscopic needle, balanced on a circus high-wire, or gathered their raw force to heave a hundred-pound sack of cement as another man might toss a football.

For all this, the mainspring of Doc Savage's amazing personality lay not in his physical development, but in his eyes. Strange eyes they were, and hypnotically compelling. Deep golden pools. The blackness of interstellar space shot through with a golden powdering of star dust. The gold flakes in his eyes swirled, seemed always alive.

Doc Savage strode forward purposely. He did not seem to walk with undue speed, yet so perfectly did those corded muscles coordinate that the bronze man reached the side of the late Phineas P. Slade in amazingly quick time. He made a thorough but efficient examination of the corpse. Doc, incidentally, was eminently deserving of the title, "Doctor." In the entire world there was, perhaps, not a man his equal in surgical ability.

Theodore Buffington volunteered, "He had been showing all the signs of a stroke before he was felled."

Doc Savage said nothing. He continued his examination. His flake-gold eyes whirling, he seemed to absorb even the most minute details. The bits of hair, clotted with blood, sticking to the oaken desk did not escape his notice.

He scrutinized this evidence, returned to the body and concluded his silent examination. Standing up, the bronze man said quietly, "It appears that I have arrived too late."

Buffington said dolefully, "Nothing could have saved him. I am quite sure of this."

Doc Savage directed, "Tell me of the events leading up to his demise."

Theodore Buffington made several twisted faces before he volunteered a reply.

"Oh, what is the use? The man is dead. Nothing can bring him back! The police are on their way, to deal with the matter.

In the absence of a duly appointed successor to President Slade, I see no further reason for your services, Mr. Savage."

"My services were requested by Mr. Slade," stated Doc Savage. "Now that I am here, and having come this far, it would be prudent to have a look around."

Buffington would have none of it. "This is an internal matter, Savage," he bit out. "We are having a rash of brake and mechanical failures in our latest model machines. This is an issue that must be investigated and settled internally. It is none of your affair."

Doc Savage replied nothing to that. His extremely active flake-gold eyes roved about the room. It was as if he were paying Theodore Buffington no attention whatsoever. In truth, Doc had heard every word and was absorbing each bit of visual evidence the pushy executive had to offer. The bronze man pointedly made no move to depart.

Theodore Buffington was not a man accustomed to being denied or refused. A hot red flush was slowly creeping across his craggy features. His fists clenched. He did not seem to know how to react to this casual defiance of his authority.

Noticing the broken pen and the profusion of ink splatters, Doc Savage studied these for a few moments. He found the other end of the broken pen on the floor, and, if the quickening of his ochroid orbs was an indication, appeared to draw some unspoken conclusions from it.

Felix Frost watched this with avid interest. He maintained his thin-lipped silence. In his quiet feline way of regarding others, he seemed more like a human cat than ever before. His trick mustaches might have been well-groomed feline whiskers.

Doc Savage at last said, "Phineas Slade spoke of a threat letter."

Theodore Buffington and Felix Frost exchanged mutual glances, but neither man spoke.

The vice-president in charge of sales was not so reticent. "A note was found in his pocket," he volunteered.

Doc said, "Where is it?"

The vice-president's eyes shifted toward Theodore Buffington. Buffington stood stolid, unmoving.

Slowly, reluctantly, Buffington removed the folded note from a coat pocket. Eyes resentful, he surrendered the paper to the big bronze man.

Unfolding it, Doc read the brief message.

"This is substantially what Phineas Slade communicated to me by telephone, when he sought my assistance," declared Doc.

No one said anything to that. In the distance, police sirens were drawing nearer, ever nearer. That seemed to encourage the employees of the Huron Motor Company to stall for time.

Doc Savage asked, "Has anything been heard of this so-called Baron in Black since this letter was received?"

Buffington snapped, "Absolutely nothing! And who are you to ask investigative questions, when you have not been officially secured for this purpose?"

Doc Savage ignored that. Theodore Buffington seemed to grow even hotter under the collar at the apparent slight. He was not accustomed to any such treatment.

Sounds out in the hallway told of an elevator door opening and the urgent tramp of feet moving along the corridor.

Hearing this, the big bronze man seem to recognize the sound of these approaching footsteps, for he turned and said loudly, "Monk, Ham—in here."

The footsteps picked up their pace, and the door was flung open by the great hairy brute, Monk Mayfair. He flashed a quick look around. His wide mouth hung open like the iron jaw of a steam shovel. His tiny black eyes popped in their gristle pits.

Monk goggled at his bronze chief. "What are you doing here, Doc?"

"Some new developments prompted me to give this matter my personal attention. Where have you been?"

"Out!" grumbled Monk. "Out like a light in the elevator

about halfway up. Answer that one, Doc."

"This frog-faced orangutan is correct, for once," snapped Ham Brooks, slipping in behind the hairy chemist. "Upon arrival, we entered the elevator and requested to be brought up to the executive floor. The elevator began toiling upward, then it simply stopped. Nothing the elevator boy or I did could do to get it started again. Then we apparently blacked out, for the next thing we knew we were all lying on the elevator floor, and the lights had returned."

Doc Savage said simply, "That was the situation I discovered upon my arrival."

Eyeing the open window, Ham Brooks came to a swift and logical conclusion. "I see the absence of a working elevator did not deter you, Doc."

Then the dapper lawyer discovered the dead man with his dark, questing eyes.

"If I am not greatly mistaken, that man is Phineas P. Slade, President of the Huron Motor concern," Ham remarked.

"Blazes!" exploded Monk. "What croaked him?"

Doc Savage replied, "The prevailing assumption is that he suffered an unexpected stroke."

"Bally suspicious," murmured Ham. "On the eve of summoning our help, to be found like this, smacks of unsupportable coincidence."

At that point, the law arrived in force.

THE DETROIT CITY POLICE were in a truculent mood when they shoved into the executive office room. No less than a uniformed captain led the new arrivals. He got right down to brass tacks.

"My name is Captain Foy. Who witnessed this death?"

Theodore Buffington stepped forward, pointed at his fellow employees and said, "We three were present before and after Mr. Slade passed away in such a lamentable and untimely fashion."

Impatience colored the police captain's gruff voice. "Do you say before *and* afterward?"

"Yes, we were all drawn out into the hallway because the scrub woman had fallen down. The sound of her falling distracted us during our conference."

This did not go over well with Captain Foy. Phineas P. Slade was a big wheel in the city of Detroit. He was politically well-connected, his assembly plant and related businesses employing a great many people during this difficult economic time. His death would have repercussions, rippling out far beyond the Huron Motor Company.

"I will want statements from all of you," snapped Captain Foy.

Doc Savage interjected himself at this point. "My preliminary examination is inconclusive," said the bronze man. "But paralytic stroke is not out of the question."

The bronze man seemed scarcely to move his lips, yet the well-modulated words flowed clearly, resonantly, in every corner of the room.

There was nothing supernatural about it. Through years of unremitting practice, Doc had succeeded in coupling maximum speech efficiency with the least possible expenditure of effort. Doc utilized this scientific principle of energy conservation in all the fields of mental, emotional, and physical activity. It accounted in part for his amazing vitality, his tremendous stock of reserve power. Anyone purposeful enough could have achieved the same development. But no one else did.

The Detroit police captain favored Doc with a challenging eye. "I take it that you are a doctor. How does it come to be that you were on the scene so lickety-split?"

Before Doc could answer, Ham Brooks pushed his way into the captain's blunt face. "My good man," he began waving his elegant cane, "do you not realize that you are speaking with Doc Savage, who holds a high commission with the New York Police Department."

"And who are you?"

"Theodore Marley Brooks, Esquire, of the Manhattan law firm of Brooks & Brooks," drawled Ham in his best Harvard accent.

"You his lawyer?"

"I am," Ham said with studied dignity.

"Well, let's hope he don't require your services any time soon."

Ham purpled slightly, began sputtering inarticulately. Monk chortled.

Doc Savage silenced them with a simple gesture, and addressed Captain Foy.

"President Slade summoned me to look into a matter," explained the bronze man.

"What matter?"

"A threat letter has been received." Doc handed over the letter in question.

Captain Foy accepted the missive, unfolded and read it, then read it again. The expression on his face told that he did not like what he had perused.

"This is starting to sound like something more serious than a man having a stroke," he concluded bitterly.

Theodore Buffington asserted, "The two incidents may be completely coincidental."

"And they may not be," retorted the captain.

The other police officers now took each witness aside, and began questioning them in private, so that their stories could be compared later for elements that might not match, should any detail not add up in the larger scheme of things.

Very soon, it came out that there had been an argument between Phineas Slade and Felix Frost, over the latter's responsibility in the chain of accidents that had plagued the day.

Frost came under greater scrutiny by the police captain himself. He answered every question with promptness, defended himself lavishly, and forthrightly stood his ground. That he was nervous was undeniable. Of course he was the type who is always nervous—nervous as an alley cat.

"So Slade fired you?" demanded Foy.

"No—but he had announced his firm intention to do so," admitted Frost.

"What stopped him?"

"Evidently the stroke that cost him his life."

"So as a technical matter you have yet to be fired?'"

"Precisely."

The captain frowned. "Convenient for you, I would say."

Felix Frost said nothing to that. There was nothing he could say that would help his position, so the catlike engineer maintained a thin silence.

During the course of this interrogation, another police officer was taking the vice-president in charge of sales' story. Once he was done, the cop came bustling over to his superior.

"Captain," he said, "this guy's story has some interesting points to it."

"Spit it all out."

The vice-president went into a nervous and rapid recitation of Phineas P. Slade's difficulty lifting his hand off his own desk, followed by his inability to extract his fountain pen from its holder, resulting in the destruction of the aforesaid pen, and the messy splattering of ink that had preceded his subsequent demise.

Learning all this, Captain Foy gathered up the two halves of the broken instrument in his handkerchief, and seemed to think they were very important.

"This fountain pen is now evidence," he announced.

Doc Savage interjected, "You have overlooked the most significant clue," he said quietly.

"Yeah? What's that?"

The bronze man pointed to the ink-spattered desk top. The exploring fly had dropped to the desk and was crawling feebly around in the black blotch of spilled India ink, trailing messy droplets.

"Notice that these fly tracks form half a circle on the desk, being heaviest along the straight diameter line," Doc pointed out.

The police crowded close. They studied the ink splatters with great interest. If any of them carried a magnifying glass in his pocket, he would no doubt have produced it and applied it to the situation.

Captain Foy lost a bit of his temperamental muscularity. He reached up and scratched his head. "I don't get this."

Doc said, "Why did these spatters end along that straight line? There is nothing in evidence to have arrested the dispersal of this spattering ink, and yet they did stop."

The bronze man was displaying to all the policeman the undeniable truth of his observation. It was something they had missed in their official scurrying about; this undeniable fact made them visibly uncomfortable.

"What's the answer?" grumbled Captain Foy.

"It is not yet possible to say with any certainty," stated Doc frankly.

"So what makes you think it is important?"

Doc Savage replied calmly, "Its significance has yet to be determined."

At this point, Theodore Buffington suddenly realized the presence of Webster Neff, the hapless Huron test driver who had accompanied Monk and Ham to the facility, but who had respectfully loitered outside in the hall, not knowing what to do or say under the present circumstances.

"Neff," he roared, "you are late! Atrociously so!"

"I—I had considerable trouble getting here," admitted Web Neff.

Theodore Buffington flinched as if stung. "What kind of trouble?"

Web Neff spread helpless hands. "I don't honestly know, but I did experience some queer brake problems."

Felix Frost, detaching himself from a corner where a police officer had told him to stand after his personal interrogation, minced up and stood between the two men.

"You mean to say that the brakes on the new Speedster failed you?" he demanded.

"I don't know what to say," replied Neff honestly. "The accident was very strange."

The Huron test driver then commenced a tortuous recounting of his long state-by-state drive in the new-model machine, ending with its ignominious destruction.

Hearing this recital, the vice-president in charge of sales groaned. "More worries!" he bemoaned, burying his haggard face in his hands.

Web Neff looked uncomfortable. "I know some of what I saw sounds crazy, but it happened exactly the way I described it."

"Huron brakes do not fail!" spat Felix Frost, evermore mindful of an angry cat. "It smacks of some fantastic plot against the company."

The desk telephone began ringing. Theodore Buffington tried to ignore it, but the ringing refused to stop. Angrily, he grabbed up the instrument, placed it against his ear, and announced gruffly, "Office of Phineas P. Slade, deceased."

The voice at the other end asked a single question. Surprised, Buffington waved the receiver in Doc Savage's direction.

"It is for you, Savage. Someone wishes to speak to you. Please do not tie up the office telephone. Important calls come in through this line."

DOC SAVAGE accepted the instrument wordlessly, spoke quietly for some minutes, then hung up. Pervading the room, an eerie trilling sound had welled up, tuneful yet tuneless, mellow and so soft that it could almost be said to be felt rather than heard.

It might have been the weird note of an evening wind seeping through skeletal tree branches. It might have been the chirring of some exotic cricket. It might have been the susurration of vagrant eddies moving across the surface of Lake St. Clair.

It might have been any of these things. But it was not.

The sound was in reality an intimate part of Doc Savage, a rare thing which accompanied him in moments of acute concentration. Only Doc's closest friends could interpret the trilling. It meant now one thing and then another.

This time it denoted surprise, puzzlement. Monk and Ham exchanged significant glances. It was clear to them that the telephone call had made a deep impression upon the big bronze fellow.

Hanging up, Doc stepped over to the busy police captain, and imparted, "Urgent call requesting our immediate departure. If you have no further need for us, we must be going."

Captain Foy did not like that at all. "You leave when I say you can leave!" he roared. "I have an investigation to run here. And until I have all my answers, nobody goes anywhere."

Ham Brooks started to protest, but once again the bronze man silenced him with a commanding gesture.

While the police captain was comparing stories with his officers, Doc Savage drifted over to the desk of Phineas P. Slade and placed a quiet call. Before long, the phone again rang, but this time Doc picked up the instrument.

He spoke briefly, then called over to the police captain, saying, "It is for you."

"Who the hell is calling me *here?*"

"The chief of police," Doc Savage said evenly.

That changed Captain Foy's demeanor instantly. He took the call, spoke a few words, then clipped his lips closed. He listened for a very long time, mouth growing grim.

Hanging up, he addressed Doc Savage in a very subdued tone. "My superior says you can go. Just make yourself available if our investigation requires it."

"Of course," returned the bronze man. "Thank you."

Proffering his business card to the captain, Ham Brooks said briskly, "You may reach Mr. Savage through my office, my good man."

Taking the elevator to the lobby, Doc Savage, Monk and Ham exited the building and reclaimed their vehicles.

Monk and Ham had arrived in a rental car. But the machine awaiting the bronze man was a powerful sedan, black as a panther. Doc had not driven all the way from New York, of course. In late months had been placing in strategic cold storage locations across the country special machines which he could retrieve whenever necessary. It was part of the exhaustive preparation for the strange work that Doc Savage did.

"Leave your machine," instructed Doc.

They had rolled down the elevator in silence, keeping their questions and conversations to themselves. But now that they were in open air, and away from prying police ears, Monk grew excited.

"What do you suppose all these cockamamie shenanigans are about?" he asked Doc.

Doc Savage did not reply. It was his way to keep his counsel when he did not wish to speak. But the fact that he declined to comment brought excitement to Monk and Ham's eager faces.

It was very likely this meant that the big bronze man had already begun formulating theories based upon available facts, few as there were.

They had come all the way to Detroit to investigate on the behalf of one of the most important industries in the nation, but now they were leaving the vicinity as if more urgent business called them.

Cruising away in Doc's powerful machine, Ham asked an obvious question.

"What was that call about, Doc?" asked the dapper lawyer.

"That was Renny. I sent him south to investigate a report

received from one of the private operatives we have stationed about the country."

"Something urgent? More urgent than this matter?"

"Something equally urgent, and possibly related," responded Doc Savage.

"Where we goin'?" asked Monk.

"Airport."

Monk's tiny eyes brightened. "Then where to?"

"Florida."

"Florida!" exploded Monk. "What's doin' down there?"

Doc Savage was slow in replying. He may have been considering whether to reply at all. If so, the bronze giant finally concluded that frank speech was better than silence in this instance.

"We may be in time," Doc said grimly, "to forestall the greatest catastrophe ever to threaten mankind."

Ham sat up in the back seat, gripped his polished sword cane tightly. "And that is—?"

"The menace behind the Baron in Black."

Chapter IV

DEATH DROP

"**THERE IS SOMEONE** riding our running board." Doc Savage spoke without emotion. It was a marked quality of his personality that he rarely showed excitement, was never given to alarm, except under extenuating circumstances.

Monk grunted explosively. Ham Brooks asked quietly, "How do you know this?"

The bronze man pointed to a tiny red light on the dashboard. It was not marked or labeled in any way. It might have been a battery warning light, or some similar contrivance.

"Capacitor-type alarm installed on the running board. Designed to reveal the presence of an unwanted person."

It was typical of the big bronze man to be prepared for any eventuality, and this instance was no exception. In the course of their many adventures, Doc Savage and his men had dealt with stowaways, kidnappers, and other such unsavory persons intent upon ambush and murder.

Ham suggested, "You've known about this unwanted passenger since we left the Huron plant."

Doc nodded wordlessly.

Monk growled, "Why don'tcha pull over so I can take him apart?"

"I was waiting until we reached an out-of-the-way spot," returned the bronze man matter-of-factly.

Easing up on the gas feed while applying the brake, Doc Savage slewed the streamlined sedan over to the shoulder of the road. It was the deepest dark of the evening now, long past midnight.

Monk lifted his squeaky voice, saying, "What a doggone place to run out of gas!"

They were not out of gas, of course. This was only a ruse to lull the unseen stowaway into a false sense of non-discovery.

While Ham pretended to fiddle with his door, Monk Mayfair slipped out the other side, and, crouched low, worked his way around to the opposite side of the stalled sedan.

He spotted a shadowy figure in the act of slipping into some roadside grass that had grown too high.

The stowaway never made it to cover. Bounding along, using his rusty knuckles to aid in his locomotion, the apish chemist descended upon the fugitive with animal ferocity, something he did only when enraged, as he was now.

The fleeing man let out a wordless screech as hairy hands clamped upon his jerking shoulders and flung him about with careless ease.

Doc Savage had pitched out of the machine by this point. He glided up, separated Monk from the other, and spun the intruder around by his shoulders.

Moonlight revealed the face of Webster Neff, the unlucky test driver for the Huron Motor Company. His blondish hair was disheveled.

Again that low trilling sound—more felt than heard—flooded the warm night air with its stirring, tremulous tone.

"An explanation of your presence would be welcome," invited Doc.

Web Neff looked somewhat abashed. He fidgeted, shifted his feet, started scratching about his person, and finally decided to unburden himself.

"You don't know me, Mr. Savage," he began shakily. "But I sure know about you. I read all about you in the newspapers. You are a great man. They say you have the strength of ten and the brains of a genius."

The bronze man began to look slightly uncomfortable. He was not averse to praise, but neither did it quench any spiritual thirst in him.

Doc eyed him steadily. "Your story please, stripped of all superfluity."

Neff ceased his fidgeting. "It's this way, Mr. Savage. I admire you. I like excitement, too. That's probably one reason I became a test driver. I kinda hunger to see new places, and always have yearned to see what's around the next corner. I don't know what's been going on today, and a lot of that I don't understand, but I have to admit it's been swell in a hair-raising sort of way."

Monk interjected gruffly, "If you're hankering for excitement, we can turn you over to the police. They'll give you all the dang excitement you can stomach."

Web Neff lifted innocent hands. "I didn't mean any harm. Honest. I just wanted to tag along and see where all this utter strangeness led."

"What did you overhear?" queried Doc.

"Nothing. Honest."

"We are headed to the airport," said Doc Savage. He awaited the test driver's reaction to that statement.

"Airport, huh? Then my hunch was right."

"What hunch?" asked Ham Brooks.

"My hunch that this thing is bigger than the Huron Motor Company—much bigger."

No one offered any response to that statement.

"Well, am I right?" demanded Neff with a wise grin.

No one, it seemed, wanted to verify that supposition either.

This left an uncomfortable silence hanging in the midnight air. Insects made steady sounds, and amid the wind and the dry autumn leaves was a disturbed rustling that was vaguely unpleasant.

"There is more to your story than that," stated Doc Savage simply.

Webster Neff did some more foot shuffling, and twisted his fingers, resuming his facial contortions.

Doc Savage's direct statement was not based on any deep intuition, but was a well-worn method of producing truth, where additional facts might or might not exist. In other words, Doc was trying a wild bluff. Or as wild as the bronze man typically got.

Such a probe usually brought forth stringent denials, which might or might not be grounded in veracity. Or they could elicit hidden motivations.

In this case, it was the latter.

"What I said just now was the plain truth," insisted Neff.

"But there is more, isn't there?" prodded Ham Brooks, fingering his cane thoughtfully.

"As you were leaving," Neff said slowly, "Felix Frost took me aside and asked me to trail you wherever you went."

"Does Frost have authority over you in your capacity as a test driver?" demanded Doc.

"No, not exactly," admitted Neff, rather sheepishly.

"So why did you comply with his request?"

Here, Webster Neff grew even more uncomfortable. It was clear that what he was about to reveal undercut his previous protests of truthfulness.

"The Cat slipped me a hundred dollar bill to do what he said," confessed Neff.

Ham frowned. "The Cat?"

"That's what they call Felix Frost—Felix the Cat. On account of his tricky whiskers and sneaky ways, not to mention his resemblance to a certain cartoon feline."

Doc Savage absorbed this in a brief silence. Monk and Ham made faces consistent with deep thinking.

Perhaps to fill the uncomfortable silence, the Huron test driver offered, "Since I was probably going to get canned for wrecking a new Speedster, a hundred bucks looked mighty tempting to me."

Interest flickered in Doc Savage's golden eyes. After a bit, the bronze man said quietly, "We are flying this night to Florida. Are you interested in tagging along, as you put it?"

Monk and Ham started to object, but Webster Neff's excited agreement drowned out their protestations.

"Boy, howdy! Would I ever! Count me in."

Doc Savage regarded the young man steadily. He was an excellent judge of character. "You appear to be a capable young man, able to handle yourself in an emergency," he commented.

"I've been in a lot of wrecks," Neff said proudly. "Kept my head in every one of them." A boyish grin cracked his youthful features. "Survived all of them, obviously."

"We will see how you handle yourself in the kind of emergencies my men and myself usually confront."

"I don't carry a weapon," said Neff, spreading empty hands.

"No weapon should be necessary," replied Doc, guiding the man back to the waiting machine.

They all got in, Monk and Ham looking a bit on the surly side. It was manifestly evident that neither one trusted the Huron test driver. At the moment, they realized it was not prudent to declaim that distrust. If their bronze chief said it was permissible to bring Webster Neff along to Florida, they were not about to argue with him. Coming events would reveal hidden motives now obscure.

Once Doc Savage put the car back into gear, Monk and Ham decided to take out their frustrations on each other.

"Why did you bring that infernal pig?" demanded Ham of Monk.

"What pig?" wondered Webster Neff.

He was ignored. The porker in question had been asleep in a carrying case in the abandoned rental machine's rumble seat. The homely chemist had retrieved him and he now rode on the floorboards, still dozing. Web Neff had not realized that the case had contained the animal.

"That pig," retorted Monk, "is my business."

"If he so much as glowers at me with his beady eyes," warned Ham, "he will adorn my breakfast plate. As bacon."

"You so much as look cross-eyed at that hog," growled Monk, "and I will personally peel you like a banana."

Ham unsheathed a glittering blade of Damascus steel from the hollow of his cane. "And I will skin you and make a rug of your miserable hide."

Webster Neff turned to Doc Savage and asked plaintively, "Are they always like this?"

Doc said dryly, "Sometimes they sleep."

THE RIDE to the airport was otherwise uneventful. There, they claimed Doc Savage's airplane. It was a big four-motored job, streamlined to the ultimate degree. It was painted a uniform bronze. At a conservative estimate, it was probably five years in advance of anything that flew.

Once he sighted this, Monk vented an explosive grunt. "I see you brought the big job."

Doc explained as he exited the vehicle and climbed aboard, "We as yet have no inkling of where this affair will take us, so it seemed foresighted to bring the largest aircraft in our fleet."

Doc fired up the motors, and they began coughing noise and exhaust. The entire aircraft started vibrating in preparation for takeoff. It was an amphibian, the hull designed like a single float for water landings, into which the air wheels folded flush.

Taxiing out onto the tarmac, Doc jazzed the throttles and started the big plane racing down the runway. Soon they were in the air, turning southeast for Florida.

Once the plane found a comfortable cruising altitude, it became apparent that Doc Savage had ulterior motives for inviting Webster Neff to accompany them to Florida.

"A thorough recitation of your experiences might be called for at this point," suggested the bronze man.

Seated directly behind the cockpit, Web Neff took a deep breath. He closed his eyes. Summoning up his memories, he began with the incident involving the little boy with the red rubber ball who blundered into the path of his Huron Speedster, nearly resulting in a tragic fatality.

"You say that your car seemed to stop of its own accord?" asked Doc.

"My foot hit the brake pedal, but they locked up," insisted Neff.

"You are certain?"

"Positive, Mr. Savage. The pedal froze."

Doc absorbed this information in silence.

Web Neff went on to recount the news reports of other strange and mysterious stoppages of automobiles, and the resulting accidents in the states of Illinois, Indiana, Michigan and Missouri.

Ham took this all in with great interest. "We have been unaware of the magnitude of these incidents," he declared. "Jove, but it smacks of something sinister."

Monk grunted, "Sounds to me like a plague of Hoodoos."

"And what, may I inquire, is a Hoodoo?" Ham asked archly.

"A Hoodoo is an Indian word for the species of parasite that mankind ain't yet gotten rid of."

Ham gave Monk a skeptical appraisal. He did not need to ask the question that was on his mind, for the hairy chemist blurted it out in the next instant.

"These days they call Hoodoos lawyers, barristers, attorneys, and other such fancy names," grinned Monk.

Face turning crimson, the dapper lawyer lifted his sword cane as if to brain the homely Monk severely.

Monk batted the shaft away with a casual gesture born of long practice, but neither man made a move against the other. For all their muscular talk, the quarrelsome pair seemed unconcerned about the threat of violence from the other.

Interrupting, Doc said, "The incident involving the blimp bears repeating."

Monk and Web both attempted to tell it their way. Inasmuch as they tried to talk over one another, neither got very far.

Ham took over the conversation, saying, "We were driving along when the blimp seem to bump into something in the sky, after which it crumpled and collapsed, falling to earth with tragic results."

Doc addressed Webster Neff, asking, "Was that identical with your own observations?"

The tow-headed test driver nodded somberly. "Before that, in the identical spot, a hawk seem to fold up and drop from the sky, dead."

Doc Savage once more made the minute trilling sound which was his signature. It filled the soundproof cabin, seeping into every corner, audible above the silenced engines. The eerie evanescence rose and fell in a musical yet tuneless manner.

Web Neff looked around, wondering what the sound was. No one enlightened him.

Very quickly, Doc discovered that he was making the emanation and suppressed it without Neff noticing that he did so.

Doc Savage spoke up. "Was there anything visible in the sky?"

Neff shook his head. "No. Nothing at all."

Monk chimed in, "Nothin' but clear blue sky, Doc."

Doc said nothing to that. He was concentrating on his flying. His silence meant that he was pondering the reports.

Web Neff continued his account.

"I was so struck with horror by what I witnessed," he admitted frankly, "that I stopped paying any attention to my driving." Neff scratched his head vaguely. "I remember feeling for the brake pedal, but not what happened after that. Guess I conked my head pretty good."

Monk interjected, "Before we knew it, this guy was about to hit us head-on. The only thing that stopped us was—"

Monk suddenly looked strange.

"Was what?" asked the bronze man.

Ham Brooks hesitated before replying. "I was driving, Doc. But I saw this man come around the curve before I could react properly. Our vehicles wrenched to a stop in the very nick of time."

"You did not apply your brakes?" Doc asked sharply.

Ham shook his head. "No," he said somberly. "For there was no time. It was all over before I could react. It was a very near thing."

Webster Neff said, "It happened exactly as Mr. Brooks says it did. We should have been killed. I almost was. My car turned turtle in a ditch."

Doc lapsed once again into a thoughtful silence. He asked no further questions.

AFTER a time, the bronze man instructed, "Ham, endeavor to raise Renny on the radio."

Renny was Colonel John Renwick, the civil engineer of Doc's tiny band of assistants. He was a hulking tower of a man notable for his dour demeanor, trumpeting voice and impressively massive fists.

There was a radio cubicle back of the cockpit, and Ham Brooks took the seat, then began tuning the dials and snapping switches on the all-wave set which could reach out across the globe.

"Doc Savage to Renny Renwick," he began chanting. "Come in, Renny."

After a few minutes of this, a booming voice made the speaker's diaphragm reverberate like muted thunder.

"Holy cow! It's a madhouse down here."

"Where are you?" demanded Ham.

"Everglades. Strange things are doing, Doc, just like that operative of yours reported. There's death everywhere!"

"Death?" snapped the dapper lawyer. "Whatever do you mean, Renny?"

"What I mean is what I just said. We landed on a small lake. And everywhere you look, there are dead alligators floating belly up in the water. It's as if the Grim Reaper himself was stalking the Everglades."

Doc Savage inserted, "Ask Renny if there is any sign of the agency dealing out this form of silent death."

Ham put the question to the big-fisted engineer. A moment later, Renny's thunderous voice shot back, *"It's as peaceful a durn day as you can imagine. No sounds. No smells. Only death."*

"Other than 'gators," inserted Monk. "Anything else dead or dyin' down there?"

Renny seemed to hesitate.

"Don't think I'm going crazy," he rumbled, *"but a while back a flock of herons shot past. Then they just seemed to drop out of the sky. It was awful. The sound of their bodies hitting the water was something to remember."*

"Jove!" exclaimed Ham. "Renny is describing on a larger scale what happened to that hapless hawk outside Detroit."

Doc Savage's voice lifted, carrying to the microphone in Ham's hand with compelling urgency.

"Renny. Stick close to your plane. Do not explore. Repeat, do not explore that zone of death."

"I hear you," thumped Renny. *"But try telling that to Pat."*

"Pat!" Monk and Ham echoed in chorus.

"Who is Pat?" wondered Webster Neff.

"Pat," explained Doc Savage with a trace of metal in his tone, "is my cousin, Patricia. She operates a beauty salon in Manhattan and has no business being in Florida."

Doc's vibrant voice prompted Renny to explain, *"She barged in just when I was leaving, and forced herself onto the plane, sassy and brassy as all get out. Sorry, Doc. I couldn't put her off without starting a dustup."*

"Do you mean to say," sniffed Ham, "that you could not handle Pat with those massive paws of yours?"

Renny grunted, *"I tried to. But she stuck that old frontier six-shooter of hers into my nose, and threatened to put me to sleep with a mercy bullet if I didn't take her along."*

Monk guffawed, "She never woulda pulled the trigger."

"That's what I thought," returned Renny, *"until she rocked back the hammer and closed one eye kinda deliberate like."*

"Well," Monk allowed, "she does have a lot of the Savage blood in her veins. So I suppose anything is possible."

"Renny," repeated Doc. "Do not stray from the plane. Wait for us. We are less than an hour away by air."

"I hear you," returned the elephant-voiced engineer. *"Renny signing off."*

Ham Brooks replaced his microphone and turned to the others, his handsome features thoughtful and concerned.

"First a rash of inexplicable accidents in the Middle West, and now wholesale death has descended upon the Everglades. What does it all mean?"

The question was not directed at anyone in particular, but Doc Savage offered a response.

"Events of the day all seem to point to trouble with the Huron Motor Company, and its automotive products. But it is obvious by now that the danger is larger and greater than the automobile industry. The menace is more comprehensive, affecting men and animals and machines in multiple localities, causing unexplained stoppages at unpredictable places."

Ham mused, "What appeared to be a vicious strike at Huron is proving to be entirely random."

Doc shook his head. "Not random."

"Then what?" demanded Ham in a baffled tone.

"Our Florida investigation should give us an inkling."

That was all the theory the taciturn bronze man was willing to put forth.

DAWN broke, clear and brilliant. During the long overnight

flight to the Gulf of Mexico, Doc Savage had maintained an altitude of some fifteen thousand feet, the altitude used by most passenger airliners.

But as they passed over the Florida panhandle, the bronze man suddenly started to climb higher. The powerful motors of the metallic amphibian strained as they searched for its service ceiling.

"Flying kind of high, ain'tcha, Doc?" wondered Monk.

"From what you and Ham described of the blimp accident, altitude may equate to safety," stated Doc.

Monk grunted, "Kinda sounds like you expect trouble in the air?"

"If so," admitted Doc, "it is trouble I prefer to avoid."

The engines began laboring at over thirty thousand feet, indicating the motors were becoming starved for oxygen. Doc Savage leveled off, and they were over the Gulf of Mexico.

It was a sunny morning, the skies were the blue of sapphires and other azure gems. What few clouds dotted the horizon were light, fluffy things, like peaceful lambs grazing by their lonesome.

As he flew along, maintaining a constant altitude, the bronze man scrutinized these cottony masses as if they concealed lurking foes.

Rolling along, they encountered no trouble of any sort. Carefully, Doc began dropping the plane, for they were approaching their destination.

At no time during this maneuver did the bronze giant fail to keep an eye on the marching clouds that looked so peaceful and serene.

This proved to be wise, as events in their turn soon became very difficult.

Swinging around over water, Doc lined up behind a particularly fluffy cloud. This particular one was of the raincloud type, in that it was predominantly the color of cotton, but tinged about the nodular edges with gray.

As he followed it, Doc raked the surrounding welkin with his searching golden eyes. The impassive mask of his metallic face never changed one iota. His features might have been cast in actual bronze.

The drone of the great engines changed key, signifying an easing of air speed. The bronze man noticed a distinct change in the cloud that he was following.

At first, this alteration came gradually. The cloud was a big woolly one, and its woolliness disguised what was actually happening.

What commenced transpiring before their eyes quickly became very apparent. The lone cloud started to spread out. It became more diffuse. Losing its shape, it seemed to come apart in stages.

The sky was otherwise unnaturally clear, and that clarity by itself was something that drew the bronze man's attention.

It was while he was switching his attention back and forth between the unusual sky clarity and the dissolving cloud that Doc Savage realized that the transforming cloud had encountered a barrier before it.

This barrier was wholly invisible. Nothing could be seen. Only by its effect upon the lonesome cloud could its existence be discerned, or even suspected.

Monk noticed it, too.

"Lookit! That shaggy dog of a cloud is breakin' up."

Webster Neff bugged out his eyes at the phenomenon, tongue momentarily paralyzed.

Doc Savage wrenched the control yoke about, stomped on the rudder pedal and flung or attempted to fling the big aircraft around in a swooping circle.

It was fast work, but not fast enough. As it turned out, the lightning maneuver availed the bronze-skinned Hercules not at all.

The others were thrown about the cabin by the suddenness of the wild turn. It was a dangerous maneuver in that the big plane was not designed to be flung about in the sky in this abrupt manner. Only a man with Doc Savage's prodigious strength could have impelled the big amphibian to respond so rapidly.

As it happened, the starboard wing sliced through this dissolving cloud, and encountered something solid. What it was, there was no telling. Everything happened so fast that even the acute senses of Doc Savage failed to comprehend it all.

The starboard wing was torn off. Just like that. It went hurtling away, engines still running, prop blades flailing madly.

Then the heeling aircraft fell into a helpless tailspin.

Chapter V

SLAUGHTER IN STRAIGHT LINES

EVERYONE WORE PARACHUTES. Doc Savage had insisted on this from the beginning of the long flight. So escape was just a matter of plunging for the exit door in time to bail out. No easy feat when the madly out-of-control bird was corkscrewing toward the Gulf of Mexico.

There was no need for words. All of Doc's aides were former military men, and accustomed to acting fast under emergency conditions.

Monk got to the hatch first, flung it open with hairy hands. Ham, abandoning all decorum, threw himself out of the aircraft, clutching his sword cane tightly.

Rushing aft, Doc scooped up Webster Neff, impelling him toward the open hatch with an irresistible strength.

The young test driver needed no such encouragement. He jumped without comment or hesitation. Slipstream snatched him away.

That left only Doc and Monk. By this time the huge aircraft had fallen into a violent tailspin. Centrifugal force began to exact its toll upon them.

Monk had Habeas the pig in the crook of one arm. Doc gave the hairy chemist a shove. Monk began spiraling away.

Lastly, Doc Savage seized the door frame in great metallic hands and catapulted himself into space.

All four men fell for a time, then one by one, they began cracking their parachutes. Ham's was deployed first. Webster was slow to get his ripcord in hand.

Monk went hurtling past him, Habeas Corpus squealing with a shrill noise that might have been fright—or delight. The scrawny porker had his adventurous side, too.

Doc Savage watched the maimed plane spiral toward the Gulf of Mexico, its sheared-off wing whirling and tumbling after it. It had been an expensive ship, costing fully as much as a modern military bomber. But that was the least of the bronze man's worries.

He was reaching for his own ripcord when he noticed that Webster Neff was struggling. The man's parachute pack had not opened. Frantically, Neff reached out, as if to claw for some kind of handhold that simply did not exist in empty space.

Falling fast, the bronze man flung out his arms and legs, and seemed to be flying. In actuality, he was volplaning, employing a time-tested method of moving about in free fall.

Reaching the flailing man, Doc calmly grasped the back of the parachute pack and yanked it open, simultaneously pushing off to clear the expected eruption of silk.

Abruptly, Webster Neff's parachute blossomed forth, and gulped air with a cracking noise that brought relief to all observers.

That relief proved to be perilously short-lived. There must have been a flaw in the parachute fabric. For now it sprouted rips and tears in the great flower-like bell.

Before their horrified eyes, the chute became a useless rag. Neff continued plummeting.

The brief braking action, however, proved insufficient to slow up the man's descent very much. This allowed Doc Savage to take corrective action.

Mighty arms outflung, the bronze man volplaned in Neff's direction, reached out with metallic hands, seizing the flailing test driver by his harness rig, pulling him close.

Gathering the frantic man up in one mighty arm, Doc Savage yanked his own ripcord. His parachute vomited out, swallowed air as it was supposed to, and yanked him up by his harness.

Webster Neff gave out a wild yelp, but the bronze giant did not lose hold of him.

Together, they descended peacefully, Web's ruined chute dangling like a distended bladder.

By tugging on their shroud lines, and spilling a little air, Doc, Monk, and Ham managed to steer themselves toward land. The sea breeze helped with that operation.

By the time their feet slammed into solid ground, the big bronze-painted bird had smashed into the Gulf of Mexico, throwing up fountains of white spray which soon subsided as it was engulfed by the surging blue waters.

THEY landed amid rolling sand dunes, decorated with a tough profusion of sawgrass.

"Boy, howdy!" exclaimed Webster Neff enthusiastically. "That was some ride down!"

"Who packed that parachute?" fumed Ham, landing hard.

"It was your turn last time," reminded Doc, hitting the ground nearby.

The dapper lawyer turned pale.

Monk was the first to shuck his chute. The minute he got loose from it, the simian chemist put forth an animalistic growling unlike anything anyone ever heard emitting from his lips before.

It is standard procedure to bury one's parachute upon landing, to keep it from billowing up and blowing away. The hairy chemist did not do that. Instead, growling and glowering, he began stamping about in circles, driving the flattened silk into the sand. Habeas Corpus wriggled out of his arms and sat down on the grit to watch his master's performance, head cocked like a curious dog.

Monk was not shy about swearing, but typically he rationed his curse words around his bronze chief. In this particular instance, he let himself fully go. There commenced a procession of imprecations which ranged from the mildly profane to the blisteringly blue.

"What is the matter?" asked Doc, mildly alarmed.

"We can't get our teeth in anything to fight!" howled Monk irately. "What can anybody do in the face of that?"

"See a dentist," jabbed Ham unkindly, slicing himself free of entangling shroud lines.

They finished burying their chutes, and Ham looked around curiously.

"Where are we?" he inquired.

"Slightly north of Tarpon Springs," said the bronze man.

"Isn't that the sea port where the old Greek fishermen go out hunting for sponges?"

Doc nodded. "It is probably the best place from which to charter a boat."

They found a road and hailed a passing motorist. The man was only too glad to pick them up, although his coupé could not accommodate them all. They had to squeeze in, Monk packing his pet pig on his lap and Doc Savage electing to ride the running board, where he could better keep his eyes on the surroundings, in the event new danger threatened.

The driver was a talkative sort. "Did you see that airplane fall from the sky?" he demanded excitedly.

Monk grunted, "See it! We were ridin' in it!"

The motorist's eyes all but bugged out of his head. "You were? What happened?"

"A Hoodoo got us. Knocked us right out of the air," Monk added disconsolately.

"A Hoodoo, you say. I never heard tell of a Hoodoo or a hex that could cause a plane to drop out of the sky like that one did."

"Well, you have now. You see us here, don't you?"

"Hear you real fine, too," quipped the driver, wincing.

The motorist was only too glad to drop them off at the Tarpon

Springs waterfront, which in this early-morning hour showed many empty docks and wharves from which the deep-sea spongers had already taken their trawlers out, to go below in diving suits along the sea bottom like fantastic farmers harvesting underwater potatoes.

Doc Savage said, "Wait here. I will see about securing a suitable vessel."

The bronze man departed in the direction of a sleek-looking motor yacht tied up all by its lonesome.

During the lull that followed, Monk and Ham resumed their perpetual argument. There was no reason for this, other than boredom and frustration—a very volatile mix where the combative pair was concerned.

Ham Brooks glared at Habeas Corpus the pig and vented a choice opinion.

"That hog," he said archly, "is the ugliest animal that was ever born. Provided he was born, and not hatched out of some infernal egg."

"This hog," Monk bit back, "is smarter than most humans."

"If he is so confounded intelligent, what is he doing keeping such disreputable company as yourself?"

"You animated hall-tree," raged Monk, making hairy fists.

"You Abyssinian ape!" countered Ham, shaking his stick at the hairy chemist's blunt skull. "I should trim off your ears!"

Monk bared simian teeth in a warning growl. Ham hastily subsided.

Listening to this exchange, Webster Neff quickly grew tired of it. He inserted himself in a vain attempt to defuse the situation.

"I grew up on a farm," he remarked. "The pigs we raised were pretty darn smart."

"Who invited your opinion?" demanded Ham Brooks.

"Nobody," said Neff defensively. "On the other hand, I slopped so many hogs growing up, I would be perfectly happy never to have any dealings with them again."

This time Monk glowered at the test driver. "Whose side are you on, anyway?"

Neff shrugged. "I am on the side of peace and quiet—which around you two seems to be in short supply."

Monk wavered on the verge of a snappy retort, but suddenly began scratching himself.

Ham Brooks noticed this and sneered, "That swine is sharing its fleas with you."

Monk, digging into his shirt, said, "I think these are sand fleas. Phooey!"

That caused an expression of profound disgust to cross the dapper lawyer's face. They retreated from the sandy spot where they had been waiting.

Doc Savage returned shortly, after concluding a lengthy exchange with the owner of the boat.

"I have secured that yacht for our trip south," he announced.

The bronze giant took them aboard the vessel, which seemed to have been composed of more brass and mahogany than they had ever seen on a boat before. And they had encountered plenty of fancy yachts in their time.

Doc took the controls, started the powerful engine, and began backing away from the dock as Monk and Ham hastily cast off the spring lines. They did this so expertly and efficiently, it became clear to Webster Neff that they were more than fair seamen.

Once out on open water, Doc Savage pointed the yacht south, advanced the throttle. The stern dug in, the prow lifted and began churning blue brine as they raced down the western coast of Florida.

Noticing the sumptuous appointments, Ham Brooks, ever with an eye toward ostentatious display of wealth, went below to check out the accommodations. He returned a moment later to report, "There is a pretty fair radio in the cabin below."

Doc nodded. "One reason why I purchased this vessel."

Webster Neff made round eyes. "You purchased it. Not rented it?"

"Under the circumstances," responded the bronze man, "we are very likely heading into dangerous waters. This yacht will be subject to anything from bullets to complete destruction. It seemed more prudent to buy the vessel outright than to possibly make awkward explanations to its owner later on."

Webster now released a silent whistle from his pursed mouth.

"You must have plenty of dough," he remarked.

This brought forth no rejoinder.

Doc Savage was, in fact, a fabulously wealthy man. But he was not prone to open or ostentatious displays of his wealth.

The source of his wealth was one of his deepest secrets. Far to the south, in the Central American jungle, lay a hidden valley lost in time. This vale of antiquity was inhabited by the descendants of the ancient Mayan race. These peaceful people maintained no contact with outside civilization. But for the efforts of Doc Savage, they would have been exposed to the outside world, and certain destruction of their ancient way of life.

As an expression of gratitude to the bronze man, the Mayans had placed at his disposal this source of gold. The mother lode of a gold mine unsuspected by civilization, it was. Doc Savage had only to communicate by radio every seventh day, at a certain hour, to request additional gold be transported by burro train to a bank where Doc had an account. Millions might be transferred in one of these clandestine shipments.

This had been a legacy of Doc's father, the man who had set him on the path he now walked. For Doc had been raised by scientists in a strange experiment to fit him for his far-ranging life of aiding the oppressed and dealing out swift justice to law-breakers who otherwise might get away with their often gigantic schemes.

But Doc never spoke of this treasure trove to anyone outside of his innermost circle.

Having advanced the throttle to its maximum, Doc Savage

turned the controls over to Monk Mayfair.

"Where we headin'?" wondered the hirsute chemist.

"The city of Sarasota," replied the bronze man.

"We'll be there in hardly any time at all!" grinned Monk. "This baby is sure fast, and she handles sweet as can be."

"She's no Huron machine," sniffed Web Neff, showing himself to be a landlubber by disposition.

Doc disappeared belowdecks to raise Renny on the radio.

THEY were making excellent time, the yacht thundering along. Day had fully broken. It was a clear sunny morning. The typical humidity of Florida did not seize them, now that they were on open water and hurtling along at a fast clip. It was too late in the fall for that, anyway.

Hairy Monk seemed to enjoy the feeling and power of the Diesel engine under his control. He was grinning from ear to ear, his small eyes narrow with excitement.

Monk's grin soon collapsed.

Ham Brooks was the culprit behind that collapse, although, in this case, it was an inadvertent thing. The fashionable barrister had discovered a pair of binoculars somewhere, and was using it to scan the waters ahead.

What he saw produced a deep notch of a frown between his sharp eyes.

"Odd," Ham muttered.

"That you are," returned Monk, "but we try not to hold it against you too much. I kinda figure you were born that way."

Ham snapped, "I am *not* joking. The waters ahead look peculiar."

Monk grunted, "The water looks blue. I don't see anything funny about it."

"Look at the waves to port," insisted Ham. "And you will see what I am speaking about."

Monk shifted his squinting gaze. Now a simian frown took over his wide, pleasantly homely features.

"Let me see those glasses," he demanded of Ham.

The binoculars changed hands. Monk began scanning the horizon ahead in the direction of port. Now his fierce grin was completely gone.

"You see it?" demanded Ham. "The water is as flat as a floor. No waves."

"Must be a strong undertow here or something," Monk muttered uneasily.

Webster Neff joined them and remarked, "I never heard of an undertow that would flatten out a wide swath of waves like this."

Monk growled, "You much of a sailorman?"

"Hardly ever been on a boat pretty much," Neff admitted sheepishly.

"Better tell Doc," Monk told Ham.

The dapper lawyer raced for the cabin hatch, but the bronze man was already emerging. His alert ears had overheard everything.

"Reverse engines!" he rapped out.

Monk threw the throttle into reverse, simultaneously throwing the wheel hard to starboard in an effort to avoid the inexplicably smooth stretch of water.

His efforts proved to be too late. The handsome yacht slid toward the zone of unnaturally flat water, and appeared to encounter an obstacle.

Thanks to Monk's quick action, the boat struck an invisible barrier broadside, and not prow on. Otherwise there might have been a calamity.

Not that what next transpired was much less in magnitude than a typical calamity.

The yacht shuddered to a stop. The engine was still racing, and Monk Mayfair frantically jazzed the throttle back and forth in a determined effort to get the boat to move in any direction at all. It refused to go in reverse. Throwing the throttle forward to advance the yacht farther into the depressingly inert zone also had absolutely no effect.

"The controls won't respond!" Monk called out, alarm in his squeaky voice.

Doc Savage rushed in, took over, and repeated Monk's futile efforts, with an equal lack of reward.

The stern engine continue to churn and complain, but the boat was stuck fast, as if encased in ice. But there was no ice. Only an eerie flat expanse of blue.

The big yacht was not wallowing in the water, as might be expected. It seemed to be pinned, or held fast somehow.

Doc throttled back the engine, with almost no alteration in their predicament.

The only consequence was it became less noisy on the water with the engine shut down. The big boat simply sat there.

"Great grief!" howled Ham. "Do you feel that?"

"What?" demanded Monk.

"The absence of rocking! The bow is sitting on water that is akin to a sheet of glass."

DOC SAVAGE and the others craned their heads over the rails of the boat at all compass points, seeking for the source of the problem. They found nothing. Whatever held them fast was utterly beyond their power to perceive it.

The bronze man's golden eyes grew animated, for he saw in the water a distinct delineation between the tossing waves of the Gulf and the uncanny expanse of glassy water.

He pointed this out to the others, saying, "The line of demarcation is as straight as a ruler and stretches far into the distance."

Ham sputtered, "But what is causing the infernal phenomena?"

No one had an answer to that. Or if they did, they kept it to themselves.

They studied the strange demarcation for several minutes as they sat helplessly on the water's surface—if it was water, which they began to doubt.

In frustration, Monk Mayfair again engaged the engine and raced the throttle, which seemed to have absolutely no effect on their position. They were stuck. The yacht was not going anywhere, its foaming stern notwithstanding.

Then, they noticed a new phenomenon.

Where they straddled the line between normal breakwater and the strange flatness, the action of the waves on the stern was pushing the boat farther into the calm zone.

This was happening inexorably, and the boat's hull continued to complain as it was being pushed into the rocks. But there were no rocks. There was nothing there. Just open air above weirdly calm water that should have been turgid with wave action.

With a combination of monkey-like curiosity and agility, Monk clambered onto the yacht's flat forecastle and probed it with a long boathook. What he expected to encounter was never known.

"Keep away from it!" ordered Doc, voice sharp.

With alacrity, Monk flung the heavy boathook ahead, and scrambled back into the cockpit.

"The devil!" howled Ham suddenly.

"Where?" demanded Monk, twisting his homely head every which way. Then the apish chemist saw what the others beheld.

The boathook was floating in midair, directly ahead of the foundering yacht! As they watched, it began sinking with an agonizing lack of respect for the common law of gravity.

Monk's eyes protruded from their sunken eye sockets, and he wiped his face with both hands as if to remove the amazed expression roosting there.

Suddenly, Doc Savage's voice crashed out, "Abandon ship!"

He rushed them to the stern, not bothering to shut down the engine.

"Swim away from the flat water!" the bronze man ordered. "Avoid it at all costs!"

They started leaping into the handiest span of naturally heaving water, after first dispensing with their coats and shoes.

Once in the blue chop, they looked about and saw the boathook land in the flat water. It sat there as if fixed in bluish glass. It was not natural.

Then the yacht, engine still straining, succumbed to the pressure on its hull.

Caulk seams split and it began taking on water.

Strangely, the boat sank stern first, but the bow refused to go down. In fact, the bow did not tilt very much. It might have been caught in something tangible but beyond the power of human sight to discern.

"What's holdin' it up?" squeaked Monk, thick voiced.

The question was directed at Doc Savage, but the bronze man merely stared at the stupefying phenomenon. He said nothing.

There was dry land within swimming distance. Doc indicated it with a silent finger.

Wordlessly, they struck out for a sandy spit of shore.

The spot proved to be one of the tiny islands that freckle the Florida Gulf Coast. Once they dragged themselves ashore, they discovered that it was nothing more or less than a sand trap.

Standing up, they watched the stricken yacht. Eventually, it sank, boiling stern first. Only then did they notice that the waves had returned to the dead zone of coastal water.

Doc Savage studied the sky for a time with a thin black monocular, but finally collapsed the telescoping optical device and put it away.

"See anything?" asked Webster Neff.

The bronze man shook his head in the negative.

Monk began scratching himself. Ham Brooks did the same, but with more dignity and less vigor.

Monk growled, "That's twice the Hoodoo wrecked us!"

Baring his ferocious teeth, the apish chemist looked as though he wanted to bite someone or something.

Seeing this expression, Ham Brooks beat a hasty retreat.

Web Neff felt about himself, but discovered no itchy spots.

He walked up to Doc Savage and admitted, "You were right about buying that boat. Too bad it didn't do us any good."

"The contrary," said Doc. "We have progressed very close to our destination."

The bronze man seemed unperturbed about the loss that the boat had engendered. Neff imagined that over a thousand dollars had changed hands in the transaction, but this big bronze fellow appeared unfazed by the wasted expense.

The sand fleas were so bad that they were forced to return to the water and complete the swim to the mainland shoreline. Not that they had any other choice in the matter, sand fleas aside.

REACHING dry land, they discovered themselves in a desolate area far from any town or city. They might have been anywhere on the Florida Gulf Coast. There were no signs or roads, or anything smacking of habitation.

Yet Doc Savage looked around, reconnoitered the swampy terrain for a few minutes, then came back to report, "We are northwest of Lake Okeechobee, not terribly far from the spot where Renny landed his plane."

Webster Neff blinked. "How can you tell?"

Doc Savage did not offer an explanation. The big bronze man was already in motion, striking inland.

Ham Brooks said rather superciliously, "My good man, Doc Savage has memorized virtually every map of every inhabited portion of the globe, and many uninhabited ones. He could land in any jungle or desert on earth, and know to a certainty where he was located after only a few minutes' study."

Webster Neff looked as if he wanted to contradict the dapper lawyer, but Doc Savage was moving inland fast. And they had no choice but to follow him.

Doc soon found a trail into the Everglades. It was very rough, but navigable. The atmosphere was warm and slightly sticky. Mosquitos started to harass them.

Slapping about his person, Monk Mayfair began growling again. His frustrations were mounting.

"Ain't there any place where I won't get bit by somethin'?" he complained.

"Maybe you should try biting back," Ham said dryly.

"Maybe I should take a chomp out of one of your ears," Monk grumbled. "Especially since I ain't eaten since last night."

Ham avoided Monk thereafter. It's not that he believed the homely chemist was liable to take a bite out of his anatomy, it was just that once Monk became frustrated, he also turned unpredictable. Anything might happen.

Meanwhile, Doc Savage had produced an object from his many-pocketed equipment vest which resembled a round device with a compass-style dial. He held this before him in the manner of a man using a compass to make his way through wilderness.

Webster Neff caught up with him, scrutinized the device, and asked a reasonable question. "What is that?"

"You might call it a radio compass," Doc Savage volunteered. "It operates on the order of a Geiger counter. It registers the presence of radioactive elements."

"Really? You don't say."

Doc nodded. "All of our planes carry a radioactive substance whose emanations can be tracked by this device."

"But it looks like an ordinary compass," Web murmured.

"It is also a magnetic compass," explained Doc. "Built into our planes is a magnetic metal that will draw the needle of any compass in its direction. Between the pointing compass and the sound and loudness of the Geiger portion of this device, it will lead us unerringly to Renny's plane."

"You're as full of tricks as a magician, aren't you?" Neff said with a trace of admiration.

Instead of replying, Doc Savage concentrated on his scientific tracking. Heretofore, Web Neff had not noticed the ticking of the Geiger device, because it had been so muted. But the farther inland they penetrated, the more distinct came the tiny clickings.

Now they were growing louder by the moment.

Doc Savage pressed on, moving more rapidly. They were entering an area where thick mats of floating green duckweed marked standing water and a lush plant called alligator flag warned of possible alligator holes among the willows and myrtle bushes.

Webster Neff voiced the question that had been causing his brow to furrow. "If this magnetic metal is built into your planes," he asked, "why doesn't it confuse the plane's own instrument compass?"

"Metal is built into the tail, and shielded in such a way that it does not affect the cabin compass."

"Swell. Did you invent that?"

"It is a combination of two previously devised instruments," Doc said modestly.

Despite that, Web Neff remained very impressed by the big bronze man. He was well aware that Doc Savage was some kind of inventive genius. By reputation, Doc was a wizard in many fields, from medicine to scientific criminology. This prompted Neff to ask another question.

"Do you think there's anything wrong with the new Huron auto brakes?"

Doc replied, "That remains to be seen. But it is becoming obvious that the problem is much larger than any mechanical malfunction which may or may not attach itself to the Huron Motor Company."

"That's good to hear," said Neff. "Otherwise, I might be out of a job." He grew thoughtful. "Come to think of it, I might be out of a job anyway."

Ham Brooks asked, "What makes you say that?"

"No one has fired me exactly, but I wrecked a brand-new Huron Speedster that was my personal responsibility. They'll probably can me for that."

"Maybe you better hope that the brakes *did* fail," suggested Monk.

"I don't know what to hope for," Neff admitted dispiritedly.

On that note, they pressed on, lapsing into silence punctuated by the intermittent slapping of hands against their bodies, as the pesky mosquitoes continued to steal nourishment from their exposed skins.

After a time, the slapping ceased. This was a welcome change from what had gone before. Florida mosquitoes rivaled their well-known northern cousins, the so-called Jersey Canaries, for voracious thirstiness.

Doc Savage lifted a hand, prompting them to halt.

"What is it?" Ham breathed.

"The mosquitoes have stopped biting."

"I'm not complaining," said Webster Neff.

"There is no reason for them to stop," said Doc. "A minute ago there were small clouds of them, now there are only a few."

Smacking his face, Ham remarked, "Make that fewer. I just got one."

Advancing with caution, Doc Savage continued along the makeshift trail, and his flake-gold eyes became even more alert than normal. He moved side to side as his penetrating gaze roved the surrounding sawgrass and cypress trees.

Soon, the bronze man happened upon an iguana in the road. It was unmoving. Gliding to a halt, he scrounged around for a stick.

This he flung at the lizard, nearly striking it. The lizard did not respond to this affront. It simply sat there, unmoving and unresponsive.

"Dead," Ham suggested.

"Without question," agreed Doc.

It was a sluggish day, not terribly steamy but without much of a breeze, either. But here and there standing reeds and rushes rustled pleasantly.

These background sounds now seemed to fade away. It was as if the volume knob of a radio receiver had been turned off.

Doc wheeled, impelled them backwards in retreat.

"What's wrong?" Monk wanted to know.

"The silence feels wrong," declared Doc.

Doc Savage urged them off the trail, and into the brush. It was not pleasant stuff to traverse, and they became very aware of the dangers of reptiles, which included cottonmouth snakes as well as alligators.

Their uneasy vigilance increased. All talk was abandoned. Their faces became grim as they picked their way through the scrubby weeds.

Separating his cane into two sections, Ham Brooks unsheathed the wickedly pointed sword that had been concealed in the hollow barrel. He used this to slice and chop his way through the underbrush.

The blade was no machete—it was very thin and fine—but it helped them through some rough patches.

Doc continued to use his strange compass in an effort to locate the landed plane.

Before long, he spotted the amphibian sitting on a patch of still water thick with sawgrass and tall reeds. It was a single-engine yellow float plane, resting on twin pontoons.

From his vest, Doc Savage extracted a small case of his own invention. This was a portable radio transceiver. Pressing a button, pitching his voice low, he spoke into the microphone set in one side of the cigarette-style case, "Renny, we are approaching. We have your plane in sight."

A steady hissing came from the loudspeaker grille, but Renny made no reply.

Doc repeated his call. "Renny. Do you hear me?"

Staticky silence followed.

"Uh-oh," monitored Monk. "I don't like the sound of this."

"Nor do I," echoed Ham.

As they advanced to the shore of the small lake, Doc Savage noticed an alligator floating in the water.

They observed that it was a medium-size specimen, which meant it was about four feet long. It seemed to be basking in the sun, not going anywhere in particular.

"Lazy lookin' critter," mused Monk.

"Not lazy," corrected Doc. "Dead."

By way of testing Doc's theory, Monk unlimbered his supermachine pistol, set it for single fire.

Aiming carefully, the apish chemist loosed a single shot. It struck the lazy-looking gator in one filmy yellow eye. The orb disappeared; the gator did not otherwise react.

Dropping his weapon, Monk muttered, "Dead all right."

The deceased alligator was not the only dead thing lurking about the amphibious float plane.

Small fish were lying atop the water, not swimming but floating on their sides, flat eyes staring upward.

"For such a small body of water," observed Ham, "that is a lot of dead fish."

But there were more dead things in the water than fish.

Doc Savage's alert eyes discovered a mound of black specks lying on and around an oak tree stump. He knelt, touching the specks, stood up again, seeming to become a larger giant than before.

"Mosquitoes sometimes buzz around in small clouds," he said. "It appears that one such cloud expired, falling to the ground dead."

"You don't suppose this danged Hoodoo got Renny and—" He gulped. The hairy chemist did not finish the thought. He was thinking of pretty Pat Savage, who at last report had been with the big-fisted engineer.

Grimly, Doc Savage moved about the edge of the lake. The others stayed close to the Herculean bronze giant.

They found other dead animals. Birds lay dead here and there. Once they encountered a pink flamingo that seemed to have keeled over by the water's edge, its open eyes weirdly blank. Doc gave this flamingo a thorough examination, finding it had not been dead for very long.

But it was very dead indeed.

"No wounds or injuries visible," he reported to the others.

This pronouncement further depressed their spirits.

"It is as if we are near a space where life cannot survive," breathed Ham Brooks, nervously jointing and unjointing his sword cane as though wishing to bring it to bear on someone.

Monk mumbled, "Well, we're breathin', ain't we?"

"So far," whispered Webster Neff, staring around uneasily.

DOC SAVAGE was raking the surface of the lake with his leonine eyes. Since it was a small lake, there would be little or no wave action. All was very placid. It was impossible to tell if that placidity was the property of a natural body of water, or if some unseen force or agency had caused the standing water to grow smooth.

The bronze man rarely revealed his thoughts, except indirectly through the way he held himself. The manner in which he stood at the lake shore, scrutinizing the quiet amphibian, rolling muscles tense, told his men that Doc was torn between leaping into the water to investigate the amphibian, or holding back lest unseen death clamp itself upon him, should he dare.

It was an anxious, agonizing situation for them all.

They moved around, circling the lake, and before long they came across an old tarpaper shack amid a stand of willows that showed signs of recent habitation.

"Seminole shack," suggested Monk.

Doc nodded. The Everglades had been the home of the Seminole Indians since time immemorial. The tribe still dwelt here, in rude habitations such as this uncouth shack.

Approaching cautiously, prepared to retreat at any outward sign of danger, they surrounded the forlorn structure.

There were no windows. And the door was not much more than a raw veneer panel on some rusty hinges.

Doc Savage eased it open. Swiftly his trilling sound filled the moist air like some fabulous insect from another realm.

Monk and Ham shoved in, striving to peer over the bronze man's shoulders.

Inside, nearly half a dozen Seminole Indians lay sprawled in attitudes suggesting sleep. But they were not sleeping. Doc Savage went from one to the other, testing for signs of life. There was none.

"Gone?" breathed Ham.

"Yes," returned Doc Savage.

Further examination disclosed no signs of violence, nor disease. The Indian family—obviously they had been a family, for there were children among the dead—was simply deceased.

It was an unnerving sight, made all the more unpleasant for the fact that the dead looked as if they had simply fallen asleep in the family dwelling.

"Some new type of death ray?" wondered Ham.

Doc Savage shook his head somberly. "No, not the conventional concept of a death ray. This is diabolically different—"

"What about Renny and Pat?" moaned Monk.

Doc Savage eschewed any reply. Plainly, the question lingered in his mind, an oppressive prospect about which he did not wish to speak. He had known Renny since the days of the Great War, and Pat Savage was his only living relative. Their loss would be unbearable.

Resuming their circuit of the lake, a strange vision appeared, regarding them from the edge of the zone of death.

"Seminole," said Ham.

"Still kickin', too," muttered Monk.

Doc Savage approached the man. The Indian refused to come near the shack. It was clear that he was fully aware of the dead who lay within.

"Are you seeking the white man and the girl?" he asked as Doc drew near.

"Yes," replied the bronze man. "What do you know of them?"

The Seminole responded gravely, "They were killed as my people were killed. Struck down by evil spirits. Other white men came, and carried their bodies away." The Indian pointed into the sky. "These men flew north."

Chapter VI
TERROR TRAIL

A STUNNED SILENCE followed the Seminole's revelation.

Doc Savage broke it. "The ones who were taken, describe them, please."

The Seminole, plainly shaken by the recent deaths of his fellow tribesmen, gathered his colorful garments about him as he mustered up his memory.

"The white man was very tall, built like a great cypress tree. His face was grim and his hands were the largest I've ever seen on any man."

"Renny, without a doubt!" exclaimed Ham.

"What about the girl?" Monk asked anxiously.

"Very young," the Seminole intoned. "Her hair and skin shone like those of this man." He pointed at Doc Savage. "I could not see her eyes, so I do not know their color."

"Sounds like Pat," squeaked Monk.

Doc Savage attempted to grill the Indian. The man, they could now see, shivered and trembled, as if he had lately encountered the specter of death itself.

To set his mind at ease, Doc Savage switched to Miccosukee, the Seminole language, one of the many dozens of tongues the bronze man had mastered over a lifetime of intensive study and training.

The exchange was not very lengthy, but appeared to be informative. Turning, Doc told his men, "This man says that a pontoon plane recently landed in another portion of the Everglades, not very distant from here. He was away, investigating it, and so was spared. The plane took off at his approach and landed at this lake, where they evidently captured our friends. The unknown persons who took Pat and Renny came from that plane."

Ham raised his sword cane. "Then let us investigate."

"First," said the bronze man, "we will search Renny's plane."

The Seminole had a canoe of sorts, a dugout. He produced this from a disordered pile of dried palm fronds which evidently served to protect it from weather and theft.

Borrowing the boat, they paddled out to the amphibian, anchored in the middle of the lake. Normally, their passing would have disturbed fish or lurking crocodiles, but all was eerily still. They found another alligator, this one floating belly up—definitely expired.

Here and there, dead fish floated, staring of eye and open of mouth. They were an eerie and disturbing sight.

The amphibian door was not locked, merely closed. Doc climbed in first.

Nothing within showed any evidence of disturbance. Renny and Pat had simply vanished.

Looking about the cabin with concern, Ham Brooks remarked, "There are no indications that they were taken by force."

Doc Savage shook his head to the contrary. "They did not leave of their own volition."

The bronze man pointed to subtle signs indicating the truth of his assertion. Slight scuff marks on the floor, suggesting the occupants had been dragged out by the heels. A dropped pencil. Other indications of a disorderly exit.

Doc Savage located Pat's impressive single-action six-shooter. It was a family heirloom, so the bronze-haired girl would never knowingly leave it behind.

Noticing the weapon, Ham Brooks made an unhappy face. "Pat would not be so careless as to leave her pistol lying about where anyone could steal it," he asserted.

Doc Savage nodded. After checking the action, in case there might be a message wadded up in one of the chambers, he tucked the frontier sixgun into the waistband of his trousers.

From a pocket, the bronze man removed a flat device resembling a folding camera. It sported a lens that was so purple it verged on obsidian. He switched this on. Nothing seemed to happen. The lens remained dark, but that was only to the naked eye. In reality, the camera projected what is known as black light.

Directing the invisible ultra-violet ray about the cabin interior, Doc left no surface unexamined. But the device disclosed nothing of interest.

Frowning, Ham mused, "They do not appear to have had the opportunity to write a message with the special chalk which glows under ultra-violet light."

Pocketing the device, Doc nodded somberly. "Renny would have left us a clue, had he the opportunity."

Monk asked, "Are we takin' this crate?"

Doc Savage considered this at length. Finally, he said, "Wherever we travel, the agency that has been causing all of this unnecessary death and destruction seeks us out. It is better to leave the plane for now, and come back to it later when we are certain that we will not be struck down from the sky once we take off."

This made perfect sense to Monk and Ham, although they did not relish the return to the waterlogged wilderness that was the Everglades.

Returning to shore, they surrendered the dugout canoe, while Doc Savage examined the lake shore for footprints or other sign that would lead them to Renny and Pat. Despite being an expert tracker, the bronze man found none.

Doc and the Seminole had a short, earnest talk away from the others. At the end of it, the bronze man returned to his men and said somberly, "I have offered to help bury the dead."

No one objected.

They spent an hour interring the family that had expired in the fragile shelter of their shack, then Doc Savage presented the Seminole with a sheaf of hundred dollar bills, which would allow him to seek a better life in the city, and put the terrible tragedy behind him.

"That was a very human gesture you just made," observed Webster Neff, who along with Habeas Corpus had kept the grieving Indian company while the float plane was investigated.

"That man could no longer dwell in these environments, having lost so many members of his family," explained Doc.

It was modestly put, but the humanity of the big bronze man was strongly conveyed by his simple words. Not for nothing was Doc Savage's name synonymous with humanitarianism.

The party pushed into the morass, working around carefully, all senses alert, although they knew the thing they were battling exhibited no sights, or sounds, or smells. It was as if they where stalking a force, not a palpable thing.

The lake where the other plane had landed was due east. This necessarily took them farther inland, and deeper into the treacherous Everglades. It was impressive going. Mosquitos returned in force. Many hands got busy slapping at the difficult-to-discourage attackers.

Actually, the pesky mosquitoes left Doc Savage strictly alone.

Webster Neff remarked on this point. "Don't seem to like your blood."

Doc Savage did not enlighten him. It was, in fact, a bit of a mystery. Doc's men suspected that he wore a chemical preparation for repelling the voracious bloodsuckers.

They came to an area of cypress trees and rank swamp choked with cat tails, pickerelweed and red maple.

A sultry breeze was pushing at the reddish leaves, and they issued forth a macabre rustling. This rustling came and went so, when it abated slightly, it was not a very noticeable phenomenon.

Came a procession of soft sounds, a slight pattering here and there.

Monk looked up, sniffing the air. "Rain drops?"

"No," stated Doc Savage. "Insects falling dead."

Louder thumps followed. Heavier things were landing all about.

A fat water moccasin uncoiled out of a tree and landed in a loose coil of scale and lean meat. It did not otherwise stir.

The serpent landed close by, but Doc Savage blocked impetuous Monk from investigating.

"Keep back," Doc warned.

"Huh?" gulped Monk.

"Too dangerous," admonished the bronze man. "Water moccasins do not normally slither up trees. Something disturbed it. Best you gather up Habeas Corpus before he wanders into a lethal area."

Another faint thud came, and they could see that this was a blue-gray peregrine falcon, which had fallen from the sky. It had not landed very far away, wings askew.

Sensitive ears hunting, Doc Savage attempted to triangulate the different sounds in the foul morass.

Suddenly, there was a commotion to the south, and a young deer routed by Habeas Corpus came bounding along.

Monk went rushing after Habeas.

He grabbed the scrawny porker just in time, for the deer blundered into an obstacle it failed to discern. Striking its head against nothing that could be seen, the tawny animal crumpled and lay still.

"Blazes!" howled Monk, clutching his pig more tightly.

They retreated from that portion of the swamp. Doc Savage led them around the sinister swath of doom to safety and decided to take action.

The bronze man toted within his carryall vest many gadgets appropriate for any occasion. This time he pulled out a metallic cartridge, which he primed and then threw in the direction of the deer.

Pallid smoke tinged with green began spurting from the cartridge. Doc watched the smoke snake out in all directions, but when it moved toward the deer, it began to spread out in a flat plane, as if encountering a stone wall.

He primed other cartridges, flung them here and there, creating a great deal of billowing vapor that crawled around, spreading, gathering and revealing by its behavior an unseen barrier that could not be penetrated.

Moving toward this obstruction, Doc Savage scrutinized the weird space, seeking to determine its extent and compass. He perceived nothing moving within the void. But farther along, perhaps fifty feet from where he stood, birds flew and dragonflies darted. The width of the phenomenon was becoming clear, but its breadth was as yet unknown.

Crowding close, the others observed what the bronze man had discovered.

"This is no natural phenomenon," Doc apprised them. "But a calculated zone, laid down by men."

"In other words, a field of force," suggested Ham Brooks.

"Possibly," said the bronze man. "The fields are of varying intensities. Some of them, such as the ones in the Middle West, simply blocked moving objects. But the zones here in the Everglades seem calibrated to snuff out the life of anything caught within their influence."

"Sounds like somebody's testin' somethin'," Monk muttered.

Doc nodded. "Undoubtedly field experiments to test the efficacy of the apparatus in preparation for whatever horrible event is to come."

"Where do we uncover the agency behind it?" demanded Ham.

"There are undoubtedly observers stationed in Florida to report results," Doc said flatly. "We must locate them."

Monk made fists and faces, ground out, "Just let me get my

mitts on them. I'll show 'em!"

They began walking along in parallel to the area of force, which did not appear to be moving. They were intent on seeing how long it stretched, which might or might not lead them to the originating point of the unseen power, depending upon the compass point from which the influence was being directed.

Suddenly, Monk bellowed, "Lookit!"

Doc Savage had already noticed the thing that Monk was indicating with a stabbing finger.

There was a man beyond the swath of stillness. He appeared to be standing on the other side of the zone, where it was presumably safe. He was shouting at them. Or so it seemed. His graying head was thrown back, his lips moving in a very active manner, but no sound issued from his open mouth.

"I can't hear a word he is saying," complained Ham.

"That's because the doggone zone is dead to sound waves," Monk elaborated.

They rushed up to get a better look at the man, taking great pains to keep clear of the edge of the static zone, which could not be determined except by inference. Where leaves in the semi-tropical trees moved in the sultry breeze, they knew it was safe to tread. Where they hung still and lifeless when they should not be, meant that death hovered under the branches of those trees.

Webster Neff was the first to recognize the silent individual. "Boy, howdy!" he exclaimed. "Look who it is!"

The shouting man who made no sound was probably one of the last persons they ever expected to encounter in the Everglades. He proved to be Theodore Buffington, Vice-President of the Huron Motor Company, who had so energetically taken charge of the investigation after the mysterious demise of Phineas P. Slade in Detroit.

Seeing Buffington, Monk growled, "I bet that bird's mixed up in this. I never liked him from the start. He's too pushy."

Ham astutely pointed out, "That's out. He evidently doesn't

understand that his voice cannot carry through the zone. Otherwise, he wouldn't be trying to talk right now."

"Strange that Buffington is prowling around these parts," muttered Web Neff.

Dryly, Ham pointed out, "Buffington is probably thinking the same of you, Neff."

DOC SAVAGE was silent throughout this exchange. The bronze man was studying the gesticulating form of Theodore Buffington intently. His powers of concentration, schooled by years of study, were remarkable. Because of the sometimes uncanny way in which Doc operated, drawing conclusions and inferences seemingly out of thin air, some uninformed persons had whispered that the bronze man possessed powers far beyond those of ordinary humans.

Indeed, certain disreputable tabloid newspapers had all but stated in print that Doc Savage possessed the far-seeing vision of a modern-day Cassandra.

Turning to address his men, the big bronze man appeared to validate those wild speculations. "This barrier ends about a quarter-mile to the north. We will go there and meet up with Buffington."

Web Neff lost control of his lower jaw. It sagged ridiculously.

"How—how do you figure that?"

Ham Brooks said nonchalantly, "Buffington just told him so. Doc Savage is an expert lip reader."

"Oh," muttered Neff. "It's not so mystifying when you know how the magician pulled the rabbit out of his top hat."

Doc Savage leading, Monk and Ham broke off their argument and trudged in his wake. Monk continued to carry Habeas in the crook of one burly arm, sometimes for variety swinging him at his side by one elongated ear. Contrary to all expectation, the ear was not uprooted, and the porker appeared to enjoy being swung by the aural appendage as they marched along.

They took extreme care not to drift near the invisible barrier whose line of demarcation could not be discerned without risk of succumbing to the life-suppressing force that lay within.

A quarter of a mile to the north, they came to a stretch where the leaves rustled freely, and mosquitoes buzzed unhindered by the deathly blanket of silence.

As he approached them, Buffington's sharp voice became audible.

He again demonstrated his aggressive nature by advancing upon Webster Neff and demanding, "What are you doing down here, Neff?"

Before the Huron employee could reply, Doc Savage said quietly, "We could ask the same of you."

Buffington snapped his gray head around, and met the bronze man's frank gaze with his own challenging glare.

"I am hunting for Felix Frost, who escaped a police manhunt last night."

Ham Brooks asked, "Frost is wanted by the Detroit police?"

"No," Buffington retorted. "But it was just a matter of time. Charges were being considered. Frost must have gotten wind of it somehow. The rascal fled."

Doc Savage said, "What charges?"

Buffington replied, "He is under suspicion for the murder of Phineas P. Slade. Not to mention complicity in the automobile accidents that are plaguing the midwest, and continue even as we speak."

"How is it you were able to trail Frost to this locality?" Doc asked.

"Frost owned a personal plane, and in this lit out for Florida. The police have been hunting it. I happen to know that Frost has a winter home near Tampa. It only made sense that he was making his way there."

Suspicion threading his voice, Ham Brooks asked, "We are quite a distance from Tampa."

"I wired the Florida authorities to keep an eye out for him," supplied the Huron executive. "Frost's personal plane was definitely sighted in this vicinity. So I came here first."

"Sounds reasonable to me," Monk Mayfair said agreeably. In fact, it was considerably less than reasonable, but hearing the suspicion in the dapper lawyer's voice, the hairy chemist naturally took the opposite stance.

"What is so reasonable about that story?" demanded Ham of Monk.

Theodore Buffington announced in a self-important tone, "It has been decided that with the death of Phineas P. Slade, I am now in charge of the Huron Motor Company."

Turning his attention to the company's test driver, Buffington repeated his question. "Neff, what are you doing in Florida? You have not made a satisfactory report, for that matter any report, on the loss of the Huron Speedster."

Webster Neff shuffled his feet uneasily, did not seem to know what to say.

Doc Savage came to his assistance. "Mr. Neff was under the impression that he had been dismissed."

"No man will be fired from Huron unless I personally fire him!" thundered Theodore Buffington.

"So he has not been terminated in his capacity as test driver?" questioned Doc.

Buffington glowered craggily at the test driver. "Not as yet."

Perking up, Web Neff said, "The Speedster was wrecked because I was distracted by a downed hawk, and then a blimp falling from the sky. Now we think that these weird invisible walls may have blocked it, not brake failure." The test driver glanced eagerly at Doc Savage, "It explains why brake pedals everywhere are locking up, too."

"I will want that in writing," barked Buffington tersely. "As for your future employment, that will be decided at a later date."

"Bunk!" muttered Neff under his breath.

Doc Savage interjected, "Have you the address of Felix Frost's

Tampa winter home?"

"Yes, I do. Naturally, I called the number, but no one answered. Otherwise, I would have gone there first thing."

Doc Savage said, "A seaplane has been reported to have landed on a nearby lake. We might assume that is Frost's ship. Since that lake lies due south of here, it is not unreasonable to deduce that the strange force that is suppressing life may be emanating from that plane."

"Then we should go there at once!" snapped Buffington.

They started back. Ham Brooks continued to question the new President of the Huron Motor works. The impatient executive became more irate the longer the interrogation went on. Consequently, the exchange produced no fruit. Buffington seemed under the impression that he was in charge of the hunt for Felix Frost.

Doc Savage did not seem to pay any attention to this, but instead watched for signs that the invisible field of death was still operating.

It was difficult to tell, so Monk Mayfair hunted up a small scarlet kingsnake, pronged it with a forked stick, and flung it toward the weird zone.

What happened next was uncanny. The snake was coiling as it arced into the air, very much alive, for it hissed sibilantly.

The red reptile seemed to have struck something, something that could not be seen, for as soon as it did, its ophidian animation seem to depart. It dropped onto the ground and moved no more after that.

"Howlin' calamities!" squeaked Monk. "That dang Hoodoo force is still active."

Eyes uneasy, they backed even farther from the invisible obstruction.

Unnervingly, as they made progress, every sense keyed up, their bodies tense and ready for action, the barrier seemed to move.

At first, the invisible void appeared to retreat from the area in which they were walking. Leaves that had been still, now began to flutter and rustle once more.

"It's retreating!" declared Ham Brooks, calling attention to a perfectly obvious state of affairs, as people will in moments of intense excitement.

Doc Savage, moving with caution, glided in that direction. His alert senses uncovered numerous dead insects and small lifeless animals in the area where the weird zone had been laid down.

What happened next was wholly unexpected.

The zone, which was definitely moving away, evidently stopped. Swinging branches and leaves indicated this. Suddenly, it shifted back in their direction like a plunging monster of invisibility.

Doc Savage detected this action first. Wheeling, he rushed back, and without a word impelled the others at right angles, away from the oncoming invisible wall.

They ran, blundering through brush. Ham extracted his concealed blade and used it to chop up obstructing sawgrass and reedy brush.

The great wall—it felt like a zone of negative pressure in the atmosphere, but was otherwise not palpable—bore down on them.

Doc reached into his gadget vest, plucked out a smooth-skinned steel grenade. Arming this, he flung it backwards.

The grenade sped through the air, encountered an obstruction and fell.

It landed shorter than Doc expected. He reached out great bronze arms and flung Webster Neff and Theodore Buffington to the ground, threw his giant frame atop them, protecting both.

Monk and Ham likewise flattened, Monk clutching Habeas Corpus protectively.

The shoat squealed in confusion.

They waited for the inevitable detonation.

It did not come.

Monk took his fingers out of his ears, and peered back in wonder.

The grenade had fallen in such a way that it could be clearly seen. It just lay there, its silvery egg shape gleaming in the morning sun.

"Dud," Monk muttered, picking himself up.

Doc was already on his feet. "No, not a dud," he imparted.

His weird golden eyes were raking the surroundings, trying to ascertain the angles of the wall. This was impossible to see directly, but changes amid foliage and clouds of mosquitoes provided clues.

Abruptly, Doc rapped out, "Move!"

The others needed no further encouragement. Scrambling, they ran and ran and ran. For the invisible wall was still moving. Charging toward them!

Glancing black, Ham saw the grenade finally explode—far later than it should have, according to its timing mechanism.

A flashing flare and resulting smoke of the detonation was the only sign. It apparently detonated on the other side of the moving wall, for the sound of its letting go did not reach their ears.

They kept running. No choice in the matter. They could no longer see or sense or guess where the wall might have stopped. So there was no other safe course of action than to keep ahead of the moving monster of invisibility.

Eventually, the wall stopped and began retreating.

They realized this only after the wall had been doing so for a minute or so.

Doc Savage signed for a halt.

Panting, Webster Neff asked, "What the heck is going on?"

Doc Savage replied, "The master of the mechanism behind this deadly phenomenon is sweeping its influence back and forth in the hope of slaying us."

Balling his fists, Monk muttered, "He ain't doin' such a bang-up job."

Ham Brooks eyed Theodore Buffington skeptically.

"You were in just as much peril as we were," he observed, pointing with his cane.

"Which proves my point," Buffington stated confidently. "Frost means to kill me, since I am the one pressing for charges to be levied against him."

Doc asked pointedly, "How does Frost know that you are here?"

Theodore Buffington momentarily lost his belligerent composure. "I—I imagine he has spies hereabouts, or other ways of knowing things. Confound it, how would I know?"

It was a reasonable statement, and accepted on the face of it. At least, no one possessed any contradictory information.

Before long, the Everglades returned to normalcy. There was a change in the atmosphere, followed by an increased rustling of leaves and a greater drone of insects. A breeze sprang up. They had not noticed it before, but now it told them that air was circulating freely and unobstructed by the unknown force.

It was impossible to say for certain, but they began to suspect that whatever machinery created the moving monster wall had been shut off.

Not long after that realization dawned upon them, a high-wing, green and white seaplane flew low overhead.

Buffington looked up, shot out an accusing finger, and yelled, "That's Frost's plane! No question about it."

Doc Savage scrutinized the buzzing aircraft. It was not flying very high, and executed broad aerial swings, as if searching the ground.

"Be prepared for anything," cautioned Doc.

The bronze man proved to be prescient.

The green and white ship circled, then began moaning in their direction.

Doc's voice crashed out, "Run in different directions. We will make less of a target that way!"

The five men scattered. Monk and Ham hastily yanked their

machine pistols from underarm holsters. Running and turning around, they unleashed a storm of slugs.

These were mercy bullets, and would have no significant effect upon the plane, being simply hollow capsules filled with a quick-acting anesthetic of Doc Savage's invention.

Curled magazines quickly ran empty, and from their pockets they produced heavier drums, filled with solid slugs, which they affixed forward of the trigger guards.

Unleashing twin streams of lead, the pair managed to clip the plane's wings and struts in such a way that the pilot decided that retreat was the better course of action. They caught a glimpse of him. He wore a leather pilot's helmet, eyes masked by aviator's goggles. Nothing definite could be said about his features.

The small seaplane moaned away, and there were no further consequences.

Once it was clear that the supermachine pistols had discouraged the attacking aircraft, they regrouped and made plans.

Doc Savage said, "Likely the pilot is headed for Tampa. Let us reclaim Renny's plane and follow it."

"I would like to go along," asserted Theodore Buffington.

Doc Savage said, "It may not be safe."

"Hang safety!" bit out Buffington. "That damn killer is an employee of the Huron Motor Company, and it is my bounden duty to apprehend him, strip him of his position, and hand him over to the legal authorities. This I will do in the name of my late employer, Phineas P. Slade. May he rest in peace."

There was so much trembling emotion in the man's voice that no one felt it necessary to disabuse him of his firm intentions.

Turning south, they marched back to Renny's plane. The whereabouts of the missing engineer and Pat Savage weighed heavily on their minds. But without a trail to follow, a search of the vast wilderness that was the Everglades would be pointless.

Chapter VII

MONK GETS HIS TEETH IN SOMETHING

RENNY'S FLOAT PLANE was still deserted when they returned to it.

This was a tremendous relief because for all they knew, their attacker—or attackers, as the case might be—might have disabled it in some way. It sat as placid as a roosting waterfowl on a millpond.

Nevertheless, Doc Savage signaled for the others to wait on the placid lake's shore before approaching the plane, and ascertaining that it was safe to board.

They climbed in, and Doc begin the procedure to start the engines.

"What about your missing friends?" asked Webster Neff as he settled into his seat.

Snapping switches, Doc Savage said, "The absence of any sign that they were carried off the lake strongly suggests that Renny and Pat were conveyed to the mystery seaplane which had lighted on this lake."

"For cryin' out loud!" exploded Monk. "Do you think they were on that other plane?"

"It is to be hoped," said Doc, impelling the madly-vibrating float plane forward. The bronze man soon had them in the air, executing a remarkable take-off considering the modest size of the lake.

Turning north, Doc pointed the howling plane toward the city of Tampa, on the Florida Gulf Coast.

The others occupied various seats distributed throughout the cramped cabin. Ham Brooks, to kill time more than anything else, begin speaking.

"What nearly happened to us back there may explain the fate of our aircraft over the Gulf."

Theodore Buffington looked interested and asked, "What befell your aircraft?"

Monk grunted, "It hit a dang Hoodoo."

The graying Huron executive looked at him with askance eyes. "Surely, you are jesting," he said crisply.

Ham snapped, "Ignore that ape. He was born with fewer brains than normal, and they never grew much."

"At least I have scruples," retorted Monk. "Scruples enough not to turn to ambulance chasin' for my meal ticket."

Buffington raised a quizzical eyebrow in Monk's direction. "Oh, and what is wrong with the legal profession?"

"What's right with it?" mumbled Monk. "That's what I want to know!"

Ham Brooks continued declaiming. "It is reasonable to surmise that Doc's plane was followed from Detroit, its distinctive bronze paint making it very noticeable, and therefore easy to track."

Webster Neff commented, "So you think that Felix Frost followed your aircraft, and ambushed you over the Gulf of Mexico?"

Ham nodded firmly. "I do."

Doc Savage offered, "A plane as small as that mystery seaplane would not be visible at a great distance. And, if we can assume he carried the diabolical device along with him, Frost could have pointed it in our direction, with the result that our aircraft struck the field of force that led to its destruction."

Monk grimaced. "I don't get it. If he was flyin' so far behind us that we couldn't see him, how could he aim the thing right?"

"He could not," advised Doc. "But he did not need to aim

accurately, since the field of force seems to be a very large phenomenon in and of itself. Just as was done back in the Everglades, it was a simple matter to sweep the deadly influence back and forth in the hope of succeeding."

Monk grumbled, "The dingus must be right powerful to put out that much death."

Web Neff commented, "If Mr. Savage's theory is correct, then the device must have been present near the Huron Motor headquarters in order to slay Mr. Slade."

Doc said, "Frost need not have been the one manipulating it, either. And he probably was not, since he was present in the executive office when the strange events transpired."

Ham said, "No doubt he had an accomplice, if not several of them."

"But what are the man's motives?" Theodore Buffington thundered. "This is what baffles me."

"His motives," reminded Doc, "remain to be discovered. Speculation would be useless at this point."

"He was, or seemed to be," amended Buffington, "a model employee. Although I will admit that Frost was not an employee for very long—considerably less than a year, if my memory serves."

Monk snorted, "That little catlike guy looked kind of foreign to me."

"I am glad you said that," said Buffington. "I have been wondering if Felix Frost is even his true name."

"Have you any proof of this?" demanded Ham Brooks.

"Only suspicion," admitted Buffington in a surly tone.

Monk decided to change the subject. "Doc, do you think Renny and Pat are—"

The homely chemist swallowed hard, unable to finish.

Doc Savage was unusually slow in replying. "It is to be hoped that they are prisoners, and that they will surface sooner than later. To have remained and searched the Everglades would have taken weeks, if not months, without any clue as to their actual whereabouts."

The bronze man's tones, usually even, rang uncharacteristically troubled. It was clear to his men that Doc Savage would have spent the rest of his life looking for Renny and Pat Savage if the sweep of events were not forcing his hand, and compelling him to fly to Tampa in the hope that their friends could be found alive as prisoners somewhere in that city.

As they approached the coastal city from the air, Doc Savage asked, "What is the address of Felix Frost's winter residence?"

Buffington replied, "It is in Ybor City, the Cuban colony."

Doc nodded. "I am familiar with it."

"Never heard of it," said Monk.

"It is a remarkable little village," said Theodore Buffington expansively. "It was founded by a man named Ybor, who had fled Cuba during one of its many periods of political unrest. He was a cigar manufacturer, and came to Florida to establish—or should I say re-establish—his lucrative cigar-making business."

Ham regarded the Huron executive suspiciously. "You seem to know a lot about this place."

"Indeed. I happen to enjoy a good Cuban cigar now and then. And cigars made in Ybor City are as fine as any rolled in Havana. Or should I say that they were. For the present business depression has made the hand-rolling of cigars less economical than it once was. Furthermore, demand for fine cigars has understandably dropped off since the stock market collapse."

Ham wondered, "You have been to this town before?"

"Ybor City? No, I have not. But I have visited Tampa. In fact, I once played nine holes on its golf course. Playing golf in Florida is a good deal different than golfing in Detroit. For one thing, it is not unusual for the first man to tee off in the morning to have to step around dozing alligators and drive away rattlesnakes with his nine iron."

"Charming," remarked Ham Brooks.

"For fifty years," continued Buffington, "Ybor City was one of the great cigar manufacturing centers in the United States. They still make cigars, of course, but now they are manufactured by machines, and not lovingly rolled by hand. You would not think that would make such a difference, but it does. Hand-rolled cigars are far superior. The machine brand produces a noticeably inferior smoke."

Doc Savage's men did not as a rule smoke tobacco, so as Theodore Buffington waxed enthusiastic about the virtues of various brands of cigars, their attention noticeably flagged.

Soon enough, but not quite as soon as they would have liked, given how the pushy Buffington dominated the conversation, Doc slanted the seaplane in for a landing at the Tampa airport.

Once on the ground, and having seen to the hangaring of Renny's plane, they rented a tasteful gray sedan, perfect for tooling around the city without attracting undue attention.

After Doc got the machine in motion, he asked Buffington for the exact address of Felix Frost's winter home.

"Number 50 Sarasota Drive."

Doc piloted the subdued sedan without consulting a map. He had memorized maps of towns and villages and cities all over the world. Without any further prompting, he knew exactly where to go. None of his men remarked on this point. They were accustomed to the bronze giant's casual wizardry.

As they approached Number 50 Sarasota Drive, Doc slowed down.

The street was not a residential one. Far from it. Dingy brick buildings pressed close to one another. Many appeared to be factories or warehouses.

Number 50 proved to be nothing less than a cigar factory three stories in height and possessing a corrugated-tin covered rear entrance that no doubt doubled for a loading dock.

A fading sign high up on the building read: EXCELLENT CIGARS.

"I do not understand," grumbled Buffington. "I have this

address on the highest authority."

Monk got out, crinkled his punch-flattened nose at the dirty brick building and said, "Won't hurt to sniff around."

Ham Brooks turned to Doc Savage and asked, "Could this be a trap of some kind?"

Doc Savage stepped out from behind the wheel and looked over the roof of the sedan, appraising the disreputable-looking brick building. Although it was broad daylight, there appeared to be no signs of activity in the cigar factory. That, and its tangible air of seediness, was suspicious.

On the other hand, it was a Saturday. With more and more companies adopting the five-day work week, perhaps the factory was not in operation on the weekend.

Doc said, "We will approach with due caution."

Hearing that, Monk and Ham unlimbered their supermachine pistols. To them, due caution evidently meant ready for battle.

Buffington and Neff hung back, uncertain whether to join the others.

Doc told them, "Although the place appears to be deserted, it might be better to remain in the automobile for your own safety."

Buffington retreated to the sedan. Neff followed him, wearing a disappointed expression. When he had earlier claimed that he liked excitement, evidently that was true. The arduous experience in the Everglades had not cooled his youthful yen for adventure.

"Boy, howdy," he said enthusiastically. "Call us if you get into a jam, won't you?"

Doc Savage decided to circle the block before attempting to enter the factory. He discerned nothing out of the ordinary.

Before long, they were moving through a back lot, which was grassy and overgrown, choked with the kinds of weeds common in Florida, predominately chickweed and goosegrass.

Doc Savage halted, looking around with a general attitude of concern, even though his metallic features remained impassive.

Ham whispered, "What do you see?"

"Grass that has not been cut in several weeks. A going concern is unlikely to leave their backyard unattended."

Monk pointed out, "Those trucks backed up to the loading docks look like they're in use."

The trucks, however, looked old and not necessarily in frequent use.

Carefully, they advanced, Doc Savage in the lead.

It was fortunate, as events developed, that the bronze man went first. For Doc's ever-active eyes ranged along the grass, rather than the building. So it was that he spied a slight stirring in the thick greenery to his left.

Ham noticed it, too. Unsheathing his sword cane, he advanced with the weapon pointed low and downward. The elegant barrister was so focused on this phenomenon of moving grass that he was caught by surprise when a metallic hand abruptly snatched the cane from his fingers.

Jumping back wildly, Ham pivoted—just in time to see Doc Savage slashing at the grass with the borrowed sword cane. But the bronze man did not attack the spot Ham had been concentrating upon, but rather another one ahead and to the right.

Something small and round leapt into the air. Ham caught only a glimpse of it. But the glimpse was grisly.

For the narrow brown head of a diamondback rattlesnake had flashed up, severed from its long body by Doc Savage's quick, certain stroke.

Shifting to the left, the bronze man employed the sword cane to impale a second diamondback—one which had darted toward him.

Doc lifted the blade, showing the unlovely serpent writhing in its death throes.

"Jove!" exclaimed Ham. "We have stumbled upon a nest of rattlers!"

"Rattlers?" howled Monk. "How come I don't hear no rattlin'?"

Doc displayed the dying snake, holding it before Monk and Ham's narrowing eyes. "The rattle has been removed surgically, so as to give no warning," he pointed out.

"Clever," gritted Ham.

Doc returned the sword cane to Ham, saying, "Walk behind me."

They advanced carefully, Monk swiveling his head from side to side, in order to miss nothing. The hairy chemist normally feared few dangers, but he had grown up in rattlesnake country and possessed a healthy respect for the vicious vipers.

Ham reached out and hacked off the head of another coiled serpent before it could sink gleaming fangs into his leg.

Doc counted two more vipers, one of which coiled itself to strike, only to discover metallic bronze fingers seizing its throat back of the head. The other hand took firm hold of the truncated tail, and Doc presented it to Ham Brooks for bisecting.

While they were doing that, a second snake crawled up from behind Doc Savage and sank its fangs into his left ankle.

Firmly, Doc lifted a foot and trampled it, crushing its tapering skull with his heel.

Monk called out, "It got Doc!"

The bronze man shook his head slowly, lifted his trouser leg and showed the alloy chainmail armor which had protected him from the poisonous fangs.

"Forgot about your long underwear," grunted Monk.

They pressed on.

SUDDENLY, a frantic squealing seized their attention.

Monk turned his bullet head, teeth gritting together.

The source of the squealing was no surprise. Habeas Corpus had cornered a diamondback—or perhaps it was the other way around. Monk had adopted the porker during an adventure in Arabia, and Bedouin legend had it that Habeas was a terror to hyenas. There had been ample evidence suggesting there was some truth to that claim in the past.

Now the shoat seemed intent upon seizing the slithering diamondback rattler in its blunt tusks.

Roaring rage, Monk Mayfair charged for the sidewinder.

Its horrific jaws distended, the snake exposed gleaming fangs like ivory needles.

As the reptile began to strike, Habeas jerked to one side. The pig was smart; he understood the silent rattler's deadly intent.

Piling in, the simian chemist grabbed the snake back of its head with one hand, seizing the dead rattles in the tail with the other, just as Doc had done.

When he came ambling back, the viper was squirming and looping in his hairy hands like a mad thing, hissing helplessly.

Ham Brooks briskly strode up, blade poised to sever the coiling reptile.

Before he could do so, Monk Mayfair did something unusual even for him. Monk was a man of unbridled passions, and one of his driving passions in life, other than pretty girls, was his pet pig, Habeas Corpus.

Without giving it any thought whatsoever, the homely chemist decided to dispatch the snake in the most efficient manner possible. He brought the writhing reptile up, stretching it to its full length, and bit down hard with his strong white teeth.

The rattler let out an angry hiss, then subsided. Monk dropped the squirming thing to the grass, watched to see what it did, and realized that all life had fled.

Eyes bugging out of his head, the dapper lawyer remarked, "Well, you wire-haired ape, you said you wanted to get your teeth into something. Now you have."

Monk did not see the humor in that. He bent down to pick up Habeas, patting the porker reassuringly on the head.

"Hog," he said gruffly. "From now on, leave all the snake fightin' to me. I got better choppers for it anyway."

They continued tramping the weedy grass, seeking more vipers. They found a final nest, halted as the vipers began hissing in warning.

Doc Savage produced from his vest a silver case containing small glass spheres, filled with a colorless liquid, removed one, and tossed it at the writhing nest.

The bronze man held his breath. It was unnecessary for Doc to direct his men to do the same, since all knew the glass balls contained a quick-acting and extremely potent anesthetic.

The thin-walled globule landed in the grass, broke, releasing an odorless vapor, which soon caused all serpentine movement to go slack. Lifting brown heads dropped from sight with cartoon alacrity.

Ham went around the yard, whacking at high weeds with his blade, then reported with grim satisfaction, "That appears to be the last of the rattlesnakes." He shook droplets of gore from his thin blade.

They resumed their stealthy approach to the old cigar factory.

It was an unprepossessing sight. There were two sets of rusting iron steps going up to the concrete loading dock, which was sheltered by an equally rusty sheet-metal awning.

Doc took one set of stairs and directed Monk and Ham to mount the other. They kept their eyes sharp for signs of human habitation. There appeared to be none.

Doc reached the loading dock first, and looked around, flake-gold orbs very active in their interior eddies.

Ham mounted the steps before Monk, and also peered about, sword cane gripped in one hand, superfirer in the other.

Glancing upward, the elegant attorney saw something that caused him to flinch and lift his sword cane defensively.

Charging up, Monk Mayfair grunted, "What is it?"

"Hideous," returned the dapper lawyer.

Monk looked up, as well. In a crack under the awning hung a bizarre, yellowish creature. It possessed eight legs and the hard carapace of a lobster or crab. But it was no crustacean. It began to move creepily on striped legs.

Doc Savage strolled over, scrutinized the thing, and said, "Banana spider. Harmless."

Monk Mayfair grunted, "Looks like it dropped down from the moon."

"It is a subtropical spider with a horny outer shell, entirely harmless as to venom," explained Doc.

Still, Monk and Ham gave it a wide berth as they moved ahead.

They crowded around an entrance door. Doc tested the knob. It was securely locked.

Removing several items from his pockets, the bronze man inserted something into the keyhole, and they drew back to a safe distance at his imperative gesture.

Soon, the lock commenced hissing and sparking angrily, then began dribbling molten metal.

Doc Savage had inserted the makings of Thermite into the lock, and the combustible combination of chemicals had made short work of it.

Cautiously, Doc pushed the door open, training ahead of him the wide beam of a powerful flashlight that was of the spring-generator type which required no batteries.

The light disclosed the gloomy and apparently disused interior. Great machines were scattered about, evidently for the manufacturing of cigars. High stacks of wooden crates and smaller cardboard boxes stood here and there.

"Place looks deserted," murmured Monk, pointing the sharp snout of his superfirer this way and that, prepared to cut loose at the slightest provocation.

There was thick dust on some of the boxes, Ham discovered by running an immaculate finger across their tops. Cobwebs in corners added to the impression of disuse.

They moved among the stacks, weapons ready for action. Doc Savage, of course, did not display a machine pistol, owing to his preference not to be reliant on firearms.

The closed atmosphere was redolent of dried tobacco leaves. There was an old conveyor belt, rotted, and obviously out of use, adding to the picture of abandonment.

"Deuced peculiar," mused Ham Brooks.

"What is?" grunted Monk.

"Theodore Buffington told us that making cigars with machinery such as this was a recent innovation."

"Don't mean that this outfit didn't go bust in the business depression," countered Monk.

"Bootleg operation," Doc suggested quietly. "Perhaps shut down by the authorities."

They began easing in the direction of a flight of old rickety steps when they heard a sound like that of a scuttling animal, possibly a rodent. Everyone froze in place.

Listening hard, they waited.

The sound did not come again.

They continued creeping toward the stairs.

The next sound they heard took them by surprise. It was a cough, not human.

The cough was almost immediately followed by an ugly chopping sound. A wooden cigar box near Monk's head jumped, shattering as it struck the cracked concrete floor.

Whirling, Monk bore down on his supermachine pistol trigger, liberally hosing the corner from which the soft noise of the bullet had come—for obviously a silenced weapon had been discharged—and filling the confines with gun thunder and powder flashes so closely spaced the result assaulted the senses.

Crates were knocked about and jostled by the stream of hunting mercy bullets, which individually carried little velocity, but collectively packed a punch.

Ducking behind a jumbled stack of crates, Ham hunkered down, peering about anxiously, seeking a target of his own.

Hissing slugs commenced knocking tall stacks of crates apart. That told Ham more than one assassin was aprowl.

Moving with stealthy ease, and a swiftness that was a little startling, Doc Savage worked his way around the maze of crates in an effort to get close to the gunmen—for the quantity of bullets coming their way told him that a second attacker was stationed well away from the first.

The bronze man had out a handful of flash bombs, which detonated with an eye-hurting light. In another moment, Doc would creep close enough to begin pegging them, in the hope of stunning their assailants.

It was a good plan, and it should have worked.

Then a man's head popped up from behind the crate, staring with huge glassy eyes. The lurker was wearing a gas mask. In one hand he held a glass bottle. He flung it in the general direction of the center of the machine floor.

The bottle struck, broke apart. Liquid splashed, and the stuff soon dispersed with an astringent smell resembling ammonia.

"Poison gas!" howled Ham Brooks.

Doc's men all carried compact gas masks of their own. They retreated to shelter and drew these on. They consisted of protection for mouth, nose and eyes, as well as a chemical filter that would prevent any noxious substance from entering mouth or lungs.

The machine shop floor began filling with the grayish vapors.

Doc flung a flash bomb, producing a blinding pop, then brought out a different type. This was a cartridge grenade. He primed it and threw it.

Black smoke began billowing. It filled the room more swiftly than the other vapor, being chemically generated.

Doc rapped out instructions in the ancient Mayan language, which they habitually employed to communicate among one another in secret. It was a method superior to any other code, inasmuch as almost no one outside of the Valley of the Vanished in Central America spoke the pure tongue. Monk and Ham raced for the stairs, joining him there.

They went up the interior stairs, sacrificing some speed for stealth. But in the end it did not matter, for the dry floorboards squeaked. Bullets began jabbing at them, making ugly pops when they struck wood.

"*Ye-e-o-w!*" howled Monk, feeling slugs plucking at his coat sleeves.

Even harassed by stinging lead, they made it to the top of the stairs, to the second floor, with the only injury being to Ham's custom-blocked hat, which was knocked off his head.

Feet came pounding up the steps in hot pursuit, and Doc grabbed a piece of junk machinery, lifted it as if it did not weigh more than an icebox, then sent it crashing down the stairs.

This discouraged their shadowy pursuers, and Doc led his men up to the third floor.

IT PROVED to be a dimly-lit loft, with heavy rafters comprising the ceiling. There were windows, but all were shuttered. Light bulbs hung bare from drop cords, Doc's questing flash ray disclosed.

Dusty spaces and empty bolt holes indicated heavy machinery had formerly reposed on the unkempt floor. These had been uprooted. Discarded cigar molds, cutting boards and drying racks lay about in cluttered fashion. Underfoot were rolled cigar clippings and scatterings of leaf tobacco that had dried in the attic-like space during the oppressive Florida summers.

Monk and Ham had their flashlights out. For Doc had closed the heavy wooden door behind them, blocking out all light.

Odd sounds could be heard. Rustling and scrapings. They were coming from a far corner. Doc Savage drifted in that direction.

There he found Renny and Pat Savage tied securely behind a cutting rack.

The trussed pair did not look particularly the worse for wear, although their faces were streaked with a combination of perspiration and dust from being held in the close humid confines. Gags were stuffed into their mouths.

Before the bronze man could move in their direction, the wooden door was kicked open and a short, wiry man inserted a silenced revolver into the empty frame.

Ham's blazing flashlight picked him out. And in the bright light the little man's eyes could be seen behind his protective goggles. They were a feline green.

That, combined with the assailant's springy body, caused Monk Mayfair to explode, "Felix Frost!"

Whoever the man was, he took a wild shot at one of the blazing flashlights. It happened to be Doc Savage's. But prudently, the bronze man, realizing his light made him a target, abruptly held it out at arm's length and off to one side.

The sizzling bullet passed under the bronze man's steady fist. It was a simple maneuver, but it took iron nerve to pull it off.

Monk and Ham's superfirers began moaning, releasing the earsplitting sounds they made, which in the close confines of the loft sounded like a titanic bull fiddle being sawed on a bass note.

The green-eyed man was nimble; he faded back. There came a rude sound of something mechanical, like a lever being thrown.

A steel panel, like a fast-moving guillotine, slammed down, sealing off the only exit door. Similar steel plates cut off the shuttered windows at either end of the loft.

Monk rushed the steel-locked door, while Ham Brooks raced to the nearest window.

"Locked in good," Monk growled.

"As much as I hate to agree with that ape," Ham returned, "these steel plates appear to be very solid."

Outside, came a muffled sound. It was laughter. It had a macabre quality of menace tingeing it.

Chapter VIII
THE CELLOPHANE CHAIN

THE FORCE WITH which the heavy steel plates had guillotined down caused the decrepit old brick building to shake and shudder. Now this vibration was fading.

Ham Brooks turned to Monk Mayfair and said waspishly, "Something more solid for you to sink your teeth into, you primitive. I trust you are happy now."

"I'll be happy when your pearly whites fall out and you can't talk!" growled the hairy chemist.

Doc Savage knelt at the end of the loft where Renny and Pat lay trussed. The bronze man removed their gags, beginning with his bronze-haired cousin.

Patricia Savage was not shy about giving forth opinions. "What took you so long to rescue us?" she flared, golden eyes snapping.

Taken aback, Doc Savage was initially at a loss for words. He stripped Renny of his cloth gag.

The big-fisted engineer boomed, "I thought we were goners for sure. They bushwhacked us in the Everglades and hauled us here—wherever it is we are."

"You do not know?" asked Doc, examining Renny's bindings by the simple expedient of grasping them in his metallic hands. They were chains, old and running to rust.

Pat Savage answered that. "We were whiling away the hours until you showed up when birds began dropping out of the sky. It was horrible. Then the air became very, very still. The way it does before a tropical hurricane. We were watching the sky when we started feeling funny."

"Funny?" asked Doc.

"My chest started to ache," Renny rumbled, "and I plumb couldn't breathe. Thought I was having a heart seizure, or something."

"I felt the same way," protested Pat. "It was awful."

"Around that time," continued Renny, "my arms and legs filled with that durn pins-and-needles sensation you sometimes get, and—Holy cow! I don't know what happened after that."

"We blacked out," snapped Pat. "That's what happened. We woke up here, trussed like a couple of prize turkeys."

Just then, a muffled voice came from what appeared to be a wall pipe designed to ventilate the hot humidor of a loft. It jutted out beside the sealed door, very high up, near the ceiling.

"Now that you have been lured here," the odd voice said thickly, "you will become the subject of a scientific experiment."

"I don't like the sound of that," murmured Pat, offering her chafed and bound wrists.

Doc ignored the bronze-haired girl, and concentrated on Renny's shackles. The chains were not heavy, and the big-fisted engineer had done a fair job of trying to pry apart the weakest links with his own elephantine strength. Perhaps with a little more time, he would have succeeded.

Doc Savage took a length of chain in both hands, and exerted his tremendous muscles. A shirt seam actually burst under the pressure of an expanding bicep.

The rusty link snapped smartly. Doc flung the loose chain away, completing the job of freeing the long-faced engineer, whose dour features actually grew more disconsolate. Strangely, this meant that Renny was very pleased indeed. He made blocks of his hands, transforming them into massive mauls that could pulverize the jawbone of any man with a single punch.

"What about me?" Pat demanded huffily.

Again, she was interrupted by the muffled voice coming

through the ventilation pipe.

"You will all die as the Seminoles died in the Everglades death swath. There is no escape from this room. This is the end of Doc Savage!"

As the bronze man began untying Pat Savage, Ham found a light switch by feel and, out of an abundance of caution for fear of booby traps, snapped it on with the flick of his cane.

Four bare light bulbs on dropcords shed feeble illumination. But it was enough to allow them to appraise their surroundings.

Monk had been attempting to lift one of the steel plates sealing a window, with a noticeable lack of success. This despite a ferocious grunting coming from deep within his barrel chest.

"Stuck good," he said, ambling over.

Pat Savage stood up, placed her bronzy fists on her hips and exclaimed, "Well, isn't anybody going to do anything?"

Doc Savage looked at her with a mixture of concern and displeasure. She was a ravishingly attractive young woman, athletic, and well-formed. Her deeply tanned skin, aureate eyes and tawny hair alone showed that she was related to the bronze man, although her coloring was her own.

Doc said quietly, "It would have been better if you had remained back in New York."

"It would have been even better," returned Pat, "if we hadn't been ambushed."

"Have you any inkling of the nature of the ambush?" asked Doc.

Renny answered that. "Holy cow! We were waiting in the plane like I said before, and we blacked out. There was nothing more to it than that. When we woke up, we were here, hogtied like animals for slaughter."

"Cast your thoughts back to the moments before you lost consciousness," suggested the bronze man. "Did you hear or smell anything unusual?"

"Now that you mention it, there was a buzzing," admitted Renny.

"I heard it, too," chimed in Pat. "It sounded like an airplane, but it was far off, and the noise came and went in a peculiar way."

Doc eyed his attractive cousin. "Peculiar?"

"It cut in and out, but not in the way an airplane motor does when it's sputtering. The sound just stopped, came back and went away again."

"I remember it that way, too," remarked Renny. "But we saw no plane, so we decided it must be something else."

"Might have been that seaplane we spotted," muttered Monk. "Flying around one of those invisible barriers, the sound of it would get blocked."

"Barriers?" Pat questioned.

Ham inquired, "Did you see your kidnappers after you woke up?"

Renny shook his big head. "They wore neckerchief masks, like old-style Western badmen. The only thing I noticed is that one of them had green eyes."

Ham exclaimed, "Felix Frost!"

Pat demanded, "Who is Felix Frost?"

But there was no time to answer that question. They all heard a low sound, a whining suggestive of machinery, or a dynamo warming up.

Pat Savage moaned, "I don't like the sound of that."

No one did, least of all Doc Savage. He became very intense in his movements.

"Each of you stand by one of these light bulbs," he directed urgently. "Make them swing about in the dark. Keep them moving."

"What good will that do?" thumped Renny.

"It may," Doc replied, "preserve our lives."

Pretty Pat grimaced. "I like the sound of that even less."

Nevertheless, they rushed to the drop lights, began putting them into motion. This created very strange lighting effects, making the clotting shadows shift and careen around them weirdly, like shadowy black ghosts chasing one another at Halloween.

Doc Savage rushed to the other end of the loft, reaching the window that Monk Mayfair had been attempting to raise.

The steel plate was stout, and it had evidently fitted into grooves in the window frame. It was a cunning bit of workmanship. Obviously, a great deal of thought had gone into transforming this spacious loft into a death trap. This suggested a very professional group of adversaries.

Monk was enormously strong. For that matter, so was Renny. But Doc Savage possessed muscles that, through lifelong training as well as due to their natural qualities, verged on the superhuman.

Doc took hold of the windowsill with both cabled hands. He applied downward pressure. The age-veined sill cracked. That it was old and the wood rotted out was beside the point. The bronze man snapped it as effortlessly as if it were punky balsa wood.

Feeling around with his steel-strong fingers, he found the bottom edge of the steel plate. Bending at the knees, the bronze giant brought his entire body lifting upward, in an attempt to budge the barrier.

It was not locked. This proved fortunate, because the plate began to lift.

Doc shouldered it clear, peered out in the wildly shifting light, and although his face did not change expression, the way in which he lowered the plate back to its original position suggested disappointment, if not defeat.

Turning, the bronze man told the others, "The adjoining building was constructed so that it presses up against this factory. There is no space between the buildings."

Spinning a light bulb around, attempting to keep out of its way, Pat Savage remarked dryly, "Things are starting to look mighty dark around here."

Ignoring the comment, Doc moved to the opposite end and repeated the operation. He all but extracted the windowsill, providing himself with easy access to the plate's bottom edge.

This one came up easily, showing sunlight and open space. Doc stuck his head out, looked downward intently, scrutinizing the wall.

"Can we climb down?" asked Ham.

Instead of replying, Doc found a piece of loose iron and jammed it into the wood to keep the steel plate in an upright position. Then he rushed back and began moving about the big loft, saying, "This side is of brick, but the brick has been faced with stucco. Impossible to climb down by using existing handholds."

This was an impressive admission, inasmuch as the bronze man possessed such finger strength that he could climb almost any brick building, simply by using the mortar spaces between the bricks for finger holds. His men had seen him do this prodigious feat many times, something even a human fly would be timorous about undertaking.

If Doc said he could not climb down the side of the building, no ordinary human could. So that was that.

Bouncing his drop light around with easy bats of his huge paws, Renny groaned, "Holy cow! That humming is growing louder!"

"What is it?" asked Ham.

"No doubt one of the force-field generating devices is warming up," replied Doc Savage in a brittle tone. He was rooting around amid the clutter and debris, seeking a rope or cord to fling out the window.

Doc carried on his person a small folding grappling hook, to which was attached a silk cord. But this cord was so slender that only someone possessing Doc's stupendous strength could safely use it. Monk and Renny might be able to slide down the line in a pinch, but Ham or Pat were unlikely to manage it.

More to the point, the punky wood of the windowsill would

doubtless give way under their weight. And they would have to go down fast, but not altogether.

Lowering them individually by the hook and cord would be too time-consuming, owing to the need to reel in the grapnel each time.

In one corner was a great roll of transparent cellophane, which was used to wrap cigars after their manufacture.

Doc pulled at the sheet, testing it with his hands, attempting to see if the heat and age had caused it to become brittle. Evidently, it had not. The bronze man seemed satisfied with what he found. The cellophane seemed like new. It had not even yellowed.

Ripping off a great swath of it, Doc Savage began twisting it, braiding it into a long, complicated rope.

"Holy cow! What the heck are you doing?" demanded Renny.

"Fashioning a means of escape," returned Doc, working rapidly.

Once he got the cellophane twisted into something resembling semi-transparent rope, the bronze giant moved toward the open window, where he tied one end to a ponderous piece of cigar-making machinery.

This naturally took time, during which the insistent humming continued to impress itself upon their nerves.

The big bronze man had almost completed his task when, at the other end of the loft, near the steel-clad door, the illuminated drop light that Monk Mayfair was making swing crazily about, did something very strange.

In the middle of one flashing arc, it suddenly ceased moving, its cord hanging stationary at a forty-five degree angle, as though seized by an unseen hand. The light bulb simultaneously extinguished itself.

Ham directed his flashlight at the spot.

"BLAZES!" exploded Monk. Beside him, Habeas Corpus stared at the phenomenon with beady eyes and began squealing with porcine unease.

Pat asked, "Monk, what are you doing?"

"I'm doin' nothing!" barked Monk, stepping back from the uncanny light bulb that hung ghostly and unnatural in the dim loft. "It's doing it itself!"

"Our adversaries are laying down their death zones," said Doc grimly. "They have not exactly hit the nail on the head with their first try. But the position of the extinguished light bulb marks the boundary of the field of influence. Everyone keep on this side of the room. It is certain death to move near that bulb."

Doc called to Pat Savage, who was manning the drop light next in line from Monk's position.

"Pat, you go out first. Monk, you manage Pat's light."

"Gotcha, Doc," said Monk, taking over Pat's swinging light bulb. He banged it about with his meaty paws as if juggling an illuminated ball.

Joining Doc Savage by the window, the bronze-haired girl cast a critical eye upon the long, twisted braid of transparent cellophane.

"Will it hold my weight?"

Instead of replying directly, Doc Savage said, "You are the lightest of us all. It will support you if it will support anyone. Down you go."

Pat looked hesitant, but Monk told her, "Cellophane is tough stuff. It has more tensile strength than you'd think by lookin' at it."

Then the apish chemist let out a howl. "The dang invisible wall is movin'!"

All heads turned sharply. Monk's light bulb had extinguished itself, and in the crazily shifting light they could see that it was hanging at an acute angle, as if transfixed by some ghostly hand.

Monk retreated, while Doc Savage gave Pat a gentle shove.

Swinging one shapely leg over the windowsill, Pat put herself in a position to go down the makeshift cellophane chain.

"Wish me luck, fellows," Pat said brightly, and began descending with the natural athletic agility of a girl who grew up out-of-doors.

Doc watched her carefully, saw that Pat was nearing the ground, and called for Ham to go next—the dapper lawyer being the lightest of the remaining four.

As Ham, with evident reluctance and not a little bit of trepidation, followed Pat down, the unseen barrier crept silently along the loft, seizing and extinguishing the third light bulb, until only one remained illuminated.

"We ain't got much time," croaked Monk urgently.

The apish chemist watched as Ham made his way down the strange chain, struck the bottom by simply letting go, rather than continue to put strain on the precarious cellophane contrivance.

Doc whipped to the anchorage to double-check it, seemed satisfied, and turned to Monk and Renny. "You both weigh about the same," he said. "It is up to the two of you to decide which one goes next."

Monk and Renny swapped looks and Renny grunted, "You ought to do better than me, being half gorilla," rumbled the big-fisted engineer.

Monk shook his rusty head. "You got bigger hands, the better to hold on, so you go ahead."

It was plain that neither man wanted to be the one to go first, with the inexorably moving invisible wall creeping forward, seeking to snuff out their lives.

Doc Savage settled the matter by giving them both a shove toward the window.

They all but fell out. It seemed to be a cruel thing to do, but the urgency of the situation demanded decisive action.

Gorilla-like, Monk swung out, began dropping down, hand over hand, while Renny swung one knobby leg over the windowsill.

Meanwhile, Doc Savage had removed his tiny grapple and

silk cord, and was hooking the sharp steel tines to the same machinery used for the cellophane chain anchor.

The final light bulb went out when he did so. Doc no longer needed the light, of course, but this phenomenon told him that the time to escape alive was now very, very short.

While Renny was still clambering down the cellophane chain, Doc Savage reached the window, tossed out his silken cord, and began descending in his own fashion. Despite the big engineer's significant head start, the bronze man beat Renny to the ground.

Once on the ground, Doc got them together and compelled everyone to keep moving, saying, "There is no telling how far that electromagnetic barrier-field can be made to extend."

They did not risk running out to the street, where they had left their machine, lest they become targets for a sniper's bullets. So they moved into the adjoining back lot of what proved to be a warehouse, where there were no overlooking windows.

No bullets found them, and Doc led the group around the massive warehouse until at last they reached the front.

Doc Savage stopped at the corner edge of the warehouse, removed a little black pipe of a device, and transformed the monocular into a periscope with some deft manipulations. He employed this to peer around the edge, until he could spy the waiting sedan in which Webster Neff and Theodore Buffington were left.

The sedan was no longer waiting. It had departed.

IT WAS a rare thing when Doc Savage hesitated in action.

The bronze man was a deliberate sort of individual. He was not afraid to plunge into danger, but he also possessed a normal ration of caution and common sense, his sometimes rash-seeming behavior in combat notwithstanding.

Seeing that the rented sedan in which he had driven to the spot was no longer there, Doc seemed at a momentary loss for a clear course of action.

Behind him, Monk Mayfair was asking, "What's goin' on?"

"The machine which Theodore Buffington and Webster Neff were occupying is no longer there."

"Blast it!" Ham clipped. "They led us into a trap, and escaped, leaving us for dead."

"Well, one of them did," retorted Monk. "But which one?"

Pat Savage wanted to know, "Who are you all talking about?"

"Never mind that now," returned Doc Savage. "That death wall may still be moving in our direction."

"Yeah, it might," Monk grunted. "But how do we tell for sure?"

Doc Savage suddenly reached into his pocket and brought out his spring-generator powered flashlight. He gave it a vigorous winding, and snapped it on.

In broad daylight, it produced an amazingly distinct glow, but it was certainly not useful illumination under the glaring Florida sunlight.

Renny Renwick frowned. Monk looked perplexed for a moment.

More quick-witted than the others, Ham Brooks suddenly realized the significance of Doc's inexplicable actions. He brought out his own flashlight, thumbed it on.

Then Monk got it. His simian features lit up. He copied the action, producing additional illumination.

Clarity dawned on Pat Savage at that point.

"If the lights stay on, we're not in immediate danger," she breathed.

"Precisely," said Doc, pointing his flash ray in the general direction of the cigar factory on the other side of the warehouse.

Doc Savage leading, they made a hasty retreat, directing their flashlights behind them, sometimes walking backwards, but traveling as briskly as they could.

When they had gotten a fair distance, Doc placed his flashlight on the ground and retreated to observe it.

Nothing much appeared to happen. Then suddenly the light

went out. It had been a dim flare in the grass, but now it was dormant.

Monk asked, "Did it just lose juice?"

"No," said Doc urgently. "The wall is still coming this way."

At that point, they began to run. They kept running. Since the thing stalking them was of great size, lethality, and entirely invisible, they did not know when to stop, so they kept going. Their legs and lungs worked strenuously.

By the time they happened upon a patrolling police car and flagged it down, it was some fifteen minutes later.

Explaining the entire situation to the police officer, who in marked contrast to the Detroit constabulary, showed him great deference, Doc Savage requested assistance, a thing he rarely asked of lawful authorities. A radio call was put out, and before long a phalanx of bluecoats, leading with their flashlights, approached the old cigar factory.

The flashlights, being battery-operated, continued up to the point that the police, with Doc Savage employing a borrowed torch, reentered the building.

It was deserted. There was no sign of the man—or men—who controlled the lethal zone of death. The culprits had escaped.

"Darn!" fumed Pat Savage. "I was hoping to sock someone on the jaw for putting me through all this hectic wild-goose chasing."

"Blame your own self," boomed Renny. "You barged into this fuss in the first place."

Blowing on her tanned knuckles, Pat grinned. "I wouldn't have missed it for the world!"

Doc Savage regarded his impetuous cousin with a flat expression and no little ire in his whirling golden eyes.

"Don't you give me that gilded glare," snapped Pat, shaking a slim finger in his direction. "You suffer from the same fever."

"Bullheadedness?" inquired Renny.

"Exciteomagnetism," retorted Pat. "Doc is as irresistibly

drawn to trouble as I am."

"There is no such condition," responded Doc Savage firmly.

"Wonderful! That means there's no antidote. So don't try to cure me, Dr. Grouch."

Renny rolled his eyes skyward. "I hope everyone understands now what I've had to put up with. Calamity Jane had nothing on Pat Savage."

"If I end up dead before this is over," said Pat coolly, "somebody kindly remember to carve those exact words on my headstone."

Chapter IX

THE LADY IN BEIGE

DOC SAVAGE ATTEMPTED to make explanations to the Tampa police. Employing swift, terse sentences, the bronze man sketched out everything that had transpired since his tumultuous arrival in Florida. He left out nothing of significance. When he came to the matter of the uncanny invisible walls of force, Doc spoke matter-of-factly.

After his difficulties with the Detroit police, it might be expected that Doc Savage would have similar complications explaining himself to the Tampa Police Department. But it was exactly the opposite.

A police sergeant, hearing his account, retrieved from his prowl car a late edition newspaper.

The headline told it all:

NATION IN GRIP OF TERROR!

The news occupied the best part of the first three pages of that edition.

Reports told of a reign of terror that was sweeping the nation. Unexplained deaths had felled large numbers of persons in scattered states. From Maine to California, no area of the country was left untouched. What was mystifying was that the victims died in zones that were long and narrow, stretching in a roughly north-to-south direction.

Doc Savage emitted a short chopping note of surprise. It was his uncanny trilling, and while it did not linger, its vehemence stilled the hearts of all who heard it.

Doc's men had rarely heard such an utterance. It meant that Doc was shocked, aghast, even dumbstruck with the unimaginable horror of the senseless slaughter.

There were other uncanny incidents. Airplanes dropped out of the sky without cause. Birds as well. Long narrow stretches passing through major cities had caused complete loss of electrical power. These blackouts dissolved as fast as they had clamped down.

It was as if a master hand of fate had control of a switch which could fell helpless human beings, bring great airliners tumbling out of the sky, and perform other awful wonders of chaos.

Rapidly, Doc Savage provided to the police concise descriptions of all the known persons involved, ranging from Theodore Buffington to Webster Neff, not leaving out the green-eyed Felix Frost.

By this time, a police captain had arrived on the scene. Hearing Doc Savage's request, he replied snappily, "I will put out an all-points bulletin on these men."

"Thank you," said Doc.

"Is there anything else?" the captain asked earnestly.

"For the moment, we will need to set up headquarters in Tampa."

"A radio car will take you and your men to any hotel you name," the captain offered. He turned and waved to a patrolman at the wheel of his parked vehicle.

The prowl car pulled up. Doc and his men, as well as Pat Savage, climbed in and they all departed for downtown Tampa.

At Doc's request, the driver turned on the dash radio, and they heard a succession of bulletins, each one increasingly hysterical, recounting wave after wave of mayhem stretching from the Atlantic to the Pacific oceans.

"Flash! The city of Baltimore today was witness to a tragedy of

a magnitude unlike any ever described. Fully a hundred persons were struck down in a park, by no known agency. Eyewitnesses report that a strange silence overtook the park just as the victims collapsed. Medical authorities on the scene insist that the dead suffered heart seizures, but whoever heard of one hundred heart attacks striking a small area simultaneously?"

"Great grief!" Ham exploded. "It sounds like the entire country is under attack!"

Pat Savage moaned, "It makes me sick listening to all of this horror."

They soon pulled up before The Grouper, a well-appointed downtown hotel. Doc rented the Presidential suite, and, since he had no luggage to speak of, headed directly for the elevators.

Moving rapidly, standing easily a head taller than anybody else in the lobby, the bronze giant naturally attracted attention.

Someone recognized him as he passed. A traveling drummer. He pointed.

"Doc Savage!" he gasped.

Others took up the name.

From lip to lip, the murmur flew. "Doc Savage… Doc Savage." There was nothing unusual about this reception. The bronze man, wherever he went, was always tendered this awesome admiration.

A matronly woman exclaimed to a companion, "He must be looking into all these strange deaths. After all, he is a doctor."

"Sure! Surgeons come clear from Vienna to attend his clinics. I've read about him in the newspapers."

Another person volunteered, "They say he knows more than any hundred university professors you could pick."

"I don't see how it's possible," expressed another. "Where does he find time for everything? He must be supernatural!"

"No," commented someone. "They say it's just a question of developing to the fullest his mental and physical potentialities. He is a product of scientific training. From his earliest youth, he studied, and put himself through an intensive routine—"

Hearing all this, Doc Savage hurried to the elevator, pressed the call button.

Ham Brooks said sharply, "Those people will have the infernal press down here before you know it."

As the elevator doors opened to swallow him, Doc said, "We cannot linger long here. Once word hits the newspapers, we will become targets for our enemies. Should that happen, innocent people could be harmed."

Doc sent the elevator whining upward to the top floor. They got out and took possession of the Presidential suite. It was sumptuous.

ANYONE who knew Pat Savage for very long would realize when she was holding her tongue. She had been holding it since they escaped from the cigar factory.

Now with the door closed, and safely ensconced in relative privacy, the bronze-haired girl aimed her clear golden gaze upon her famous cousin and demanded, "Are you going to say it, or am I?"

"Say what?" wondered Renny.

Pat ignored the big-fisted engineer. She never took her sharp regard off Doc Savage.

"You always know what's what ahead of anyone else," Pat accused. "Only this time, I'm not far behind you."

Fingering his cane, Ham Brooks asked, "What is she talking about, Doc?"

"We have encountered the phenomenon of these moving fields of force before," replied Doc in a matter-of-fact voice.

"Sure," said Monk, snapping thick fingers. "That time a couple years back, when we all got involved with the Elders."*

Pat commented, "I was along for that little caravan, too, in case everyone has forgotten. In fact, I was part of it before any of you Johnny-come-latelies showed up."

---

* *The Motion Menace.*

Renny, who had not been involved in that adventure, rumbled, "Somebody fill me in."

Doc Savage recited, "There was an inventor who developed a device which could shut down inertia in limited areas, on the theory that inertia is a separate force of nature, rather along the lines of gravity. Within those electronic fields, all motion ceased, whether mechanical or biological. Under certain circumstances, a person caught in the standing field would perish, owing to the stoppage of the heart and other vital organs."

Ham mused, "I was beginning to wonder if there is a connection between that device and the weird power we are facing presently. They struck me as uncannily similar."

Monk asked, "What happened to the weapon we captured? Didn't you store it up at your Fortress of Solitude, along with the other deadly weapons we glommed over the years?"

The bronze man shook his head slowly. "Ever since the affair involving John Sunlight, I have ceased to place any such dangerous device in my Fortress, lest it be stolen."*

"So what happened to the doodad?" asked Renny, blocking his big fists.

"I suggested to the inventor, Captain Cutting Wizer, that he donate the device to the United States Department of War, inasmuch as its potential as a defensive weapon would be unparalleled in human history. So far as I am aware, the generator is safely in the hands of the War Department."

Frowning deeply, Ham wondered, "Could somebody else have perfected a similar contraption?"

"It is entirely possible," replied the bronze man. "Throughout history, there have been many examples of inventive minds developing identical contrivances at approximately the same time. This could be another such instance."

Pat said bitingly, "Well, we're up against a weapon bigger than the one you defeated back then. This one seems to be able to reach out and affect any city in the nation."

---

* *Fortress of Solitude.*

"This," agreed the bronze man, "appears to be a much more powerful version of the death dynamo we confiscated."

Ham twirled his ebony cane thoughtfully and remarked, "That will make this present threat all the more difficult to defeat."

Pat said, "Well, just so long as I'm along for the buggy ride."

"You are not," said Doc Savage firmly. "We are putting you on the next commercial passenger plane to New York. That is final."

Pat blocked tanned fists on hips, stuck out her pretty jaw, and said, "Try and make it stick, why don't you?"

Monk cautioned, "Now, Pat, you know these little shindigs are usually too dangerous for you. And this one is shapin' up to be a beaut."

"I came this far," Pat said firmly. "I'm going the distance. And that's that."

Doc Savage seemed about to engage in an argument, when the bronze-haired girl abruptly decided to turn on the radio, a large console model sitting in a corner.

"Why are we standing around arguing, when the whole country is in peril?" she demanded. "I want to hear the latest news flashes."

Pat snapped on the radio, dialed around until she got an excited voice, and listened intently.

An announcer was going on at length about the terrible event that had taken place in Berkeley, California. Many had perished, but no one understood the exact nature or source of the calamity. The disaster seemed to be on the same order of the inexplicable park deaths in Baltimore.

They listened as the hoarse-voiced announcer went into considerable detail about this latest tragedy.

Then, another voice cut in sharply:

"Attention, Doc Savage. Calling Doc Savage. If you are listening, Doc Savage please call radio station WNAN in New York

City. This is an urgent summons for Doc Savage. If you are within the sound of my voice, call station WNAN immediately—"

"My goodness!" Pat exclaimed. "Aren't we important today?"

That dig was directed at the bronze man, who switched off the radio. Doc Savage went to the telephone and spoke to the hotel operator.

The operator put in a long-distance call to the radio station in question. As the others stood around, Doc launched into a very low and urgent conversation about which they could make neither heads nor tails.

The exchange lasted nearly ten minutes, which was long for the big bronze man, who preferred to get to the point.

After Doc had hung up, Pat asked, "Who was that, oh long-winded one?"

"The President," replied Doc.

"President of what?"

"The United States."

"Dang me!" exploded Monk.

"Holy cow!" thumped Renny, his rumbling vocal thunder blending in with Monk's squeaky, childlike expostulation.

Doc Savage explained, "It appears that the President has received a communication from the author of these nationwide tragedies. This person is communicating threats, making demands, and has set a deadline for compliance."

"Who is this scoundrel?" demanded Ham.

"The unknown is calling himself the Baron in Black," responded Doc somberly.

Ham drawled, "That was the name signed to the extortion note received by Phineas P. Slade in Detroit."

"The President has requested that I immediately fly to Washington to confer with him," added Doc.

This simple statement was so impressive that a breathless hush fell over the group.

"What do you want us to do in the meanwhile?" asked Ham tightly.

Doc Savage clipped out concise orders. "Renny, you return to New York and man our headquarters. Endeavor to discover anything you can about the direction from which these electronic emanations are coming. Monk and Ham, you will remain here and supervise the search for Theodore Buffington, Webster Neff and Felix Frost. It would be advisable if you change hotels every few hours, given the risk to yourselves and others. As yet we have no defense against these sinister zones of force."

"What about me?" wondered Pat. "Remember, I'm sticking."

"You will accompany me to Washington, D.C., in order that you remain out of mischief."

"Mischief!" blazed Pat. "You mean danger, don't you? Admit it. You're afraid for my life."

The bronze man's reply put a chill in every heart.

"I fear for the life of everyone in this country."

DOC SAVAGE left the suite only minutes later, taking a reluctant Pat Savage along with him.

Once the bronze man had departed, Renny hauled off with one monster fist and demolished an inner door of the suite with a resounding crack resembling a splintery thunderclap. It was his eternal boast that he had yet to encounter a door he could not thus treat.

Monk growled, "What was that for?"

"Frustration," thumped the big-fisted engineer. "Everybody gets to go in for some action, while I'm stuck playing nursemaid to our headquarters."

With that, long-faced Renny charged out the door to hunt up a taxicab, and claim his float plane at the airport.

After he had slammed the door behind him, Monk and Ham, predictably, got into an argument.

The cause of that argument was occasioned by a knock at the door. Ham Brooks answered it. A smartly uniformed bellhop proffered him a crisp white envelope bearing the crest of the hostelry.

"For Mr. Mayfair," announced the bellboy, putting out a white-gloved hand for his tip.

"Monk, tip this fellow," snapped Ham.

The hairy chemist flipped a half-dollar coin in the bellhop's direction. The latter caught it snappily, touched his emerald pillbox hat with a glove, and left for the elevator.

Monk tore open the envelope. Inside was a folded note that smelled faintly of a woman's floral perfume. It read:

> If you are interested in meeting a man who knows all about the attackers of our country, meet me in the park by the bay.

The note was signed, *The Lady in the Beige Beret*.

"What does it say?" demanded Ham.

Monk, tiny eyes narrowing in their pits of gristle, said guardedly, "A lady wants to see me about somethin'."

"What lady?" asked Ham suspiciously.

"She didn't sign the note. But I'm gonna go meet her."

"At a time like this?" flared Ham incredulously. "I had better go along in the event that it is a trap. You are so slow-witted sometimes it is a wonder you haven't been ambushed and ended up in a zoo somewhere."

"Not a chance," insisted Monk. "I can't have you beatin' my time in case this is an admirer who has a crush on me."

Ham twirled his sword cane. "Personally, I never saw woman yet you couldn't be sold on."

"Listen, you bar fop, I choose my women careful."

"Is that so?" Ham sniffed superciliously.

"Yeah. I got a good eye for the femmes."

"You have a good eye for fists," the dapper lawyer retorted. "I would not be at all surprised if you are walking into a bunch of them, all directed at your thick skull."

"Well, that's my lookout," grinned Monk, barging out the door before Ham could utter another word of warning. Habeas Corpus the pig trotted in his wake like a loyal, if spindly, dog.

"Drat!" fumed Ham. "That reckless ape is going to get his fool neck broken."

Picking up his sword cane, the dapper lawyer put an ear to the suite door, listened intently until he heard the sound of the elevator doors clicking shut, then slipped out into the corridor, determined to follow the homely chemist wherever he went.

Chapter X
PARK AMBUSH

IT WAS RAINING lightly when Monk Mayfair exited The Grouper Hotel, Habeas Corpus the pig clicking his heels happily behind him. The rain was warm, a pleasant drizzle in the Florida evening.

Monk attempted to hail a cab, but the first taxi driver to pull up took one look at the homely chemist and his equally homely porker and said, "No soap, buddy. I'm taking no pig anywhere. No offense."

Undaunted, the apish chemist raised a hairy paw and beckoned for another hack. This driver, like the first, made a pained face when Monk opened the rear door and attempted to boost Habeas into the back seat.

"I don't take animals," the hackman said apologetically. "You'll have to find another ride. Sorry, buddy."

"Suit yourself," Monk said amiably. He was used to being treated thus, Habeas having cost him many cab rides during his travels.

The third taximan to pull up took one look at the pig, cocked an eye at the five dollar bill Monk was waving under his nose, and shrugged, saying, "A passenger is a passenger."

"Swell," beamed Monk, slamming the door shut as the cab scooted off in the rain, tires whining on pavement.

"Whereto, my good fellow?" The cabby was polite. Since this was not yet the tourist season, fares were understandably scarce.

"Park by the water," said Monk. "Whatever it's called."

"I know the spot."

The cab catapulted into the traffic, slammed in the direction of Tampa Bay.

Monk cranked down one of the windows, and Habeas got up on his hind legs and stuck his long snout out in the fashion of a dog enjoying a ride.

They made quite a sensation as the taxi rolled through the rain-slickened Tampa streets. More than one female driver flashed the pig a laughing smile.

An accomplished ventriloquist, Monk made the pig appear to say, "Hello, you beautiful babe! How's about a date?"

Presently, the cab pulled up before Bayside Park. Palm trees were growing slick in the drizzling rain, fronds hanging heavy and dripping.

Climbing out, Monk paid the driver. Picking up Habeas by one coal-scuttle ear, and whistling a cheerful show tune, the hairy chemist made himself conspicuous in the park.

There was no immediate sign of the mysterious woman who had sent him the enticing note.

Monk had a good idea who she might be. That is, when Doc Savage's party first entered the lobby of the hotel, Monk had noticed a stunning brunette out of one corner of his eye. He'd given her a broad smile. She had winked in return. Ham had not noticed this byplay, and naturally Monk was not about to call his attention to it, lest the dapper lawyer stir up unwanted competition.

The woman had been wearing a charming beige frock set off by a rakish beret of matching hue.

Monk kept his eyes peeled for such a vision, for she was one of the most attractive women he had beheld in quite some time. Monk was perpetually fascinated by stunning examples of femininity, and the attraction was often mutual, much to the hairy chemist's immense pleasure—not to mention Ham Brooks' often apoplectic frustration.

Before long, a tan coupé slid into view, and pulled over to the side of the road. The driver's door opened and out stepped a lovely young thing swathed in beige.

Smiling invitingly, the woman approached Monk, her beige beret canted saucily to one side of her fluffy brunette hair. She carried a stylish umbrella; it, too, was beige.

"I am so glad you came, Mr. Mayfair," said the vision in beige. Her accent had an intriguingly foreign lilt, and her eyes were as dark and lustrous as polished opals.

Monk beamed back. "Hiyah, toots," he squeaked. "I came as fast as I could."

The woman's smile widened, showing nearly perfect teeth.

"My name is Shari," she said by way of introduction. "Shari Phoenia."

Monk asked, "What's this about a guy that knows the scoop on all these tragedies?"

"You get right to the point, don't you?" retorted the woman, losing her smile. Now there was a dark gleam in back of the opal orbs.

"I don't exactly beat around the bush. Right, Habeas?"

Monk lifted the pig to chest height. The porker squealed amiably.

"Is that your pig?" the woman asked, momentarily amused.

Monk beamed proudly. "His name is Habeas Corpus. I named him after a certain shyster's profession. Now who is this guy you want me to meet?"

Shari Phoenia turned serious of face and demeanor. "Actually, the man I wrote you about wishes to meet you. He has information for Doc Savage—important information which the world must know about."

Monk grunted, "The whole world, huh?"

"Exactly."

"Then take me to him," said Monk.

"You have read my mind," smiled Shari, taking the simian

chemist by the arm.

Monk liked that. He grinned widely. "I see you're the impetuous type."

"I am! Do you approve?"

Monk's grin now threatened his ears. "Sounds like you're the kind of dish that's right up my alley."

Together, they walked toward the waiting coupé. Monk carried the beige umbrella to keep off the pattering raindrops.

Monk could not take his eyes off the woman. She was the vibrant, exotic type, undefinably foreign. She was not hard on the eyes, either.

They had almost reached the waiting coupé when a nearby rain-splattered oleander bush shook itself in a way that had nothing to do with the warm breeze coming off the bay.

A tube slid out of that bush, pointed directly at Monk Mayfair's barrel of a chest.

The tube was of a dull metal; its front sported a gun sight. It was a rifle barrel, so wet that it shone dully. Rainwater was dripping off its lower edge.

The unseen man behind the rifle squeezed the trigger. There was a report, a brief flare of saffron, followed by a forceful puff of smoke.

Fifty feet stood between the muzzle of the rifle and the ambling, long-armed chemist. At that distance the marksman could not miss.

Nor did he. Not exactly.

The spinning round sped true, but flattened in the air two feet from Monk Mayfair's pushed-in nose, hung there like a dull coin, and dropped harmlessly to the sidewalk.

The sound of the rifle shot failed to reach Monk's ears, but the sudden phenomenon of the flattening bullet caught his eye.

Growling like an animal, Monk dropped the umbrella, lowered Habeas to the ground and watched, eyes popping in their tiny pits of gristle, as the flattened bullet sank to the ground with agonizing slowness.

"I'll be danged!" he exclaimed, blocking the girl to protect her. "It's one of them death-zone screens!"

MONK hunkered down, grabbed a handful of gravel, flung a gritty cloud wildly ahead of him. The stuff struck the invisible barrier, became stuck, and began floating downward, caught in the anti-inertia field.

Peering intently, Monk could see where rainwater was running down, as if against clear glass. This made the near edge of the force field semi-transparent.

"I do not understand—" the woman began.

Herding the lady in beige with one burly arm, Monk began retreating from the half-visible threat.

As he did so, bushes on this side of the barrier began to shake and shiver. Men emerged. They wore hats yanked down low, almost over their eyes, shielding their faces. They toted pistols, and one brandished a rifle. They had the unsavory look of low-class crooks.

Stepping in front of the woman in beige, Monk reached into his coat, and yanked from its underarm holster his supermachine pistol. Unlatching the safety, he directed the muzzle toward the oncoming men. They had yet to get off a shot. They never would, either.

Pressing the firing lever, Monk began spraying mercy bullets. The machine pistol started to bawl like a frightened calf. The bawling increased in volume until it hurt the eardrums.

Men began succumbing to the quick-acting knockout pellets. Two dropped immediately. Two more beat a hasty retreat, firing wildly behind them. Their sizzling slugs missed Monk by a country mile and lodged in the force field at his back with strange thunking noises, as if wooden mallets were at work.

"Wait here," Monk warned Shari, charging after the men on his bowed legs. Habeas was galloping at his heels, making angry snufflings and gruntings.

It was Monk Mayfair's intention to catch up with the men,

to wring the truth out of them about the motives behind the ambush. He was destined never to accomplish that muscular feat.

The two men raced away, suddenly collided with something that could not be seen.

The way they struck the invisible barrier was almost comical. They appeared to run into a spider web composed of nothing at all. The gunmen became entangled, or possibly glued. One tried to pull his hand out of the eerie morass. He could not. He was stuck fast.

This man became upset, began crying and moaning in a kind of helpless agony.

The other had been running low like a football player, his hatted head leading. It was the head that entered the anti-inertia field first. And it was the head that became stuck in it.

The man swiftly assumed the posture of an individual who had gotten his head caught in a hole in a plaster wall. He was using his hands to press against the wall, and lever his head out. It was a bizarre sight, and could conceivably have worked had the wall been composed of plaster, and not some inexplicable electromagnetic force.

The man's hands became stuck in the force field, and his body struggled to disengage itself. If he was yelling his head off, as was likely, no such sounds reached Monk's ears.

Then, inexorably, both men ceased to move. Slowly, they began to sink to the ground like wet rag dolls.

Monk skidded to a halt. He could see clearly the running film of rainwater that showed the nearest edge of the force field. It was creeping closer.

Retreating to Shari's side, Monk shouted grimly, "We're not safe anywhere. There's one of them on each side of us, like invisible jaws… what if they bite together?"

Then they did exactly that!

Monk stood braced on his bowed legs, shifting back and forth, trying to ascertain the length of the wall at their back, in an effort to go around it.

Behind him, Shari was fumbling with her beige umbrella, which she had recovered. She got it open, directed the circular canopy before her as if to employ it as a shield. It was an absurd notion, but panic often produces odd behavior in the threatened.

The apish chemist saw that he could only retreat so far, so he grabbed Habeas by one oversized ear and took Shari by her elbow, and rushed them down the path between the closing walls of invisibility. It was his clear aim and intention to reach the point where the unseen fields ceased operating.

Despite his pumping legs, Monk never made it. First, he got tangled up in the umbrella, whose sharp ferrule dug into one hairy forearm. This inhibited his headlong flight. Angrily, he flung the beige contraption away, resumed his flat-footed race.

But it was too late.

The walls closed inexorably. He could feel them approach. The bristling hairs on the back of his neck started lifting. Whether this was due to goosebumps or the action of an electromagnetic field, was impossible to tell.

But before he could do anything about it, Monk was swallowed by the closing jaws that could not be seen, touched, or avoided.

In mid-stride, Monk and Shari Phoenia, who had been swinging along, simply stopped moving. They stood frozen, like a motion-picture reel that had gotten stuck in its projector, their faces growing paler by the moment.

Somehow, Habeas the pig had managed to shake free and go charging off, his curly tail bouncing like a spring.

A sinking sensation overtook the hairy chemist then. There was a sick feeling of being bogged down and helpless, as if he had been swallowed by some swampy morass that was palpable in an uncanny way. A pins-and-needles sensation crept along his frozen limbs.

Slowly, like candle wax melting, they slid to the ground, inert, utterly helpless, unable to move except insofar as gravity pulled them slowly to earth.

After they succumbed to the closing mandibles of force, neither of them twitched. Nor did a drop of the falling rain touch them. It was as if they had been encapsulated in the etheric substance of another realm.

Hunkered under a rain-soaked bush, Habeas Corpus observed this tableau with his dark beady eyes and the hackles along his scrawny frame raised. The trembling shoat did not venture to investigate; he only sniffed the air with his quivering elongated nostrils.

Chapter XI
MILK TRUCK TRAIL

THE TERRIBLE EVENTS that befell Monk Mayfair and the mysterious Shari Phoenia at Bayside Park did not go unnoticed.

There were, of course, the usual scatterings of passersby—pedestrians and motorists driving along the palm-lined boulevard that fringed picturesque Tampa Bay.

Many of these did not see anything clearly, owing to the steady drizzle mixed with the invisible fields of force, inasmuch as the latter were not detectable to the naked eye.

One of the witnesses was no less than Brigadier General Theodore Marley Brooks, otherwise called Ham, a nickname he detested, but to which he had grown accustomed over long years of use.

Ham had been a late arrival, owing to the difficulty in securing a taxicab from The Grouper Hotel and the further difficulty in convincing the driver to follow the cab which had ferried Monk Mayfair to the park overlooking Tampa Bay.

The hackie had been reluctant to follow the dictates of a complete stranger and, when Ham had informed him that he was a noted New York attorney, the driver had been even more hesitant, saying, "I don't cotton much to lawyers. I got sued once over a collision."

Sputtering, Ham expostulated, "I also happen to be an associate to Doc Savage."

"Doc Savage!" the cabby exclaimed, reaching back to fling

open his rear passenger door. "Why didn't you say so? Doc Savage is a right guy. I hear he's in town to look into these terrible deaths."

Ham had climbed in, and they had trailed Monk's cab at a decorous pace, keeping their distance, the fastidious barrister hunkered low in his seat, holding the shiny head of his sword cane down and out of sight. His immaculate attire—not so immaculate now—and signature cane would have been a dead giveaway had Monk glanced out his back window, which he almost certainly was in the habit of doing, since danger followed the aides of Doc Savage wherever they went.

"Doc Savage," ruminated the driver. "I've heard things about that guy! He hit one of Snag Ravelli's muscle men once, about two-three years back. Popped him in the nose with his fist. Just once. After that, there wasn't nothin' left to the guy's nose. It was smeared in against his face. I seen that bohunk the other day. He ain't got no nose yet—only holes where he breathes through."

"Mind your driving!" Ham directed curtly.

There had been a near collision a time or two when the hackman almost lost the taxi they were tailing. But Ham's driver doggedly stuck to the trail, balancing caution with tenacious wheel work until they arrived at the broad boulevard overlooking Tampa Bay.

Still hunkered down in his seat, Ham began looking about when the earsplitting bullfiddle roar of a supermachine pistol smote his eardrums.

"Brake, driver!" howled Ham.

Flinging a twenty-dollar bill at the cabby, Ham pounced out of the fast-braking machine, sword cane in one hand, oversized superfirer jumping into the other.

The dapper lawyer was sprinting toward the commotion of combat when he spotted gun flashes, then saw Monk and an unfamiliar girl in a beige beret suddenly freezing in their tracks, against all laws of physics.

"Monk!" called out Ham. "Watch out!"

But the hairy chemist was beyond hearing. Ham's immaculately shaven jaw began to sag as he saw Monk Mayfair and the mystery girl succumb to what he suspected was a deadly void of death.

Suddenly, Ham realized his own peril. He did not comprehend along exactly what compass lines that death field lay. He only knew that it hovered before him, and was possibly moving.

Sliding to a stop, the fast-thinking attorney lifted his elegant cane, and used it to probe the way ahead. He crept one step forward with great care and deliberation, not advancing any more than an inch at a time, trusting in his stick the way a blind man negotiates a road with his white cane.

Ham understood that he had encountered the field of force when the stick suddenly became fixed in midair, and no amount of yanking could cause it to be removed. Ham let go of the knob, and the cane stood rigid in midair, horizontal to the ground. His eyes widened in horror.

Feeling helpless, Ham backed away, and for the first time noticed the flat streams of rainwater running down the transparent barrier. It was clear once he knew where to look, and his dark eyes fell into focus upon that plane. Moving parallel to it, Ham tried to find the defining edges of the thing, but he knew it was futile. Monk and the unknown girl were held fast within the zone, and there was no reaching them unless he entered the ominous barrier, which most assuredly would cause him to succumb to its irresistible influence.

Frustrated, anxious, Ham raced about, lifted his superfirer and sent a burst of futile shots into the invisible wall. This produced nothing more resultful than the sight of several smashed mercy bullets freezing in midair and then slowly sinking to the ground as if in heavy oil, incapable of motion other than that exerted by the pull of gravity.

Determined to accomplish something, Ham took hold of the knob of his slim cane, gave it a twist, and removed the sword from its sheath. It came free only because the blade was not as long as its black barrel, which remained fixed in the wall of invisibility.

By this time, a police prowl car came hurtling around the corner, siren wailing. Another was careening from the opposite direction. They slewed crazily on the slick blacktop as they braked. Ham rushed over to greet the arriving officers.

"Do not advance into the death zone!" he pleaded.

The police by now had become familiar with the phenomenon occurring nationwide of bands of force in which men and machines fell dead. The officers prudently heeded the dapper lawyer's excited injunctions.

Ham identified himself as a Doc Savage aide, and attempted to explain what had just transpired in Bayside Park.

The officers were as interested as they were cautious. They asked many questions. They showed great respect for the zone of immobility, having noticed the unmoving forms that were slumped within.

"I think I recognize one of those bodies—assuming that they are dead," ventured patrolman. "That one in the gray hat is one of Snag Revelli's torpedoes. You can see he's got almost no nose left."

Ham frowned. "Doc Savage had a run-in with one of Ravelli's gang a while back, and the gunman's nose got the worst of it."

The officer said, "Maybe Snag is trying to even the score by putting one of Savage's men on the spot."

"Rather doubt that an old bootlegger like Ravelli would be embroiled in such a wide-ranging plot as this affair," mused Ham thoughtfully.

Another bluecoat chimed in, "Since Repeal, Snag has fallen on hard times. He hires his boys out to whoever needs muscle work."

While they were discussing the problem, a new machine came roaring up, this one a long black touring car as shiny and sinister as a coffin.

A man's head and shoulders stuck out of the back-seat window, cradling a ponderous Tommy gun. This began chattering. A ghoulish cackling preceded the resulting hail of bullets.

Hot lead commenced chipping away at the royal palm trees lining the boulevard, thick oleander bushes and a concrete seawall. Greenery of all types showered down.

Ham and the startled bluecoats ducked behind the police machines as automobile window glass shivered into tiny fragments and a front tire exploded, releasing air with a gusty cough.

More hot lead lashed the air. The vicinity might have been buzzing with angry wasps.

Clutching his machine pistol, Ham dared to peer over the police hood, and attempted to return fire.

The windows in the side of the touring car that roared past them hastily rolled up to keep out the rain. Furious mercy bullets sprayed against tempered glass and the steel car body, harmlessly splashing their potent contents, which then mixed with the falling rain.

"Confound it!" fumed Ham.

A fierce-eyed police officer lifted his head, and let loose with some solid lead from his smoking Police Positive.

The slugs broke apart one window of the touring car, which careened into a wild slide on the rain-scoured boulevard, but was otherwise unhindered.

The funereal touring car slewed about, braked sharply, and the sound of doors opening with a dull clap came. The submachine-gun recommenced snarling in their direction.

A virtual storm of slugs began chewing up the police machines as if they were made of cardboard and candy canes, not glass and steel and chromium.

Ham and the three police officers hunkered down as best they could until the leaden hurricane abated.

There came the sound of fast feet and a sense of men rushing about, followed by a noise that Ham recognized as his walking stick falling to the ground with a loud *click*. Peering out from under the chassis of the police machine that had offered him shelter, he saw a scramble of feet. Then, with a low whine, the touring car slipped into gear and went moaning away.

After the automobile had departed, and it seemed safe to do so, Ham poked his bare head up again, saw that it was safe, and stepped out into the moist thoroughfare.

The dapper lawyer retrieved his cane from where it had fallen, angrily sheathed the blade. Lifting the stick, Ham used it to probe his way toward the spot where Monk and the girl had fallen.

They were no longer there. Habeas Corpus also was among the missing.

There were others, however—bodies of the gunmen. Ham went from one to the other and discovered them all to be stiff and lifeless.

Standing up from where he crouched to examine the last of these deceased persons, the frustrated attorney turned to the approaching police officers, and said, "These men are all dead."

"Yeah," said one officer breathlessly. "And all of them members of the Ravelli mob. It doesn't figure. What's their angle?"

"Whatever it is," grated another, eyeing the faces of the dead gangsters, "Ravelli is back of it. That was the big boss himself behind that chopper. I recognized his face."

Ham Brooks was also studying the pile of deceased crooks. "Not a mark on any of them," he observed grimly.

"What does that mean?" asked one of the police officers, tilting back his uniform cap to scratch at his head.

"It means," choked Ham, "that Monk Mayfair and the woman who was with him were also killed by the deathly force."

"Are you sure?" asked the other officer.

Ham looked sick. "All of them were trapped in the paralyzing field, and these men are dead, without a wound upon their bodies. That means their heart muscles were arrested by the force fields. If their hearts were stopped, what could possibly protect the hearts of Monk and the unknown woman?"

There was no sensible answer to that. But one officer wanted to know, "If they did both die, why did the damn gunmen carry off their corpses?"

"Perhaps," returned Ham thoughtfully, "they hoped we would believe that Monk and the woman were still alive, so they can use them as bargaining chips. But they cannot be alive. Not after what just happened here."

There seemed to be no arguing the point. The police officers radioed headquarters for morgue wagons to take away the dead. Headquarters was alerted to be on the lookout for the murder car of Snag Ravelli.

"We'll get him," promised one officer, brushing pebbles of broken glass off his blue uniform. "They've already got a dragnet set up for that coffin car."

WHILE Ham Brooks was considering his next move, Habeas Corpus trotted out from under a sprawling philodendron, looking agitated.

There was no love lost between the dapper lawyer and the skinny porker. In fact, for many years now, Ham had been threatening to carve up the homely shoat into racks of breakfast bacon with his sword cane.

Habeas, who was named to rankle the noted barrister, and who understood the fastidious attorney's possibly feigned animosity toward him, walked in cautious circles around Ham's expensively-shod feet, awaiting a reaction.

Looking down at the spindly-legged creature, Ham remarked drolly, "I imagine that I've inherited you, the way matters have turned out."

Habeas sat down and cocked his unlovely head at Ham with beady-eyed interest.

"I must get you back to the hotel, where I can communicate with Doc Savage and tell him the terrible news," added Ham.

Habeas following in his wake, the grim barrister went in search of a taxicab.

He managed to flag one down, but when Ham attempted to urge the porker in the back seat with the tip of his cane, the taxi driver naturally objected.

"No animals! And that's final."

Ham Brooks was a normally polite and well-bred sort of fellow. He was the product of a Harvard education; in fact he was Harvard Law School's brightest light.

Nevertheless, Ham shucked his sword cane of its protective barrel, and placed the tip of the gleaming blade to the pugnacious nose of the cabby.

The driver crossed round eyes at the wicked-looking blade.

"You will take us to The Grouper Hotel, and you will make it snappy," Ham grated out.

"Yes, sir!" said the cabby. "And if you want, your pet pig can sit up front here with me. He's welcome to ride in my cab at any time."

"Very well," returned Ham in a mollified tone, holding open the door for Habeas and urging him into the front seat with the polished tip of his shoe.

Closing the door, Ham leapt into the back, and told the driver, "Hurry, my good man."

The hack got into gear, and began moving along the boulevard. The cabby drove decorously, careful of his balding tires in the relentless but pleasantly warm rain.

In the back, Ham Brooks was sunk in the cushions, at a loss for words. The murder of his friend and perpetual sparring partner had taken the starch out of him. His eyes had that queer inward look of the shocked and grieving.

Before long, passing in the other lane, barreled an ordinary milk truck.

It was a very late hour for a milk truck to be about, since they ordinarily made early morning deliveries. But that was not what caught Ham's sharp-eyed attention at first.

The man behind the wheel, although attired in the regulation white service uniform belonging to his trade, was noticeable for the greenness of his eyes.

The rest of his face was unfamiliar. But those eyes were unmistakable. Ham had seen them glowing behind the goggles of a gas mask back at the cigar factory, and before that, similar eyes had belonged to the Huron chief engineer, Felix Frost.

Abruptly, Ham banged the lean barrel of his black cane on the driver's shoulder saying, "Follow that milk truck wherever it goes."

"Is this a gag, buddy?" demanded the driver.

Once more, the dapper lawyer shucked his long blade of its barrel. He placed the edge of it so that it rested atop the cabby's left ear, dislodging an unlit cigarette that sat balanced there.

"One downward stroke," warned Ham bitingly, "and your ear will be a souvenir."

The driver piloted the hack around in a sharp turn, and obediently fell in behind the midnight milk truck.

"Maintain a discreet distance, my good man," advised Ham. "We want to follow that truck, but not be noticed by it."

"You're the boss," quipped the driver sincerely.

In the front passenger seat, Habeas Corpus sat staring out the window, ears wilted, eyes downcast, unusually subdued, as if contemplating the unhappy prospect that he would never see his master again.

Chapter XII
WHITE HOUSE CONFERENCE

DOC SAVAGE HAD chartered a plane in Tampa, a speedy ship that ate up the air miles to the District of Columbia. While it was not one of his fleet of super-planes, it was serviceable and made fair time.

The bronze man flew in a mute silence. The gravity of the situation facing the United States of America appeared to weigh heavily upon his high metallic brow.

In the co-pilot seat, Pat Savage fidgeted uncharacteristically. Doc had barely spoken to her. Pat knew she was in for a tongue-scalding at the bronze man's hands for having barged her way into the crisis, which was now looming of vaster proportions than anything she could have imagined when the bronze-haired girl first stuck her intimidating six-shooter muzzle in Renny Renwick's mournfully disappointed face.

"You don't have to say it," Pat clipped at one point over the noisy engine drone.

The bronze man did not reply.

"Very well," said Pat snappily. "Then *don't* say it!"

Again there was typically characteristic silence from the bronze man.

He had the plane engines running at their maximum. The cabin was not soundproofed in the way the bronze giant's fleet were. It was possible that the motor noise overwhelmed his supersensitive hearing, making it difficult to distinguish her voice from the unremitting blade scream.

With an entirely understandable female objection to being ignored, Pat exclaimed, "I don't give a flying hoot if you never speak to me again! You were always leaving me out of your busy affairs. A gal likes to get her blood going once in a while. Can't you understand that?"

Abruptly, the bronze man motioned for silence. He began working the cabin radio.

"Doc Savage calling Long Tom Roberts. Doc to Long Tom."

Presently, a querulous voice began issuing from the loudspeaker.

"Long Tom here," said the voice. *"I've been trying to reach you. What is going on?"*

"Your assistance is needed," answered Doc. "Where are you?"

"Flying to Florida."

"There is no need for you there, Long Tom. Can you rendezvous in Washington, D.C.?"

"Sure, I'm more than halfway there," reported Long Tom.

"Meet us at the airport."

"Us?"

"Pat is with me," clarified Doc.

Long Tom's voice turned sour. "How did she blunder her way into this mess?"

Doc Savage said with just a trace of weariness, "In her usual inventive manner. I am certain she will tell you all about it."

"See you there, Doc," Long Tom said, signing off.

After Doc had replaced the microphone on its hook, Pat inquired, "Blunder! I like that!"

Doc Savage offered no comment.

Pat then asked, "What about Johnny?"

Johnny Littlejohn was the archaeologist of Doc Savage's band of fighters. He had a secondary specialty as a geologist as well.

"Johnny is presently in Iran, looking into a Persian tomb that was discovered there," stated Doc quietly.

"So I guess he won't be joining our little soiree?"

"Not this time."

Pat brightened. "That means you're shorthanded," she said cheerily.

Doc Savage did not take the bait. He tuned the receiver to the commercial radio frequencies, and attempted to obtain some news.

There was plenty of it. In Detroit, the Huron Motor Company was attempting to defend its battered reputation in the face of a hurricane of mysterious accidents and car stoppages. The disappearance of new president Theodore Buffington, followed by the company's chief engineer, Felix Frost, made the situation seem all that more suspicious and inexplicable.

In British Columbia, a plane had fallen out of the sky over Vancouver. Witnesses reported that it was flying along when one wing simply sheared off as if wrenched free by a giant hand. The passenger airliner promptly corkscrewed out of the sky, and, fortunately for those below, landing in water—in this case, Burrard Inlet.

There were other such reports. All horrific.

One bulletin, presented as unconfirmed, had it that the President of the United States was convening an emergency meeting at the White House. Joining him was the Premier of Canada, the President of Mexico, and a handpicked group of military officials, politicians, and important industrialists.

Hearing this, Pat Savage wondered, "What is to stop this Baron in Black from targeting all those high mucky-mucks at the White House?"

"Nothing whatsoever," said Doc Savage grimly, giving the throttle another smack.

The fast ship droned north, miles of greenery unreeling beneath its flashing wings. Here and there below, there were touches of an early snow. Winter was still some weeks off.

"First snow of the season," remarked Pat. "I was planning on getting in a little bit of skiing before Christmas."

Doc Savage said tightly, "It would have been better if you had."

Pat Savage looked miserable. She could tell her cousin was angrier at her than he had ever been before. His lack of communication verged on the impolite.

How angry Doc Savage actually had become was demonstrated after the bronze man set his aircraft down at the Washington airport.

Long Tom had beaten them to the ground by twenty minutes and was awaiting their arrival. He was an undersized fellow with a sallow complexion and looked as if he should be in a sanitarium somewhere, recovering from a long illness. In actual fact, Long Tom Roberts was in top physical condition. He was also one of the great lights in the field of electrical engineering.

Doc Savage and Long Tom conferred for several minutes, pointedly ignoring Pat, who stood to one side with her tanned arms folded, tapping one tapered foot impatiently.

"What a swell way to treat your only cousin," she fumed.

Presently, the bronze man came over and said shortly, "You will accompany Long Tom back to headquarters."

Pat's delectable face grew angry. "Don't I get to meet the President?"

"It is too dangerous for you here," Doc advised, voice softening.

Sparks ignited in Pat's golden orbs. "That's not so—it's too dangerous everywhere! You heard those bulletins. Your argument plain does not wash, and you know it!"

"Long Tom has important work to do and will need an assistant," Doc told her firmly. "You will assist him. This way you cannot complain that you are not involved in the present undertaking."

"Sitting around a stuffy old lab is not my idea of action," Pat retorted.

Brooking no argument, Doc Savage said, "The President is waiting on me."

"Fine thing! You get to meet the President for the first time, and don't take your only living relative along!"

Doc reminded quietly, "I have conferred with the President on other occasions."*

"Oh," said Pat, duly impressed.

Then, Long Tom Roberts took her by the arm and said impatiently, "Let's go. We're wasting valuable time here."

Pat allowed herself to be squired over to the electrical wizard's speedy little ship, and they were soon in the air.

A long-nosed official town car, which had been standing quietly nearby, motor idling, rolled over to pick up the bronze man. Doc got in, clapped the door shut, the limousine drove off.

ON HIS way to the White House conference, Doc Savage made a request that would have struck anyone familiar with him as odd.

"There is a tobacconist shop on K Street," the bronze man advised the chauffeur. "Please stop there for a moment."

"We are running a bit late, Mr. Savage," the man insisted. "And the President is waiting."

"It is vitally important that we make this stop," Doc told him firmly.

The driver shrugged, and piloted his limousine to K Street, where Doc Savage entered the tobacco shop and made a purchase.

He returned to the waiting limousine carrying a wrapped package.

"Proceed," instructed Doc.

The limousine resumed its official route, and was soon pulling up to the circular driveway in front of the White House.

There were armed Army and Marine guards everywhere. The executive mansion itself had the air of a place under siege. Eyes under steel military helmets stared grim as stone.

---
* *Haunted Ocean.*

A dignitary met Doc at the door and swiftly conducted the bronze man to a long conference room deep in the innards of the executive mansion.

The assembled dignitaries were already seated when Doc Savage was ushered into the Cabinet Room. The President of the United States, looking grave of face, was seated at the head of the massive conference table.

A hush fell over the assembled gathering when Doc Savage entered the room. Despite the quiet manner in which the bronze giant entered, his impressive height, the smooth flow of his cabled body in motion, drew all the attention.

The President waved the bronze man to an empty seat at his right hand and said, "Pray be seated, Mr. Savage. I was just explaining to these fine gentlemen the origins of our problem before going on to a discussion of solutions."

"Thank you, Mr. President," Doc Savage said, taking his seat.

The President began addressing the gathering. "As you all know, our nations are under an intensive attack by an unknown party who calls himself the Baron in Black. This individual has come into possession of the secret plans for a weapon which, when fielded, could well end war as we know it. This frightening contraption lays down fields of force which arrest all motion within said fields, including all by biological processes, shutting down heart action, respiration and circulation."

Doc Savage added, "My men and I encountered a similar threat in Manchuria only a year or so back."

The chief executive nodded sagely. "I have been briefed about that situation by my advisors. They tell me that you arranged for a captured example of this dynamo of death to be deposited in our own War Department's secret archives."

Doc nodded. "Has that device been stolen by an enemy power?"

The President shook his head gravely. "No, but our military scientists had been examining the device, and devising ways to duplicate and improve it. It was these improved plans that appear to have been stolen."

"How far back?" asked Doc.

"Less than three months ago," admitted the President.

A general spoke up. "We have conducted an investigation, and have determined that a woman was involved in duplicating these plans."

"The woman's name?" queried Doc.

"She was calling herself Diana Frost. She became friendly with one of our officers and, by this means, acquired the secret information that has now been turned against us. All of us," he added, waving to the leaders of Canada and Mexico.

Doc Savage absorbed this information without changing expression. Reaching into his coat, he produced a brand-new pipe, as well as a pouch of excellent tobacco.

"Do any of you mind if I smoke?" he asked politely.

No one objected, so the bronze man methodically filled the bowl with fragrant tobacco and applied a wooden match to the mixture.

Had anyone who knew him well witnessed this, they would have been astounded. For Doc Savage eschewed the use of tobacco in all forms. He was not known to smoke. But now he was puffing on a pipe as if it was a daily habit.

As the President continued speaking, Doc Savage blew out long plumes of aromatic smoke in various directions, taking care to avoid sending any fumes into the faces of the assembled group.

Soon, the room began to fill with pleasant tobacco smoke. This was very visible under the overhead lights. For although it was broad daylight, this conference room was heavily curtained.

The President of Mexico wanted to know, "Tell us of this Baron in Black who is blackmailing us all."

The President lifted his hands helplessly. "I have no conception of his identity, whether he is a foreign enemy, or simply some type of super criminal. At present, he is only a fanciful name."

The Premier of Canada offered this: "My government, as yours, also received a demand note from this so-called Baron in Black. Although we have had only one incident, the Baron promises that the wave of destruction now sweeping the United States could be moved north at a whim, plunging the Dominion of Canada into chaos."

The President of Mexico added, "We have had no such incidents, but a similar note received at my Presidential palace warned that the menace could creep south at any moment, unless certain demands are met."

"What are these demands?" asked Doc Savage.

The President of the United States replied to that all-important question.

"They are identical in every particular. Our combined countries must surrender to the Baron in Black within five days, under pain of scientific annihilation of our entire population. This mysterious Baron claims to be able to lay down fields that could, in effect, bring all modern-day activity to a dead stop, whether it be mechanical or biological. The terrors that have been transpiring these last few days, this haughty Baron insists, are just a small taste of what is to come."

The chief executive handed Doc Savage the demand letters.

Doc perused them quickly, then said, "When this matter began, it appeared as if the Huron Motor Company was the object of blackmail, but it has now swiftly escalated to involve virtually the entirety of North America."

"That," said the President somberly, "speaks to the utmost gravity of the situation facing our combined nations. The question before us is: How do we combat this madness?"

Doc Savage was blowing tobacco smoke behind him, attempting to spread the aromatic mixture about the room. His flake-gold eyes were very actively searching the room.

An orderly knocked politely, then entered the room, conveying a message for the Commander-in-Chief of the United States.

The chief executive received this message, then carefully opened the note. He read it silently, eyes bleak behind his famous pince-nez glasses.

Turning to Doc Savage, he said, "I regret to inform you of this news that has reached us from Tampa, Florida. It appears that a member of your personal brain trust, Mr. Monk Mayfair, has succumbed to one of these infamous force fields."

Doc Savage's trilling leapt out of him, racing about the room like an angry shrike. When he got it under control, the bronze man asked in a tensely controlled tone, "Has this been confirmed beyond a shadow of any doubt?"

"There were multiple eyewitnesses, although the body, along with the body of an unidentified woman, were carried off, possibly by the slayers," reported the President.

"Thank you for that information," Doc Savage said with only a trace of repressed emotion in his vibrant voice. The bronze man resumed his methodical smoking. His metallic eyes were unreadable.

"That reminds me," offered the President. "The note I received from the Baron in Black warned us that should Doc Savage be called into this crisis, it would result in his death, as well as the deaths of those who summoned him. I am obliged to tell you gentlemen this. I know that your notes did not contain this proviso."

Doc Savage volunteered, "Unquestionably, this was why Phineas P. Slade was felled by one of the life-nullifying zones. It was learned that he had requested my help, and the Baron in Black ordered his slaying. His heart was stunned, leading to the outward appearance that he had succumbed to a sudden stroke."

The President of the United States mused, "That would suggest to me that this Baron has or had a spy in the Huron plant."

"This is my theory as well," admitted Doc. "The point is that the Baron in Black has the power to strike at any of us, at any time. And there is no known defense against the awesome power he wields."

Ashen of face, the Premier of Canada asked, "So what is it that we can do?"

To which the President of Mexico interjected, "But is there nothing we *can* do?"

All eyes went to the premier scientist of their time, the wonder-worker known as Doc Savage.

Strangely, Doc Savage did not seem to be listening very attentively now. He was entirely absorbed in his smoking, and making sure that the plumes of tobacco smoke he was furiously jetting about the room did not unduly bother the other conferees.

After releasing one elongated cloud, which quickly drifted over to a far corner of the room, incidentally demonstrating that the big bronze man possessed wonderful lung capacity, Doc Savage's flake-gold eyes sharpened.

Abruptly, he came to his feet, saying, "Gentlemen, I suggest as our first defensive act an immediate withdrawal from this room. No doubt measurements for the laying down of a lethal field to encompass the White House have been carefully worked out in advance. And our gathering has not been very secret."

This stunned the assembled dignitaries. They appeared slow in fully grasping the dangerous import of the bronze man's words.

The President barked, "On your feet, gentlemen! Mr. Savage knows whereof he speaks."

As the others climbed to their feet, looking somewhat confused, Doc Savage pointed to the corner of the room that he had just filled with pungent smoke.

"Look!"

In that far corner, the roiling smoke began to behave queerly. A portion of it seemed to freeze, to turn into frozen gray cobwebs. Smoke rolling in that direction banked against a wall that could not be seen, showing that all motion had ceased in that corner of the room.

"To the door!" snapped Doc.

Giving the President a hearty shove, Doc impelled the chief executive before him. The man stumbled momentarily, so the bronze giant simply lifted him up in his great cabled arms and bore him off as if he weighed no more than a small child.

The rest of the assembled notables instantly rushed for the exit door, away from where the palpable but unseen field seemed to be materializing. This led to a side entrance, and the dignitaries, assisted by their personal bodyguards, were rushed to their vehicles, all of which took off at high speed, departing in every possible direction—for no one knew along which compass lines the sinister field was creeping.

DOC SAVAGE and the President of the United States found themselves in the back of the latter's official limousine. The vehicle, its siren wailing under the hood, fled for the airport.

Overhead, a small seaplane buzzed about. Doc Savage noticed it. It resembled the ship which had harassed him over the Florida Everglades. Dipping a wing, it streaked off, losing itself among the low-hanging clouds.

The bronze man recognized that pursuit, even if it could be promptly organized, would probably be futile.

Doc turned to the President and advised, "Mr. President, have the Army send up a flight of fighter planes to force down a seaplane now fleeing the District of Columbia. There is good reason to suspect that the attempt on our lives emanated from that aircraft."

"Confound it!" snapped the President hotly, smacking one fist into the other. "How are we to combat this insidious menace that strikes with such impunity?"

"Leave that to me," Doc told him. "It is best that you remain safely out of Washington, D.C., until this crisis has been resolved."

"Agreed," nodded the President of the United States. He was

very thoughtful for a time. "You have no weapon to combat this menace?"

"None," admitted Doc candidly. "But allow me to work on this situation. Let it be understood that you will give your answer to these demands on the morning of the fifth and final day of grace."

"I gather that you hope to conclude this horrid emergency by that time?"

"If my men and I survive," admitted the bronze man.

At the airport, the President and Doc Savage shook hands firmly, and the chief executive was hustled off to a waiting airplane where he would be conveyed to a secret location from which he could ride out the present crisis, presumably in safety.

Doc Savage reclaimed his chartered aircraft and launched it into the air, pointing howling motors north to New York City. As he flew, the bronze man worked the radio, endeavoring to raise Ham Brooks and learn more of the fate of the fallen Monk Mayfair. But he was not successful. Ham Brooks was clearly not near a radio receiver, so Doc Savage remained in the dark about the terrible events in Tampa, Florida.

Chapter XIII
FIRE ON THE WATER

THE SUSPICIOUS MILK truck drove south, out of the metropolitan Tampa area, farther down the Gulf Coast several miles, until it reached the Gandy Bridge, which took it across the causeway into the sprawling city of St. Petersburg.

By this time the steady rain had abated and night had fully descended upon Florida.

Behind the wheel, the nervous cabdriver remarked to Habeas Corpus, "This is going to cost your master a pretty penny."

Habeas grunted noncommittally, and gave one long ear a good scratching.

"But as long as he's got the dough, what do I care?" shrugged the cabby, who had started talking to Habeas after failing to get a rise out of the grieving attorney.

In the rear seat, Ham Brooks sniffed, "There will be no difficulty about the fare."

"From the way you're all duded up," the driver said conversationally, "I wouldn't doubt it."

"I happen to be wearing the finest clothes any man could afford," snapped Ham, who was sensitive about his apparel.

"Didn't I just say that?" quipped the driver.

The milk truck, surprisingly, found its way to the waterfront, and a cramped dockage for private boats and pleasure yachts.

Ham was not greatly surprised to see the coffin-hooded black touring machine that had spirited Monk Mayfair away only hours before parked nearby. It appeared to be empty.

The dapper lawyer said abruptly, "Pull over here. I will walk the remaining distance."

The driver quoted a very substantial fare.

Ham paid by peeling out a crisp fifty dollar bill, saying, "You may keep the change."

This impressed the driver, who got out and opened the door, not only for Ham but for Habeas the pig, with a rather elaborate flourish. He tipped his uniform cap, then wheeled his cab away to seek the nearest saloon.

Gripping his slim sword cane in one hand, Ham moved through the moonlit darkness, and observed the milk truck jerk into a parking space. The driver doused his lights and slipped from the vehicle and made his way to the dock of a particularly sumptuous looking cabin cruiser, whose length neared sixty feet.

With Habeas following him on clicking hooves, Ham went to the dairy truck, saw that the back was padlocked, and picked the lock with practiced ease.

Throwing open the doors, he discovered two complicated electrical devices that looked as unfamiliar as they were disquieting. They appeared to have been built around transformers.

"No doubt these are the devilish contraptions that generated the fields of force with which we have been contending," mused Ham aloud.

Habeas grunted as if in agreement. He sat down to resume his vigorous scratching.

Alone among Doc Savage's men, the dapper lawyer was no scientist. He understood electrical and mechanical apparatus sufficiently to be cautious around them. The temptation to disable these unfamiliar devices was strong in him. Greater still was his caution. He did not wish to risk electrocution, and furthermore understood that Doc himself would prefer that any scientifically-advanced machine fall into his capable hands for study.

Relocking the doors, Ham began to creep toward the cabin

cruiser, which rocked gently in the lapping waves of Tampa Bay.

There were lights on the cruiser; cabin portholes glowed with a warm illumination. Despite the late hour, the craft was clearly occupied. Shifting shadows could be seen, silhouetted by the interior lights.

Looking about, the fastidious barrister sought a safe spot from which to observe the vessel more closely. Ham saw that a sailboat on the other side of the dock was unoccupied, and he carefully picked his way toward that. Gathering Habeas under one elegant arm with distaste written all over his face, he cautiously stepped aboard.

Crouching low, Ham looked about the empty cockpit. He soon found a pair of binoculars, and carefully trained them on the portholes that shed inviting light.

"Jove!" he exploded.

For through the powerful lenses the dapper lawyer beheld an astounding sight.

THREE persons were seated around a table. One was the exotic woman in beige. Although she was no longer wearing her saucy beret, she was immediately identifiable by her luxurious black hair and lustrous opalescent eyes.

Facing her across the table sat a green-eyed individual who was vigorously rubbing theatrical makeup off his narrow face, revealing the catlike countenance of none other than Felix Frost.

Most welcome was the third person at the table. It was apelike Monk Mayfair, sitting up, big as life.

The trio were talking with the ease of casual acquaintances.

Ham blinked, as if disbelieving what his optics communicated to his brain. Using the binoculars, the dapper lawyer attempted to eavesdrop on the conversation.

A porthole was cracked open, which allowed their murmuring voices to waft outward. Not all of it was understandable, but Ham had some practice at lip reading, and this helped him fill in the gaps.

The woman in beige was saying, "This is the man I promised you would meet."

Monk growled, "I already had the pleasure. Your friend tried to kill us only this morning."

"Not I," retorted Felix Frost firmly, his feline whiskers quirking with bristling indignation. "I swear to it."

"The guy who tried to kill us had green glims, just like yours," returned the hairy chemist.

"Green eyes are not common, I will admit," retorted Felix Frost stiffly, "but neither are they unique."

The woman inserted urgently, "Mr. Frost wants to tell you things of importance. You must listen to him. You must hear him out. Many lives are at stake."

With evident reluctance, Monk said, "Spill, friend. If I don't like your line of talk, maybe I'll work you over some."

Felix Frost sighed in a manner that verged on purring. "The whole thing is horrible. My story is a complicated one. But first tell me—are you feeling any aftereffects from your encounter with the life-suppressing fields?"

Monk made a simian face. He felt of one hairy forearm. "Something must've bit me," he complained. "I got some kinda bite mark on my arm."

"Even this late in the year," the girl reminded, "bees and hornets abound in Florida."

"This must've been some hornet," muttered Monk. "It left a pock mark that won't quit stingin'."

"But are you feeling in good health?" pressed the former chief engineer of the Huron Motor works.

"Yeah, sure. But how come I'm alive? The rest of them all died back there in the park, didn't they?"

"They did," admitted Felix Frost sadly.

"So what's the answer?"

"That is only one of the many things I am prepared to tell you," informed the spring-jointed man nicknamed The Cat. "Things that will save America—perhaps the entire world—from terror. You must get this news to Doc Savage. I cannot reach out to him myself. For I am under suspicion for the murder of Phineas P. Slade in Detroit. I cannot expose myself to arrest, you understand. I must clear my name first."

"Gotcha," said Monk impatiently. "But get to the point. How come I didn't die?"

"There is a way to survive when encompassed by the fatal fields—"

"It is true, Mr. Mayfair," added Shari urgently. "Otherwise, I would have died with you back in the park. As you can see, I did not. This is why we brought you here. So that you may hear the truth, and understand the salvation of the world."

Various puzzled expressions crossed Monk's simian features. He appeared to be trying to recall how he was brought to the vessel, but without success.

Felix Frost had been fingering his feline mustaches as the woman spoke. But now it was his turn to explain further.

As Ham Brooks watched, completely intent upon the tableau visible through the cruiser's porthole, the sudden bark of a revolver shattered the brief interval of silence.

"Blazes!" howled Monk, reaching into his coat for his superfirer. His hairy paw flashed out again, brandishing the powerful machine pistol.

Ham perceived a shadow creeping along the wall of the cabin. Monk pointed the muzzle of his weapon at that shadow, and began firing. The cruiser interior filled with stuttering bedlam, synchronized with eye-hurting gun flashes.

Heaving up, the dapper lawyer charged up from the dock and pitched toward the open cockpit of the cruiser. He was racing for the vessel when a masked figure in black thrust his head out of the lower cabin, saw him, and began blazing away.

Scorching lead pierced the air on either side of Ham Brooks' head. He was forced to duck, yet in doing so managed to loose short bursts of bullets. But his aim was wild, owing to the need to dodge hunting lead.

The mercy bullets began splattering their chemical potion all over the cabin cruiser's sides and brass brightwork.

A streak of shiny black leather flashed in the night, and the assassin leapt over the port rail, on the opposite side from where Ham was approaching. There came a great splash.

Monk and Ham reached the cockpit at the same time, smoking weapons in hand.

They traded startled glances. Monk barked, "Did you get him?"

"No, did you?"

"No, he ducked back before I could get a bead on him."

They lunged for the port rail, leaned over, and saw oily water gurgling and bubbling.

Monk sent a spray of mercy bullets into the disturbed brine, but to no apparent effect. Nobody surfaced, conscious or otherwise, and Ham invited Monk to jump in after the fleeing man.

"*You* jump in," Monk complained.

"My clothes will be ruined," Ham retorted tartly.

Monk looked as if he was prepared to plunge in, when suddenly the cruiser's engines begin to churn and boil water at the stern.

They looked about. The woman in beige, Shari Phoenia, was attempting to get the boat underway.

Monk and Ham rushed to her side. Monk demanded, "What are you doin'?"

"We must escape! Felix Frost is dead, and we will be next if we do not fly."

Anxiously, Monk looked about, and spotted a furtive figure in black moving in the direction of the milk truck. All that could be seen of the assailant in ebony was his head, which appeared to be swathed in a pilot's helmet of wet black leather, to which was attached smoked goggles that completely masked his features.

The apish chemist attempted to down him with a burst of mercy bullets, but to no satisfactory avail, for he had exhausted his drum capacity in the earlier skirmish. The powerful pistols went through rounds with frightening efficiency. That was one of the few drawbacks of their design.

Ham shouted, "She may be right, you hatless ape! The back of that milk truck contains the generators for producing the force fields that are so lethal."

"That means we're sittin' ducks!" roared Monk.

Hastily, the pair begin casting off lines. Once this was done, Shari ran the motors ahead, and the cruiser surged out of its dockage.

They moved out into the heart of Tampa Bay. Monk and Ham, stationed at the stern, prepared to a loose a flurry of mercy bullets if necessary, Monk having reloaded.

But it was so dark, with lowering clouds obscuring the moon, so they could not pick out the masked man in black, wherever he was.

The milk truck suddenly snorted to life, and lunged around in a circle, only to back up so that its rear doors faced the retreating vessel.

A shadowy figure jumped out, began to throw open the doors. That was when Monk and Ham resumed firing.

But it was no use. The range was too great for the superfirers, which depended upon close quarters and a fierce concentration of firepower to do their work.

The vibrant woman piloted the cruiser out into the bay, and began steering erratically, saying, "This will make us less of a target!"

"Who are you?" demanded Ham. "How do you hook up with all of this?"

"Time enough for that later," she flung back urgently. "We must get as far away as possible, before the fatal field clamps down on us and snuffs out our lives."

Monk looked around, and spotted Habeas Corpus who, in

following Ham, had leapt into the cockpit during all the excitement. He grinned happily.

"Hiyah, hog," said Monk. "I see you're still among the livin'."

Habeas commenced trotting around in happy circles, clearly overjoyed to be reunited with his homely master.

"Will you stop playing with that uncooked pork chop!" snapped Ham. "Our lives are in danger."

Mention of that undeniable fact caused Monk to jump back into the cabin below, where Felix Frost was lying in a welter of crimson. He appeared to be dead. But the dying man had dipped his finger in his own blood, and scratched out a brief message:

> *Find Theodore Buffington. He knows—*

"Knows what?" muttered Ham, who had followed Monk down.

"I dunno," admitted Monk.

Suddenly a shrill scream tore the night from above, and they rushed back to the pilot house.

There, Shari was pointing a quivering finger toward the water directly ahead.

Tampa Bay was alive with a milky blue phosphorescence. Witch fire churned beneath the waves, making the water glow eerily in the absence of moonlight.

"That's just natural phosphorescence," Monk reassured her. "Sea fire, sailors call it."

"I know this!" Shari snapped back. "Look over there. Where I am pointing!"

Their eyes followed the line of her jabbing finger. Up ahead, off to starboard, there was a flameless section of water—a long deep bar of it. It was coming into view now.

Ham observed, "It is the churning of the water that excites the organisms that produce the phosphorescent glow. See where there is no luminosity?"

"Yeah," said Monk. "That means there's no motion in the water, or above it."

Shari clarified, "That dark line denotes the boundary of a static death zone."

All could see that the dark water was unnaturally flat. The chop of waves was entirely absent. It was, by contrast with the surrounding surge, an unsettling sight.

Dead fish became visible on the water's surface. They sat, still as silvery stones, neither rising nor falling with the tides. For the bay water sat immobile, as if frozen.

Grimacing, Monk took the wheel from Shari, and yelled, "Hang on!"

Using every ounce of the animal strength in his burly upper body, the hairy chemist attempted to sheer off from the invisible wall of energy.

The Diesels responded smartly. But the trim ship was hurtling along at high speed. The leaping prow knifed toward the last patch of electric phosphorescence, and seemed ready to strike the unseen barrier.

The terror of the force fields was great in their minds. For a thing that cannot be seen is somehow more fearsome than something that can be clearly discerned. Out in the dark of night on Tampa Bay, with the phosphorescent patch demarcating the end of the zone of safety, a sense of malevolent menace seized their brains.

Growling, Monk spun the wheel madly. The dead-looking water loomed. There seemed to be no avoiding a collision.

With a shrill shriek, Shari cried out, "I refuse to die like this!"

Before either man could react, she leaped over the rail and into the milky blue waters, then began swimming through the phosphorescence, away from the dead, dark patch.

Monk, growling ferociously and showing bared teeth like a maddened gorilla, swerved the boat until it scraped along the edge of the motionless field.

"Did we miss it?" howled Ham.

"How do I know?" Monk yelled back. "It's invisible, ain't it?"

They looked, but could not make out the line of demarcation

now that they were so close to it. There were no visual clues in the air to aid them.

Ham picked up a life ring, flung it over the port rail. It struck the invisible wall, became fixed, and as it fell behind them, began to sink toward the dead-looking expanse of waveless water.

"We made it!" chortled Monk, putting the awful zone behind them.

"It might move," reminded Ham. "It can follow us at any point, if the controllers of the field are able to fix our position."

Suddenly, Ham realized that the cruiser's illuminated portholes made them sitting ducks. He raced for the electrical switches, began turning off lights, but he didn't know where everything was, and stumbled about. Finally, the frantic lawyer doused every conceivable light and rejoined Monk at the stern.

As they watched from the stern rail, the line of dark water inexorably crept toward them, dousing the azure phosphorescence in its path. It was moving at a fair clip, like some underwater creature composed of black void.

Wide-mouthed, Monk raced forward on bandy legs, batted the throttle, advancing it all the way, and sent the sharp-prowed cruiser hammering along the waves.

"We can't outrun it!" he bellowed.

"Well, we cannot outswim it, either!" barked Ham.

Eyes wide, Monk yelled, "We gotta do something!"

In the end, with the dead-looking water creeping up behind them, Monk and Ham decided to abandon ship.

But first, Monk turned the cruiser in the direction of the wall, while Ham restored the lights.

"This might work, at that," commented Ham approvingly.

Monk gathered up kicking Habeas, and together the three dropped into the water.

The speeding vessel charged directly into the looming wall that could not be seen, and the boat came apart at the prow.

Noisily, it crumpled as if it struck a stone wall. The keel split with a tortured crack like a great sequoia tree crashing down. There was not much recognizable in a nautical way after that.

Swimming away from the cruiser, they called out for the missing Shari.

But there was no answer.

In the end, they gave it up. The water was cold. Grimly, they struck out for shore, and when they pulled themselves out of the water, there was no sign of the mysterious milk truck.

The long black coffin of a touring car belonging to Snag Ravelli, underworld leader, had not moved from its parking spot, however.

Cautiously, superfirers drawn, Monk and Ham approached the vehicle.

Streetlight glow disclosed a dark figure seated behind the wheel.

Waving the dapper lawyer to hang back, Monk went ahead on all fours, crouching like a gorilla, and sidled up beside the passenger door, below eye level. He had taken his machine pistol between his teeth by the trigger guard.

Now Monk sprang into sight, simultaneously yanking the door open while training the gun muzzle on the unsuspecting driver.

"Stick 'em up, you!" snarled Monk.

The driver did no such thing. Instead, he tumbled out of his seat and fell across Monk's oversized shoes.

There was sufficient illumination to show the dead man's face. There was no question that he was dead. Staring dark eyes had the glassy quality found only in corpses. The mouth hung open, displaying the unlovely snaggle-toothed grin which had given the man his nickname in life. That broken grin that had dried to a dull ivory hue in an unshaven jaw.

Rushing up, Ham blurted, "Snag Ravelli!"

"Yeah," muttered Monk. "And not a mark on him. What do you want to bet someone rubbed him out?"

"The driver of the milk truck must have turned one of those deadly machines on him," Ham intoned.

Monk grunted, kicking the dead man off his brogans. "What'd he look like?"

"That goggled assassin had green eyes the last time I saw him."

"Figures," muttered Monk. "A green-eyed killer for that green-eyed Felix Frost. What the heck could that mean?"

Ham only shrugged.

The hairy chemist looked around angrily. He bared his teeth in a ferocious grimace.

"This night," he said bitingly, "has been a total and complete bust."

This time, Ham Brooks did not disagree with him.

Monk sought a pay telephone in order to inform the police of their grisly discovery while Ham stood guard over the late underworld mobster.

Chapter XIV
DOOM IN FIVE DAYS

THE HOUR WAS past midnight when Doc Savage slanted his chartered airplane in the direction of New York City.

Owing to the urgent need for speed, Doc's plane was not one of his preferred amphibians, but a regulation craft equipped with retractable wheels. This made it impossible for him to land at his Hidalgo warehouse establishment on the Hudson River. The combination of boathouse and aircraft hangar was designed for seaplanes only.

Consequently, Doc was forced to land at the North Beach Airport in Long Island, and hire a taxicab to take him into the city.

By the time the taxi was rolling across the Queensboro Bridge, a light, fluffy snow had begun falling, signifying that winter, still many weeks off by the calendar, had arrived early.

Doc paid careful attention to the drifting flakes, knowing that they might betray any sign of a deadly force screen coming into being. He saw no such signs.

When the cab deposited him before his towering headquarters in midtown Manhattan, the bronze man strolled through the lobby as rapidly as he could, in order to avoid undue attention. Due to the lateness of the hour, he was very fortunate in that respect. There was hardly anyone about.

Doc took the superspeed elevator to the eighty-sixth floor, which moved upward with such tremendous velocity that he was all but thrown to his knees. The lift had been known to bring unwary passengers crashing to the floor with distressing consequences but, owing to the height of the building, which was New York's tallest, and the often blinding speed with which the bronze man sometimes needed to reach street level, Doc had built the lift for maximum efficiency.

Stepping out into the eighty-sixth floor corridor, Doc approached the plain bronze door on which was the modest legend: CLARK SAVAGE, JR.

This substantial portal opened as if by magic at his approach, a consequence of a radioactive compound he wore concealed in the heel of one shoe, which triggered a sensitive relay which in turn opened the door mechanically.

Striding into the reception room of the office suite, then passing through a very large library dominated by an oversized globe of the world, Doc entered the great enamel-walled laboratory, which glittered with fantastic machinery, glasswork of the type commonly employed by chemists, and other wondrous devices. This was the fabulous workshop of Doc Savage, in which he performed wonders beyond the imagination of the ancient alchemists.

Long Tom was over in the section devoted to electrical work, dominated by an immense electrostatic generator. Pat Savage hovered around him. The unhealthy-looking electrical expert appeared to have assembled a number of disparate instruments on a spacious work bench, and was monitoring them with a concerned expression on his sour features.

"Doc!" said Pat excitedly. "Thank goodness you're here. I was about to die of sheer boredom."

No smile of acknowledgment or recognition crossed the bronze man's metallic face. His eyes were very still, and there was a haunted look in them that was strange to see.

"What have you to report, Long Tom?" asked Doc.

"Less than nothing," groused Long Tom. "I have every electromagnetic detection apparatus operating, but so far nothing has happened. No one has attempted to strike at our headquarters with any electrical weapon of any kind."

"Do not take your eyes off those instruments," cautioned the bronze man. "Our lives are very much in peril every hour that we remain here."

Looking up from an array of engineering tools spread over a glass-topped table, Renny Renwick boomed, "I think I'm getting somewhere."

Instead of inquiring further, Doc Savage reported, "In Washington, a report was received detailing the death of our good friend, Monk Mayfair."

Pat Savage's hands flew to her mouth, choking back a cry. "Oh, no! It can't be!"

"Holy cow!" blurted Renny. "I'll believe that when I see it!" He made and unmade great knobby fists in his consternation.

Long Tom's sallow face paled. He spoke one word, softly, bitterly, "Damn."

No one had anything more to say.

The bronze man walked over to the tabletop where Renny had been working. His flake-gold eyes scrutinized a map that the big-fisted engineer had laid out. There was a compass. Ruler. Protractor. Other drafting implements. It appeared that Renny had not been working on anything other than attempting to plot the lines of the various death zones which had descended upon the United States. There was a considerable number of them.

Doc Savage said quietly, "The trend is becoming apparent."

"So you agree with me?" asked Renny.

"As a working theory, this bears further investigation."

The bronze man began picking up the compass and a protractor and began adding lines to the complicated map.

These lines had been trending in one direction, but as the bronze man worked, they converged on a certain point in the Northwest Territories of Canada, above the Arctic Circle, in the general vicinity of Great Slave Lake and the remote outpost of Yellowknife.

All was quiet, until Pat Savage could be heard seated in the library, quietly sobbing. In the many years of their association with the masterful bronze man, they had never lost a companion. And now it appeared that Monk Mayfair was dead.

"It's too much to bear," sobbed Pat.

Long Tom whispered to Doc, "She's taking it pretty hard."

Doc Savage nodded, intent upon his work. He seemed very focused in his concentration. Except for the metallic look in his eyes, he might not have been greatly moved by the loss of his friend of long association.

But those chilly eyes spoke volumes. Noticing them, Long Tom knew in his heart that the perpetrators of Monk Mayfair's demise would face the kind of wrath that would make the fury of Thor and his thunderbolts seem like a spring rain in comparison.

When his anger was aroused, the mighty Man of Bronze was nothing if not single-minded in his pursuit of justice.

"Have you heard from Ham?" asked Doc suddenly of Long Tom.

"No. Do you think he's all right?"

"Try to raise him on the radio," requested Doc.

The pint-sized genius of the juice hustled over to the great all-wave transceiver standing in the electrical corner of the oversized laboratory. It was already warmed up. Now he grabbed the microphone and began calling Ham Brooks' name on their special wavelength.

Fifteen minutes of this produced no results. Long Tom broke it off, and returned to where Doc Savage was finishing up. His pale eyes rested on the map before Doc began rolling it up.

"I take it we're moving fast on this Baron in Black?" he asked.

Doc nodded firmly. "The nation has been given five days to surrender. Therefore, we have less than that much time to get to the heart of the matter, and uproot this conspiracy at its source."

"I pity this Baron in Black, once you catch up with him," Renny said grimly.

Pat Savage sat up suddenly and her voice was steely. "I'm going along for this hell ride. Don't think you can stop me! Monk Mayfair didn't deserve what happened to him. He had the biggest, kindest heart of anyone I ever knew. And I aim to track down those who slew him."

The cold vehemence of the bronze-haired girl's words made such an impression that Doc Savage, for once, did not object to her demand.

"It will be dangerous," he reminded gently.

Pat's golden eyes grew cold. "Right now, I'm feeling mighty dangerous."

That seemed to settle that.

Suddenly, Pat asked, "Anybody seen my grandfather's sixgun?"

"It wasn't in my float plane when I left Florida," said Renny.

"I'll die if it doesn't turn up," fumed Pat.

Saying nothing, Doc Savage made preparations to depart.

First, he handed out wristwatches to Long Tom and Pat Savage. They were larger than the usual commercial items, and sat on the wrist rather heavily.

"What are these?" asked Pat, puzzled.

Long Tom explained, "These are special wristwatches Doc confiscated from a spy ring a while back. They flash infra-red messages triggered by a radio signal. You can feel them on the back of your wrist where the watchcase rests."*

As a demonstration, the puny electrical expert began stabbing at the winding stem, which produced the sensation of hot flashes on the back Pat Savage's wrist, precisely where the watchcase sat.

"I can feel them!" exclaimed Pat wonderingly. "Morse code?"

"Exactly," said Doc Savage. "These instruments will allow us to communicate silently should we become separated. We are up against a very great threat, which has the ability to shut down all life, all electricity, all motion."

---

* *Merchants of Disaster.*

"We've tackled this type of menace before," Pat said grimly, "and come out on top. We'll do it again."

The degree to which Doc Savage's grief and preoccupation over the danger threatening the nation and the sudden loss of Monk Mayfair was shown when he gave his head a slight shake and reached into his pocket and produced a pipe and pouch of tobacco.

As they watched in amazement, the bronze man lit up, began releasing streams of tobacco smoke from his mouth.

Methodically, but with restrained urgency, the bronze man moved among the fabulous equipment of his laboratory, and then into the commodious library, blowing out billowing smoke so rapidly he might have been a brazen steam engine in human form.

"What's he doing?" demanded Pat of Long Tom. "Has he lost his reason?"

Long Tom shook his head. "No. I get it, though. Doc is laying down a smokescreen to see if one of those lethal zones is operating."

After fumigating the reception room, the bronze man rejoined them in the laboratory.

"All appears normal," he reported. "Smoke, if it ceases its rolling motion, instantaneously betrays the presence of a standing field of lethality."

"Do you think our enemies will attack us here?" asked Pat dubiously.

"They fear nothing. They attacked the White House itself. We barely got away with our lives."

Renny grunted, "They must have a lot of these gadgets."

"Undoubtedly," agreed Doc. "But it stands to reason that there is one single powerful broadcasting station located in an out-of-the-way place, which is laying down the larger and more potent fields that are scourging the nation."

"That's where we're heading, eh?" muttered Long Tom.

"Knocking out that central sending station is our primary objective," Doc told him flatly.

Doc moved to a wall of the vast laboratory where a special pneumatic capsule, designed to convey passengers to the Hidalgo warehouse just a few city blocks away, awaited them.

Pat Savage hesitated, saying, "Do we have to ride that whirligig?"

The answer proved to be a resounding no. For suddenly the laboratory lights went dark.

DOC SAVAGE abruptly halted, flashed into reverse. He charged straight for Pat and Long Tom like a football player rushing opposing players.

Before they knew what hit them, Pat and Long Tom were each taken up in the bronze man's great irresistible arms.

Doc raced through a forest of scientific paraphernalia, headed for the door to the spacious library, carrying them with him. It was a breathless few minutes. Reacting only seconds behind, Renny pounded in their wake, swallowing his habitual expression of disapproval while he focused on flight.

The terrestrial globe which sat in the center of the library would have honored a university library. It was immense, fully eight feet across and twenty-five feet in circumference.

That it was not entirely ornamental was demonstrated when the bronze man leapt to the pedestal, tramped a foot on one spot, causing the face of the globe depicting the Americas to split and open up in two sections.

This disclosed a cavity within. Doc jumped up, springing into it, taking Pat and Long Tom with him. Not that they had any choice in the matter. Renny clambered in after them.

Doc slammed down into the hollow space, whereupon the two sections valved shut. A greater darkness clamped down on them. It was utterly impenetrable.

"What's going on?" demanded Pat, untangling herself from Doc's massive arm.

Long Tom explained, "The lights went out. Probably means an anti-inertia swath cutting across the skyscraper."

Renny finally released the pent-up pet expression that passed for an oath. "Holy cow!" The interior of the globe actually shook in response to his vocal thunder.

Doc Savage added quietly, "This globe was constructed so as to shield persons encased within its circumference from all manner of deadly rays."

"Will it protect us from the lethal electrical fields?" asked Pat breathlessly.

The bronze man's reply was not reassuring. "I confess that I do not know," he said. "It is lined with lead, as well as a metallic mesh and other substances, designed to defeat electromagnetic fields, of which the zones are known to be comprised. But it has never been tested against exactly this penetrating force."

Long Tom muttered, "I helped Doc construct this Faraday cage. We have encountered more than our share of death rays in the last few years, you know."

Searching the intense blackness with her eyes, Pat asked reasonably, "Should we start saying our prayers right about now?"

No one replied to that. They held their breath and waited.

Doc Savage passed the time by manipulating his signal watch, which caused Pat to react as if she had received the equivalent of a hotfoot in her right wrist.

"Why are you fooling with that at a time like this?" she flared, shaking the offended hand.

"If you want to accompany us on our mission, you will need practice decoding the heat impulses," explained the bronze man in the absolute darkness.

"Oh," said Pat, who seemed suddenly reassured by the bronze man's relatively calm demeanor. She began paying attention to the intermittent flashes.

"I think it's saying, stay calm," Pat reported.

Doc signaled in code, E-x-a-c-t-l-y.

They all calmed down at that point.

The bronze man tracked the time by consulting the radium dial of his oversized wristwatch. They could hear it ticking in the immense blackness of the interior of the terrestrial globe, for the devices also told time rather accurately.

The fact that the watch continued to tick, as well as the fact that their hearts managed to beat more or less regularly, made them feel more and more confident that the special shielding properties of the sphere were functioning as designed.

DOC SAVAGE waited twenty long minutes. Then, locating a secret stud above his head, he caused the sphere to crack open.

Their light-starved eyes were assaulted by the fluorescent lights of the library.

"Juice is back on," muttered Long Tom.

Doc Savage helped Pat climb down, while Long Tom leaped nimbly to the parquet floor. Renny landed like an ungainly elephant with only two legs.

Pat sighed forlornly. "I guess I'll have to resign myself to taking a spin in that infernal go-devil, as Monk liked to call it."

Doc shook his metallic head.

"Not necessarily." He strolled over to a bank of windows which overlooked the Hudson River. There in the sky danced a monoplane of unusual coloration. It was white on the top, and a cool bluish-gray on the bottom.

The craft was making acrobatic turns in the midnight air. Snowflakes drifted all about it like pursuing fireflies of some cold otherworldly ice kingdom.

Renny asked, "You spotted that ship before the lights went down, didn't you?"

The bronze man admitted that he had, adding, "It was flying in a peculiar manner. Now it seems to be buzzing our warehouse hangar by the Hudson."

"That means we don't dare go there, do we?" frowned Long Tom.

"Not if we hope to preserve our lives. Whoever this Baron

in Black is, he is determined to knock us out of the picture."

"Sounds like he's afraid of you!" suggested Pat.

Doc Savage said grimly, flake-gold eyes tracking the pirouetting plane, "He has good reason to be."

His words brought a chill to everyone in the room. Everyone understood that the bronze giant had the fate of Monk Mayfair on his mind, as did they all.

Abruptly, the radio transceiver in the laboratory began speaking in Ham Brooks' cultured voice.

Swiftly, Doc surged to the large set. Taking up the microphone, he said crisply, "Doc Savage here."

"Doc! I'm here with Monk. We had a number of close shaves. But we're O.K."

"Monk is alive?" demanded Doc sharply.

"As much as I regret to say it, yes," returned Ham coolly. *"The clumsy ape stumbled into more trouble than he could normally handle. But I personally saved his worthless hide."*

Monk's squeaky voice intruded, adding, *"Don't listen to the shyster, Doc. It's nothin' like he says."*

"What has happened down there?" asked Doc, relief underwriting his tone.

Swiftly, Ham Brooks relayed all that transpired, beginning with Monk receiving the summons from the mysterious woman in beige, Shari Phoenia, leading up to the battle aboard the cruiser in Tampa Bay, from which they escaped by the narrowest of margins.

Doc Savage asked, "You say that Felix Frost is dead?"

Ham replied, *"He was shot, and then he went down with the boat. No one could have survived that combination."*

To which Monk added, *"We don't know what happened to the girl, Shari. We couldn't find her in the bay. She must've drowned. Too bad, she was quite a looker."*

Pat Savage scolded, "A woman dies and all you have to say about it is that she was pretty?"

Doc Savage inserted, "What else did you uncover?"

Monk replied sheepishly, *"Truth is, we don't know a heck of a lot more than we did before."*

Ham naturally contradicted the hairy chemist, saying, *"There were two death-zone dynamos in operation down here, Doc. Someone got away with them. That someone was the assassin wearing black and who had green eyes, similar to those of Felix Frost."*

"What about Webster Neff and Theodore Buffington?" asked Doc Savage. "Have there been any sightings of either of them?"

"Yeah," piped up Monk. *"We got hold of the Tampa police and they found Neff in a vacant lot. He was in rough shape. Not a mark on him. We think his heart got temporarily stopped by one of the electrical fields. They got him in a hospital now. Doctors think he'll make it, but he ain't talkin' to anybody any time soon."*

"Since he was last seen in the company of Theodore Buffington," remarked Ham, *"it does not look good for Buffington."*

"As much as I hate to agree with this shyster," Monk offered, *"I gotta admit he's right. Felix Frost wrote in his own blood that Buffington had the answers to everything. Now that Frost is dead, that leaves Buffington."*

Doc Savage advised, "It does not make sense for Theodore Buffington to be involved with the Baron in Black."

"If this is so," returned Ham in frustration, *"who else is left?"*

"That," stated Doc Savage emphatically, "is the question of the hour."

Chapter XV
THE GREAT LONE LAND

DOC SAVAGE RAPPED out instructions to Monk and Ham in Tampa, Florida.

"Charter a fast plane and fly north as rapidly as possible. Do not land at the Hidalgo warehouse hangar, but continue north. Stay in touch by radio."

"Gotcha, Doc!" returned Monk, signing off.

Replacing the microphone, Doc Savage gathered up the charts and mapping tools which Renny had been using to plot the zones that had striated the nation with their powerful wedges of unseen death and destruction.

Doc went to a wall, pressed a stud, opening two sets of doors, which slid back to disclose within a vertical steel pipe larger than a sewer tunnel.

Hanging suspended within was a double-ended bullet-shaped form. A hatchway opened automatically. Doc assisted Pat into the capsule, then followed Renny and Long Tom inside.

The capsule was padded within. There were no seats, only subway style straphangers. The bullet car—for that was what it was—was designed for a fast escape, not for comfort. Passengers tended to get banged about the padded interior walls unceremoniously.

"I hate this claustrophobic thing," complained Pat.

"I thought you liked riding roller coasters," Renny questioned.

"I do. What of it?"

"Think of this gimcrack as a subway roller coaster."

"No, thank you," sniffed Pat. "I can bail out of a roller coaster and take my chances on landing alive. This whirligig of a hurtling coffin frightens me."

Doc actuated the controls. The capsule hatch closed, then the massive steel pipe hermetically sealed itself. The conduit was actually a gargantuan pneumatic tube.

Doc set the controls. They were not complicated. "Everyone brace themselves."

Pat grabbed not one, but two straphangers. With her attractive face gathering into a grimace, she squeezed her golden eyes shut.

With a frightening *whoosh!*, the capsule let go, dropping the entire height of the skyscraper in less than ten seconds. It was a breathtaking experience.

It stopped in the sub-basement, coming to an abrupt halt, flinging them against the padded cushions, which absorbed the shock.

Doc opened the hatch, and stepped out of the commodious pipe into the sub-basement garage that housed a diverse fleet of automobiles, ranging from expensive limousines to streamlined coupés and a taxicab used to shadow suspects without their knowing anyone was on their trail.

"It is much too dangerous to go on to the Hidalgo warehouse," advised the bronze man. "We will drive to North Beach Airport instead."

Doc selected a black sedan possessing a special motor of his own engineering, and they all piled in. By this time, Pat Savage had pried open her eyes and it was to be noticed that her gait was wobbly.

The drive to North Beach Airport in the late-night snow took the better part of an hour. The winter tires were constructed so that they could run in heavy drifts without benefit of snow chains for added traction. As they barreled along, Pat and Long Tom in the rear were studying through binoculars the strangely-hued aircraft as it orbited Manhattan.

Long Tom muttered, "It's almost invisible against the snow."

"If you look closely," Doc Savage stated, "you will notice that it is fitted with skis."

"Skis!" rumbled Renny. "That means—"

"Exactly," rapped Doc. "We are going north."

AT the North Beach Airport, they stopped before a hangar at the far end of the field, and entered it.

Inside was a four-engined transport plane, which was equipped with skis. This was one of Doc Savage's spare buses, which he kept at the municipal field for just such a contingency as this. Inasmuch as it was not an amphibian, it could not be hangared in the Hidalgo warehouse without removing the skis and fitting pontoons in their place.

Since the operation to fit ski runners over the wheels was a time-consuming one, Doc kept this ski plane in constant readiness for emergency use. It could take off in a flash.

Doc took the controls, as Renny sank into the co-pilot bucket. The others distributed themselves about the spacious cabin.

Doc began stabbing switches and coaxing the great engines to power. Lurching into life, the big aircraft rumbled out onto the tarmac, and lined up for takeoff.

There was sufficient wintery accumulation already coating the runway that the airport had closed to ordinary craft and their pneumatic landing wheels. Conditions were perfect for the ski plane.

Long Tom took his customary spot in the radio shack. Pat Savage occupied a comfortable seat in the rear, saying, "Exactly how many planes do you have stashed here and there?" she demanded of Doc.

Long Tom grumbled, "Pipe down. You know Doc is always prepared for any emergency."

Pat made a wry face. "I wish I had half his dough."

Revving up the engines, Doc ran the big aircraft down the runway. Its tail lifted, wings slicing air. There had been no side-to-side slipping as the ski runners flashed along the snow-coated blacktop. Takeoff was smooth.

Climbing rapidly, Doc flew in the direction of the city, seeking the marauding ski plane. But it had already vanished in the maddening swirl of wind-blown snow.

"No tracing it now," fumed Long Tom.

"We'd be sitting ducks if we did," rumbled Renny, making frustrated fists. "One wrong move, and he could knock us clean out of the sky with that blamed devil device."

Reluctantly, the bronze man turned the aircraft south, surprisingly enough, not north as expected, and flew on. The ski plane made tremendous time.

"Correct me if I'm mistaken," said Pat to no one in particular, as she watched the familiar landmarks roll beneath her wings. "But aren't we going the wrong way?"

Doc replied, "We are going to rendezvous with Monk and Ham to pick them up. They will make better time flying with us than trying to follow in their chartered craft. We can easily make up for the lost time in this bus."

This was done at a prearranged airfield in Maryland, outside of Baltimore. Long Tom radioed instructions to the other plane.

Both aircraft landed within thirty minutes of one another. Monk and Ham hastily abandoned their chartered craft, which, while fast, was not capable of flying the vast distances involved. Habeas Corpus accompanied the hairy chemist.

Pat Savage greeted Monk warmly, "Well, look who's here—the man who died and came back to life."

At sight of the bronze-haired girl, Monk beamed broadly. "Hi, Pat. You know nothin' can keep me down."

To which Ham Brooks inserted archly, "You can thank me for this ape's salvation. As much as I hate to admit it, without Monk I would have no one to test my wits against."

Renny thumped, "Not to mention the fact that you'd fall heir to that ugly pig."

Once they were all safely aboard, and the aircraft doors closed,

Doc Savage turned the plane into the wind, and sent the craft thundering into the early morning sky. For a new day was dawning, the beginning of the third day of the five allotted to the President of the United States to come to terms with the mysterious and ruthless Baron in Black.

Once they were in the air, Ham Brooks put forth a question. "Doc, if time is of the essence, why did you expend the extra time to come and pick us up?"

Doc replied simply, "For this operation, we will need every hand. My plan calls for us to separate before going into action. Also, by flying south, any suspicious eyes would assume we were tearing off on a wild-goose chase."

"Makes good sense," remarked Monk. "But why are we splittin' into two groups if we have only one plane?"

"For what I have in mind, I will need to make my way to the Fortress of Solitude, where several inventions in various stages of completion could prove useful. One device, perhaps with some refinements, could serve to foil these lethal fields."

"Speaking of that," inserted Long Tom. "What if we ram smack into one of the monster-sized zones on our way up north? If we can't see the fields, how do we avoid them?"

"That possibility is ever-present," replied Doc. "It is a chance we will have to take."

It had not been snowing much in Maryland but, as they hammered north over New England, aerial snowflakes were abundant. They filled the skies in fluffy flurries illuminated by spectral moonlight.

Doc instructed his assistants to man windows with powerful binoculars and even a small telescope that was kept on board.

Doc directed, "Keep an eye peeled for any void or cessation of the whirling snow, or any ski plane such as the one spotted over New York."

That kept everyone busy, although Monk and Ham managed to direct a few cutting remarks at one another.

Ham was complaining, "Only a nitwit like yourself would

go off and rendezvous with a lady of questionable motives."

Monk growled back, "If you're referrin' to Shari Phoenia, I think she was all right."

"That remains to be seen," sniffed Ham "In any event, if she truly drowned, we will never discover the truth about her."

"The truth," rejoined Monk, "is that she gave me the glad-eye, not you. You're just jealous, is all."

Frowning at the hairy chemist's disreputably loud suit, the dapper attorney commented dryly, "Perhaps she was merely eyeing those ridiculous glad rags you call clothes."

"You Fifth Avenue scarecrow! I don't need no sissy clothes to set me off."

Ham snapped back, "Listen, you flat-brained jungle brute—"

"Knock it off," boomed Renny. "Or before you know it, my fingers will be squeezing your throat muscles closed."

"Ditto," added Long Tom sourly.

The dueling duo fell back on trading hostile glares.

From time to time, Doc Savage questioned Ham closely about the events in Tampa. He did not seem satisfied by the answers—or at least appeared to struggle with making sense of the mystifying crosscurrents that took place down in Florida.

The involvement of notorious Tampa gang leader Snag Ravelli came out. Doc Savage had not previously been aware of this development, having been in Washington during the fracas there.

"After our trouble in Tampa Bay," Ham was saying, "we discovered Snag Ravelli in his touring car, dead as a doornail, not far from the dock to which I trailed him, and turned the body over to the authorities. They promised to let us know what they discovered. While we were flying north, we heard by radio from the Tampa police. The medical examiner pronounced him dead of natural causes."

"Heart attack, you mean," scoffed Monk. "Sounds like Ravelli got double-crossed, but good. What do you make of that, Doc?"

Doc Savage said carefully, "It appears that the Baron in Black, or possibly an accomplice, engaged the Ravelli gang to do some dirty work, and was not too careful about what happened to his hirelings during the electronic ambush."

Ham spoke up. "Why would he deliver Monk and that mystery woman to Felix Frost? It does not makes sense, unless Shari Phoenia was tied up with the Baron in some way."

"Not a chance in Hades!" scoffed Monk. "She was as much a victim as Frost."

"The role of Miss Phoenia in this matter remains unclear," offered Doc. "As does that of Felix Frost."

Simian wrinkles shrank Monk's tiny forehead. "If the idea was to kidnap me at that park, why did the Ravelli gang try to gun me down the way they did?"

Doc said, "It seems likely that they were instructed to feign a typical underworld rubout, in order to make the demonstration of the fields appear more dramatic, the better to impress you, Monk. Then they were slain in order to cover the Baron's tracks, if not to trick the police into believing that an underworld feud lay behind the ambush."

"Heck," grinned Monk, "Tampa cops say the whole gang got rubbed out. So none of 'em will be talkin', at least not this side of Perdition."

"What I fail to understand," Ham drawled at one point, "is how this misbegotten tree ape survived his encounter with two fatal fields focused to crush him like the beetle-browed insect that he is."

Rolling up one shirt sleeve to display a hairy arm, Monk muttered, "Speakin' of insects, I got me a fierce bite down there in Florida. Stings worse than a blasted yellow jacket."

"Let me see that," requested Doc. Examining the mark, which was visible through the tangle of rusty hair adorning the apish chemist's arm, the bronze man saw that swelling had set in. A flicker of interest stirred the golden flakes that ceaselessly swirled in his eyes.

"It does not look serious," was his only comment.

"Beats me what a wasp or hornet was doin' buzzin' about so late in the year," complained Monk, giving the wound an annoyed scratching.

"Count yourself lucky," reminded Ham. "Consider the fate of poor Webster Neff, who will be fortunate if he pulls out of his ordeal with his health intact."

One wary eye on Renny and Long Tom, Monk muttered under his breath to Ham, "We were dopes for ever takin' that guy for anything but what he really was—a harmless lug who liked to drive cars fast and had a yen for adventure."

"Yes," agreed Ham. "He was no conspirator, merely another regrettable victim of the Baron in Black—whoever he is." Then, catching himself, he added, "Speak for yourself, you dope!"

Pat Savage commented at one point, "Why were so many people who were employed by the Huron Motor Company involved in this affair in the beginning?"

Doc Savage usually did not broach theories without foundation, but in this case he felt satisfied enough of its likelihood to make one point.

"It is reasonable to suppose the Baron in Black initially targeted the Huron Motor Company as a test," he said. "Remember that the first attempted extortion was directed at one of the most important industrial centers of the nation. This may have been for the psychological impact of such an attack."

"Make sense," quipped Monk. "So why did he expand operations so quick?"

"Our arrival on the scene could have precipitated an escalation of the master plan," suggested Doc. "Once we were involved, the Baron in Black may have feared our ability to track him down to his hidden headquarters."

"If that's true," mused Pat, "he's not exactly running scared now, is he? He's got the entire nation fired up, and he's threatening everyone from the President of the United States to the average man on the street."

"The Baron in Black is an audacious plotter, to say the very least," commented Doc Savage. "While his motives may be as simple as wholesale blackmail and even conquest, his underlying motivations remain murky."

"What do you mean?" asked Long Tom from the radio cubicle.

"The Baron in Black could blackmail individual companies without stirring up as much a fuss as he has by challenging the government of the United States. Perhaps there are other motivations compelling him to strike at America in the way that he has."

That supposition made them all feel as chilly as the perpetually swirling snow outside the cabin windows.

Upstate New York soon fell behind them, growing more and more covered in a white shroud. They were over Canada, and the Province of Quebec began unreeling below.

"How far north are we headed?" asked Pat Savage. She had been playing with Habeas Corpus, much to the annoyance of Ham Brooks, who preferred to have the bronze beauty's attention showered upon himself.

Doc replied, "In plotting the electronic fields, Long Tom and Renny have noticed that they are distinctly wedge-shaped, and converge toward a point in the upper reaches of Canada. By improving upon their calculations, it is my inescapable conclusion that the anti-inertia zones are being radiated by a powerful broadcasting station secreted in a region known as the Northern Barren Lands."

Ham frowned. "That is up in the Arctic Circle, isn't it?"

By way of answering, Doc Savage said, "You will find a supply of parkas and snowshoes and similar equipment in lockers at the rear of the plane."

Although the big aircraft was electrically warmed, not to mention soundproofed so the conversation could be carried out normally, one by one the group began scrounging up and assembling appropriate winter outfits.

As they dressed, Ham wondered, "Canada is vast. How will we ever track the Baron in Black to his lair?"

Long Tom the electrical genius answered that one. "In order to lay down such elongated and powerful electronic fields," he pointed out, "requires a broadcast antenna as large, or larger, than anything constructed for commercial purposes. Once we get a fix on their signal, it won't be too tough to spot the mast from the air."

Hastily, they bundled up, just in case of an emergency.

ONE soon came.

An aircraft barreled out of the sky. Pat was the first to notice it. The unmarked ship was painted a bone white from prop spinner to stabilizer, and so was not easily discerned amid the whirling snowstorm. The storm was more in the nature of a roving blizzard, they realized.

The plane barreled up from the north, and along the leading edges of its wings, lurid crimson sparks began to wink.

"Company, boys," sang Pat.

All heads turned.

"Warplane!" shouted Ham in warning.

The big ski plane was not designed for combat maneuvers. Still, Doc Savage booted rudder until the ship rolled off one wing, avoiding the smoky line of tracers that would have punched through the fuselage and wings.

Like most of Doc Savage's craft, this one was unarmed. There would be no dogfight. That did not deter Monk Mayfair from rushing to the back of the cabin, then pounding back with an ungainly contraption that no one recognized.

"What is that?" barked Ham suspiciously.

"You just watch," returned Monk, throwing open the hatch door.

Cold air and whirling flakes blasted in, making everybody glad they had on their wolverine-fur lined parkas. They watched while the apish chemist set himself.

The contraption that Monk had hauled forward possessed some of the qualities of an old-fashioned blunderbuss. That it was thoroughly modern was evident due to its unusual and intricate workmanship.

Monk waited for Doc to maneuver the thundering ski plane into position, then he excitedly pulled the trigger. Incredible noise resulted. Monk was kicked backwards—all the way to the opposite side of the cabin.

The hairy chemist climbed to his feet grinning, set himself to fire again.

It proved to be unnecessary. For the flaring muzzle had exploded, expelling a great black ball that went flying in the direction of the climbing warplane.

The sphere was probably half the size of a basketball, but the warplane flew directly into it, and the ominously round thing broke apart against its white snout.

The result was something that not everyone saw clearly, owing to their positions around the hurtling aircraft.

But in the co-pilot cockpit, where he observed it clearly, Renny's thundering voice reverberated in the noisy cabin.

"Direct hit!"

The projectile did not explode so much as it was torn apart by violent contact with a four-bladed propeller. Whirling blades flung about a mixture of viscous black substance, some of which splattered the warplane's windshield.

Some of that was sucked into the engine. And the spinning propeller promptly stalled, its blades becoming fixed.

After that, the pilot realized he could no longer control his fighter. Throwing back the greenhouse cockpit canopy, he bailed out, shaking a fist at them.

A tiny figure, he cracked silk in time to save his life. All that could be seen of him was that he wore a white uniform of military cut.

The warplane spiraled downward to mash itself into the side of the snowcapped mountain, most of its ammunition unexpended.

"What the heck was that?" Long Tom wanted to know, after slamming the cabin door shut.

"A concoction of my own invention," said Monk, promptly climbing to his feet. "It's a thin ball of composition that easily ruptures on impact. Inside is a bunch of chemicals, some of which act like paint and smear an airplane's windshield so the pilot can't see out of it. The rest of the gunk, if it gets sucked into an engine, will clog it up good. With one shot I did both." He stuck out his barrel chest, and gave his biggest grin. "One-Shot Mayfair, that's me."

Ham Brooks, who usually had a cutting remark for anything that Monk accomplished, instead allowed, "Rather fair shooting for a jungle monkey like you." It was almost a compliment.

The ground below was too rugged to land and investigate. So Doc instructed Long Tom to radio the Royal Canadian Mounted Police to investigate.

Then, Doc Savage pointed the nose of his aircraft back on a northerly heading. He did not have to voice what the others had noticed. The warplane was not an American ship. Nor a Canadian or English one. It was European. Many distant nations had that model in their air forces.

They flew farther and farther with unending monotony until Doc Savage announced, "We are within the Arctic Circle."

Renny was poring over a map, saying, "This is a plenty wide area to be combing through. How are we going to know where the sending station is located?"

There was no easy answer for that, but they had resumed searching the snowy atmosphere with their binoculars. The blizzard seemed relentless, the snow inexhaustible.

"For a first snow before winter," muttered Monk, "this one is shaping up to be a real doozy."

After a while, Ham Brooks abruptly shouted, "Off to starboard! The snow is not moving. It looks frozen in place!"

Doc Savage swiveled his head around, and saw what Ham was pointing out.

The snow nearest them was swirling as normal, but beyond that one could see flakes in suspension, as if fixed in clear amber. It was a weird sight, as if starry galaxies of snow hung suspended in space.

Doc rapped out, "Try to get a directional fix on how it runs."

Everyone moved to the starboard side of the plane and trained their binoculars on the uncanny phenomenon.

"Looks like there are far fewer flakes in the dead zone," Ham ruminated.

"Makes sense," said Long Tom. "Fresh snow can't enter the field and add to the flakes already frozen inside of it."

Renny, with his engineer's eye for angles and planes, was the first to get a sense of how the electronic field was oriented. He got out his map, and begin sketching what he perceived. This he showed to Doc Savage, who nodded. The bronze giant muscled the droning ski ship slightly to the west.

"Take the controls," Doc directed Renny.

Renny seized control of the big aircraft. Doc Savage accepted the map from him and began bisecting the angle on the wedge.

"Take us higher," directed Doc. "It may be possible to fly above the zone of immobility."

"Sure," rumbled Renny. "It would only run as high in the air as the top of its broadcasting tower, wouldn't it?"

"Not necessarily," supplied Doc. "But it is worth trying, since we have to assume the people controlling the direction of the fields are not accustomed to hitting moving targets they cannot see."

Everyone held their breath as the big-fisted engineer sent the plane climbing higher and higher.

After Renny finally leveled out, they discovered that they had reached the atmospheric zone where no snow blew at all. They were flying above the clouds.

"No way to tell anything by the air up here," remarked Long Tom, craning his head about.

They flew on and on and on until it was reasonable to assume that they might have escaped the grip of the inertialess zone. No doubt it had been directed their way by the downed pilot. As such, it had been a blind and, as it turned out, futile stab at them.

Regaining control of the aircraft, Doc Savage brought it down under the clouds and back into the realm of unending blizzard. He sent the plane in a slow sweeping turn, then pushed it in the opposite direction, widening his area of exploration.

By methodical maneuvering, the bronze man finally located the weird aerial spot marked by an absence of swirling snow.

"Looks like we overshot the thing," rumbled Renny.

Doc nodded. "It stands to reason that we are due east of the broadcasting center. Conceivably, by flying west you will happen upon it."

"How are we going to sneak up on the sending station without being spotted from the ground?" wondered the big-fisted engineer.

Doc Savage replied, "It would be best if you found a safe spot to land, and, once you have fixed its exact location, travel on by snowshoe. I am counting on you to accomplish that part of the mission."

"Holy cow!" thumped Renny. "What are you going to be doing?"

Standing up from the controls, Doc Savage said, "It is my intention to fly on to the Fortress of Solitude alone, there to retrieve apparatus that might be useful in our campaign against the Baron in Black."

"How the heck are you gonna get there?" demanded Monk from the back.

Instead of replying, Doc Savage went to the rear of the plane, where large wooden crates hung secured in heavy cargo netting. The bronze man opened these with his steel-strong fingers, not bothering with a pry bar, the thin wood separating under his ministrations.

Out came sections of what at first appeared to be a clumsy but unidentifiable contraption.

To their astonishment, Doc Savage began assembling something that resembled a miniature glider. Some of it was doped fabric, but much of it—the framework and other sections—proved to be balsa wood. It was very light, but clearly constructed along sturdy lines. Glue was used for lightness.

The wings were hinged, like those of aircraft that are designed to land on aircraft carriers and be stored on the decks with the wings folded against the fuselage.

They could see that there was a parachute pack affixed to the back of the complicated arrangement, where it would lie along the bronze man's spine.

"I get it now," yelled Monk excitedly. "You strap that thing to your back, jump out, pull the ripcord, and work the wings into position until you've got yourself a handy glider."

"Once I am safely aloft, I will jettison the parachute," commented Doc, finishing his assembling.

"Sounds horribly risky," muttered Pat nervously.

"I have repeatedly tested this glider-parachute," informed Doc. "It has performed well in the past."

Doc Savage gave Renny directions on which heading to fly. The big-fisted engineer obliged by pointing the ship's nose to the northeast, in the direction of the distant Beaufort Sea.

None of them knew the exact location of Doc Savage's Fortress of Solitude, but most of them had visited the fabulous place. They would be very interested to see it again, but under the present circumstances all understood that this would be impossible.

The big-fisted engineer called out position after position. Doc Savage threw open the hatch, allowing bitterly cold slipstream to swirl about the cabin, and forcing the others to hastily grab for gloves and tighten their clothing.

In this confusion, Doc calmly donned the compact glider arrangement. Without any warning or farewell, the bronze giant leaped out of the plane.

"Just like that, not a word? Not even a good luck?" blurted out Pat Savage.

Rushing to the hatch, Monk thrust out his blunt bullet of a head, and watched the bronze man fall toward the earth below.

Tumbling wildly, Doc Savage struggled to maneuver the cumbersome glider arrangement into position. The sight was heart-stopping. Monk's pounding heart leapt into his mouth and his blunt jaw sagged, revealing its enormous capacity.

Finally, Doc pulled his ripcord.

The parachute erupted out of its pack, jerking Doc into a vertical position. As they all watched, he flung out his mighty arms to deploy the hinged balsa wings.

Once the bronze giant had them in position, they locked into place by an ingenious mechanism. Doc released his parachute by cutting the shroud lines with a sharp knife.

Watching from a window, Pat gasped as the bronze man began falling without a parachute.

Doc Savage twisted and squirmed in midair, until he got the wings where he wanted them to be. The next thing they knew, he was swooping around the snowy skies like a human hawk.

As Renny pushed the hammering aircraft on a westerly course, the bronze man rode the prevailing winds serenely northeast, confident that they would carry him to his faraway Fortress of Solitude.

"I wonder if we'll ever see him again?" murmured Pat Savage, her golden eyes fixed and staring.

Monk Mayfair squeaked genially, "Doc knows what he's doin'. He'll catch up with us all right."

Flashing his infra-red wristwatch for the bronze-haired girl to see, the simian chemist added, "He'll let us know when he's comin' through these here gimmicks."

Pat Savage did not look reassured. Her well-tanned face grew a full shade paler.

It began to dawn on the others that the pretty cousin of Doc Savage was beginning to regret volunteering for this campaign. Not that she would ever admit it.

Chapter XVI
ARCTIC ATTACK

AS THE STREAMLINED ski plane droned over the frozen treeless plain of the Canadian Barren Lands, Long Tom was busy in the radio shack, headphones clamped over his sail-like, oversized ears. The slender electrical genius was dialing around the commercial stations, repeating news reports from the forty-eight states.

"The zones are clamping down as far south as New Orleans. People are dying by the thousands. Everyone's in an uproar. From coast to coast, it's pure panic."

"Talk about howlin' calamities!" cried out Monk, who had replaced Renny in the co-pilot position. Ham's firm grip on his sword cane tightened. Everyone in the cabin felt the immense weight of the task that Doc Savage had entrusted to them.

Long Tom added, "When I tune to static, it has a violin-like sound that seems to accompany the laying down of the electronic fields."

Ham suggested, "When that noise goes quiet, that will be the correct time to sneak up on that broadcasting station."

"But *can* we sneak up on it?" asked Pat Savage anxiously. She had Habeas Corpus sitting on her lap, which she seemed to find reassuring. The porker did not appear to mind, either.

Monk suggested, "When we think we're close, we'll chop the motors and come in on a dead-stick landin'. This bird is painted white, so in all this blasted blizzard it probably won't be noticed."

"What if it is?" returned Pat suspiciously.

The homely chemist shrugged ponderously, saying, "No tellin' what may happen then."

Long Tom returned to fiddling with the radio dial. After a time, he barked, "Fly twenty miles north, then cut around to the southwest," the puny electrical expert directed. "I ought to be able to triangulate the exact location of that sending station using the directional loop antenna."

Renny rumbled, "Are you sure about that, you curdled runt?"

"You'll know when I do," returned Long Tom sourly, who did not like his expertise questioned.

The sheer monotony of the long flight over desolate unforgiving prairie had gotten to them all. Even Renny and Long Tom were getting on each other's nerves.

The big-fisted engineer pointed the lumbering brute of a ski plane north, traveled several miles, then swept to the southwest, in accordance with Long Tom's instructions.

"Keep going," Long Tom encouraged, as he traced marks on a paper map covering the small table before him.

Renny circled around for a time, while the others intently scanned the terrain below with their binoculars. It was hopeless. The blizzard had proven to be a monster. The rugged tundra and ridges of the great Barren Lands were all but indistinguishable. Even the immense body of water that was Great Slave Lake could not be discerned, this despite the fact that it approached Lake Superior in size.

"Even if we find it, where are we going to land?" complained Ham.

Renny rumbled, "We'll sweat that once we know where we're landing."

"Speakin' of landin'," muttered Monk. "I wonder how Doc is doin'?"

No one ventured an opinion. The thought of Doc Savage piloting a tiny man-glider deep into the North Polar regions in search of his Fortress of Solitude was a sobering thought. It was a daring, even reckless, quest. But only the immense gravity of the situation facing the nation, if not the entirety of North America, compelled the bronze man to take the incalculable risk of becoming lost in the frozen, forbidding wasteland.

After circling and circling, Long Tom announced, "Think I've found it!" He called out a heading to Renny, who wrestled the big plane smack onto that directional.

Long Tom added, "Try to sneak up on it from the northwest."

"Why the northwest?" Renny questioned.

"You'll see why, you fistic freak," Long Tom grated back, returning to his calculations.

IT TOOK nearly an hour for the truth to become apparent.

They were flying beneath the snow clouds, but high enough that the sound of the four great motors was unlikely to be heard on the ground. The super-silencers reduced the engine noise to a steady hissing. Still, up in the immense quietude of the north, with the snow falling silently, it would be impossible to gauge the acoustics of the situation.

The big ivory-hued plane might not be spotted; then again it could become unexpectedly visible against the lowering cloud cover, which showed signs of darkening.

After a time, Ham cried out, "I spy frozen snow! It is suspended in the air like tiny white spiders hanging on their webs."

"Look!" Pat Savage was indicating the air to the port side now. They all looked.

The phenomenon manifested itself in an unusual way this time. They were looking down upon it. Snow began to accumulate along the top of the projecting wedge of inertialess energy, making it distinctly visible.

"The devil!" exclaimed Ham. "Snow is piling up on the roof of the void, as if it were solid."

"It *is* solid," countered Long Tom. "Solid energy."

Monk muttered, "If it keeps pilin' up like that, once the zone drops out, a heck of a lot of snow is gonna come smashin' down to the ground all at once."

Before long, they saw it do exactly that.

A long snow bank stretching miles in the distance, it abruptly collapsed, turning into a long narrow avalanche of powdery accumulation. Some of it seemed to dissolve into smoke, adding swirling ghost genies to the existing blizzard.

During the interval of time in which the zone had persisted, they made out undulating stretches of snowpack where it would be possible to land.

That gave Monk Mayfair an idea. He called back to Long Tom, "How close do you think we are to the broadcastin' station?"

"Close enough that we could overfly it any time."

Monk turned to Renny, and asked, "What say we put her down right now, and mush along on foot?"

Renny made faces for a minute, then came to a firm decision. "Suits me. I'm getting tired of being cramped up in this cockpit with the rest of you noisy birds."

Pushing forward on the control yoke, the towering engineer put the plane into a slanting dive, and concentrated on the process of dragging the snowpack, looking for a suitable landing spot.

It was not as easy as it looked. The white stuff had piled high, but there was no telling how dense it was, or whether it was the powdery kind, or the heavy, wet stuff. The light was not good, the sun hanging so low in the Arctic sky that it produced a perpetual gloom of twilight that got on the nerves after a while. This time of year the duration of actual day was less than six hours.

With binoculars, Ham scrutinized a solitary spruce tree, looking to see how heavy the branches were hanging with snow. That would give an indication.

"Looks powdery," he reported. "Good ski cover."

"That settles it," thumped Renny, and attempted to set the plane down.

Cranking the flaps, the big-fisted engineer brought the ski plane around in the final turn. He cut power to the engines, and an unnerving silence filled the cabin. Tundra whizzed past; a flashing tawny blur that looked like an antelope raced away. Ahead, a flock of nesting ptarmigan exploded into frantic flight.

For a rough weather landing, it was pretty smooth. There was a sweeping plain of unobstructed snow forming a natural runway. Renny took full advantage of it.

The ski plane ran and ran and ran while Renny fishtailed the rudder, attempting to bring the hurtling aircraft to a smooth halt.

As the looming ridge of a granite esker approached, the long-faced engineer was forced to jockey the plane around, in order not to plow into a wall of snow-smeared obstruction.

He succeeded by a comfortable margin, which caused Monk to say admiringly, "That was the best dead-stick snow landin' I ever lived through."

Grunting in acknowledgement, Renny got out of his seat, launched himself down the aisle and joined Ham at the hatch, which the dapper lawyer was in the process of opening.

It was still snowing, naturally, and the air was very cold and bitter. Their breath produced pale fogs that turned into brief, dissipating ghosts.

Monk spit experimentally, and the sound of the frozen droplet pinging off the plane's hull was as if he had employed a pea shooter.

"Dang cold!" he muttered.

They got together packs of equipment, which included catgut-strung snowshoes.

Renny turned to Pat Savage and asked, "Are you sure you're up to this?"

Pretty Pat scoffed back, "I was raised in British Columbia, in case you've completely forgotten. I practically learned to walk in snowshoes."

Shrugging, Renny used a big paw to push Pat out of the plane, precipitating her into a snow bank, whereupon everyone laughed with relief.

"What do you mean by that, you big lummox?" demanded Pat, scrambling to her feet and glaring back with molten gold eyes.

Renny rumbled, "I owed you that for sticking your sixgun in my snoot. So we're even."

The fire went out of Pat's glare. She laughed good-naturedly and said, "I guess we are, at that."

They sat down in the snow and put their clumsy snow shoes on.

When that operation was concluded and they found their feet, Renny closed the hatch, set the alarm system, and they took off in the direction Long Tom's quivering compass needle was pointing.

Monk refused to leave Habeas Corpus behind, the snowpack proving unable to support his hoofs. There was a momentary argument. The homely porker emitted a brief whine until his owner packed him in the customary manner—toting him by one oversized ear. That solved the issue until the scrawny shoat commenced shivering, whereupon the apish chemist cradled him in his padded arms.

They trekked north, slightly to the west, and Pat Savage began fiddling with her signal watch.

"I'm letting Doc know we've landed," she explained.

"Good idea," said Long Tom, exposing his own watch. "Better let me give him the longitude and latitude."

Eyeing Habeas Corpus cushioned in Monk's burly arms, Ham drawled, "Don't lose that animal. I understand that pig fat smeared under the eyes protects one from snow blindness."

"You touch that hog," snarled Monk, "and you'll be wearing one of those snowshoes around your neck. And after that, I'm gonna play tennis with it."

The vehemence of Monk's colorful threat convinced Ham Brooks to break off his ribbing.

They trudged along doggedly until their legs ached. It was good trekking snow, but that didn't make the going any easier, especially since they were in one of the greatest wildernesses on the face of the earth. The surrounding drifts sparkled with that jeweled radiance only fresh snow seems to possess.

As they approached a tall hillock of snow—it was too large be a drift—they were astounded to see a familiar figure waving to them wildly from beneath a rare snow-laden spruce tree.

"Who is that?" demanded Long Tom Roberts.

LIFTING his sword cane in a gesture that might have been a greeting or a threat, Ham Brooks shouted, "My word! Theodore Buffington!"

It was the former assistant to the president of the Huron Motor Company. He was not garbed in businessman's attire any longer, but wore a heavy parka, mittens and mukluks, and came striding up on substantial snowshoes.

The assertive Huron executive was probably the last person they ever expected to see, and Monk was about to remark to that effect, when out from behind the tree trunk emerged an even more astonishing figure.

It was a black-haired woman. This feminine apparition wore an emerald sport frock under a matching parka, set off by a jaunty crimson beret. Her mittens perfectly matched her beret. The entire affect was quite Christmassy.

What was not seasonal was her exquisite form beneath the parka, whose entrancing curves were only mildly thickened by the heavy garment.

Monk and Ham particularly were struck speechless by the wholly unexpected sight of fluffy-haired Shari Phoenia.

She came rushing up to them, smiling with white teeth and opal eyes as if they were the most welcome sight in the entire world.

"Jove!" bleated Ham, lifting his cane, which he had been using as a makeshift ski pole. "Am I seeing a snow mirage?"

"Somebody," growled Monk, "has some mighty tall explainin' to do."

"Is that the woman who drowned?" demanded Pat, frowning.

"No," returned Ham Brooks suspiciously. "That is the woman who did *not* drown."

Monk and Ham took the lead, promptly accosting their greeters in a muscular way.

"What the heck are you doin' way up north?" demanded Monk.

"Yes, please explain yourselves," added Ham.

Neither Theodore Buffington nor Shari Phoenia knew which of them was being addressed. They both started speaking at once. Their words became entangled. They were very excited.

"One at a time," suggested Ham sharply.

They subsided, looked at one another, shrugged. Theodore Buffington commenced a long narrative.

"As you might have deduced, Webster Neff and I were kidnapped by persons unknown to me as we were waiting outside of the old cigar factory in Tampa. They stuck guns in our faces, demanded that we drive off. We had not gotten very far when we were compelled to drive to a vacant lot, whereupon Neff was taken into the scrub brush. They came back without him. I asked what happened to him, but no one would answer me." Buffington's voice turned ragged. "I fear he is deceased."

"Sounds fishy," muttered Monk.

"Indeed," echoed Ham. "Why would they spare you?"

"They did not. At a traffic light, I managed to flee the kidnap car, and disappear into an ordinary neighborhood. They failed to find me, thanks to a friendly Floridian, who answered my frantic knock."

Everyone stared as if inspecting the gray-haired man for symptoms of prevarication.

Theodore Buffington spread helpless hands. "I am well aware how my participation in this sordid affair might look to other eyes."

"Go on, Buffington," encouraged Ham.

"In my capacity as temporary replacement to our departed

president, Phineas P. Slade," resumed the abrasive executive, "it is my duty to look out for the welfare of the company. I suspected both Felix Frost and Webster Neff of complicity in the attempt to extort the Huron Company. When I learned that Frost had bribed Neff to follow Doc Savage to Florida, I naturally followed. That much you already know."

"When are you going to get to the part of your story that explains how you ended up here above the Arctic Circle?" snapped Ham impatiently.

Buffington blinked, made a thin, craggy mouth, composed himself, and resumed speaking. "As I said, I managed to escape from my captors, and found myself at liberty. This woman here phoned me at my hotel, by sheer luck, it seems, and informed me she knew what was behind the entire mad affair."

All eyes went to Shari Phoenia.

"My story is a complicated one as well." The exotic woman looked around nervously. "This is hardly the ideal spot to hold a long conversation. We have been hiding in a cave nearby. Perhaps we should go there, and get out of this weather."

Pat Savage interjected, "The last time anybody went with you, they wound up in a hot jam."

Monk, always ready to defend a beautiful damsel, turned on Pat Savage and said, "That wasn't her fault. She almost got killed, along with the rest of us."

"Didn't you say she drowned?" Pat asked pointedly.

"I am an expert swimmer," Shari returned frostily. "I managed to get away, but was unable to find Mr. Mayfair or Mr. Brooks. I found my way back to the hotel where I first met with Felix Frost, discovered Mr. Buffington's name on the register, and called upon him. We put our heads together, and decided to join forces."

"Against whom?" sniffed Pat.

"Against the terrible people behind these tragedies," snapped Shari Phoenia in an equally disdainful tone. "They have their headquarters very near to this spot."

Renny grunted, "How do you know this?"

"I—I am not who I seem to be," the opal-eyed woman stammered. "Would you believe that I am a secret operative for your F. B. I?"

"A G-Woman?" scoffed Pat. "With your hoity-toity accent? That's rich. Tell us another, why don't you?"

Ham Brooks said, "I am hearing a lot of words, but understanding very few of them."

"We can continue our conversation on our way to the cave," reiterated Shari.

Reluctantly, they decided to take the suggestion. It was sensible. They were too exposed out here on the drifting snowpack.

Trudging on, they fell into a single-file march. Pat Savage took up the rear, commenting, "Is it smart to follow these two anyplace?"

Monk popped a mittened thumb against his chest and remarked confidently, "We outnumber 'em." As if that settled everything.

MAKING their way west, the group moved along in the general direction of the sending station that was emitting so much death and destruction. There was no sign of the antenna mast, but the hazy atmospheric conditions and obstructing ridges would account for that.

Ham resumed his interrogation of their surprise greeting party, demanding, "How is it you come to be here?"

"Oh, it was the only suitable landing spot," Buffington returned, as if no other explanation was necessary.

Feeling he was receiving a runaround, Ham insisted, "You might explain your motivations in mixing up into this tremendous matter. You're an executive of an automobile company, not an official investigator."

This comment struck a sensitive nerve, and Theodore Buffington began to unburden himself.

"In the aftermath of the murder of Phineas P. Slade," he said, "I looked into the background of Felix Frost, and did not like what I discovered. His last name was not really Frost, but Fretz. He was born Felix Fretz. This naturally aroused my suspicions, and further caused me to suspect him of complicity in the blackmail attempts against the Huron Company."

"Go on," encouraged Ham.

"Given the flock of legal threats, and the terrible publicity attending these inexplicable motorcar stoppages, I knew that if his involvement came out, it could ruin us. Tracking down Frost—I mean, Fretz—and bringing him to justice, was the only way out. Otherwise, the Huron Motor Company would be finished."

"I can see that line of reasoning," admitted Ham.

"It still don't explain what you're doin' way up here," grumbled Monk, stepping carefully along.

"I am getting to that," said Theodore Buffington impatiently. Suddenly, he stabbed a mittened hand ahead. "Look, we are almost to the cave."

Still suspicious, Pat Savage looked around with frosty golden eyes, and remarked to no one in particular, "I don't see any sign of their plane."

That astute observation was just sinking in when they rounded a sharp-spined granite esker, and came upon the mouth of the cave in question. It was in the side of a snow-covered hillock which they had not noticed in the swirling flurries, thanks to the camouflaging qualities of its frosty covering.

But now the black maw of the cave became clearly visible. Icicles hung at its entrance like gleaming teeth ready to snap shut. It was an unpleasant prospect out here in the pristine wilderness.

But that was not the worst of it. Standing arrayed in the shelter of the cave were about two dozen men attired in ivory-white uniforms, eyes brittle under bone-colored helmets, pointing modern military rifles at them.

Everyone stopped dead in their tracks, caught flat-footed.

Theodore Buffington alone expressed verbal surprise. He gasped audibly. The sound struck the ears as sincere.

In that frozen moment, Monk dropped Habeas Corpus behind his back and whispered hoarsely, "Hide, hog."

The ungainly shoat employed his long snout to excavate a burrow and swiftly disappeared under the snowpack, undetected.

Shari Phoenia strode up forcefully and regarded them with chilly opal eyes, saying fiercely, "You will all place your hands over your heads, or you will be shot dead."

The first one to react was Pat Savage, who said contemptuously, "Hah! I knew it all along. You're a fourteen-caret phony."

Shari Phoenia looked Pat Savage dead in the eye and sneered, "One more utterance out of you, and I will have you liquidated on this very spot."

Pat subsided. But the banked fire sparking in her golden eyes was a sight to behold.

Chapter XVII
FORTRESS OF SILENCE

RIDING ALONG THE prevailing northwesterly winds, Doc Savage became covered in powdery precipitation. Snowflakes coated his parka, mittens and mukluks like some species of pale, otherworldly fungus.

The air was very bitter. Surprisingly, the bronze man was completely comfortable riding along the air currents.

His parka, hood, and protective cloth mask were all electrically warmed. Battery current supplied the juice from tiny dry-cell packs sewn into the lining. Thus his face and extremities were well-protected from frostbite.

Had it been the middle of winter, it is unlikely that the bronze giant, even with his tremendous physical conditioning, could have withstood the arduous aerial journey to his Fortress of Solitude. But it was late in the fall, and not nearly so frigid as the winter months would become.

As he rode the frosty currents, the bronze man occasionally dipped into a pocket, and then removed tablets, which he swallowed. These were concentrated food capsules, which provided him all the nutrients he needed, without having to consume a meal. Water came from an insulated pocket canteen.

Two hours passed. Doc Savage steered by his wrist compass, noting certain natural landmarks below. In anticipation of having to make such a challenging journey one day, the bronze man had arranged certain stones on the ground so that they marked the way to his Arctic retreat.

To pass the time, he reached over to activate his infra-red signal watch, and transmitted a query to his men back at the plane.

The first time Doc did this, the warm electrical impulses against his cool skin communicated back that all was well. Monk sent the message, which ran:

"D-u-l-l f-l-i-g-h-t. H-a-m a-s-l-e-e-p. H-a-b-e-a-s m-a-k-i-n-g t-i-m-e w-i-t-h P-a-t. P-h-o-o-e-y o-n t-h-e-m b-o-t-h."

The second time Doc did so, Renny reported:

"M-o-n-k a-n-d H-a-m f-i-g-h-t-i-n-g a-s u-s-u-a-l. M-a-y h-a-v-e t-o s-o-c-k o-n-e o-r b-o-t-h i-f t-h-e-y d-o-n-t k-n-o-c-k i-t o-f-f."

Doc, not wishing to wear out the tiny watch batteries, communicated to Renny to keep him up-to-date. After that, he left the ingenious watch alone. The bronze man's inventive skill had greatly improved the original design, giving the mechanism great range and power, but at the cost of shortened battery life.

It was late in the afternoon when Doc Savage sighted the rocky island which held the great blue dome.

It resembled a gargantuan polished gem encrusted in snow. This was Doc's fabulous Fortress of Solitude, the place to which he could retreat for weeks or even months on end, toiling there in tranquility. For it was in intense solitude that the bronze man developed his greatest inventions.

Twisting his body, Doc caused the glider frame to begin spiraling down toward the azure blister on the icy isle.

This huge structure looked as if it were composed of some type of blue glass. It was not strictly speaking glass, but a new material of Doc's creation, which combined the qualities of tempered glass with the hardness of tool steel.

Seen from the air, gleaming strangely in the stubborn twilight, the Fortress of Solitude looked like neither of those substances. In truth, it appeared unearthly, as if it had been built by beings from another plane of existence. The fabled Frost Giants of Norse legend might have constructed it.

Doc maneuvered so that he commenced circling the immense dome, and prepared himself for the shock of landing.

The glider was simply constructed, which allowed for ease of operation. Provisions for landing were simple. Doc would have to come in on a flat glide, and select one of two methods of extricating himself from the glider.

If the ground was not rocky and dangerous, he could release the glider straps, much as he would shrug off a parachute harness, and simply tumble out and roll in the heavy, cushioning snow until he lost momentum.

If the ground was not so comfortable, the second method was much more dangerous. Doc would then have to swoop in low and as slowly as possible, then tilt his body back, stalling the glider, and either land on his feet, risking injury, or by once again releasing the harness, and smashing to earth as best he could on his booted feet, which were reinforced so that they could act as brakes.

Neither prospect was anything to look forward to.

Since the island around the dome was packed with snow, some of it fresh, Doc elected to attempt a gliding landing.

This is no by no means without risk, for Arctic winds might drive him up or down, causing him to strike the ground headfirst, possibly breaking his neck.

Balancing carefully, the bronze man set himself.

The snowpack came up to meet him. Doc arced his body to make the wings flare, thereby reducing his headlong speed. His snow goggles had become caked with snow, and although he had wiped them clean many times, they were still somewhat hazy. He gave them a last wipe with a gloved palm.

Doc was hurtling along, barely two dozen feet off the ground. When he calculated that he was moving as slowly as he thought possible and yet remain airborne, he hit the glider harness release catch.

Thus freed, the bronze man dropped into the snowpack hard.

He careened along on his chest, sliding this way and that, keeping his arms and legs up, trusting to brace himself against any obstruction he might encounter. Although that was the safest thing to do, he risked breaking if not shattering an extremity.

At the end of the tumble, Doc threw the kinetic energy of his landing into a sideways roll, until he had slid to a slushy stop.

Carefully, the bronze man stood up, felt of his legs, tested his arms and, although he felt bruised here and there, was reassured that nothing had been broken.

Doc looked over to where the glider had impacted the ground. It was a sad ruin of balsa wood and tubular aluminum structural supports, like some artificial pterodactyl.

It had not been designed for reuse, so the bronze man was not concerned about its fate.

Walking up to the strange blue dome, the bronze man circled it until he was in line with a certain dark stone that stuck up from the snowpack. This told him that he was near the entrance door, which was entirely invisible, owing to the seamless construction of the great agate-like skin.

Doc lifted his radium-dialed wristwatch to the glassy face as he approached. Miraculously, the door cracked open, allowing him to enter.

When he disappeared within, the door resealed itself, presenting a seamless surface. No one examining the outer shell with a magnifying glass could tell that a door had been there. That was how wonderfully the Fortress of Solitude was constructed. It smacked of magic. In a way, it was. For the place was one of the greatest products of the bronze man's scientific wizardry.

Had an Eskimo wandered into the Fortress, he might have thought he had died and translated to the next world. For the interior was along the lines of a gigantic super-igloo—wonderfully insulated from the cold, and stocked with many provisions.

The dome was divided into arching segments by insulated

white walls, designed along the lines of a halved grapefruit. There was a small kitchen, bedroom, and a great hangar with several aircraft waiting in readiness. Hot water pipes underlay the composition floor, heating the Fortress of Solitude to a pleasant degree of warmth.

Other rooms ranged from the most well-equipped laboratory on the face of the earth, to a full gymnasium, where Doc could obtain sufficient exercise during the sometimes lengthy periods when the bronze man marooned himself at this Arctic fort. This gymnasium was equipped with a regulation boxing ring. To keep in fighting trim, the bronze giant often fought three or four hardy Eskimos at the same time, besting them easily. The Eskimos belonged to a tiny band who guarded the Fortress of Solitude during Doc's absences. Currently, they were away, no doubt getting an early start on their winter walrus hunting.

Doc stopped at the kitchenette, and prepared himself a warm meal consisting of a reindeer steak and several portions of healthy vegetables, then took his plate into the laboratory. This laboratory-workshop was fabulous beyond description. It made the arrangement back at the eighty-sixth floor of the skyscraper headquarters in New York look under-equipped by comparison.

There were instruments and devices that could not have been accommodated in the New York laboratory, for they were of prodigious size, but were in evidence here at the Fortress of Solitude. These included a cyclotron more advanced than anything produced in America or Europe and a wind tunnel for aeronautic experiments.

Doc Savage got immediately to work. He became very busy. The laboratory was divided into specialized sections. One was chemical in nature, another electrical and so forth. Doc began by working in the chemical section. He commenced preparing what appeared to be a solution of many diverse ingredients. While it was simmering, he moved to the electrical area, and plunged into a mass of complicated devices. He selected two of these, items that were dense with coils, condensers and vacuum tubes and whose purposes would be impenetrable to any but the most advanced technical mind.

Over these the bronze genius labored intently.

Several hours later came another message through his infrared watch:

H-a-v-e l-a-n-d-e-d. W-i-s-h y-o-u w-e-r-e h-e-r-e. L-o-v-e P-a-t.

Doc flashed back, B-e c-a-r-e-f-u-l.

Then came Long Tom's confident signaling, giving their precise location.

After that followed a very long silence.

AS the hours passed, one advantage of the Fortress became quite apparent. In addition to being insulated against the Arctic cold, it was also soundproofed to the point where no noise, not even the howling wind, nor the moan of a passing airplane, could intrude upon the bronze man's complete absorption in his work.

Assembling various items of apparatus, Doc Savage got them into working order. Then he returned to the chemical section and began charging several syringes with the product of his finished distillation.

The electrical devices were bulky, so Doc put them into a large white duffel bag. Going to a locker, he changed his clothes, putting on an insulated suit that had some of the properties of a regulation parka, except that it was proof against the elements. This included hooded tunic, gloves, boots, a facial mask, and other accessories.

When Doc Savage was finished donning this garment, he was encased in white from head to toe. Over his golden eyes he threw a set of smoked goggles designed to protect them against the glare of the sun on the snow, and prevent snow blindness.

There were other outfits in the locker, including one that was an alarming red and trimmed with white rabbit fur.

Seemingly on impulse, the bronze man took this garish outfit, which included a long red stocking cap, and stuffed it in the duffel bag. Then he slung the bag over his shoulder, and moved through several doors, which opened for him as if by magic but were really actuated by photoelectric cells, until he found himself in the great hangar at the other side of the high hemispheric dome.

There were only two airplanes in the hangar—a robust amphibian, a small two-place ski plane. Off in one corner stood a streamlined gyroplane that was the most advanced in the world. This was unpainted, perfect for operating in polar conditions because its silvery skin tended to blend with the snowpack. Mounted in the rear were two burnished aluminum tubes. These were experimental rocket engines which, when engaged, were capable of propelling the tiny windmill ship at speeds exceeding five hundred miles an hour.

Doc Savage selected the gyroplane, climbed aboard, stowed away the duffel bag, and started the forward engine, which got the prop spinning until it was almost transparent. Tapping a dashboard switch, he actuated a radio signal that opened the great hangar door, which lifted skyward in a manner as miraculous as the opening of the smaller entrance door.

Doc advanced the throttle and the nose propeller yanked the vibrating gyroplane out onto the ice, which was insufficient to allow for an ordinary takeoff. That did not matter since one of the properties of the windmill plane was that it could lift straight up into the air.

Doc waited for the hangar door to finish closing, then he engaged the windmill rotor. Like a silvery grasshopper, the nimble gyroplane leapt into the air, went winging over the frigid Arctic waters.

Doc Savage set a course for the spot in the northern Barren Lands where the secret sending station of death was thought to be.

The Arctic sky had clouded over and grew ominously dark. A jagged fork of lightning painted an incandescent tattoo against the gathering thunderheads, as if warning of impending events. Strangely, no rumble of thunder accompanied the electric display. Nor did a second bolt materialize.

Once he was on course, the bronze man reached for his special watch, and tapped out a message.

There was no response. Doc repeated the transmission. Again, the watch failed to communicate the series of hot flashes which signaled that his men were able to communicate with him.

Overhead, the twilight sky looked restive and threatening, but remained forebodingly quiescent.

Grimly, the bronze man disengaged the forward prop and overhead rotors, then fired up the twin rocket engines, sending the whirligig craft beating madly toward his objective. The speedy ship became a silvery meteor that ate up the empty sky miles, traversing the vast distance to Western Canada with breathtakingly unbelievable velocity.

Behind the lenses of his snow goggles, flake-gold eyes scanned the glimmering horizon with machinelike relentlessness, seeing all, missing nothing.

Chapter XVIII
THE LETHAL LABORATORY

THE SOLDIERS IN immaculate white quickly surrounded the aides of Doc Savage. Dozens of military-style rifles ringed them. There was no escape. That was very clear.

By this time, everyone had their hands up in the air. Including, Monk and the others saw to their surprise, Theodore Buffington.

Ham Brooks eyed the Huron executive skeptically, and asked, "Whose side are you on?"

Buffington jerked his craggy, gray-haired head in the direction of Shari Phoenia and said helplessly. "I was on her side—or so I believed."

The woman in emerald, her dark eyes glowing, sneered, "You were but a dupe. And now you are my prisoner."

"Exactly who are you?" demanded Ham.

"A secret agent of a certain power," she replied. "A spy, if you will."

Pat Savage snapped, "A thief is more like it."

The Christmas-clad woman ignored that. She turned to a man who seemed to be in charge of the ghost-white squad, and barked out a crisp order. "March them to the sending station."

Rifles prodded the prisoners in the back, and with arms upflung, they were impelled through the blustery snow for the better part of a mile. The swirling flakes began to ease off, and visibility became clearer.

As they marched along, Ham interrogated Theodore Buffington.

"Your role in this is unclear."

Theodore Buffington cleared his throat uncomfortably. "That treacherous woman assured me that she could take me to the Baron in Black, and bargain with him for relief, so that the Huron Motor Company could emerge from this terrible legal predicament."

Renny rumbled, "Don't you know the whole blamed country is under siege?"

"I only know what my responsibility to the Huron Board of Directors is," returned Buffington sheepishly.

Ham Brooks snapped, "This woman is nothing more than a modern-day Mata Hari."

Buffington sighed. "I know that now."

Shari Phoenia, overhearing this, turned her dark-haired head and bit out, "Silence! You will march! You will say nothing. Or bullets for your brains will be the penalty."

She sounded as if she was accustomed to being obeyed.

Before long, they began to discern a structure ahead in the great snowy wasteland that was the Canadian Barren Lands. It was approximately square, and had very few windows. What windows they could discern were barred by iron.

"Looks like they're taking us to the local hoosegow," muttered Monk.

When they reached the main entrance, which was also barred, they realized that was exactly what it was. A jail or prison of some kind, belonging to some long-forgotten outpost of the Royal Canadian Mounted Police.

The structure had been made of cinderblock and mortar, but now it was whitewashed in an effort to camouflage it against the snow cover. Even the flat roof was white.

Rising from that roof reared a tall derrick-style tower, also painted as white as polished bone. Atop this was a parabolic form, which appeared to be made of aluminum mesh or some similar reflective metal.

Long Tom said to no one in particular, "That's the terror

antenna that broadcasts the electronic nullifying zones."

Except for the parabolic portion of the mast, it might have been an ordinary radio broadcast antenna. There was nothing sinister about it. It generated no discernible noise, nor electrical corona. It was simply a broadcasting tower, painted so white it was virtually invisible in the snowy swirl.

They were marched to the entrance. The barred gate was pulled aside, and they were conducted through a wooden door into a big empty receiving area, where they were relieved of their mercy pistols and other items. Ham reluctantly surrendered his innocent-looking cane, his face wearing a disgusted expression.

Lastly, their oversized infra-red signaling watches were confiscated.

"No way to get a message to Doc now," murmured Pat to Monk.

The hairy chemist grumbled under his breath, "I tried to work the gadget while they were marchin' us along, but no soap. I hadda keep my hands wide apart, otherwise they woulda shot me down."

The crestfallen expressions on the faces of the others told that they, too, had failed to manipulate their watches to any useful effect.

It was reasonably warm inside, once the doors were shut tight to keep out the Arctic cold.

A man in a black uniform met them. Unlike the other soldiers, who wore white and whose sleeves bore no national insignia, this man sported a uniform that was distinctive, and belonged to an established nation of some notoriety.

"You may refer to me as Commander Igor," greeted the man. He spoke in a distinctive foreign accent that sounded half familiar.

Long Tom was the first one to catch on. "Unless I miss my guess, and I don't think I do," offered the puny electrical wizard, "that uniform belongs to the Balkan nation of Egallah."

"Precisely," purred Commander Igor. "Our leader, the illustrious President Boris Ocel, conveys to you his very best—or should I say worst—regards."

Renny thumped, "Holy cow! What's this all about, anyway?"

Monk answered that. "You missed out on that fracas. Back when we charged off to the Balkans to recover those war weapons hijacked from Doc's Fortress of Solitude, we found ourselves smack in the middle of a dustup between Egallah and the two-bit country that bordered it, Tazan. They were fussin' over a frontier called Ultra-Stygia. We put a quick stop to everything before a young war broke out. I don't think either side is happy with the way things turned out."*

"That," intoned the Commander, a steely tension creeping into his politely cultured voice, "is what you Americans call an understatement."

"This is beginning to make sense," offered Ham. "This isn't just about blackmailing the United States. The saboteurs also seek revenge against Doc Savage."

"Speaking of the famous bronze meddler," said the Commander, looking over the assembled prisoners, "where is he?"

"Where you can't reach him," retorted Ham.

Shari Phoenia strode up, and whispered, "Could it be that the bronzed one is hiding in his Fortress of Solitude? Perhaps he sent his men in his stead, not daring to risk his own life."

Pat Savage laughed musically. "You don't know Doc Savage if you believe that applesauce!"

Commander Igor interjected, "Perhaps this man is in hiding, but possibly also he is attempting to develop a weapon to use against us."

This statement was not a question, but it hung in the air as if it was.

The Egallan commander regarded Doc Savage's men steadily, awaiting a response. None came.

---

* *Death's Dark Domain.*

"Perhaps we should shoot one of you in order to make the others talk," he murmured finally.

Shari Phoenia offered a rather frosty smile, showing unpleasantly chilly teeth.

"An excellent idea. Allow me to execute the girl."

She produced a sidearm, trained it on Pat Savage. Her gun hand was as steady as stone.

The bronze-haired girl made tight brown fists. It looked as if Pat was about to leap like a tawny tigress despite the rock-steady gun muzzle trained upon her.

Monk Mayfair normally spoke in a squeaking childlike voice. But when angered and aroused, he could bellow like an enraged elephant.

Monk commenced bellowing now. He put all of his lung power into it. He made a ferocious face, snarled in a manner befitting a jungle gorilla, and grew so ferocious that the semi-circle of soldiers, despite holding military rifles on him, instinctively took a concerted step backward.

"Anybody who harms a hair on Pat's head, I will wring their neck!" he snarled.

It was very convincing talk. And Shari Phoenia hastily trained her weapon on Monk, lest the apish chemist suddenly spring and overpower her.

That seemed to settle, for the moment, any talk of shooting Pat Savage.

"Take them to the laboratory," snapped Commander Igor. "Perhaps a demonstration of our power will loosen their tongues."

They were prodded through a monotonous maze of cinderblock corridors, past empty jail cells, to a central room which was outfitted as a laboratory. The latter space was virtually the size of a barn interior.

There was a huge transformer set in the center of this spacious area, a bulky black housing festooned with sprawling induction coils reminiscent of something out of a movie thriller. Insulated electrical cables ran from this machine through holes in the walls to a dynamo or generator situated elsewhere in the building. The base of the rooftop broadcasting tower was anchored into the heart of this device. A reinforced hole had been cut through the high roof for this purpose.

Seeing the apparatus for the first time, Long Tom was so impressed that he blurted out, "I'll be damned!" This meant that the slender electrical expert was very impressed indeed.

There was a sprinkling of scientists attired in white smocks, goggles over their eyes and earmuffs protecting their ears, for this room was unusually cold. They looked up briefly, then went back to their work monitoring the impressive apparatus. Their faces could not be clearly seen. One boasted a bushy white beard, further concealing his features. He kept his head down, intent upon his work and attracted no more attention.

Commander Igor smiled broadly. "Here you see the master device, the all-powerful weapon by which the mighty nation of Egallah will bring the United States of America to her knees. And incidentally, make her very, very wealthy, in reparation for the meddling interference by America's greatest champion, Doc Savage."

"You're all nuts if you think this cockeyed stunt will work!" snapped Renny Renwick, blocking his upraised fists.

"It *will* work!" snorted the Commander. "It *is* working, rather. Hundreds of miles to the south, your nation is in panic. The death toll is now in the thousands. If we do not receive our just compensation, the dead will soon be numbered in the millions."

Theodore Buffington, silent up until this point, emitted an audible groan of despair. "I was a fool to come here," he admitted gruffly.

"All American men are fools," sneered Shari Phoenia. "It was a love-sick fool working in the United States War Department who fell for my pretty smile and my empty promises. From him, I obtained copies of the plans that enabled my homeland to build this magnificent weapon."

"Like I said before, a thief," murmured Pat Savage.

The two women exchanged frosty glares. But nothing more

was said or done. Commander Igor was clearly in charge here. The vibrant Shari was obviously subordinate to his authority.

Ham addressed the Egallan officer. "I take it that you are the infamous Baron in Black?"

The Commander inclined his head in a gesture of respect. "You have a well-deserved reputation for being very clever, Mr. Brooks. But in this case, you are not quite clever enough. But to answer your question, no, I regret to inform you that I am not the terrible Baron in Black."

One of the men in the white lab coats turned and addressed them for the first time saying, "He is very correct. *I* am the Baron in Black."

ALL EYES went to this new speaker, and their faces remained blank.

The man lifted his goggles, which were evidently worn to protect the eyes from stray sparks or other electrical discharges, revealing his features.

Ham Brooks yelled, "I know that face! You were the man driving the milk truck down in Florida, the one who controlled the deadly zones."

"Was that the masked guy who shot Felix Frost—I mean Fretz?" demanded Monk.

Ham nodded. "The very same. Notice the color of his eyes."

Everyone focused on the individual's orbs. They were a distinctive green—a very familiar hue, too.

"Allow me to introduce Baron Edgar Fretz," purred Commander Igor.

"Did you say Fretz?" asked Theodore Buffington, craggy features puzzled.

"Any kin to Felix Fretz?" Monk wondered, eyeing the man's very verdant optics.

The individual to whom the question was addressed bowed graciously in a courtly old-world manner. "My late and unlamented brother."

"You shot dead your own brother!" Pat said in undisguised horror.

"Regrettably so," returned the green-eyed man. "For he had betrayed our cause, and so it was my profound but distasteful patriotic duty to silence him. But all of that lies in the inglorious past now."

Long Tom made narrow eyes, and snapped one of his upraised fingers. "Wasn't there an Edgar Fretz, a scientist in the Balkans, who earned a reputation working with magnetic fields?"

"*Electromagnetic* fields," corrected Baron Fretz. He clicked his heels together in an aristocratic manner. "I had been making progress along certain experimental lines, when I learned of the events in Shanghai and Manchuria, into which Doc Savage inserted himself many months ago. Investigating these rumors, I discovered the existence of an astounding new dynamo that could perform wonders."*

"So you stole it!" snapped Long Tom.

The Baron shrugged. "It was known all through Ultra-Stygia that Doc Savage hoarded inventions that he devised or captured from his enemies, and these were among the greatest war weapons imaginable. Some few of them, as you all know, were stolen from his so-called Fortress of Solitude in the Arctic, and dispersed by a human fiend named John Sunlight. This Sunlight of course, perished. And Doc Savage entered the Balkans for the express purpose of reclaiming those weapons—which I regret to say he succeeded in accomplishing."

Doc Savage's men listened to this recital without response. Their stony faces failed to betray that they knew this to be the truth. The location of the Fortress of Solitude was a very deep secret, but the late John Sunlight had spread word of its existence when he attempted to sell the stolen death machines to warring Balkan powers, such as power-hungry Egallah.

Baron Fretz continued, "However, among the weapons known to have been liberated from Doc Savage, the machine which

---

* *The Motion Menace.*

generated the inertialess zones did not belong. We wondered what had become of it. And so dispersed spies throughout the world, hoping to ferret out its location. No other nation seemed to have acquired it, so it seemed reasonable that the bronze man might have turned it over to the American War Department, since it was reputed to be a defensive weapon without equal."

"That was where I came in," smiled Shari Phoenia, dark eyes flashing.

Commander Igor now interjected, "Now that you know the full story, it is time for our demonstration."

The Egallan officer snapped his fingers and pointed to Theodore Buffington, saying coldly, "You are of no use here. You may go."

Theodore Buffington looked puzzled, then became very uncomfortable. "Go? Just like that?"

"Yes, yes. What are you waiting for? If you please—at once!"

As if to encourage him, rifle muzzles were trained on the jumpy Huron executive.

"But—but," he sputtered. "Where will I go? We are in the middle of nowhere!"

"That," sniffed Shari Phoenia, "is entirely your affair. Take your leave, or accept a bullet in the brain."

Hands still raised in the air, but trembling now, Theodore Buffington began backing out of the laboratory room. Two snow-white soldiers seized him by the upper arms and escorted the trembling executive outside, into the gloomily bitter Arctic day.

Out of the side of his wide mouth, Monk said to Ham, "Five will get you ten they stand him up against a stone wall and just shoot him."

Thoughtfully, the fastidious lawyer hissed back, "Somehow, I do not think so."

The truth of Ham Brooks' pronouncement came when a boxy device was wheeled out and switched on.

It proved to be a large television receiver, remarkably advanced, which showed an angle from the roof of the sending station structure. Obviously, a television "eye" was stationed up there.

As they watched the frosted screen, the two soldiers who escorted Theodore Buffington outside came into view, and gave the trembling and confused man an encouraging boot in the direction of the United States of America, thousands of miles to the south.

Buffington began running, throwing fearful glances over one shoulder, as if anticipating a bullet between the shoulder blades. No such bullet sought him, however. He kept running.

Gesturing to Baron Edgar Fretz, Commander Igor gave the signal.

"By now," the Baron said conversationally, "you are all aware of the power of the lethal fields of force. But there is something that you do not know. Observe."

Turning to the Bakelite control panel of the great electromagnetic generator, the Baron began manipulating it. The bulky contrivance was set on a raised platform. At the touch of a lever, this commenced to revolve, rather in the fashion of an astronomer's observatory telescope, on some type of hidden gearing.

It presently became clear that one of the hideous death zones was about to be directed at the fleeing Theodore Buffington.

All eyes naturally went to the oval television screen on which the tableau of death was being displayed.

It took some minutes for the machinery to shift the rooftop mast into the correct orientation. This created unnerving, if not unbearable, suspense among the prisoners.

By contrast, the white-uniformed forces of Egallah seemed only to anticipate what was to come. Their eyes gleamed with an eager light.

Monk caught Renny's eye. The big engineer nodded glumly. He flicked a thick finger, catching Ham's attention. The dapper lawyer nodded his chiseled chin briefly. Neither of these exchanges were noticed by their captors, whose entire attention was fixed on the pictures appearing on the frosted screen.

MONK MAYFAIR kicked off the fireworks. From a standing start, he sprang at the nearest two soldiers, smacking rifles out of their hands with his great hairy paws, then crushing their heads together like two white-helmeted coconuts.

Renny whirled and brought gigantic scarred knuckles to bear against the face of another man. His foe's head was knocked back and around so forcefully it threatened to tear his skull off his upper vertebrae.

Everyone jumped into the fray at that point. Pat Savage spun on a startled Shari Phoenia, and began doing punishing things to the unprepared woman with fists and feet.

It was a sight to see. Pat blackened an eye, barked both shapely shins, grabbed hanks of hair, yanked, and otherwise pulled everything possible in order to disable the female spy.

Long Tom was the only one who didn't mix it up. He was rushing toward Baron Edgar Fretz and the humming apparatus of death. His intention was to switch off, if not permanently disable, the monstrous machinery.

But it was not to be. Seeing the confusion, the Baron snapped the master control lever.

A tremendous whine filled the cool confines of the laboratory, and, in an instant, the running figure of Theodore Buffington froze in mid-step—and smashed face down into the snow. He did not rise again.

Commander Igor pulled a silver whistle from a pocket, and gave forth a shrill blast.

This brought fresh soldiers running from other parts of the prison complex, men who had been held in reserve, but who now entered the noisy battle.

They charged in, shooting, first firing over the heads of the combatants, in some cases causing pieces of ceiling plaster to come cascading down. Plaster grit turned into a snowy, choking swirl.

By this time Monk, Ham and Renny had seized rifles, and were using them as clubs.

A few shots were exchanged, but to no discernible effect. Quarters were too close for accurate shooting.

The reinforcing supply of Egallan soldiers were overwhelming in their sheer numbers. The order was given to surrender, or be cut down. Commander Igor issued it.

Monk, Ham, and Renny each swapped stark looks, and their faces assumed differing expressions of hopelessness verging upon despair.

Without a word, they mutually agreed to drop their weapons. The rifles clattered to the concrete floor, barrels still smoking.

"Holy cow!" rumbled Renny. "We're sure in for it now."

The last to surrender, and only because Monk Mayfair hauled her off Shari Phoenia with his long, hirsute arms, was Patricia Savage. That she had gotten her licks in was proven by the fact that the exotic female spy did not get to her feet afterward, but merely lay there, chest heaving, attempting to get air back into her tortured lungs.

Dragged back to her feet by Monk, Pat flung a clump of curly black hair in the beaten woman's general direction.

"You talk a swell fight!" accused Pat. "But that's all you are—cheap talk."

The hairy chemist positioned himself in front of the bronze-haired girl, muttering over his shoulder, "Take it easy, Pat. If they start shootin', stay behind me. I'm wearin' my chainmail undershirt."

Pat murmured, "Thanks."

"It's nothin'," breathed Monk.

Once the prisoners were bunched together, Commander Igor seemed satisfied. His flashing eyes went to those of Baron Fretz.

The Baron shut down the great generator. Its unpleasantly climbing whine abruptly cut out. A strained silence filled the chamber.

The Baron stepped over to the television receiver, and watched the fallen figure of Theodore Buffington.

After a bit, the stricken man began to stir, and thrash about in the snow. When he was done shrugging off the aftereffects of his experience, Buffington climbed to his feet and looked around in a dazed and puzzled manner, as if not certain what to do next.

"As you can see," the Commander said, "we are able to control the ultimate fates of any caught in the grip of the inertialess fields."

"Holy cow!" thumped Renny. "He didn't die. How is that possible?"

Monk reminded, "I didn't croak when those fields swallowed me down in Tampa. But I ain't completely figured it out yet."

The Commander said smoothly, "Those we wish to protect from the fields, live. Those we wish to die, perish in their awful clutch. Only we determine who will live and who will die."

"You convinced me," snapped Pat Savage. "But what's the point of these shenanigans?"

"The point," returned Commander Igor, "is that you will tell us where we can find Doc Savage—or you will be the next ones to suffer in the zones of electronic death. This is your last opportunity to live. Speak up!"

Long Tom spoke for them all when he said, "Go to hell!"

"Ditto," said Pat.

The Commander looked at them as if not believing his own ears.

"Very well, then. March them out. Send them on their way. Let them feel the tingle and bite of Egallan justice."

They were roughly prodded and herded toward the door by the white-uniformed soldiers of the modest Balkan power that had risen up to challenge the United States.

Suddenly, a soldier came rushing in from outside.

"Commander! An autogyro has been sighted, beating this way."

Baron Fretz rushed to the television receiver and began flipping switches. It became evident that the device was connected to several cameras situated on the parapets of the whitewashed former prison outpost.

Finally, he picked up an image of a whirling aerial vehicle approaching from the east.

Monk muttered, "Looks like one of Doc's experimental gyroplanes. It can land on a dime."

"Halt!" thundered Commander Igor. "Bring them back. Stand them before the television receiver. Before they are executed, let them first witness the death of their leader, the vaunted Doc Savage."

Chapter XIX
GLIDING DEATH

PRODDED BY THE muzzles of enemy rifles, Doc Savage's aides were forced to stand before the large television receiver, on which it was possible to observe the approach of the ultramodern gyroplane in flickering images of black and white.

Standing behind them, his foreign-sounding voice triumphant, Commander Igor proclaimed, "Watch the great one die! It will not be the same as when an airplane runs into a lethal zone, crumples to a stop, and the aviator, his body not quite within the zone, is able to bail out and slope his parachute safely down. In this instance, the zone will be turned on full force in his direction, enveloping him in its irresistible vise. Need I remind you that within the zones, no motion is possible, other than that exerted by the inexorable pull of gravity? Doc Savage's parachute will not open. For it cannot open—all kinetic energy being forbidden within the zones we now control. The bronze nemesis will fall like a lead plummet." He eyed the prisoners, smiling thinly. "To his doom."

As they watched, a growing horror inscribing itself on their features, the gyroplane, rotors beating, approached silently. Silently—for the television apparatus did not receive sound transmissions.

The entire room was hushed—other than the rapid breathing of the watchers, who feared what might come next.

The haughty commander threw a sharp hand signal. Baron Edgar Fretz moved his hand toward the actuating lever.

There seemed nothing Monk and the others could do, for cold rifle muzzles pressed into their backs with an insistent prodding, lest they repeat their rebellious activity.

As the gyroplane grew larger and larger, and the tremendous whine of the dynamo rose in frequency, Monk Mayfair began growling under his breath. It was not the growl of an angry man; rather it was the deep, fierce noise of a wild animal, expressing its ferocious frustration.

Finally, Monk snapped. With the roar, he whirled, and the soldier who had kept his rifle pressed into Monk's back, naturally reacted as he was trained to do.

Three bullets roared out of the military weapon, striking the hairy chemist in the spine and left side as he pivoted wildly.

Monk managed to fling a wild, flailing swipe against the side of the man's head, knocking off his bone-hard helmet, upsetting him. That was all the apish chemist managed to accomplish. Coughing, he went down, holding one side and twisting on his back, as if mortally wounded.

"Monk! Monk!" sobbed Pat, racing to his side.

"Nix!" gritted the hairy chemist. "Bulletproof vest. Slugs bounced off my ribs!"

"Oh, thank goodness!"

Meanwhile, Ham Brooks seized the opportunity to reach out and reclaim his sword cane, which had been confiscated by a soldier, who had held it loosely in one free hand.

With this weapon, Ham knocked the man senseless with the gold-headed knob and, clutching the slender cane in both hands, rushed the Baron at the controls.

Coming up behind him, Ham swept the sturdy stick down over the man's head, caught it up under the other's chin sharply, capturing the throat.

Exerting pressure, the dapper lawyer began choking the man, simultaneously wrestling him away from the controls.

Commander Igor shouted an order to cut Ham down.

Hearing this, Ham wrestled the hapless Baron around in

front of him, turning him into a human shield. No one dared fire.

Ham aimed to snap off the switch, but dared not release his hold. Long Tom rushed in to do that for him. The puny electrical wizard lunged for the controls, but a volley of bullets snapped in his direction. One struck him in the shoulder, spun him around.

Long Tom lost his balance, went careening into the machinery. He attempted to reach up and grasp at anything that could shut down the death machine but, before he could, hard rifle muzzles were pressing into his sour face, distorting it like soft clay. Long Tom subsided. He threw up his hands, and there were near tears in his pale eyes.

Then, Pat Savage gave out a long scream.

Everyone who could, looked.

While the whine of powerful machinery filled their ears, making their skeletons vibrate in sympathy, they saw the silvery gyroplane, falling helplessly, its rotors frozen.

"Behold!" roared the Commander. "An autogyro, without power, will glide to a safe landing through the braking action of its rotor vanes. But here the fatal field prevents that safety operation. The blades refuse to spin. The gyro tumbles like a stricken thing. It cannot glide. It can only fall."

As the gyroplane plummeted, its fate seem to be exactly as predicted.

Except for one particular.

All eyes were on the stricken gyroplane, so when the parachute opened, everyone was surprised, if not astonished.

"It cannot be!" complained the Commander.

Baron Edgar Fretz had extricated himself from the strangling cane crushing his windpipe. Clutching his injured throat, he gave Ham Brooks a remonstrating kick while coughing his lungs clear.

Watching the big screen, the scientist said with croaking difficulty, "Very clever. It is obvious that the bronze man has perfected a device which signals when the first faint emanations enter the air. This somehow warned him that an inertia-nullifying zone was being laid down, and while we were preoccupied with your fruitless revolt, Doc Savage bailed out of his gyroplane prior to the field taking firm hold. Before it clamped on full force, his parachute had already opened."

Commander Igor interjected, "No doubt the parachute, which was not fully visible against the clouds until we looked more carefully, has preserved his life."

The Baron nodded. He was getting his voice back. "In the case of Doc Savage, this maneuver will avail him nothing, for that is a dead man you see parachuting down. The zone, at the intensity I have created, has the power to kill instantly. For it will arrest his heart and lungs before he reaches the ground."

As they watched, the tiny white figure at the end of the parachute shrouds seemed to be struggling. The bronze man— for they were virtually certain it was he—suddenly grasped at one arm, much like a man who is experiencing heart failure.

When the helpless man struck the ground feet first, he toppled over with a strange rigidity. It took a long time for him to hit the ground. The gray bell of his silken parachute stood upright for part of this, then with uncanny slowness, as gravity overcame the anti-inertia field, it enveloped him like a shroud.

Eyes sick with horror, Monk, Ham, Pat and the others were transfixed by their helplessness. The television images made the scene seem real and immediate, but at the same time, they fully understood that they were too far away from the tragedy to avert or affect it in any way.

Only Pat Savage uttered anything. "He—he can't die this way..." she moaned.

Many minutes passed, as they watched for any signs of movement or lingering life. But not even the silken parachute fluttered, for it was fixed fast in the powerful electronic zone in which nothing could move.

After ten minutes, the signal was again given, and the Baron shut off the awesome device, causing the dynamo to whine down until a grim silence returned to the chilly laboratory.

Commander Igor said simply, "Doc Savage is undoubtedly dead."

The scientific staff arrayed around the inertia-field generator broke out into a smattering of impolite applause. There were congratulatory handshakes all around.

A hot tight feeling arose in the throats of the fighting friends of Doc Savage, but they said nothing and displayed no other emotion in silent salute to their stoic chief.

HOURS later, the seemingly perpetual twilight had deepened to a smothering darkness.

Two white-uniformed pickets were patrolling a half-mile along the eastern approach to the great prison-turned-laboratory-sending station.

They shivered in the biting winds, pacing and marching, staring out into the snowy immensity of the forbidding Barren Lands. This was a duty they detested, but one that was very necessary, for Royal Canadian Mounted Police swept this frigid desolation from time to time.

Far in the distance, great glacier-carved eskers stood, their sand and gravel ridges heavy with the recent snow. From time to time, the crushing weight of the white stuff caused swatches of snow to slide off, to land with silence-shattering thumps and thuds.

One man detected colorful activity among those rugged, snow-smeared ridges.

It seemed, at first, to be a trick of the eye—or perhaps a manifestation of snow blindness, which every winter soldier feared. But the sun had not been out in hours.

Pitching his voice low, the sentry called his fellow picket's attention to the strange furtive movement among the drifts.

After they conferred in their native language, the emboldened pair commenced creeping closer and closer to the ridge. Under skull-colored helmets, their squinting eyes grew sharp.

They detected no further movement—not until they were nearly upon the looming ridge.

Then, the awestruck pair beheld the most astounding sight of their entire lives.

A figure stood up from a snowdrift, as if rising from a nap, and brushed snow off his impressive form. It was a familiar figure, but hardly one that would be expected out in this great frozen wilderness.

This new arrival wore a fire-engine red suit which was trimmed in white rabbit fur. A crimson cap, also trimmed in white fur, covered the man's head. Black boots and mittens completed the ensemble.

This crimson apparition was prodigiously large, especially about the waist, which was belted by a wide leather belt, also black. His snowy grandfather's beard was very long and white. Across one scarlet shoulder was slung a great white sack.

To say that the two soldiers were startled would be to put it mildly. They stopped dead in their tracks, and leaned forward to scrutinize the intruder more clearly.

Their round eyes actually bugged out of their heads, and their mouths opened wide. As they stared, their jaws sagged even lower, until chins were practically resting on their chests.

This was an exaggeration, of course, but the attitudes of the men were that of utter dumbfoundment.

One man found his tongue, and bleated out a name well-known in his distant part of the world.

"Kris Kringle!"

To American eyes, the fantastic figure would have gone by the name of Santa Claus. The jolly figure smiled in his great white beard, and raised a black-mittened hand in a friendly salute.

The two men got control of their jaws, swapped startled looks. They began jabbering at one another.

"It cannot be!" one gulped.

The other replied, "He is said to live up in the North Pole. We are very near the North Pole."

"But he is a myth, a child's fable!" insisted the first.

To complete their confoundment, the roly-poly figure greeted them in their native tongue, in which he was obviously fluent.

There ensued a vigorous argument over whether or not to shoot this preposterous intruder dead in his tracks. One man insisted that this was their solemn duty, while the other sentry vociferously objected, claiming that to kill the benevolent elf would be a crime unspeakable.

In the end, the matter was taken out of their hands.

The great figure—he had not seemed so tall until he was almost upon them—drifted up, dropped his fat sack in the snow, and reached out great arms as if to hug the two soldiers in welcome. His smile was very generous, his teeth pearly and perfect.

This naturally disarmed the two soldiers—which gave Doc Savage time and opportunity to seize skulls and knock their heads together, rendering them completely unconscious. They collapsed in the snow, weapons unfired.

Taking up the fallen rifles, the bronze man removed all ammunition, and scattered it in every direction. Removing a hypodermic needle from his pocket, he injected both men with the preparation.

Satisfied, the bronze giant removed his Santa Claus outfit and beard, revealing the white coverall garment beneath it.

Pulling a snow-colored hood over his head, which concealed all but his golden eyes, Doc Savage retrieved his dropped sack and advanced cautiously, all but invisible against the undulating snowpack.

The only sound of his coming was the soft crunching of boots in snow....

Chapter XX
SIX MUST DIE

IT WAS BRUTALLY cold in the spacious cell into which Monk Mayfair, Ham Brooks, and the others had been confined. There was a single window, heavily barred, but without glass. So the frigid Arctic air had free rein. It made their skins slowly turn blue.

Why they had been consigned to this cell was unknown to them. They expected summary execution. Nothing less.

After the shocking demise of Doc Savage, witnessed through the medium of a television receiver of great sophistication, they had been herded together and marched through a dank maze of corridors until they came at last to the largest cell in the forlorn complex. Into this they were hurled, rather unceremoniously.

The only gesture toward decency was that Pat Savage was given a smaller cell of her own. It was otherwise no more comfortable.

After a time, Shari Phoenia strode up the corridor, the heels of her snappy winter boots clicking ominously.

Ignoring the chamber in which Monk and the others huddled for warmth, Shari wheeled to a halt in front of Pat's solitary cell.

"You," she hissed venomously, "will not die as easily as these others."

"Make me believe it," returned Pat, golden eyes flashing. She fully understood that her famous cousin was dead, even if deep in her brave heart, she harbored a small smoldering ember of hope.

"You *will* believe it, tawny one," sneered Shari Phoenia. She snapped a lean-barreled black pistol out of its holster, trained it through the iron bars, and added, "I threatened to shoot your eyes out before. I will do this. But I will slay you last of all. You will witness the deaths of your comrades, and so understand you have no hope—nor any future."

The ebony-haired spy seemed about to make good on her threat, but rage was making her pistol muzzle shake in her red-gloved hand.

Shari was a sight. One eye was a purplish-black, and nearly closed. Her hair was in total disarray, and clumps of it were missing. The lower lip was twice the size of her upper lip and was not the inviting rouged curve that it once was. To add to that miserable picture, the tip of her formerly well-formed nose had grown rather flat.

Pat Savage sidled up to the bars and said, "Any time you want to put that thing away, come in here and fight, woman to woman. I'll teach you a few more tricks."

That was more than Shari Phoenia could endure. Bruised face working with fury, she stepped back and yanked the trigger of her weapon. As it happened, the bullet sparked off one of the iron bars while Pat, ducking, retreated to a corner.

The bronze-haired girl had no place to hide. The next bullet would almost certainly find its mark.

But there was no next bullet. Shari Phoenia, quaking with rage, attempted to squeeze off another shot. But the weapon jammed.

Beating at it with her palm, she tried to get the mechanism to unjam. But the weapon refused to function.

In the other cell, Renny rumbled, "Cold must've got to it."

Whether that was the case or not, Renny had no idea. The big-fisted engineer was simply attempting to discourage the furious female spy.

It seemed to work. Snarling and hissing, Shari Phoenia stalked off, muttering incoherent threats under her steaming breath.

"She'll be back," Ham warned Pat.

"Don't think I don't know it," Pat murmured shakily, creeping back to her barred cell door to peer down the dim-lit corridor. "I do not understand what got into me. I'm just so riled at that treacherous she-devil."

Monk grumbled, "We know how you feel, Pat. We want to wring all their necks, too."

They settled down to contemplate their fate.

"We are certain to be executed," remarked Ham.

"Is that a legal opinion?" wondered Long Tom sourly. "Because if it is, it stinks."

The puny electrical wizard was nursing his shoulder, which had been severely bruised by a bullet. Like Monk, he wore a bullet-proof undershirt, which preserved him from serious injury.

"Maybe they're holdin' us for ransom," offered Monk, pacing his cell on bandy legs.

Ham retorted, "These fiends are holding the entire nation hostage. By comparison, we are very small potatoes to them."

"Doggone," muttered Monk, "they must have some reason for doin' what they're doin'."

"But what is it?" thumped Renny, slamming one knobby fist into the waiting palm of the other.

There was no puzzling it out. They sank into a profound gloom, and awaited future developments.

Developments would not be very long in coming.

THE SPECTRAL darkness of the northern reaches made the snow-covered expanse surrounding the former prison a morbid place. Thunderclouds had crowded in from the east, obscuring a brilliant moon, transforming the lunar-lit landscape into a smotheringly oppressive domain of midnight murk.

Through this darkness, moving low so as not to be visible against the night sky, moved a gigantic figure in white.

This Herculean form lugged a heavy sack over one shoulder, and left only distinct footprints in its wake.

Approaching the whitewashed wall of one side of the installation, the figure set down the sack, extracted from its interior two very long icicles. These he clamped between strong white teeth. Then mittens came off strong hands, revealing the corded bronze fingers of Doc Savage.

The spaces between the blocks of the prison wall were shallow, but this did not seem to hinder the giant bronze man. Doc began climbing, using only these minute finger holds for purchase.

Up he went, soundless as a snowball rolling downhill—except that in this case the snowball rolled *uphill,* gathering momentum as it did so.

Reaching the roof, Doc slipped over the parapet, and glided toward the pale, skeletal antenna which had been transmitting terror and death to the continent below this polar latitude. He moved with an utter soundlessness that was as ghostly as his shrouded figure.

Doc Savage circumnavigated the antenna, flake-gold eyes scrutinizing the insulated power cables which adorned it. When he found a set of cables that seemed to intrigue him, the bronze man removed the icicles from his mouth, taking one in each hand.

First, Doc pitched one icicle. It sailed through the air, striking two black cables, making a momentary connection between the parallel wires.

A shocking blue-white light flared up, died. Purple-blue sparks splashed about, followed by flickering orange flames as the shorted wires burned. Swiftly, the bronze man threw the other icicle, producing a similar result.

Scooping up roof snow with both mittened hands, Doc flung the heavy stuff onto the burning wires, extinguishing the smoldering insulation. He paused, listening.

Under the roof beneath his black boots, a sudden mutter of concerned voices swelled into an outraged uproar.

A voice cried out in the Egallan language, "The power! It has gone out."

"A short circuit!" bit out another voice. "See to it. *At once!*"

Hastily, the bronze man drifted to the parapet, and slid down the sheer side as nimbly as he had climbed it.

Moving to the wall below, traveling close to it, Doc came to a set of iron-barred windows, and employed a tiny black periscope of a device to peer within without being seen. This was his transformable monocular.

The first cell he found proved to be empty, but when he eased up to the second, he perceived his cousin, Pat Savage. She was alone in her cell. She lay upon a rude wooden cot, her face turned to the wall. Her shoulders shook, whether from the intense cold or some inner emotion was difficult to discern.

Moving on, Doc came to another barred window, and again employed his ingenious periscope.

This revealed Monk and the others, pacing and shivering in the cold night air.

They were complaining, "What happened to the durn lights?" rumbled Renny.

Monk grumbled, "What does it matter? There's no heat. There's no nothin' here. We're all gonna freeze to death if they don't hurry up and shoot us."

Doc Savage, his lips grimly sealed in part so that he did not produce any telltale breath exhalation through the thin vents in his face covering, but also so he did not inhale too much of the bitterly cold air which could burn a man's lungs if exposed to it for too long a time, now parted those lips. From them issued forth a weird evanescence. Tiny, vague as a wayward polar breeze filtering through evergreen boughs, it traced its notes in the frozen air, a haunting yet tuneless melody.

"Wind sure kicked up awful sudden," muttered Monk.

"You dim-witted dunce," hissed Ham. "That's no wind. Listen."

Silence fell over the moonlit cell. The eerie sound wafted in through the bars, caressing their ears, and made their hunting eyes grow wide.

Long Tom said it first, "Doc! He's here."

They rushed to the bars, where they were greeted by a hooded ivory figure, wearing a pale face mask. The only things recognizable about the frosty phantom were his compelling golden eyes, for Doc Savage had lifted his goggles to reveal his eerie orbs, in order that there be no mistake about his identity.

"Stand back," undertoned Doc.

He was wrapping pale cords of an unusual type around the tops and bottoms of the bars. Once he was finished, the bronze man ignited them in some way, producing an eye-hurting white glare that began turning the ends of the bars sunk into mortar into hot slag.

The sizzling heat ate away at the cold metal, and just before the bars could fall out, the bronze giant wrapped white mittens around their cool centers, and extracted them, flinging them to either side to avoid being splashed by the molten ends. Landing in the snowpack, they hissed and sizzled, producing clouds of palpably warm steam.

Doc piled snow on the windowsill, which produced a ferocious hissing, but which swiftly cooled the remaining slag.

Ham breathed, "The lights went out just a few minutes ago."

Doc explained, "Short-circuit. Produced by bridging live power lines with icicles."

Long Tom grunted, "That must have fouled the electrical system pretty good. It'll be hours before they can get their devil's dynamo running again."

"We do not have hours," said Doc firmly.

He passed a compact contraption to Monk and gave quick instructions in a low, urgent tone. The others caught only a glimpse of the thing, but saw that it was gray and bulky, and patently electro-mechanical in nature.

"Gotcha," said the hairy chemist, grinning.

While the bronze man began helping Ham Brooks to squeeze through the aperture, Monk set the mysterious device in one corner of the cell so that its square edges touched both walls. Once he had the thing firmly in place, he pressed a red button on the top.

The device was very plain looking, and commenced making a steady pulsing a bit like a metronome. That was all.

Pat Savage had dozed off, but now she sprang to life. Owing to a dividing cinderblock wall, she could not see into the adjoining cell, but her ears detected interesting commotion.

Presently, she recognized her cousin's distinctive voice.

"Doc?" she gasped. "I must be dreaming—or have I landed in the Great Beyond?"

"Neither," came the bronze man's confident tones.

Pat seized the bars of her cell window, called out eagerly, "What is going on? A jailbreak? I want in! Out, I mean!"

Doc Savage said sharply, "Hold your horses. We will get to you directly."

"If I had horses," Pat said archly, "I wouldn't be holding them, I'd be spurring them." But in the gloom of her prison cell, she grinned, and wiped away a tear of relief she did not wish the others to see.

Doc finished pulling Long Tom out, then it came time for Renny to exit.

It quickly became evident that the big-fisted engineer was too large to slip through the aperture. That meant that Monk Mayfair, with his barrel chest, was also not going to slip through.

Doc instructed, "Wait there. All of you."

"Stinker!" hissed Pat from the cold confines of her cell.

But Doc Savage was gone.

Gliding around the corner in the direction of the main entrance, the bronze man reached a point where he could peer around the corner with his monocular-turned-periscope. Ghost-colored soldiers were spilling from the place. They fanned out, taking positions where they could look over the roof from a safe distance.

The soldiers of Egallah were attempting to ascertain the nature of the problem, which was very difficult given the unhelpful darkness.

In that midnight gloom, Doc Savage removed his ivory parka, showing that it was reversible. All of it. Including his electrically-warmed face mask.

Very quickly, Doc Savage stood in an ebony black parka which enabled him to blend with the inky shadows, of which there was a great abundance. For racing clouds had swept in, swallowing the lunar orb whole, and extinguishing its spectral effulgence.

Slipping into the entrance gate unobserved, the fur-trimmed black shadow disappeared into the incredibly dark interior of the former prison, undetected and unchallenged.

Previously, interior illumination had been on the feeble side, but now the corridors were an ugly and unrelieved black.

Doc Savage produced from his person a flashlight and strange goggles, both of which operated on the infra-red principle. Covering his golden eyes with the goggles, he clicked on the torch. No visible light came forth.

This allowed the bronze man to traverse the corridors virtually unseen, while leaving him capable of seeing others as well as would a prowling cat.

There did not seem to be an abundance of electric torches distributed among the soldiers working their way through the building in a state of confusion. Occasionally, a flash ray licked out, but failed to disclose the stealthy shadow.

Doc Savage moved unseen, unsuspected, and unchallenged through the frigid corridors, a looming fragment of blackness.

Once the bronze giant turned a corner and, while he stopped in time to avoid bumping into a man, the fumbling soldier collided with what appeared to be an anthracite wall. The "wall" reacted violently.

Unable to use his skilled fingers to render the man insensate by manipulating neck nerves due to the thick black bearskin mittens, Doc sent out a fist, which rocked the man's head back on his shoulders. Doc caught him before the unfortunate one made a clatter on the cold flagstones.

SETTING his victim to one side, Doc Savage moved on. By unerring instinct, he made his way to the side of the building where Monk and the others remained trapped in their prison cells.

Reaching Pat's cell first, he discovered it unguarded.

Doc tested the barred door, found it too solid to be dislodged by main strength alone. He removed from a pocket a blackened device resembling a darning needle, and went to work picking the lock. It surrendered in a ridiculously short amount of time.

"I could have done that," sniffed Pat, stepping out into the darkness. "If only I had had a bobby pin."

"Stick close," warned the bronze man, moving on to Monk's cell.

This lock proved more challenging, owing to the fact that the mechanism had acquired a coating of rust over the seasons. It fought him a little, but Doc produced from one pocket another device which proved to be a tiny oil can, which he liberally applied to the innards of the lock.

After that, the lock mouse-squeaked once and the heavy door fell open.

Monk came barging out, rusty fists knuckling. He grinned in the darkness, showing amazing teeth. "Looks like we get to fight our way out, huh?"

"Stealth would be a better method," warned Doc.

Monk, Renny, and Pat followed the shadowy giant form through the unpleasantly cold and dark place.

Pat wanted to know, "However did you survive?"

The War Makers / 247

"Later," cautioned Doc.

The place was in an uproar, verging on pandemonium. Evidently, many soldiers had been asleep in their barracks bunks, and these were now being mustered in an effort to get to the bottom of the inexplicable power loss.

Renny muttered, "Just a matter of time before they check our cells, figuring we might have escaped."

Doc said, "It is urgent that we leave this building as soon as possible."

"No fooling," sniffed Pat anxiously. "These boys are no chocolate soldiers."

Monk put in, "Doc ain't funnin', Pat. He's got a rabbit he pulled out of a hat. It's about to start hoppin'."

Pat frowned in the chilly murk. "Rabbit? What rabbit?"

Moving toward the main entrance, they found it choked with milling soldiers, most armed, and all being hectored and lashed by the words of their commander, who was urging them to action in their native language.

Doc translated quietly, "The invaders are under the misapprehension that they have been discovered by Canadian authorities. They are all but panicking."

"Good," said Pat. "Serves them right."

Doc, in the act of moving through an open door, suddenly reversed himself. Great black-mittened hands reached out for their shoulders, spinning them about, gently but firmly.

"Back that way," he urged.

Everyone careened into reverse. Doc flashed around them, again taking the lead.

They ran smack into a small knot of soldiers, who were picking their way along with flashlights. The torches filled their hands; in other hands, sidearms jutted out.

Doc Savage waded into them with the silent ferocity of a grizzly bear catapulting from a cave.

He grasped heads, brought them together with the resounding bell sounds of clanging helmets. There was a soldier who happened to become caught between the two heads that were being brought together. Thus, three heads collided with an almost comical bonking sound.

The men fell into a disorderly pile, stunned by the abrupt and irresistible attack.

Monk and Renny stepped up, bent over, and applied terrible knuckles to exposed jaws. That put the trio of foes out for good.

Everyone collected a flashlight, but doused them at a sharp suggestion from the bronze man.

They worked their way around, hugging bitterly cold walls, letting Doc Savage peer ahead through half-open doors with his periscope.

There was a rear entrance, of course, and they found their way to it, and then out into the darkness and the snow. The temperature difference was not very great, but the wind in their faces made them feel as if they had stepped into an icebox.

Doc emitted a sharp exclamation in the Mayan tongue.

Back came a similar bark.

Soon, they rendezvoused with Ham and Long Tom, then started moving away from the prison installation.

"Go ahead of me," directed Doc Savage.

"What have you got in mind?" wondered Ham.

"I will catch up," said the bronze man, giving the dapper lawyer a motivating shove.

They got moving. They still wore their snow gear, sans the handy snowshoes, and this enabled them to move relatively unseen against the snowpack, for the moon had wandered out of the wintery cloud cover, illuminating a sweeping, spectral landscape.

Hanging back, Doc Savage again reversed his parka outfit until he was wearing white, and began to float in their wake. It became evident the bronze man did not want to present a dark shape against the shimmering snow that might draw attention, and worse yet, enemy bullets.

The bronze man had also collected his plump sack of devices.

One of these he extracted and manipulated until its tubes began to warm. It was rather large, and shaped like a basketball, but with an aluminum skin.

After Doc determined that the device was operating, the bronze man placed it in the snow, and smoothed that patch over in a rough fashion, making it look as natural as possible.

Only when he was satisfied that the device would not be discovered, did Doc Savage start moving in the direction of his fleeing aides.

SOON enough, Doc caught up with his men, and they began peppering him with questions.

Ham, naturally, opened the interrogation. "We saw the death swath clamp down on your gyroplane. How on earth did you survive that?"

"You will all remember that, in our last encounter with these electronic fields nearly a year ago, Habeas Corpus had the misfortune to be caught in the influence of one motion-dampening zone."

Monk grunted, "He almost died. But you saved him."

Doc advised, "With an adrenaline and strychnine injection. It restarted his heart, which had stopped beating as a result of the life-suppressing field. While at my Fortress of Solitude, I prepared a similar injection, this one a concoction of adrenaline, strychnine and cobra-venom derivatives which effectively combats the tendency to depress the heart under the force of the anti-inertia radiations."

"I get it!" Monk said. "You injected yourself before the power got you."

Doc nodded. "You will remember what you thought was an insect bite on your arm, which you acquired in Tampa, Florida."

"It still itches somethin' mean," complained Monk, scratching one arm vigorously.

"When I examined that so-called bite," returned Doc, "I

recognized it as the injection site of a hypodermic needle."

Ham exploded, "Is that why Monk didn't die down in Florida? He was injected with something similar?"

"Exactly," returned Doc. "No doubt the so-called woman in beige surreptitiously injected Monk when she was pretending to be his friend."

"Come to think of it," muttered Monk, "I did start feelin' that sting around that time." Monk snapped hairy fingers. "That dame had an umbrella with her. I remember gettin' poked by it when we were runnin' away from the two closing fields. That's how she musta pulled it off! There was a hypo needle in the ferrule!"

Pat shot a withering glance at the apish chemist. "Chalk it up to another woman making a fool of you."

"My sentiments precisely," sniffed Ham.

Monk groaned, "How was I supposed to know she was on the devilish side?"

"If she was attracted to you," said Ham waspishly, "her hair should be checked for horns and her shoes for cloven feet."

Long Tom asked Doc Savage, "Do you have any more of that cobra juice?"

"Enough for all of us, should it become necessary."

DOC SAVAGE glanced over his shoulder, and saw a sprinkle of white-clad soldiers questing about the grounds of the old R.C.M.P. prison-turned-terror-station.

They wielded flashlights, whose backglow made them resemble roving ghosts.

At the moment, Doc and his crowd did not seem to have been spotted. But they were moving against a flat snowy landscape that was barren for miles around. It was just a question of time before their empty cells were discovered.

"Keep moving," urged the bronze man. "I will attempt to inoculate you all while we reach a point of relative safety."

Monk growled, "I'll take mine now."

Doc tossed him a hypodermic. The hairy chemist caught it in freezing fingers.

Homely face determined, Monk jabbed the needle into his arm, pressing the plunger home.

Watching with horror, Pat shivered and exclaimed, *"Brrr.* I hate the very idea of needles."

They churned across the great Barrens, handicapped by a lack of snowshoes, but spurred on by the knowledge that so many trained soldiers would soon be in hot pursuit.

As they rushed along, Doc Savage distributed additional charged syringes. Finally, everyone had been inoculated, except Pat Savage.

Looking back, Doc was able to discern a lone figure in black standing on the parapet of the former prison's roof. He had something in his hand that was long and dark. Moonlight glinted off one end of it.

Wrenching to an abrupt halt, Doc Savage arrested Pat Savage in her headlong flight.

"Lift your sleeve," he directed.

Hurriedly, Pat complied, and Doc Savage injected her with a quick jab of a hypodermic needle.

Ham Brooks looked back, spied the glint of moonlight, and his eyes sharpened.

"Commander Igor is employing a telescope to search for us," he warned.

Then, a siren began wailing. It was one of the hand-cranked types, often used in military air fields to awaken sleeping pilots.

The caterwauling was drawing even more soldiers out of the prison complex, and out into the billowing snow. For a stiff wind had picked up, scouring fresh flakes off the snowpack and hurling them around.

Renny boomed out, "That does it! Now they're all going to be gunning for us."

Doc nodded grimly, but there was a flicker of something that was almost satisfaction touching his metallic bronze features.

Noticing this, Ham asked, "This is going to make it difficult for us to reach the plane."

Doc Savage did not seem concerned by that. Instead, he directed them with a pointing finger in the general direction where their white ski plane stood waiting on the snowpack.

They plunged along, and behind them the sharp crack of military rifles started echoing. The range was not good, but that did not dissuade the soldiers from peppering them, or attempting to pepper them, rather. For they demonstrated themselves to be indifferent marksmen. Darkness helped.

As they pounded through the crusty snow, Doc Savage led them around the two sprawled sentries he had overcome earlier.

The soldiers were still unconscious.

"What happened to them?" wondered Long Tom.

"What do you think?" flung back Pat. "Doc Savage happened to them."

The bronze man did not reveal to them his earlier subterfuge. Truth to tell, he was slightly embarrassed by it. His childhood was spent living around the world. Being handed off through a succession of scientists and other masters of knowledge had left little time for the ordinary run of fun that most young boys get to enjoy. As a consequence, a peculiar prankishness sometimes manifested itself. Doc could not decide if it was entirely healthy or not.

The bronze man had kept the Santa Claus costume at his Fortress of Solitude for a very practical reason. While it was rare for an aircraft to wander near the remote spot, it was not out of the question. Doc had instructed his Eskimo friends to don the outfit and wave at any passing plane, on the theory that should the pilot report that he had sighted a large blue dome near the North Pole, apparently inhabited by old Saint Nick, he was unlikely to be believed and the Fortress would be consigned to legend and remain uninvestigated.

The hard-charging group continued on. Their objective was the great cave in the side of a hill, not far from which was staked their big ski plane. The bronze man had earlier spotted it from the air, and thus knew in which direction to run.

No one spoke. They put all their concentration, every muscular ounce of effort into running. With each churning of their arms and legs, their lungs seemed to be on fire. Cold condensation streamed out of their open mouths in ghostly plumes.

They reached the cave first, and moved past without giving it much attention.

Ahead lay their plane, looking frosty with a fresh coating of snow.

Renny bellowed, "Sure hope those durn motors will fire in this cold."

"We'll know soon enough!" puffed Long Tom.

Doc reached the plane first, yanked open the door. Up popped Habeas Corpus from a nearby snowbank, squealing with delight. The homely pig had burrowed deep into the white stuff, awaiting the return of his homelier master. Monk had taught him to survive in extreme cold in the same manner Eskimos did—by taking advantage of the insulating qualities of deep snow.

Grinning, Monk caught the bounding porker, while Doc Savage held the door aside for the others to clamber on board.

He barely started this exodus when the close crack of a rifle split the night.

Turning his blunt head, Monk roared, "They're closer than I thought!"

They were indeed. Much closer.

For out of the great cave stepped a pair of ghost-white soldiers, one of whom held a smoking rifle, the other of whom pointed a weird device at them which they did not at first recognize.

Ham exploded, "I know that devilish machine. Down in Florida—"

Abruptly, uncannily, Ham's voice was cut off, although his wide, mobile mouth continued working excitedly.

The device did not hum or whistle or omit any other sound that impinged upon their eardrums. In fact, no sound reached their ears.

The world became suddenly very quiet and very still. It was an unnatural stillness. It was as if a great maw had swallowed their surroundings.

All sound ceased. And all movements ceased. They froze in mid-gesture.

Pat Savage had been the first to climb into the plane. She stood poised on the door frame, when suddenly every limb went still.

Unable to move, completely enveloped in a weird soundless void, the bronze-haired girl lost her balance and tipped backwards.

Pat fell with the slowness of a feather falling to earth. Frozen of features, helpless of limb, gravity pulled her to the snow-packed earth, where she landed without making any noise, or otherwise reacting in any way.

Her golden eyes stared upward, helplessly. Their light was stark.

The others stood around in attitudes of arrested action, as if some polar Gorgon had turned them to stone.

They did not move; they could not move. Movement was impossible.

When the device pointing at them was shut down, they simply fell to the snow in stunned heaps.

By this time, the first advance contingent of winter-clad soldiers had arrived from the prison laboratory.

A sergeant barked out a quick order.

"Carry them back to the base. They will not be able to resist."

HAULING them all that distance proved to be more of a challenge than any of the soldiers of Egallah had at first thought. Monk and Renny particularly proved too cumbersome to be carried, even by two husky soldiers.

Three men attempted to lift Doc Savage, and simply sat down in the snow, coughing and heaving in their exertion, expressing defeat.

One complained, "The bronze one weighs as much as if he were actually cast out of metal."

It might be suspected that this soldier of Egallah was a slacker, inasmuch as Doc Savage actually weighed less than either Renny or Monk. But the metallic lines of the bronze giant's massive form suggested otherwise.

Nevertheless, sledges were fetched, and bindings made out of coarse army blankets. The prisoners were laid upon these, and dragged laboriously back to the prison compound.

The prisoners were rudely flung into a single prison cell. This was not one of the cells they had previously occupied, but a new chamber. They were left there for many hours.

Deep into the Arctic night, but an hour before dawn, Baron Edgar Fretz appeared, Shari Phoenia at his side. They studied the unmoving prisoners for some time.

"We should execute them at once," snapped the opal-eyed woman spy. Her face had been repaired by makeup, but it still bore the discolored marks of her rough treatment at the hands of Patricia Savage.

"They will die at dawn," announced the Baron. "Once I devise a method appropriate to their crimes against our patriotic plans."

"Why not simply turn one of the zone-creating devices upon them?"

"It will accomplish nothing," retorted the Baron. "The bronze devil managed to inoculate them from the heart-stopping power of the fatal fields."

Shari curled her bruised upper lip. "Will it not wear off by dawn?"

The Baron shook his head. "We do not wish to drain the storage batteries of our portable devices. Not until the master dynamo is back in operation."

"What do you suggest then?" asked Shari Phoenia.

The Baron shrugged negligently. "Perhaps we will hang them. Perhaps we will stand them against stone walls and shoot them. But I am thinking that the likes of Doc Savage and his men deserve a more memorable death than those commonplace executions."

Shari Phoenia spat contemptuously onto the stone floor, saying, "Good riddance to them all!"

At that, the two departed in silence.

When they had gone, Doc Savage stirred, and sat up carefully.

The bronze man had heard every word prior to volition returning to his vital form. His returning hearing had told him that the paralysis induced by the inertia-dampening field had begun to fade.

Doc went about reviving his men, beginning with his cousin Pat. As he worked, his golden eyes were very active.

Doc Savage's supersensitive ears detected the sound resembling a metronome, which now showed signs of speeding up. It was coming from a cell down the block, the one in which Monk and the others previously had been held. The sound was like the ticking of a strange clock, marking time that was in some bizarre way accelerating.

What it portended was unknown, but the manner in which the giant Man of Bronze redoubled his efforts showed that he expected something momentous.

Chapter XXI

THE MAD MAZE

IN THE PRISON cell where Doc Savage and his five men were confined, gloom hung as thick as an Arctic fog, both physically and spiritually. Renny paced steadily, as Long Tom expressed it, like a starved giraffe. Monk and Ham sat staring at each other, too disconsolate to quarrel. Even Pat Savage looked like someone had taken the gleam out of her golden orbs.

Pervading the place, the inexorable metronomic clicking of the gray device Monk Mayfair had planted in their old cell did its part to deepen their gloom. The tireless machine was ticking away their lives.

"How soon is it going to be, you figure?" Renny blurted out.

"According to Doc, the Baron did not say exactly," Ham clipped. "He only threatened to execute us eventually."

"No sense not taking him at his word," commented Long Tom.

"And how," added Monk.

Renny ceased his pacing. "You said it," he rumbled noisily. *"How.* That's what I want to know."

Long Tom mused. "If I had my choice, I'd rather be shot than hanged by the neck until I strangled, or my neck broke."

"I don't know," Monk answered dolefully. "I ain't never been hung."

"Are you trying to be funny?" demanded Ham.

"I never felt less funny in my life," admitted Monk.

"I wish you all would stop arguing like this," complained Pat. "All this gloomy doom talk is getting on my nerves."

Doc Savage's flake-gold eyes roved the cell. He no longer wore his protective mask, for it had been confiscated. The solitary window had been cemented over for some reason. The barred door was the only exit. Doc stood speculating.

"There is nothing to be gained by fooling ourselves," he stated. "We are up against a serious proposition. It is now clear that these machinations are a direct result of our role in stopping the war over Ultra-Stygia last year. While neither nation won that struggle, President Ocel of Egallah continues to hold a grudge against us, and intends to prosecute it by bringing the United States to its figurative knees."

"That's about the size of it," Long Tom confirmed. "Looks like he's got us right where he wants us, too."

There was not much more to add, or clarify their predicament. The cell fell silent. Renny recommenced his pacing.

IT WAS approaching what would have been a delayed dawn in the land of the midnight sun when Edgar Fretz, the self-styled Baron in Black, put in a return appearance.

With him marched a contingent of white-uniformed soldiers, armed with snappy modern rifles.

Renny rumbled, "Looks like the execution squad is early."

But the big-fisted engineer had jumped to a premature conclusion. For the soldiers were prodding two of their fellows ahead of them. These men were unarmed; moreover, their hands were held above their bare heads, pale faces showing misery.

These were the sentries the Doc Savage had earlier overcome, having taken them by surprise while disguised as jolly old Saint Nick.

These distraught men were clapped into a cell of their own. The barred iron door slammed shut with a final ringing that echoed through the chilly cinderblock confines.

Baron Fretz wandered over and approached Doc Savage,

maintaining a respectful distance from the bronze man, whose terrifically strong hands could easily reach through the cold iron bars and seize an unwary man in their unbreakable grip.

The Baron remarked casually, "Those men of mine told a rather fanciful story."

Doc Savage vouchsafed no reply.

The Baron continued, "They claimed to have encountered on the tundra no less than the Father Christmas of legend. The crimson-clad grandfather walked up to them and then they saw stars. They remember nothing else. Very strange."

Again, Doc Savage offered no comment.

The Baron rocked back on his heels and said flatly, "It has not yet been decided how to dispose of you all."

When that brought forth no reaction, the Baron asked a disarmingly simple question. "Would you and your men care for a last cigarette?"

Pat Savage emitted a derisive laugh. "You're barking up the wrong conifer. Doc wouldn't—"

"A final cigarette would be appreciated by all of my men," said the bronze man without emotion.

The Baron brought forth a pack of foreign cigarettes, shook the pack until several slender white tubes popped up. He held this out, maintaining a respectful distance from the strangely-calm Man of Bronze.

Doc Savage took cigarettes sufficient for each of his men, including one for Pat Savage. Without comment, he distributed them, one to each person.

The Baron tossed a pack of matches, which Doc caught easily.

"It might interest you to know why your execution is being delayed," purred the Baron.

Doc inclined his head as if to show interest.

"My men captured a wild pig in the wilderness. They are at this exact moment reducing him to bacon and other eatables. As you can imagine, breakfast fare here below the North Pole is not always fresh."

Monk Mayfair came charging to the bars, grasped two in his hairy hands, and began shaking them vigorously. He roared. His growl of ferocity was such that the Baron hastily retreated in spite of his position of supreme authority.

As he turned on his heel smartly, leaving the prison corridor, Baron Fretz chuckled to himself, having elicited the desired response at long last.

Monk Mayfair's howls of rage followed the black-clad noble many yards before he closed sufficient doors between them to shut out their protests.

After a time, the homely chemist subsided. He sank down onto a bench, and buried his bullet head in his hairy paws.

No one knew what to say. But Pat Savage gamely tried. She wanted to get the hairy chemist's mind off the loss of his pet.

"I thought I saw Habeas dive into a snowbank when they got us," she said. "Maybe the pig they have is a wild one, and not Habeas."

Long Tom bent a pale eye in the direction of the bronze-haired girl.

"A wild pig? In the Arctic?"

Pat sent a scathing glance back at the puny electrical genius. "Are you saying it's impossible?"

"No," countered Long Tom. "I'm saying it's ridiculous. Pure, unadulterated bunkum."

"Have it your way, then," murmured Pat.

"Leave me alone, willya?" moaned Monk.

Silence fell over the chilly cell.

After a time, a frantic squealing could be heard. The squealing went on and on and on until Monk groaned, "I can hardly stand it!"

Finally, the squealing protests died off.

It was a long time before anyone spoke.

Ham Brooks sidled over to the disconsolate chemist, laid a comforting hand on his apish shoulder. "So sorry, Monk. I think

I liked Habeas Corpus as much as you did," he admitted. "He could do more things than a dog, even. That pig had intelligence."

"Yeah, yeah," Monk mumbled, shifting his big feet. "Guess it's silly of me to take it so hard, but when you like an animal well enough to risk your life for it—"

"I know, Monk, I know," commiserated Ham.

Gesturing with her unlit cigarette, Pat Savage asked, "What am I supposed to do with this? You know I don't smoke. In fact, none of us do."

Doc Savage said, "Hold onto them, all of you. They will become important later."

The bronze man offered no further explanation.

There was no sunrise as such, only a perpetual twilight, but about mid-morning the low-wattage electrical bulbs shed sudden illumination.

"Looks like they got that blamed generator working," thumped Renny.

Doc Savage paid no attention to that. He had been listening very intently to something. Suddenly, he shifted position. The bronze man placed his ear to the walls of the cell, as if listening for termites or other subtle interior sounds.

Pat Savage placed her hands on her hips and demanded, "Are you waiting for the cavalry, or are you going to do something about this mess we're in?"

Doc waved for her to be still.

Curious now, the bronze-haired girl drifted up to the wall and began listening, too.

"Sounds like a metronome, only it's going very, very fast," she observed.

Monk looked up from his morose gloom, tiny eyes gleaming with sudden interest.

"How fast?" he muttered.

"Ticking to beat the band," responded Pat. "Whatever does that mean?"

"It means," returned Monk, standing up and making menacing fists, "all heck could break loose any second now."

Everyone looked at him.

Ham walked over and demanded, "What do you know that the rest of us don't?"

Monk said only, "Doc's got somethin' up his sleeve."

Before anybody could press the matter further, Shari Phoenia made a dramatic return appearance.

She came strutting up the corridor, eyes ablaze.

"I see that you are all awake," she taunted. "Just in time for your executions."

If she expected Doc Savage and his group to tremble, or protest, she was very much disappointed. They just regarded her skeptically.

Long Tom asked negligently, "Figured it out yet?"

"We're getting kinda curious," grunted Renny with elaborate nonchalance. "Been making bets on whether it will be bullets or a rope."

Slightly deflated, the dark-eyed spy sneered thinly, "That is not up to me. If it were up to me, you would all be boiled in a hot liquid, possibly whale oil."

"If it were up to me," snapped Pat Savage, "I would give you a whale of a tarring."

The exotic woman ignored Pat, and turned her full attention on Doc Savage.

"It is known in my country, bronze one, in fact known throughout the region, that the last Balkan war that you interrupted was waged with weapons stolen from a secret laboratory that you are rumored to maintain somewhere near the North Pole."

Everyone went silent. This was one of Doc Savage's deepest secrets. But the theft of the various war weapons from Doc's Fortress of Solitude by John Sunlight so many months ago, while not generally known to the world, had managed to infiltrate the territory in the Balkans around Ultra-Stygia.

Shari Phoenia went on, "It is obvious to anyone that you flew your gyroplane from a hidden location. No doubt there are many strange secrets remaining in your reportedly fabulous hideaway."

She paused, met Doc Savage's gaze with frank opalescent eyes. "Perhaps your lives might be spared if you could be persuaded to divulge the location of this special vault?"

"Time is growing very short," commented Doc Savage, apparently in regard to nothing in particular.

Rebuffed, the woman spy abruptly changed the subject.

"I imagine you would all enjoy a last meal," she quipped. "By chance, we have a surplus of ham and bacon this morning." She laughed nastily.

This brought Monk Mayfair roaring and thrashing about in such a way that Shari Phoenia decided that the iron bars might not be as stout as they appeared and quickly betook herself away, boot heels clicking a brisk tattoo.

IT WAS not very long after that the walls of the old prison began shaking.

The shaking started rather offhandedly, commencing as a sense of growing discomfort in the air that was hard to put a finger on, followed by a noticeable tremor in the thick walls.

This tremor persisted, grew in intensity, and it was then Doc Savage said, "Be prepared to make a break for it."

"What's happening?" Pat asked in alarm.

Monk leaped for the cell door and tried to jar the iron bars loose. They refused to budge. Grimacing and baring clenched teeth, Monk's muscles audibly crackled with his extreme exertion.

Doc Savage stepped in and attempted to assist.

While they were twisting the bars, endeavoring to make them turn in their sockets, a section of nearby wall cracked like a thunderbolt. A rift appeared, tracing a jagged path along the mortar lines. Cinderblocks began cascading with a noisy thudding.

This came unexpectedly. It was the corridor that collapsed, but part of that included the upper portion of the door to their cell.

Iron bars groaned under the weight of the falling ceiling. Much of it was stonework and coarse cinderblock. These shattered.

The result was that the door was twisted violently out of its frame.

Doc Savage, Monk and Renny, the strongest of the band, begin working on the twisted tangle of iron and steel. Their combined strength was prodigious. They began wrenching an aperture open.

All the time they worked, the great prison building shook and shook like a mad thing.

"This must be an earthquake," moaned Pat.

"It's an escape," shouted Monk. "Come on. Let's go!"

They squeezed out of the aperture thus created, and began creeping down the gloomy corridor.

Ham elbowed Monk and demanded, "What deviltry did you pull this time?"

"Explain later," snapped Monk, rolling up his sleeves. "We got some fightin' to do first."

"Watch out for the anti-inertia zones," warned Doc Savage sharply.

He paused to light his cigarette, got it smoldering, then applied the flaring match to those of the others. Soon, all seven cigarettes were burning like miniature coals.

"What possible good will these things do?" demanded Ham impatiently, waving his smoke.

Instead of answering, Doc Savage uncharacteristically drew deeply on his cigarette, and produced blue cigarette smoke. He directed it ahead of him in a concentrated stream.

The smoke rolled down the corridor uninhibited.

Advancing a few yards, the bronze man repeated the operation.

"Great Scott!" Ham said suddenly. "I believe I understand now. If blocked, the smoke reveals the presence of an invisible barrier."

Understanding dawned. They began smoking furiously, exhaling tobacco in all directions, looking for any signs that one of the death zones had clamped down, or, worse, was seeking them.

Meanwhile, the old prison building continued shaking nervously.

One nearby wall tumbled, exposing a ragged opening. It was difficult to determine where it led. For the lights were flickering and winking out at intervals.

Doc climbed through, leading the others.

The place proved to be constructed in the fashion of a great labyrinth. Originally, of course it had been no such thing, but the Egallan military staff had remodeled the structure for their own purposes.

Negotiating the tangle of dim corridors was a challenge. They had to keep moving, lest they bunch up and fall over one another.

"Like threading the maze of the Minotaur," complained Long Tom sourly.

Very quickly, all sense of direction was lost. The fact that they were negotiating an interior section, devoid of windows, added to the confusion.

PAT SAVAGE was bringing up the rear, popping out tobacco smoke in spurts from her pale but delectable lips. When she released a stream of gray smoke, it rolled a few feet, began banking against nothing that could be seen.

Pat whirled, called, "Doc!"

The bronze man wrenched to a halt, and scrutinized the strangely behaving smoke.

The small cloud was mushrooming, and began to wash

backward toward the bronze-haired girl, who started backing away in horror.

Beside Pat, Ham Brooks cried out, "It's an invisible wall! It's coming this way!"

"Follow me!" urged Doc Savage.

They moved along the corridor, which had no light whatsoever. Only the lurid coals of their burning cigarettes showed anything. It etched their tense faces into harsh lines.

From ahead, the tramp of booted feet charged in their direction.

Finding a door in the darkness, Doc tested it, found it to be unlocked, and pushed inward. It was a stroke of luck that he did so.

Leading them in, the bronze giant stood guard while the others packed into what proved to be a small storage room. He pressed his considerable weight against the panel, just in case the approaching patrol tried to force it open.

Monk let out a low growl of delight. He used the glow of his cigarette to show them what he had found.

"Our stuff—it's all here!"

Strewn around shelves were their superfirers and other equipment taken from them after their capture.

Each man grabbed for a weapon, checked the magazine indicators, and began stuffing extra ammunition drums into his pockets. Ham found his sword cane, whipped forth the wicked blade, and inspected it critically.

Pat reclaimed her frontier revolver, checked the action and announced, "Six shells. I'm ready for anything." To underscore her point, she gave the cylinder a snappy spin.

The oversized signaling wrist watches were also here, and these were hastily donned, although what use they might be in close quarters was doubtful at best.

Pat suddenly made a strange sound in her throat. "I just realized. What is my six-shooter doing here? The last time I had it was at Renny's plane down in the Everglades."

"From which I retrieved it," explained Doc. "Neglected to return it to you."

Pat made a dubious mouth. "Neglected?"

Doc told her, "You are sometimes too free with your lead. I had been holding it for you—until we fell into the Baron's trap."

"For your information," advised Pat, "I mix up my ammunition now. Every other slug is a mercy bullet."

By this time, the patrol sounded outside the closed door behind Doc Savage's blocking back.

Booted feet went rushing past. Just like that. No one thought to check the closed door.

Monk said grimly, "How's about a little target practice?"

Renny grunted, "I'm all for blasting our way out of here."

Stepping away from the door, Doc Savage said, "We need to find a way out of this building before it comes tumbling down."

That was enough for the others. Monk threw open the door, jumped out into the corridor, and began firing. Muzzle flashes illuminated the gorilla-like chemist as if he were surrounded by exploding firecrackers.

Renny, Long Tom, and the others tumbled out, adding their fury to the combined assault. The superfirers made a deafening noise in the cramped passage.

Searching soldiers spun about, unable to save themselves from the storm of hollow shells and their anesthetic contents. They collapsed, arms and legs entangled, to the cold floor. Not a return shot was fired.

Doc Savage stepped out, collected the rifles, and removed all ammunition. He took a moment to take the rifle barrels in hand and bend them double, showing strength that defied imagination.

Dropping the useless weapons, the bronze giant led the way down the corridor.

The old building continued to shake, and the manner in

which the cinderblocks groaned in agony was alarming in the extreme.

Continuing along the nerve-testing maze, a familiar odor reached their frozen nostrils.

"Bacon!" said Ham, pinching his nose shut.

Monk ground out, "Lemme get my hands on whoever cooked that bacon."

Using his simian nostrils to guide him, Monk followed the familiar scent.

Doc cautioned, "We have very little time."

"This will only take a minute," Monk said fiercely.

Seeing that the hairy chemist could not be dissuaded from his grim intent, they followed Monk as he moved along the trail of the tangy odor.

The pungent smell came from behind a closed door, and Monk put one burly shoulder to it. The effort proved unnecessary because the door surrendered readily under his pressure.

Monk stopped on the threshold, and let out a wild whoop.

"He's been shot!" Ham screeched.

But that was not what brought that apish chemist's powerful lungs into action.

Peering past one of Monk's sloping shoulders, Ham Brooks saw a table set with ham and bacon, garnished with what appeared to be fried potatoes.

Off in one corner stood a small cage, and in the cage sat a grotesque-looking animal they all recognized. It lay stretched out, its eyes closed.

"Habeas!" shouted Monk, lunging for the cage.

The thing was locked, but the lock could not resist Monk's clamping fingers.

The homely chemist wrenched off the door by brute strength, reached in with both paws, then removed Habeas Corpus.

The homely porker had been asleep. Now he woke up, and began grunting with a mixture of fear and curiosity.

"He's alive?" blurted out Ham Brooks.

"What does it look like?" returned Monk, holding Habeas up to get a better look at him. The shoat was acting strangely, as if someone had taken the curl out of his tail.

Then Monk let out an angry bellow. For Habeas Corpus had not been harmed, but the reason for his painful grunting became evident upon close inspection.

Someone had twisted his ridiculously long ears into a painful bow!

Setting him down, Monk carefully undid the ridiculous knot, restoring Habeas' ears to their normal length and attitude.

Thus freed, the pig happily pranced around the hairy chemist's feet.

Gathering up the liberated porker, Monk turned and barked, "Let's get the heck out of here!"

They moved back out into the perpetually shaking corridor maze, groping their way to an exit.

It wasn't long before they confronted a contingent of Egallan soldiers, diligently searching for them. Their white uniforms made them resemble moving blobs in the poor light.

Doc had been leading the way, blowing tobacco smoke ahead of him, in order to make certain that the way was clear. But it was no longer clear, at least not as far as danger was concerned. The glowing tip of Doc's cigarette, which provided sufficient glare for him to see the rolling smoke, gave him away.

Turning, Doc Savage clipped to the others, "Retreat!"

They hastily reversed course, firing at the approaching soldiers in order to drive them back. Superfirers hooted voraciously, spitting out shells and spent brass cartridges amid a profusion of muzzle flashes that lit up their determined faces, making them look like a band of demonic warriors from some hyperborean place.

The soldiers had not yet turned the corner, so no mercy bullets struck them. But the frightful thunder of the superfirers instilled a great amount of caution in their advance.

Moving rapidly, Doc and his band turned another corner, only to find themselves confronting another searching patrol of white-clad soldiers.

This squad was led by no less than Baron Edgar Fretz. He brought his men to halt, and called out, "Savage! You are surrounded! It is time for surrender!"

Doc Savage appeared to hover poised between two decisions, whether to surrender or to fight. Eyes chilly, he took a puff of his now very short cigarette, drew in tobacco smoke, and released it carefully.

The cloud, tinged blue, rolled in the direction of Baron Fretz. It struck the Baron in the face, causing him to cough slightly.

"What is your answer, Savage?"

Pivoting the other way, Doc Savage repeated the action, as if considering the proposition.

That smoky cloud also rolled along the corridor unobstructed.

"It appears," the bronze man commented, "that escape is out of the question."

Monk spoke up. "Doc! We can't just give up!"

"That's right," Long Tom inserted. "They'll execute us for sure."

Doc Savage addressed the Baron in Black. "Have you found the device that is causing the building to shake?"

The Baron looked startled. "Device?"

"Do you think that you are experiencing a natural earthquake?"

The Baron's eyes grew queer. "Are you claiming that you are producing this maddening shaking?"

Doc nodded. "A device based on the theory that if the structure's vibration and internal resonance can be found, it can be brought down entirely. That device, which we planted before our capture, has been operating all along. It is seeking the resonance pitch of this building, which, when found, will cause the entire structure will come tumbling down on our heads. It is urgent that we all flee before this happens."

A new voice spoke up.

"A lie!"

THE VOICE was the sharp-tongued Shari Phoenia, who was shouldering her way through the group of soldiers headed by the Baron.

"The bronze one lies! He is trying to trick us! Do not listen to him."

The Baron assumed a torn expression. For the cinderblock walls continued to vibrate in an unsettling manner.

At last he said thickly, "I do not think he lies."

"Then shoot him! Shoot them all!" insisted the furious woman.

But no one did any such thing. For a fresh contingent of soldiers led by Commander Igor suddenly entered the scene, arriving from the opposite direction.

The commander toted a strange contraption that could not be clearly made out.

It consisted of a stainless steel tank slung over one black-uniformed shoulder, which was connected by an insulated hose to a pistol-like nozzle arrangement. The mouth of the nozzle seemed to be smoking faintly, as if it had just been fired.

"If anyone is to shoot, it will be I—and with this."

If the commander expected anyone to inquire what this was, he was disappointed. This caused him to offer an explanation of sorts.

"This is the latest secret weapon devised by the finest war scientists in all of Egallah, if not the world," he boasted. "I have only to release this inhibiting valve, and death will cover you in a frost of morbidity."

Monk Mayfair, scrutinizing the whitish smoking nozzle of the thing, sniffed the air curiously and squeaked, "Blazes!"

"In typical blundering American fashion, you have it backward," spat Commander Igor. "No doubt you mistake this nozzle and pressurized tank for a primitive flame thrower."

Doc Savage stated, "That comment suggests a weapon employing one of the coldest substances known to science—liquid oxygen."

"Liquid air!" Long Tom said seriously. "That's worse than liquid fire! One drop of it on a man's skin will burn a hole in him quicker than the most corrosive acid."

Renny looked toward Doc Savage. "Bad as that?"

Doc nodded. "It does not burn in the sense that acid burns," he explained. "But it has an even more annihilating effect. Liquid air is cold enough to freeze the mercury in a thermometer so hard that you could drive a nail with it."

Doc paused and looked at Monk, who had been the first to recognize the nature of the weapon. "Isn't that right, Monk?"

Monk nodded firmly. "If you stuck your finger in some liquid air and left it there a bit," he elicited, "you could break it off as easy as pickin' a dandelion."

"Well, what are you waiting for?" screeched Shari Phoenia. "Spray them!"

"Who is in charge here, woman?" snapped Baron Fretz testily.

"It is not you!" raged Commander Igor. "Now stand aside!"

The commander looked to Baron Fretz for assent before unleashing his hideous weapon.

A nod passed between the two men of Egallah.

Doc Savage had by this time palmed some of the anesthetic bombs he habitually carried—thin-walled gas spheres which released a volatile brew once they shattered. He was on the verge of pegging them in all directions, in hopes of overcoming every one of their massed foes. The unique gas on more than one occasion had proved to be a life-saver to Doc and his aides.

The bronze man paused only to offer up a curt warning to his friends in the Mayan language, so they could hold their breaths the necessary minutes until the potent stuff dissipated, and not succumb.

But he never got a syllable out.

Pat Savage had her rather large six-shooter gripped in one tanned fist, and she brought it up in such a way that no one noticed the cumbersome weapon.

Rocking back the hammer, the bronze-haired girl lined up on the insistent woman spy. Pat let the hammer fall on the waiting cartridge.

The report, when it came, was deafening and unexpected in the confined space.

A mercy bullet struck Shari Phoenia in one shoulder, very high up. She slapped at that wound with one hand, as if swatting a hornet that had stung her. Her dark eyes were wild, now they became insane.

Screeching, she reached for the pistol portion of the liquid oxygen dispenser.

Her mad intent was clear. She was going to avenge the insult to her person.

The potent brew in the mercy bullet usually kicked in within seconds, dropping the victim. In this case, perhaps the dosage was weak, or old. Several seconds elapsed before the overpowering anesthetic reached the woman's brain.

In those fateful moments, she seized the barrel of the terrible weapon, yanking it from Commander's Igor's stubborn fingers.

During the frantic exchange, two fingers sought the trigger. Shari's won.

The smoking nozzle suddenly gushed a blast of cold white substance that sprayed in the wrong direction.

For the weapon was momentarily directed, not at Doc Savage and his men, but at Baron Edgar Fretz and his personal guard!

The unprepared group absorbed the full brunt of the horrible liquid concoction.

Their bodies were instantly coated in dazzling white, as if they had become men of frozen ice or snow.

The terrific force of the wintery blast knocked them backward. Sounds like blocks of ice breaking and shattering could be heard amid the cold clouds of condensation that filled the man-jammed space. But that was only the beginning.

A softer thud told that Shari Phoenia had finally succumbed to the mercy bullet that had so enraged her.

Through the pale, ghostly clouds, Doc Savage discerned the figure of Commander Igor desperately scrambling for his fallen weapon.

Moving so quickly that he seemed like a streaking bronze shadow, Doc thrust out a boot-shod foot to kick hard against the side of the commander's leg, simultaneously avoiding the shifting nozzle of freezing doom. He struck with such accurately calculated force that Igor was knocked off his feet and turned completely upside down in the air.

An average man would have been laid out cold by the whack on the head which the Egallan officer sustained when he struck the concrete floor. Commander Igor was no ordinary man.

Flat on his back, with his hand on the trigger of his weapon, Igor struggled to line up the smoking nozzle with his towering foe, viciously cursing the obscuring haze of visible cold fog.

Charging in from another direction, Monk made a desperate long-armed grab for him. Igor eluded hairy hands for a second, redirected the nozzle once again.

Renny had also flung his huge bulk into the fray, massive fists poised to pummel.

This brought the smoking muzzle shifting once more.

"You must all die!" Commander Igor raged, shaking finger constricting on the trigger.

"You first!" bellowed Renny, monster fist descending like a wooden maul.

Before the big-fisted engineer knew what hit him, an irresistible vise of a hand seized him by the collar and yanked him forcibly backward.

Monk Mayfair discovered himself to be in the identical

position. He was traveling backward so fast that the nails in his dragging boot soles struck sparks.

Both men had time to comprehend that only one power on earth possessed the sheer might to manhandle them in such a masterful manner.

The bronze man's voice crashed close to their ears. "Keep clear!"

What would have transpired next was destined never to be known. For the rumbling and grinding of the surrounding cinderblocks suddenly turned into a cascade of earsplitting noise, broken concrete, spilling grit, and confusion.

At the last ditch, Doc Savage made a desperate lunge in the direction of his cousin, as if to shield her with his powerful body. The bronze man never completed the leap. A section of ceiling smashed down upon him.

Then the roof caved in, burying them all.

Amid the clatter of settling debris, a sinister hissing could be heard. It persisted for many minutes, finally trailing off into a final choked-off gasp.

A profound absence of sound followed. It smacked of the silence of death....

Chapter XXII
SINISTER GENIUS

THE UTTER AND complete stillness that persisted in the aftermath of the prison building's collapse was not disturbed for several minutes.

Then, a dust-smeared bronze hand emerged from the rubble. Followed by a bare head, the hair of which was darker than the protruding hand and as metallic as a close-fitting skullcap. Animated flake-gold eyes surveyed the surroundings.

Doc Savage saw that not all of the former cinderblock structure had collapsed, but a great deal of it was now whitish rubble. A dusting of disturbed snow had already coated much of the settled debris.

The central laboratory area with its towering bony antenna, which had broadcast unremitting terror over a defenseless population, still stood upright in the moonlight.

A flicker of disappointment touched the bronze man's impassive features. He inhaled deeply. Bracing air went into his nostrils, emerging as cold clouds of breath steam.

Shrugging off rubble, Doc Savage began excavating through the chaotic tumble of cinderblock, mortar, and pulverized plaster. His movements verged on the frantic.

Pat Savage was the first to be extracted from the rubble. She appeared to be dazed, her golden eyes dull, and Doc Savage silently checked her limbs with his sensitive hands. Finding no breaks, sprains or serious contusions, he seemed relieved.

Batting her eyes suddenly, Pat came around. Doc helped the

shaken girl to her feet.

"I guess they'll have to hold off inscribing my headstone a while longer," she said weakly. She was still gripping her six-shooter.

Doc Savage eyed her without change of expression, but a warm light seemed to smolder in his eerie eyes. He returned to the task at hand.

While the bronze giant was working, an immense monster fist smashed upward, followed by Renny's dour head.

The big-fisted engineer peered about, blinked, saw Doc Savage and Pat, then bellowed, "Holy cow! Where are the others?"

"Dig for them," advised the bronze man.

Renny struggled to his feet, shaking off dust and debris.

Together, Doc and Renny commenced slinging broken blocks and other clutter this way and that, seeking their missing comrades. It was no easy task.

"Where the heck are they?" bellowed Renny in frustration.

Abruptly, the bronze giant paused, lifted his special watch, stared at it intently. He stabbed at the watch stem with a thumb.

This prompted Renny to pay attention to the warm flashes striking the back of one thick beam of a wrist through the medium of his own watchcase.

S-O-S came the signal.

Doc signaled back. W-h-o?

L-o-n-g T-o-m.

T-r-y t-o m-o-v-e, communicated Doc.

Came a crackling commotion not far away. It was not much of a disturbance, but it was sufficient to draw their attention.

Doc and Renny dug in, hurling cinderblock chunks from the spot. Soon, they discovered assorted limbs, coated in a mixture of plaster dust and snow. They began pulling these free.

Monk was out cold, but Long Tom had only to shake plaster dust out of his pale hair before he was on his feet, fists clenching, looking around for someone to pummel.

"Looks like those watches finally came in handy," guffawed Renny at the comical sight.

"Anyone left to fight?" demanded Long Tom.

"If there is," grunted Renny, "they haven't emerged from their holes."

Long Tom dropped his balled fists unhappily.

They fell to finishing the task of finding their friends.

Ham Brooks was excavated last. He appeared to be dazed but, when Habeas Corpus, digging himself out of the debris with his long snout and sharp hoofs, trotted up and began sniffing him, the dapper lawyer—no longer quite so dapper—reacted indignantly.

"Get that infernal insect away from me!" he snapped.

This woke up Monk, who bounded to his feet, blinking small eyes and grimacing as if he wanted to take on all comers.

"What fell on us?" he mumbled, looking and sounding like a punch-drunk pugilist.

"Everything," snapped Long Tom.

Monk frowned, rubbing the bristly crown of his bullet head. "Everything?"

Long Tom nodded. "And then some."

"Felt like it," mumbled Monk, who suddenly collapsed.

Renny rushed over to examine him. "Holy cow! Out like a light again."

It was obvious that the hairy chemist had been out on his feet in the manner of a prize fighter who had taken too many shots to the head, and toppled back into a stupor. Habeas trotted over and applied his pink tongue to Monk's homely face in an effort to rouse him.

Doc helped Ham to his feet and they looked around.

Nothing else stirred in the piles of rocky rubble. Doc went to the spot where Shari Phoenia had last been seen.

He dug around, found a soldier, determined that he was dead. His skull-hued helmet had been crushed, pulping the head within. A shadow crossed Doc Savage's metallic features. He preferred to avoid fatalities whenever possible. In this particular instance, however, death had been unavoidable.

Doc's aides pitched in, picking up shattered debris, pulling together until they found the woman spy.

She stared upward with a dazed expression, eyes like dusty and dulled opals.

Pat Savage marched over, gave her the once-over and said snippily, "She's still breathing, the hussy."

Doc nodded, testing her pulse, noting the stream of cold condensation coming out of her open mouth. The bronze man felt of her scalp, pried eyelids wider, and announced, "Concussion. It is difficult to say how bad at this point."

"If you asked me," Pat snapped, "she earned that knot on her noggin."

Doc did not criticize his strong-willed cousin, but it was clear that the bronze man was displeased with the significant loss of life, even though the destruction of this end of the prison building had undoubtedly save their lives.

"It had been my hope," he said slowly, "to engineer a panic during which every inhabitant would escape the building before it collapsed."

Renny eyed his bronze chief sympathetically, and rumbled, "You took a calculated risk. That inertialess-zone generator had to be shut down. It just didn't work out the way you hoped it would."

Doc Savage said nothing. They stood virtually outdoors, with open sky overhead and fragments of walls still standing here and there. Doc surveyed the scene. It was clear that there was more work yet to be done to quell the menace. For the whine of the dynamo powering the sending station could be heard. It was still in operation. But it sounded weirdly off-key.

Moving along the shattered corridor was useless; the surviving part of the building appeared to be sealed off by heaped detritus.

As Ham applied fistfuls of cold snow to Monk's slack features, Doc Savage looked up and saw that it would not be difficult to gain the surviving roof by climbing across the top of a mound of wreckage.

In this awkward but efficient fashion, the bronze man reached the roof, and swept it with his golden eyes.

There had been a trap door near the spidery antenna—obviously an inspection hatch—and this was intact.

Motioning down for the others to follow, Doc moved toward that aperture. The building beneath his feet was surprisingly quiet, but the muffled sound of someone moving about could be detected.

Renny joined him, with the others trailing close behind.

Monk had been restored to consciousness and was the last to clamber up onto the roof. He windmilled his freakishly long arms like a movie cartoon character winding up to throw a wild punch. His simian features wore an eager-for-battle look.

Renny said to Doc, "That field generator dingus is still operating."

Grimly, Doc Savage moved to the base of the antenna, and examined coiling wires and other electrical components.

Observing this inspection, Renny offered, "If we had some rubberized gloves, we could take hold of those wires and yank them out."

Doc used his feet to toe around in the snow, until he found what he was looking for.

It was a long gleaming icicle—one of the two used to cause a short circuit earlier. The icy fang had been significantly melted, and proved too short for a repeat operation. Doc tossed the thing away.

The bronze man reached into his equipment vest, and was going through the pockets. There were numerous grenades, and other handy gadgets. But nothing contained therein seemed to satisfy him.

Renny grunted, "Demolition grenades will do for this tower

well enough."

"Better to save them for the destruction of the transformer itself," replied Doc. "Without the field generator, the antenna will be useless."

"Good thinking," nodded Renny.

Removing a pair of cylinders from his equipment vest, Doc Savage moved with an almost inhuman soundlessness in the direction of the closed roof hatch.

Lying down on his stomach, the bronze man lifted the hatch door, and employed his ingenious collapsible periscope to see what could be seen.

"Man at the controls," he told Renny.

"We can jump him," Renny assured the bronze man.

"Let me at 'im," said Monk, pushing up. "I got me a score to settle with these babies for tryin' to scare me with all that hogwash about Habeas bein' turned into breakfast bacon."

Without saying another word, Monk reached out with his long arms and flung the hatch open. Then, he jumped down.

It was an entirely unexpected action, and probably prompted by a combination of having been knocked out, and his anguish over his beloved pet.

As it was, the impulsive action caught Doc Savage entirely unprepared. So the bronze man was forced to jump down after him.

Doc's men began tumbling down, Pat Savage last. After landing, she brandished her six-shooter as if eager to fling lead about.

They found themselves before the monster black housing which was studded with serpentine induction coils. The individual at the controls had his back to them all, but hearing the commotion of a flurry of feet landing in the great laboratory chamber, he whirled.

Gaining sight of the man's thin, feline features, Monk Mayfair exploded, "For the love of mud!"

Renny boomed out his favorite expression, "Holy cow!"

Long Tom added a blistering, "I'll be whiskered! The black cat is out of the bag."

FOR THE man at the complicated controls was no less than Felix "The Cat" Frost, whom they knew now to be in reality Felix Fretz, the former Huron Motor Company chief engineer, who had seemingly perished on a boat in Tampa Bay, Florida.

Monk demanded, "Ain't you supposed to be croaked?"

Fretz scowled in such a way as to bristle his white beard, for he had allowed it to grow in order to hide his catlike whiskers. His emerald orbs narrowed. "A ruse, engineered by myself and my brother, Baron Fretz. For it was he who pretended to shoot me, after the gangsters we hired brought you to me. Once the boat sank, I remained under water through use of a diving helmet, later swimming to safety—as did the one you know as Shari Phoenia."

Ham said, "Very clever. You tried to conceal your tracks by making the world believe your corpse rested at the bottom of Tampa Bay."

"I had hoped," Felix Fretz returned tightly, "to change my name yet again and continue my work against the hated United States of America."

Fretz reached out for the master lever controlling the inertia-suppressing field generator.

"It is no use, Fretz," warned Doc Savage. "You cannot kill us because we are standing too close to you. It would be impossible to define an inertialess zone precisely enough that you can surround us without also encompassing yourself within the fatal field."

The cat-green eyes of Felix Fretz flamed with an insane light. "Doubtless. But I can turn on the zones beyond us. In New York and Chicago and San Francisco, by the pressure of my fingers I can slay ten million people!"

At those words, Pat Savage screamed. She looked ready to

bring her six-shooter to bear, but recalling that the next round in the cylinder was lead, and not a quick-acting mercy slug, hesitated to risk a shot. The others appeared to be frozen in place, fearing to move lest the death lever be thrown.

Doc Savage lifted a cautioning hand. "The destruction of a portion of the building has no doubt affected the electrical system supplying power to the field generator. You will sign your own death warrant if you pull that switch."

The bronze man's chilling words sunk into the engineer's fevered brain. For a moment it seemed as if Felix Fretz would hesitate. His bushy beard bristled.

Then, with a sharp slicing movement, he snapped down the master lever.

"Back!" Doc Savage shouted, as lurid electrical fire began crackling from the transformer in elemental displays.

The entire chamber filled with a terrible whining and careening crescendo of sound. The awfulness of it assaulted their senses. It was like a mad song of death being howled out by an enraged monster composed of transformer, induction coils and vacuum tubes.

Screaming at the top of his lungs, Felix Fretz proclaimed triumphantly, "Ten million people are now dead!"

On that last grim word, the whining of the dynamo reached a crescendo. Suddenly, sparks began spitting, long blue-white snapping and snarling things that seemed alive.

A terrible ozone stink filled the chamber and Felix Fretz continued caterwauling, but now his screams were wordless and tortured, as his body jerked and danced fixedly in a coruscating halo of sizzling electrical display.

The distinctive smell of ozone was quickly replaced by the horrible odor of burning flesh.

By this time, Doc Savage had rushed his aides to the handiest door, and thrust them out into open terrain.

Knowing from the death smell that nothing could save the maddened engineer, Doc Savage primed two of his highly potent hand grenades, and hurled them in the general direction of the screaming dynamo. He clapped the steel door shut, and rushed the others as far away from the building as fast as humanly possible.

The grenades were quite potent. They let go almost seconds apart, with the result that a tremendous detonation followed.

That brought down the remainder of the roof, toppling the great skeletal antenna with its parabolic dish, and burying the diabolical apparatus of doom in its entirety. The commotion of its collapse started as a tortured groaning of metal twisting unbearably.

The sinister genius that they now knew to have been the mastermind behind the death dynamo was undoubtedly dead. No one mourned.

DOC SAVAGE watched the building collapse and cave in with a strange grinding of masonry punctuated by spiteful electrical snappings.

Soon, it was once again quiet.

"It is over," intoned the bronze man quietly. There was a touch of disappointment in his voice, and all who knew him well understood that the terrible loss of life was something that Doc would have preferred to avoid—even if the dead had been for the most part enemy combatants.

"But ten million people were killed!" Pat Savage said in undisguised horror.

"No one was killed," Doc Savage reassured her. Without another word, he went through the south-facing wall, and dug around the snow until he had excavated the compact aluminum sphere he previously concealed there.

Monk came lumbering over, regarded it with interest. "What the heck is that?"

As he turned off the device, Doc Savage replied, "At my Fortress of Solitude, I perfected an invention I have long been working on—an inertia equalizer. In the short time I had to work, it was not possible to make the apparatus function in the zones far from this sending station. But within a short arc outside of the building, blocking the settled regions of Canada, encompassing the Atlantic and Pacific Coasts, it functioned perfectly."

Long Tom wanted to know, "What exactly did it do?"

"It was set up to automatically disintegrate the lethal inertia fields as fast as they were created. None of the electronic zones were able to penetrate it. Therefore, wholesale death could not be broadcast beyond the radius of this building in the direction of America."

Monk grinned. "So no one died?"

Looking back at the ruined laboratory-broadcasting building, Doc Savage intoned, "No one who did not deserve it."

And that was as close as any of them have ever heard their bronze chief speak of evildoers as having earned their just deserts.

They spent the gloomy morning picking through the rubble and satisfying themselves that there were no survivors, other than battered Shari Phoenia.

They located the stiff bodies of the unfortunate Baron in Black, Edgar Fretz, and his personal guard. After they had been quick-frozen by the ferocious frost that was liquid oxygen, each man had fallen dead, with the result that their shattered remnants were almost indistinguishable from the white-washed and broken cinderblock rubble of the inner prison walls.

The Baron's icy head lay apart from his rigid body.

Realizing her timely role in precipitating all this human destruction, Pat Savage's golden eyes widened in shock and she clapped both hands to her mouth before turning away.

Monk and Ham attempted to comfort her.

"You did the right thing, Pat," assured Ham.

"Yeah," added Monk. "Saved our bacon for sure."

"Speaking of bacon," muttered Long Tom. "Where's Habeas?"

At the sound of his name, the long-eared porker poked his anteater snout out from Monk's coat. He squealed as if to say, "Here!"

"Had a special pocket sewn into my coat for Habeas to hide in," explained the hairy chemist. "That roof cavin' in musta got on his nerves. He decided to stick close to me for now."

Pat remarked, "More likely, he's upset because that's twice now he thought you were killed."

"The day I'm killed," boasted Monk, "the ones that done it had better light out for parts unknown. Because once I catch up to 'em, I plan to slaughter the sorry lot of 'em."

The thought of hairy Monk pursuing his own murderers from beyond the grave evoked musical laughter from Pat Savage's throat.

At this juncture, Renny's steam-shovel hands had upflung a mound of mixed material that included the mortal remains of Commander Igor. It was evident at first glance that in falling, his pressurized tank had been ruptured by the avalanche of construction materials, and hissed out it awful contents, freezing him solid.

His head, too, had separated from his shoulders, owing to the sudden brittleness of his thick icicle of a neck.

They reburied the dead, and attended to the still-unconscious Shari Phoenia. Alone of all, she had not suffered the hideous fate of her countrymen, a fact explained by the freakish way in which the roof had come down, separating her from the others.

When she was brought around by a stimulant administered by Doc Savage, the exotic woman spy sat up and began spitting and snarling at them like a feline who had been roused in her den.

"You live?"

"Obviously," replied Doc Savage.

"Only through blind, stupid luck," she spat.

Pat Savage marched up to her and snapped, "That will teach you to buck Doc Savage."

Screaming madly, Shari Phoenia sprang to her feet and made a lunge at Pat Savage's face with her sharply manicured nails.

Pat dodged, put out a trim ankle, and tripped the spitting spy, making it look as if she put no special effort into the job.

Shari Phoenia went skating on her face, and attempted to get up again.

Pat Savage planted a slender boot in the small of the struggling woman's back, preventing her from rising. Pinned in the snow, Shari Phoenia turned the frosty air blue with her profane expostulations.

Only Doc Savage, who spoke her mother tongue, recognized them as lurid profanity. His ears actually turned a little red, although that might have been the result of the frigid Arctic wind acting upon his skin.

When Shari Phoenia had exhausted herself in word and action, Pat lifted her boot and allowed the defeated woman to stand up.

Only then did the enormity of her situation sink in. The dark-eyed Egallan spy looked about, saw that there were no soldiers in formation about, and said in a deflated voice, "I am your prisoner then."

"You will be treated humanely," returned Doc Savage in an earnest tone.

"Unless you get out of line again," added Pat Savage, pointing her sixgun at the woman. "Now march!"

Scavenging snowshoes for the trek, they trudged through the cold morning to the cave at which they had been ambushed the day before, where the bronze man's ski plane stood waiting.

The great streamlined ship had been left unattended, and the hatch was slightly ajar from the time they had been struck down by the inertia-dampening field.

After sniffing the cold air briefly, Doc Savage silently signaled a halt.

"What is it?" asked Ham Brooks.

"Someone inside the plane," said Doc. His sensitive nostrils had imparted to him that information.

Supermachine pistols came up, and their muzzles were trained on the hatch. Fingers constricted on triggers.

Renny had the loudest voice, and he unleashed it now.

"Whoever is in there, you had better come out right now."

THERE was a bit of clatter, and a parka-hooded head poked out. Rabbit fur framed a craggy face they all recognized. It was Theodore Buffington, the new President of the Huron Motor Company.

"What the devil are you doing there?" demanded Ham.

Buffington climbed down, shivering as he blew on the tips of his frostbitten fingers.

"I was hiding in the cave when you were all ambushed," explained the nervous executive. "After you were taken away, I went to the plane, but of course I could not get it off the ground. I am no pilot."

Doc Savage seem satisfied and approached. His men trudged behind him.

Doc imparted to Buffington, "Developments have shown that Felix Frost was the sinister genius behind all this wholesale death and destruction."

"Frost! Whatever was his motive?"

"He was the brother of Baron Edgar Fretz, the Baron in Black. Apparently, he was planted in your company in order to extort it for financial gain. As the scheme fell apart, it was expanded into a gigantic undertaking to subjugate the United States of America, which was their ultimate aim, after all."

Buffington trembled the length of his parka-clad body. "Incredible!"

"It was one of the most audacious schemes ever perpetrated upon America," intoned Doc. "But it has failed utterly."

Silently, they climbed on board the plane, and the hatch was secured. Doc Savage dropped into the control bucket, and began warming up the motors. Because they had gotten so cold, it took quite a while to get the engines running properly.

Soon, the bronze man was sending the ski plane skidding over the desolate Barren Lands, and vaulted up into the air.

Once aloft, everyone settled down. Everyone with the sole exception of Shari Phoenia, whom they had to strap into her seat because she was becoming unmanageable. Foreign invective filled the cabin.

Monk snarled, "Pipe down!"

Shari spat something back in her native tongue, which prompted Pat Savage to step up and glare at her with sparking golden eyes.

"Whatever is eating you now?" Pat demanded hotly.

"I overheard your talk."

"So?"

"The man you knew as Felix Frost was my husband."

"Oh," said Pat, genuinely nonplussed by the news. "I had no idea."

"I do not wish your condolences."

"I wasn't offering any," said Pat tartly, returning to her seat.

Up in the cockpit, Doc Savage turned the controls over to Renny Renwick, who guided the climbing plane in a southerly direction, toward the United States.

Renny undertoned, "I take it you're going to turn her over to the college for rehabilitation?" he asked of the bronze man.

"It is the humane thing to do."

Renny did not contradict the bronze man, although the disapproving expression on his long face told a different story. The "college" referred to was, in its way, a secret as deep as that of Doc Savage's fantastic Fortress of Solitude. At the beginning of his career roaming the globe in search of adventure and evildoers to bring to justice, the bronze man realized that modern justice left a lot to be desired. Prisons often served as accidental schools that fostered habitual criminals once the period of lawful incarceration ended. Execution was no certain path to rehabilitation, either.

So Doc Savage had constructed in the wilderness of upstate New York a hidden institution where he consigned the felons who fell into his merciful hands. There, a process of relieving them of their criminal habits was inaugurated. First, through the surgical wizardry of the bronze man, their memories were banished from their criminal brains. After that, they were given a fresh start in life through a healthy program of reeducation and job training. Finally, they were released into society with new names and identities, their wicked pasts forever abolished.

Renny reminded, "A lot of people died because of that hellcat, and her husband."

"That is all over now," said Doc. "It belongs in the past."

Doc Savage went to the radio cubicle and squeezed his gigantic frame into the space allotted. He worked the radio for some time, speaking in a low but urgent tone. When he was done, he took off the headphones, and returned to the control cockpit.

Renny asked, "Settling up business?"

"The President of the United States has been apprised of developments, and a contingent of the Royal Canadian Mounted Police has been dispatched to the scene to the secure the Egallan sending station, and complete its destruction."

Renny grunted, "I take it the matter is being hushed up."

Doc Savage nodded. "The President was informed that there were no survivors of the battle."

"What about the situation with Egallah?"

"That nation will have to find a new prime minister, and I suspect they will not be seeking to create mischief for a very long time to come."

"You mean now that they were caught red-handed, they are going to get a severe talking to?"

"The matter will be settled through diplomatic channels," responded Doc. "Otherwise, it would be war. For many thousands have already perished in the lethal zones which touched so many states with their deadly influence."

That news caused every tongue to become still as they took in the enormity of the threat they had defeated. The unbelievable loss of life had taken some of the satisfaction of victory out of them.

The cabin remained hushed for quite some time as the snowy fir-dotted landscape of the Northwest Territories rolled beneath their wings. After their series of ordeals, which had taken them from Detroit to the Arctic Circle, Doc Savage and his men were glad for some quiet and the time to reflect upon the last few days, with their hectic rush from peril to peril.

Not so Pat Savage. She bustled up to the front of the cockpit and, using no greater leverage than her cocked thumb, jerked Renny back into the cabin.

Pat sank into his seat, and enjoyed the scenery from the cockpit for a few minutes. After a while, she turned to Doc Savage and asked, "I suppose you want to give me a severe talking to, as well."

Doc Savage shook his head. Instead, he said, "After all you have been through, perhaps now you understand why you cannot be allowed to join us in our undertakings."

"Undertakings! That's a mousey word for it. This was an adventure. One of the swellest. And I loved every minute of it!"

"Good," returned the bronze man steadily. "You will have to harbor these memories for a long time, and I hope they satisfy you. Because this is your last adventure with us."

Pat Savage frowned. "Didn't you notice back there that I pulled my own weight?"

"Perhaps you might want to reconsider your way of thinking."

"I might at that," returned Pat lightly. "I'll make you a deal. You reconsider your thinking and I'll reconsider mine."

"What do you mean?" asked Doc.

"How about a nice fair swap?"

"What kind of swap?" Doc Savage asked suspiciously.

"I'll stop barging in on your adventures, if you invite me to every third one."

"Nothing doing," said Doc flatly.

Pat folded stubborn arms. "Fine. Have it your way. That was a fair bargain I just offered you."

"It was no deal I would ever make," said Doc.

"Well, you had your opportunity," snapped Pat. "From now on, I'm going to try to horn in on every single adventure possible, to make up for all the ones I lost out on."

"That will never do."

"My offer still holds, if you want to take me up on it," Pat asked hopefully.

Doc shook his metallic head gravely. "Too dangerous, for a woman."

At that point, Habeas Corpus trotted up and hopped onto Pat Savage's lap, a thing the porker liked to do whenever he had the opportunity.

Scratching at Habeas' long ears, Pat observed, "If it's not too dangerous for a pig, it should be O.K. for a woman. Habeas gets to go along on almost every adventure."

"Habeas," returned Doc reasonably, "happens to be Monk's pet. Monk takes him wherever he goes."

Pat turned around and hollered back into the cabin, "Hello, Renny! How would you like to have a pet to take with you wherever you go?"

Renny, who had been dozing in his seat, roused and asked grumpily, "What kind of a pet?"

"The kind who won't get in your hair."

"Say again?"

"And I won't eat much, either," added Pat, laughing.

Renny's booming "Holy cow!" made the entire cabin interior shake.

About the Author
RYERSON JOHNSON

WALTER RYERSON JOHNSON was born in the coal town of Divernon, Illinois, on October 19, 1901. His father, Simeon Johnson, was a physician and his son was expected to follow in his footsteps, but never did, although he flirted with dentistry, later working briefly in the local coal mines. After graduation, a wanderlust seized him and he rode the rails in the famous fashion of hobos of that era on and off between 1921-26. His nickname in those days was "Doc," but over time people called him Johnny.

Johnson once wrote:

> I graduated from the University of Illinois with a degree in Foreign Commerce, but I never did work a day at it. One of the themes I wrote in an English class turned out to be a salable short story, and I haven't been much good for anything except writing ever since—writing and a little editing and teaching.
>
> I did make a stab at a life of business. As a warehouse manager for a plaster company, I got along so well it scared me—foreseeing a long life ahead with nothing but plaster to be interested in, I asked for a doubling of my salary, which was promptly refused, but which gave me the courage to quit. I went to Europe on a one-way ticket because I didn't have enough money for the round-trip. I kind of sawed my way through Europe with a musical saw, and landed in the Balkans where I stayed six months, and on one occasion played the saw at the Bulgarian National Opera House. I kept writing

and sending stories back to the U. S. None of them sold, and I worked my way home from Antwerp, Belgium nursemaiding a bunch of horses quartered on the open deck. We ran into a three-day storm; the horses' stalls were washed overboard and the horses were screaming around... I played the saw to the horses; maybe it soothed them. We didn't lose any overboard and we did eventually get them to Iowa.

I found when I got home that I'd sold several stories, so I knuckled down to the sober business of perfecting my craft, and have made a living from free-lance writing ever since. I'm beginning to think I must be the last of my tribe—writing catch-as-catch-can all over the place.

In the beginning I was impressed with a writer: H. Bedford Jones. I, too, had an uncommon family name and a common last name. So I started out writing under the name of W. Ryerson Johnson. Later I dropped the W as being pretentious.

Johnny's first sale was "Nimble Fingers," which appeared in *Detective Tales* in 1923. That was the manuscript written in college. He only found out that it had been published many years later, and never did receive a check. His first serious sale, "The Squeeze," went to the prestigious *Adventure* three years later. He wrote coal mine stories, hobo yarns, and Mountie tales in the beginning, moving on to Westerns when the Mountie market faded.

In 1938, Johnson had an opportunity to go to Venezuela with pulpster Arthur J. Burks as "resident expedition reporter" to search for the missing aviator, Paul Redfern, but his interest in Minnesota artist Lois Lignell exerted a stronger pull. They met in the New York studio of artist Gozo Kawamura and married that year in a Japanese American Dutch Reformed Church. Later, they collaborated on many illustrated children's books. Johnson never did get to Venezuela.

"Johnny is one guy who never lets anything interfere with the pleasant ambling business of grazing through life," Lester Dent once observed.

Over the next several decades, Johnson freelanced everything from TV scripts to comic books, and contributed to the *Encyclopedia Britannica*. His final sale was "No Tinsel, No Humbug," which appeared in *Louis L'Amour Western Magazine* in 1994, marking the end of a 71-year career. During that period, he wrote or ghosted stories featuring famous characters ranging from The Phantom Detective to Mike Shayne, but he is best remembered for his contributions to *Doc Savage Magazine,* all in collaboration with series originator Lester Dent.

When Bantam Books announced plans to reprint the Doc adventures in 1964, Johnson reached out and offered his services to modernize the long out-of-date pulp novels. The publisher politely declined, believing the stories would hold up unchanged.

Johnson was astounded. "I thought they were crazy. Didn't think the crude pulpiness could possibly go in today's market. How wrong can you be?"

The Bantam revival went on to sell millions of copies, ultimately reprinting all 181 original stories, as well as new installments.

"What happened just baffled me," Johnny later admitted. "People give attention and significance to Doc Savage that Les didn't at the time feel at all. He just turned out a story, got the money, and did another one."

About the Author
WILL MURRAY

BEFORE THE THOUGHT entered his head to write Doc Savage novels, Will Murray was interested in learning more about the men behind the house pseudonym of Kenneth Robeson. It became a long, strange quest.

Reading in Ron Goulart's *Cheap Thrills: An Informal History of the Pulp Magazine* that Ryerson Johnson ghosted *Land of Always-Night* and *The Fantastic Island,* and a third unnamed Doc Savage story, Murray undertook a search for him. Luck or fate played a significant role. Reading in a 1930s issue of *Writer's Digest* that Johnson had once roomed with *Superman* editor Mort Weisinger, Murray reached out to Weisinger, whom he had interviewed a year before, and was provided with three addresses—in Illinois, Maine and Hawaii. Murray wrote to all three.

Back came a long, friendly letter containing the astounding information that the mysterious third Ryerson Johnson Doc Savage novel was *The Motion Menace,* and a warm correspondence began. That was in May of 1976. Murray was attending college. Johnson was in his late 70s. Neither imagined that one day they would co-author a Doc Savage novel, albeit posthumously, nor that it would sequel *The Motion Menace.*

That autumn, they met and Murray introduced the veteran freelancer to the world of pulp magazine collectors. Johnson became a guest at the annual Pulpcon, and enjoyed himself so much that he continued attending as a regular, winning over all he met.

Periodically, they got together and, as Murray's writing career grew, Johnson cheered him on. In 1979, Murray visited Johnson in his rambling Civil War-era home in Lubec, Maine, which Lester Dent had visited back in 1946. Murray signed the kitchen wall where Dent, Mort Weisinger, Otto Binder, Kurt Schaffenberger and others had inscribed their names back in the 1940s. Johnson took him on a tour of the rugged coastline and other spots which had served as the locale of Lester's final Doc Savage novel, *Up From Earth's Center*.

When Murray was offered the assignment to write Doc Savage novels in the 1990s, suddenly the two friends became brothers in pulp—the only surviving 1930s Doc Savage writer, and the newest Kenneth Robeson. Reading Murray's manuscript for *Python Isle,* Johnson grinned and cracked, "Man, Dent would have loved to have known you!"

It was without doubt the greatest compliment the young writer could have received.

The friendship lasted nearly twenty years, ending only with the passing of the perpetually youthful 94 year old. The Bantam Books Doc Savage series had recently gone on hiatus. It seemed for a very long time that an era was over and Doc Savage would fight no more. But Murray never lost faith. When he brought back the Man of Bronze for Altus Press, he looked forward to the day he could finally bring to life Ryerson Johnson's lost Doc Savage adventure.

That day has finally come.

About the Artist
JOE DeVITO

JOE DeVITO WAS born on March 16, 1957 in New York City. He graduated with honors from Parsons School of Design in 1981 and continued his study of oil painting at the city's famed Art Students League.

Over the years, DeVito has painted many of the most recognizable Pop Culture and Pulp icons, including King Kong, Tarzan, Doc Savage, Superman, Batman, Wonder Woman, Spider-Man, *Mad* magazine's Alfred E. Neuman and various characters in World of Warcraft. Throughout, his illustration has had an accent toward dinosaurs, Action Adventure, SF and Fantasy. He has illustrated hundreds of book and magazine covers, painted several notable posters and numerous trading cards for the major comic book and gaming houses, and created concept and character design for the film and television industries.

In 3D, DeVito sculpted the official 100th Anniversary statue of *Tarzan of the Apes* for the Edgar Rice Burroughs Estate, *The Cooper Kong* for the Merian C. Cooper Estate, Superman, Wonder Woman and Batman for Chronicle Books' Masterpiece Editions, as well as several other notable Pop and Pulp characters. Additional sculpting work ranges from scientifically accurate dinosaurs, a multitude of collectibles for the Bradford Exchange in a variety of genres, to larger-than-life statues and the award trophy for the influential art annual *SPECTRUM*.

An avid writer, Joe is also the co-author (with Brad Strickland) of two novels, which he illustrated as well. The first, *KONG: King of Skull Island* (DH Press) was published in 2004. The second book, *Merian C. Cooper's KING KONG*, was published by St. Martin's Griffin in 2005. He has also contributed many essays and articles to such collected works as *Kong Unbound: The Cultural Impact, Pop-Mythos, and Scientific Plausibility of a Cinematic Legend* and *Do Androids-Artists Paint In Oils When They Dream?* in *Pixel or Paint: The Digital Divide In Illustration Art*.

In regard to the creation of the *War Makers* cover, he writes:

> *The War Makers* is the eighth collaborative effort between Will Murray and me in *The Wild Adventures of Doc Savage* series, and officially pushes us past the seven-book mark established in our initial run together in the 1990s.
>
> Working with negatives from the original James Bama photo shoots is always fun. For this one we chose a parka scene appropriate to the North Pole climate out of a selection of unused stills depicting super-model Steve Holland as the Man of Bronze. Both Will and Rick Scheckman (who commissioned the cover) were happy to revisit the fleece version of the parka that was used on a previous Bama Doc cover, *Haunted Ocean*. As for the locale, Doc's fabulous Fortress of Solitude, it's a conscious follow-up in spirit to *The Miracle Menace*, which showcased Doc's Hudson River hideaway in New York City, the Hidalgo Trading Company warehouse. It was my intention to stay close to the original description of the dome possessing a glassy or jewel-like reflective surface. The sliding hangar door has the property of disappearing completely when closed, the way the walkway to Klaatu's flying saucer disappeared seamlessly when closed in *The Day The Earth Stood Still*.
>
> Each time we concept a new cover scene, Will and I like to include something new. For *The War Makers*, I created an ultramodern autogyro, with polished aluminum aerodynamic lines and rocket tubes. Advanced for the '30s time frame, without being too Flash Gordonish. The action is staged so that we do not know whether Doc has just arrived, or is about to

leave on another mysterious adventure. Either way, the scene is frozen in time, strobe-lit by a massive lightning bolt that starkly contrasts against the stormy sky. At Will's suggestion, I painted an extinct volcanic cone into the background. This is Lester Dent's original, unused conception of the Fortress of Solitude. Rick and Will were both approving of the apparent simplicity of the scene, which heightened the tension from the electric bolt all the more.

The actual painting is 30" x 20", and it took a month or so to finish while working on other projects. Again, my sincere thanks to Rick for the commission, and I hope he enjoys it!

www.jdevito.com
www.kongskullisland.com
FB: Joe DeVito-DeVito Artworks

About the Patron
RICK SCHECKMAN

RICK SCHECKMAN HAS worked for David Letterman's *Late Night* shows since 1982 and has been a Doc Savage fan since 1970, when he found a Bantam Books reprint at his local bookstore hidden behind a few other paperbacks.

He grew up during the Golden Age of local New York television—*Courageous Cat and Minute Mouse* in the early morning followed by *The Little Rascals (Our Gang)* on Channel 7. On Channel 5 at the same time, Sandy Becker with his puppets and Bugs Bunny. Then there was Officer Joe Bolton on Channel 11 with The Three Stooges, Captain Jack McCarthy with Popeye, Claude Kirschner on Channel 9 with the Spunky and Tadpole cartoons. Let's not forget Chuck McCann whose Sunday morning show was called *Let's Have Fun*. Every Sunday McCann would dress up as the characters from the Sunday *Daily News* comics: Dick Tracy, Little Orphan Annie, The Dragon Lady, etc. In between he ran cartoons, *Superman*, *The Three Stooges* and old serials. Each week would be a chapter from *Flash Gordon, Buck Rogers, Tim Tyler, Ace Drummond, The Phantom Empire* and more. Thus began Rick's love of everything from the past and adventure heroes.

"A few years later, Bantam had the short-lived series of reprints of The Shadow's early adventures and the world of pulp heroes opened up to me," Rick recalls. "Now it is 1970, I was nosing around my local bookstore "The Book Mark" on Union Turnpike in Queens, New York, and behind some other paperbacks was a copy of some pulp hero that I never heard of called Doc Savage, featuring an eye-catching cover by—as I later learned—James Bama, and I was hooked. That reprint was *The Feathered Octopus* and after reading it, I noticed that it was number 48 in a series, so began the quest to find the other 47. It took a few years of combing bookstores in New York City but as I added the monthly new adventures that Bantam was publishing, I was able to fill in the missing, often out-of-print books, and now have a full set of the Bantam reprints."

Before long, Rick began to research the life of Kenneth Robeson and found out that he was actually a writer named Lester Dent who wrote under a pen-name. For years, he thought that a man named Franklyn W. Dixon wrote his then-favorite series "The Hardy Boys." Who knew back then that they were all house names and often multiple authors?

As the years went along, there were the comic conventions which gave Rick the opportunity to meet many of the pulp and comic book creators and to fill in his collection of any and all books and comics that featured Doc's adventures, as well as the fanzines that featured research into the history of the Man of Bronze, Lester Dent, and his publisher. Having purchased all the reprints of the Doc Savage adventures that were published by Street & Smith, he began to buy some of the original pulps. Then there were the statues and cover reprints from Graphitti Designs, Joe DeVito's iconic statue of Doc fighting a giant python, and more.

Rick Scheckman's collection now includes an original Doc Savage cover by Bob Larkin, an oil painting recreation by Jerome Rozen of Walter Baumhofer's cover for the 1936 Doc adventure, *The Spook Legion,* from the collection of Phillip José Farmer, and now the cover for the Doc Savage book you hold in your hands.

"I'm so grateful to Will Murray for allowing me the opportunity to purchase the original cover painting for *The War Makers,* and of course, to the artist, Joe DeVito, for creating it," Rick concludes. "In my opinion, this is in the all-time Top Ten of Doc Savage covers and am proud that it hangs on a wall in my home."

DOC SAVAGE

LIMITED EDITION FINE ART PRINTS!

WWW.JDEVITO.COM

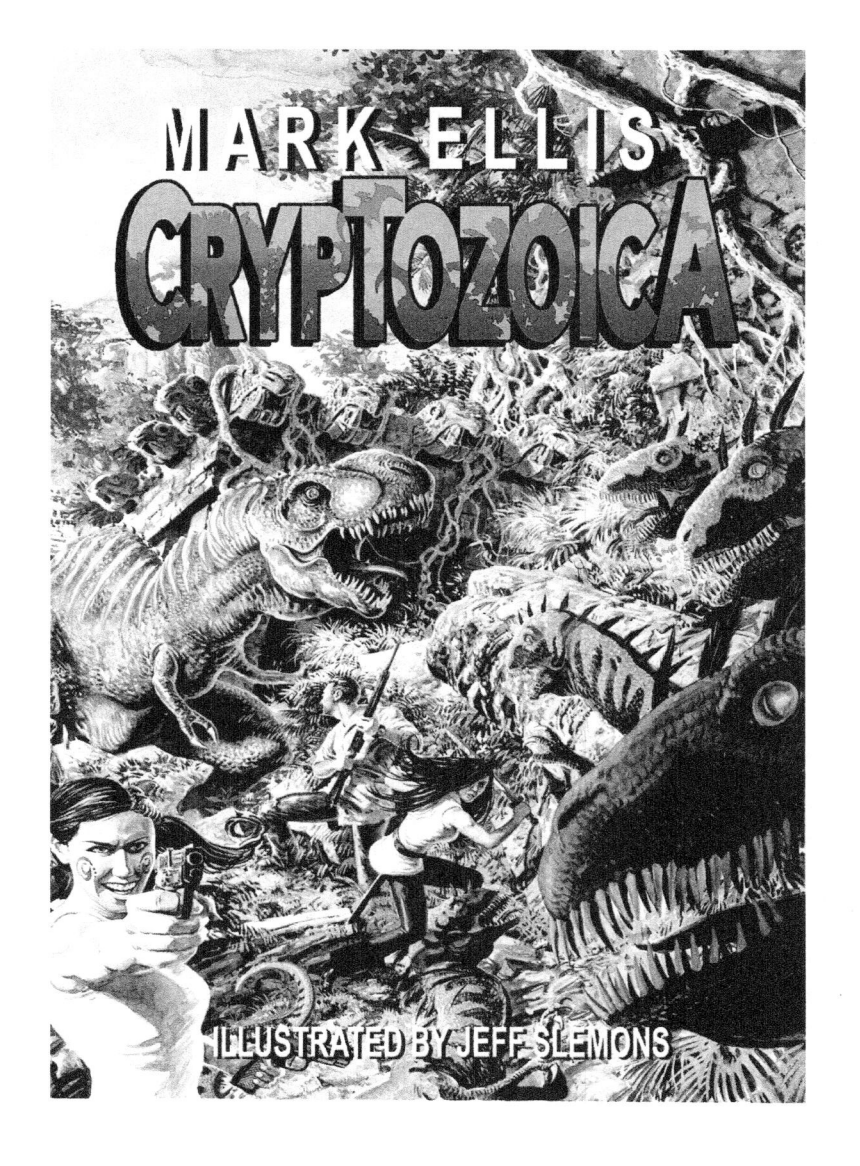

From Mark Ellis, the Creator of OUTLANDERS & THE SPUR!

"CRYPTOZOICA is a novel for those who really want to sink their teeth into something engrossing to the finish. For a modern take on pulp adventure, you would be hard-pressed to find one that delivers like this!"
--Bookgasm

Available in trade paperback at all online booksellers, and as an ebook exclusively at Amazon.com

THE BRONZE Gazette

Unofficial Magazine for the Fan of Bronze

For over 20 years, The Bronze Gazette has been bringing Doc fans insightful articles, extraordinary artwork, and all of the latest information about all things Doc Savage. Today, Doc is having a rebirth. Current projects include a new comic, new novels, audiobooks, reprints, and there may even be a new movie in Doc's future. If you want to keep up with all of the latest Doc news and events, subscribe today!

Subscription info:

US $15.00/3 issues, Canada $16.00/3 issues, Overseas $20.00/3 issues
Green Eagle Publications / 2900 Standiford Ave 16B / PMB #136 / Modesto, CA 95350
For more information, email: rrenwick@sbcglobal.net

Will Murray's Skull Island Is Now An Audiobook!

Doc Savage vs. King Kong!

Order any of the six Doc Savage Audiobooks at RadioArchives.com or by calling 800-886-0551

Printed in Great Britain
by Amazon